Symphony of the Dead

Abbas Maroufi

Translated by Lotfali Khonji

First published in 2007 by Aflame Books
2 The Green
Laverstock
Wiltshire
SP1 1QS
United Kingdom
email: info@aflamebooks.com

© Abbas Maroufi 1987
This translation is published by arrangement with
Qoqnoos Publishing House, Tehran, Iran

This English translation copyright © Lotfali Khonji 2007

First published in Persian in 1988 as *Samfoni-e Mordegan*

Note: Italicised words are explained in a glossary on page 269.
A superscript number after a word or phrase indicates a translator's note to explain items of historical or cultural interest.
These notes can be found on page 271.

ISBN: 0955233968
ISBN-13: 9780955233968

Cover design by Zulu Spice/www.zuluspice.com

Printed by Guangzhou Hengyuan Printing Co, Guangdong, China

Symphony of the Dead

Abbas Maroufi

Translated from Persian by Lotfali Khonji

Prelude

In the name of Allah, the Almighty, the Magnanimous, the Compassionate.

... Cain said: "Of course I shall kill you." Abel said: "I have committed no sin. God will accept a sacrifice of the innocent. If you raise your hand to kill me, I shall not raise my hand to kill you, as I fear God of the World. I want you to be guilty of killing me and, at the same time, guilty of disobedience so that you reside in Hell, as that eternal furnace is the ultimate chastisement for all oppressors of the world."

Following this dialogue, Cain's inner demon persuaded him to kill his brother. By doing so, he became one of those who are led astray and, thus, join the losers.

Therefore, the Almighty caused a raven to dig at the ground with its claws, showing Cain how to bury his brother's corpse. Cain said to himself: "Shame on me; am I less able than this raven? Can I not hide my brother's corpse beneath the soil?"

Thereupon, he buried his brother and deeply regretted what he had done.

Holy Koran, the Sura of Ma'ida, v26

To my wife and daughter,

who endure my fatigue

First Movement

Symphony of the Dead

A thin plume of smoke floated beneath the barrel arches and domed vaults of the nut-sellers' souk and forced its way out through the front gate. At the other end of the souk, a number of porters burnt wood in a brazier. A blanket covered their hands and occasionally, whenever they dared bring them out, they cracked watermelon seeds. Behind them, in a place looking somewhat like a crypt, three men were roasting the seeds in cauldrons. A mixture of smoke and steam rose into the air.

All the oil lamps, even the stronger *zanbouri* lamps, had been lit. From a distance, the souk resembled a village enveloped in mist. On the right hand side of the hall, in the trading chamber named "High Quality Nuts and Dried Fruits", two men were content with the heat emanating from the oil lamp on the table. Urhan Urkhani was sitting behind the table. Ayaz the policeman was sitting beside him.

Ayaz the policeman came to the shop every Thursday, sat on a big chair and placed his feet on a small stool. Whether it was winter or summer, he had the habit of frequently wiping sweat from his brow. If there were no big chair nearby, he would sit on a sack of watermelon seeds. He said: "How can I sit on a small chair with this huge body? Tell me."

If he wanted to, he could even lift Father, awe-inspiring as he was, with two fingers and hang him from one of the hooks suspended from the ceiling. Ayaz had a plump, fleshy face, a small head and a skin abrasion, wrinkled like the rest of his face, on his left cheek. He had the habit of buying a single seer measure of pistachio nuts and actually paying for it, although the nut sellers insisted that he should help himself. He shelled the pistachio nuts and placed them on the table in a row. He then ate them in one go. It was at this stage that Urhan had to bring him a glass of cool water.

Father was very fond of him because he was the veteran policeman in town and also because he knew a lot. He had a wealth of information about every person and place, and could tackle any sort of problem. Father said: "This man is not an ordinary person." Father paid him his due every week and, every New Year's Eve, sent about a dozen kilograms of nuts to his house. Even now, several years after Father's death, Urhan kept paying the policeman his weekly dues.

On the other side of the chamber, behind the counter, there were two young workers with their hands in their pockets. They were wearing their *papakha* sheepskin hats. They had covered their ears with the raised collars of their overcoats. They were whispering, exactly as Urhan and Ayaz were doing: calmly, and with their mouths close to each other's ears.

Ayaz said: "I am standing behind you like a lion; have no fear."

Urhan was hesitant. He did not know what to do. He said: "Are you sure this won't be an own goal?"

"Finish the job and get rid of the whole problem."

"But what am I to do if some piece of evidence betrays me?"

"You've got to be clever. You should avoid leaving any clues."

Urhan pondered for a moment. Then he turned his eyes away from Ayaz and said: "Like Yusef?"

"Has anybody suspected anything? After the passage of several years, no problem has arisen."

"They refer to the case as fratricide. I have heard it with my own ears."

Ayaz shouted: "Let them fuck off." He then lowered his voice and said: "People talk, even behind God's back."

"But my dear Ayaz, are you sure that this one won't be a bottomless pit? Are you sure that I won't fall into it, head first?"

"Just tell me, was I not a friend of your father's?"

"This is all true, but ..."

Ayaz said: "You remind me of your father. He was a coward."

Urhan passed his hand over his bald head, brought his face nearer to the lamp and said: "I am not a coward. On the contrary, I have the courage to do anything."

"You asked me to tell you what to do with that whore, didn't you? I told you to divorce her. Did you not benefit from the advice? You are now asking me to tell you what to do with this son-of-a-bitch. I am telling you to finish him off. One of these days, when his daughter is seen in this vicinity, you will no longer he able to carry on your business. You might suddenly see some blonde asking whether this is her father's shop."

Urhan was silent.

Ayaz said: "Now that the matter has came to a head, don't wait any longer. Act right now. Get going."

Symphony of the Dead

Urhan said: "In this snow? Where do you want me to go?" He looked outside.

Such heavy snow had fallen that for years to come people would refer to this winter as the terrible one. Half the people had crept into their shelters and the other half had no choice but to struggle in the cold and snow to make ends meet. The snow had let everybody down. A curious silence reigned over the streets and alleys, pipes had frozen, cars could not move, the snow was piled high in the streets, shopkeepers had swept the pavements but the previous night's snowfall, to a height of about half a yard, was still there.

In the narrow alleys, doors to homes had disappeared behind snowdrifts. People had dug out interconnecting paths along which they moved confidently. Had a disaster struck? Perhaps. Many winters had come and gone and there had been numerous snowfalls, but no-one could remember one such as this. The ravens had taken over the town and several of them could be seen on every tree. They were to be found indoors as well. They landed comfortably on balustrades and veranda railings and flew off again. The house with high walls, cornices and double windows had been buried under the snow. It was forgotten, cold and lifeless. The ceilings of the rooms on the upper floors were sagging. The stench had reigned for many years on the lower floors. No-one lived in it, no lights were lit, nobody swept the snow from the roof. The lantern at the entrance was broken.

In the good old days, mother brought flour from the pantry, made dough and baked bread in the oven at the centre of the kitchen. The pleasant scent of baked bread and burning wood rose from the oven. When the bread was ready, Mother wrapped six loaves in a piece of cloth in order to send them to Uncle Saber. Ideen and Urhan rode in the five-horse carriage and sped towards Uncle Saber's. Before their return journey, Uncle Saber's wife filled their pockets with delicious things to eat.

There was also a time when Father, ascending the staircase, held the rounded railings and counted. When he reached 21, he doffed his *papakha* and hung it on the coat stand. He also took off his overcoat, shook it and hung it up. He wiped his trousers down with a handkerchief but did not hang them. Instead, he placed his trousers under his mattress so that they would be "ironed" while he was asleep and would acquire neat, sharp creases.

There was also a sister called Ida. She roamed about in the kitchen, in the cellar, other places in the house, enduring the severity of the rheumatic pains which were burning her. Eventually, she did burn up.

And now, in the stale silence and cold of the rooms, there was no Urhan to sleep under his worn-out, dirty quilt and think that he could sleep comfortably. No. Everyone was dead. And this last one?

He said: "He should be got rid of by whatever means necessary."
Ayaz said: "What are you waiting for then?"
"Where is he?"
"As always, at Shoorabi[1] lake, at the teahouse."
"In this snow?"
"You weren't born in Arabia were you. Whoever has been brought up in Ardabil[2] lives with snow. Besides, he might be dead."
"No. I know that he is alive."
"How do you know? After ten days, how can be he alive?"

Urhan said firmly and with confidence: "Ideen is alive. I can't believe he could be dead. Just yesterday, I found out that he had a 15-year-old daughter. I also found out that they were holding her birth certificate. If he lives, we will soon have hundreds of claimants and litigants on our hands. Do you understand, Ayaz?"

"Go then. Go. I will be standing right behind you like a lion. Nothing will happen to you. Pay no attention to my age. I am still Ayaz the policeman".

Urhan listened to the hissing of the *zanbouri* and thought of a 15-year-old blonde who would one day appear on his doorstep.

Ayaz bent his head, gazed at Urhan's face and said, in Azeri Turkish: "Hurry up brother."

Urhan was silent. Ayaz said: "If I had been in your father's position, God bless his soul, during the years when Ideen was too proud and tried to be a poet, I would have taken him to the frontier and let him go."

Urhan said: "My Father? My Father was afraid of him."
"You are afraid of him too."
"No. I am not afraid. I just can't be cruel".
"If you had done it last week, you would be happy right now. A man must say 'water' and drink it, must say 'air' and breathe it. Otherwise, he'll be dead".

Ayaz donned his *papakha* and stood up, fastened the buttons on his overcoat one by one, from the bottom upwards and checked that his appearance was completely neat and tidy. Then, as if talking to his subordinate, he barked: "What are you going to do?"

Urhan pulled himself together, raised his head and said: "I will go."
Ayaz stamped his foot on the ground: "Yes, like me. Get up and go." And he left.

He forgot to collect his weekly due. Or may be he didn't want it. Urhan was left feeling deeply troubled. One feels so lonely at times like this, as if a spell has been cast on one. He was sitting there, dumbstruck, motionless as a mountain. But was it possible to remain there?

Symphony of the Dead

A few moments later, at exactly at two o'clock in the afternoon, Urhan, contrary to his usual practice, was not able to transfer the daily accounts into the overall ledger, although he wanted to tidy up and close the weekly account. Anxiously, he counted the banknotes earned and pushed them into his trouser pockets. He placed the account books in the framework of the abacus but forgot to put the abacus in the drawer and lock it up. But he would not forget his *papakha*. He would keep it on his head whether it was summer or winter. While working, he would keep the hat on the desk and, on leaving, he would put it on his head again.

He donned his *papakha* and fastened the buttons on his overcoat. He looked around the shop and, without giving them any work, told the employees they were free to go.

He stood there until the employees had picked up their empty lunch plates and left the place. For a moment he felt that he should pick up something or perform some particular task. But the more he thought and the more he looked around, the less he remembered what he was supposed to do. He let out the compressed air of the *zanbouri* and left the office. He secured the top and bottom locks of the door and looked around him with great care. He went to entrance of the souk and gave a five-*tooman* note to Martha, the beggar sitting on the steps at the corner of the hall. He said to her: "Martha, you're shivering like a dog, aren't you?"

The old woman said: "It has turned very cold" and quickly hid her hand, holding the banknote, under her chador. She continued: "May Allah bring you abundance and prosperity."

Urhan turned back. He saw the porters at the end of the souk, burning wood in braziers. Smoke had spread everywhere. He pointed at the large sacks of pistachio nuts and watermelon seeds under the arches and said to Esmayol: "You fire-worshipping fools will one day set this souk on fire". He didn't wait for an answer. He went through a row of arches under which sacks of roasted and salted watermelon seeds had been placed and, without addressing Esmayol directly, said: "Keep an eye on the shop too." He then walked towards large sacks of pistachio nuts that had been stacked on the left hand side and filled the space under the arches. Within the next day or two, the sacks had to be taken to the retailers. The money earned would no doubt arrive by the New Year. He touched the bulging sacks of pistachio nuts and, once again, looked towards the other extremity of the souk. The porters, who had turned down the flaps of their hats, lowered their heads as a sign of greeting to Urhan. Their eyes looked tired and sleep had accumulated at the corners. He passed slowly through the hall of the souk. He heard someone saying: "Hello Urhan." He didn't want to look. He just said: "Hello." Whoever it was did not matter.

He neither knew them nor needed to. They passed him quickly, like wind.

Father used to tell him: "When wind pushes upwards against the rim of your *papakha* it will lift it. Be very careful."

Times were more peaceful in those days. When Father was around, sleeping on the terrace was more pleasant than one could imagine. Even the night sky was blue. One was able to dream in colour. Until quite late at night, one could hear Mother and Ida washing up in the kitchen. Ideen, tucked up in his bed, turned from side to side until everyone was asleep and he was able to open his book and keep reading. Sometimes I thought that he was eating the pages. And, eventually it was reading that finished him. One could imagine that it was possible to hear the movements of his eyelids and the sound of his thinking from his room at the end of the corridor while the cats were meowing loudly on the high wall of the courtyard.

Father used to ask: "What is it you are reading Ideen?" And Ideen used to reply: "I am studying. I am learning my lessons Father." I suppose he was telling the truth.

"Carry on reading. We will see what achievements you will make and what regions you will conquer by doing so".

He had reached the street. He pounded his feet harder so that no snow would settle on his boots. Rotten oranges floated on the water's surface and then submerged, the water flowed fast and the cloudy sky looked like dark velvet, in a single piece, without a break. Urhan stopped and looked towards the end of the nut-sellers' souk. He was hesitating. He didn't know what to do. Apart from the problems of business at the shop and afternoon customers and scores of such headaches, the ten-day absence of 'Sooji' was irritating him.

Since that morning, even since the night before, he had struggled with himself about whether or not to go. Could he refrain from going? Every night, when he entered that big, cold house, the distant hubbub of bygone years suddenly became as silent as a wall; it turned into a pine tree and stood motionless in the middle of the garden; it turned into a door and remained closed. The distant hubbub of the past acquired the shape of Yusef who gazed, with eyes wide open, and stood like a huge chunk of meat. If Ideen could overcome his restlessness and stay in the house, all I had to do was to say: "Where are you Sooji?" Immediately, a man wearing a long overcoat, a scarf and a worn out *papakha*, all having belonged to father, would creep out of the hole upstairs like a wild bear and declare his presence without making the slightest noise. He said: "Don't chain me Urhan".

Symphony of the Dead

I said: "Don't say Urhan. Say brother," and slapped him across the face. The *papakha* fell off his head. Father's old hat brings back memories and restrains me. Sometimes I want to slap him in the face or chain him to the railings of the balcony. But his smiling face, topped by the old, discoloured hat, softens me. What can be done? Mother said: "You have no feelings or affection." I replied: "I do." And I really do. Oh, mother, you, too, would be fed up if you were in my place. You would not set foot in a house with a pond containing water green with dirt and moss, with pine needles covering the courtyard, with cold air trapped behind dusty windows and with open wood-burning ovens, in the kitchen hidden under loads of useless objects. The dead kitten embedded in the ice in the gutter at the end of courtyard is still there. It has been frozen in the gutter for two months. There is no life in it and no-one cares to push it so that it falls down. No-one is in a mood to light the fireplaces. The bricks at the top of the walls fall down one by one, as if the building has caught a cold. No-one sweeps the rooms. No guest arrives. The glass that held the lightbulb at the front door is broken. The rooms, devoid of furniture, look overly large and, when one walks on their floors, reverberations of one's footsteps hit one's head like a hammer. The sound of one's breathing floats about. You wouldn't dare even sneeze, as the sound would turn around in your own head. From all the hubbub of the past, only the harsh sound of the ravens has remained. They move about on top of the pine trees.

Their ear-splitting noise sounds like the shouting of "snaw, snaw", as if acknowledging the white surroundings.

He gazed at the leafless trees along the pavement. The snow had bent their branches. They would no doubt break with the next snowfall. The people, too, resembled the trees. A heavy load of snow was constantly on their shoulders and its weight would be felt until the beginning of spring. What was bad about it was that the people, unlike the trees, died only once. And this unique occurrence was a painful catastrophe.

He pushed his hand into his overcoat pocket and felt the ball of rope that he had picked up that morning. He felt at ease and buried himself in the crowd. When he reached Qanat Crossroads, he pulled out his silver pocketwatch, looked at it only by way of habit, without noticing the time, closed it and put it back in his pocket. Mother used to say: "Ideen is fading away. We must do something." She even used to ask me where the Armenian girl was and suggested that it could be because of her. And I used to reply: "No Mother. It is tiredness. I will take him to Villa Darreh. The fresh air will invigorate both of us".

When he was passing Dorostkar's, the watchmaker, he felt like stopping for a moment and looking through the window. He must have passed that shop a thousand times but now he looked closely at Mr Dorostkar's big, circular clock. The frame was made of oak and the hands of high-quality Persian ironwood. The round, convex face had artistic illustrations. The glass in front of the face was also convex. So was the shop window. Between the window and the big clock, there were about a dozen mantelpiece clocks. The big clock was a truly beautiful one. Mr Dorostkar himself had made it ages ago, but it had been out of order for the past 30 years. It had stopped when Mr Dorostkar's heart had stopped beating for just a moment. Or perhaps it was the other way round and the heart had stopped beating when the big clock stopped working. In either event, the two failures had been more or less simultaneous. The only difference was that Mr Dorostkar's heart had started beating again, albeit with some difficulty, whereas the clock's stoppage had been so serious that Mr Dorostkar, despite his great skill, had not been able to reverse it. It had stopped exactly at half-past five. To be more exact, it had stopped at half-past five in the afternoon, on a hot summer's day, in the year 1325, or 1946 if one went by the Christian calendar. And, now, alas, after so many years the big clock was still dormant. Mr Dorostkar was manipulating the gears of a wristwatch and, no doubt, dreaming of the day when he would revive the big clock and, with the sounding of its beautiful cuckoo chimes, would prove to everyone that anybody can do what they desire, provided that nature is not against them. Father had told these things to Urhan and Urhan used to tell them to other people. "And when the big clock is revived, Mr Dorostkar, with no further wishes, would lie down on his shop floor and surrender to death." This, too, had been related by him to everybody in the town over the past 30 years.

Father used to say: "This, too, is a big misery." Mother used to reply: "Don't talk about that madman any more."

Now that I am no longer young and vigorous, there are many things I can't stand. As soon as I reach the house and open the door, all those living people, with their hubbub and noises, run away. At the doorstep, a dreadful silence embraces me, lifts me up, takes me upstairs, and makes me lie down on the ramshackle wooden bed, under the old quilt, pale with its years of dirt. Before I feel warm, midnight arrives and submerges me in further fatigue and worry.

I used to enter Mother's room in the afternoon, when I returned from the shop. She must have been breathing her last. She was all skin and bone. It would be enough for somebody to squeeze her nose; and that would be the end of her. Her room was the same room of the past with its three doors, on the lower floor. It smelt of garlic and staleness. It smelt of the breath of someone suffering from tuberculosis. The teacups and the saucers were saturated with

Symphony of the Dead

these smells and the taste would go down one's throat with the tea. I sat at mother's bedside. I avoided eye-to-eye contact. I said: "Hello Mother." I touched her hand and caressed it without any feeling.

From the depth of their sinking, mother's eyes were gazing at the ceiling. They resembled a swallow's nest on an old tree trunk. She said: "Ideen ... where is my Ideen?"

I reacted with rapid blinking. I just kept gazing at the floral patterns on the carpet, or perhaps at nothing. I, too, was her Urhan, or maybe I was not. And nothing could be done about it. I had accepted the possibility that I might not be her dear Urhan. I said: "He must be around here Mother."

Mother turned her head for a moment and released my hand. Her white, long fingers were hanging from the edge of the bed. She said: "Go and get him here straight away. Do you understand? If you can't take care of him, chain him here, right in front of my eyes."

I said: "How can I find him?"

Mother sat on her bed. Every now and then she displayed some strength and this was peculiar. It was as if she had a hidden reservoir of strength. She shouted: "You are unfair." Tears rolled down her pale face. She said: "Who have you inherited your habits from? Where is my Ideen?" Her voice sounded like a piece of cloth being torn.

I said: "Don't worry yourself, Mother. It'll damage your health. I'll find him this very evening. I promise".

She said: "Do you understand? Where is Ideen right now?"

He was behind the Anooshirvan the Just School. A child of 12 or 13 was playing some sort of a makeshift mouth organ and he was looking at him. Saliva was running down his face. I said: "What the hell are you doing here, you big good-for-nothing?"

He replied: "I was just wandering around and I ended up here."

I said: "You should be ashamed of yourself, you silly ass. I warned you not to do this sort of thing again. Get moving".

Mother was nervous and worried. She was bony. She was shaking. She pulled on my jacket sleeve and said: "Where is he? Can't you hear me? Are you deaf?"

I said: "He must be wandering around and will end up somewhere. In Akhavan Garden."

After crying for some time, she had regained some of her calm but she had a trembling voice: "He is no kid, is he? He's 29-years old."

I said: "Do you think that I don't want my brother to be wise and well-behaved? Why do you hold me responsible for everything?"

She lay on her bed and drew the white sheet up to her chin. She was clutching the sheet so fiercely. It was as if she was crushing me. She said: "I don't know what you have done to him. Anyway, I order you to take good care of him. He doesn't expect anything from you. He just has some food and lies down."

I said: "Mother, please don't talk like that." And I wept.

She said: "In that case, sell some property and spend his share on him. Take him somewhere."

I wish I could take Father's will out of my pocket and read it aloud. I said: "Mother, I promise to take him to Tehran or abroad. I will also spend money on him. Show some patience and let me get things done. I promise."

In his will, Father had formally stipulated that none of the beneficiaries was to transfer their inheritance, in part or in whole, to anyone else during the lifetime of that beneficiary. On the other hand, what was Father's estate after all? It was the entirety of the nut shop in the hall at the souk, a house covering 480 square metres, at Sheikh Safi-od-din e Ardabili Street and a garden, with trees and a total area of 1,240 square metres, to the north of Sardab. Father had transferred the ownership of his apricot orchard to mother at the time of their marriage so that he would not be indebted to her in any way.

Mother put her handkerchief to her eyes, wiped her wet cheeks and said: "I just don't want him to die like a stranger in the middle of mountains or deserts. That is all I want."

"Please don't say that sort of thing Mother."

"What's going to happen to him after my death?"

She was sobbing. I got up and fetched her a glass of water. She sat up with my help, took a sip of the water and leant against the headboard. Her silence was killing me. She just looked and blinked. I wondered whether to stay or to go. But during those last days, she was no longer restless. Now, after nearly a year, she had forgotten the disaster. She was getting used to it. She had neither the breath to shout nor the strength to stand up in front of me and yell: "What have you done to him, you scoundrel?"

I said: "I didn't have anything against him, Mother. Did I?"

She wailed, she pounded her chest with her clenched fists, and her tears were always rolling down her cheeks or, at least, could be seen in her eyes. She kept saying: "May God make you fall to the depths of misery and degradation."

"Don't curse me mother."

"How can I help cursing you, you infidel, you heathen? Do you think that you'll come to a good end, you ..."

Gradually, her mournful temper subsided. One day, when Ideen and I had returned from the souk, she had cooked us a delicious meal of stuffed vine leaves. We ate and I talked about my trip to Astara on the Caspian coast. I said it would be a good idea if Ideen and I went there together to see the dense forests. I kept tempting: raspberry bushes are everywhere along the road, one can see the sea-bed, and there is a 19-year-old girl who would agree to marry Ideen if he promises to behave. Afterwards, Ideen, giddy and sleepy, stretched out. With Mother's help, we took him to the basement room. She said: "Ideen, would you like to go back to your previous room and stay with Urhan?"

He said: "What are you up to this time?"

We helped him on to the bed. On the stairs, Mother said: "I hope he doesn't wake up again. I can't bear seeing him like this any longer. What happened to all that dignity, all that strong personality, all that compassion?"

She wept again and progressed up the stairs by holding on to the railings.

I said: "Why do you exhaust yourself, Mother? Do you think he's really suffering? Rest assured that he is the most comfortable person on earth. He has no sorrow, no worries, no cheque to get cleared, no bills to pay. He enjoys absolute comfort and bliss."

He was going up the stairs, two steps ahead of me. I laughed. And as soon as he heard my laughter, he slapped my face so hard that I felt dizzy. He said: "Who are you laughing at, you scoundrel?"

His voice was cold and devoid of feeling, exactly like Father's commanding voice. For me, it was as if the walls were cracking and the cracks extended to the ceiling. The seed had been sown very early in childhood. After Ida's death, our lives resembled a great avalanche plunging into the depths of the valley of death, with no-one able, or willing, to stop it. It was as if destiny had decided that from childhood I should carry this incorrigible brother of mine on my shoulders and carry him up through a mountain pass. Despite all this, he pretended to be so self-sufficient that he made not only me desperate, but Father as well.

He meddled with my toy car and took it to pieces, climbed walls, and mocked everybody. I could not convince my parents that they should try to stop him.

Helplessly, all I could do was to hit my head against the wall and shout until someone paid attention to me. One day, he got hold of my bicycle which I had left against the wall. He cycled around the pond with such speed that it must have made him dizzy, exactly like a wasp sprayed with insecticide. Was it my fault if Father had not bought him a bicycle? I shouted from the veranda: "Get off my bike." But he kept pedalling around the pond, faster. And he guffawed.

I sat in corner of the courtyard and kept banging my head against the ground until I fell, exhausted and motionless.

Father was having some watermelon on the veranda. He did not budge when I banged my head on the ground. But when he saw my face covered in blood, he came down and started slapping Ideen on the back of his neck. He hit him so hard that Ideen could not move his head for three days. Mother cursed both Father and I. The kind mother, who had devoted all her affection to Ideen, did not utter the phrase "my Urhan" even once.

During the day, she used to send us off to the area around Lord's Electric Fan Factory to loiter about. We used to go to the end of the alley where the factory was situated in a kind of huge quarry, surrounded by a barbed-wire fence. The two flaps of its gate kept moving to and fro with the wind. A steep dirt road led to the area in front of the factory buildings.

We stood there as a matter of habit and, from the alley, looked down. The factory kept purring, making electric fans at an astonishing rate. We looked at broken blades piled up in a corner of the area in front of the building.

I said: "Let's go."

He replied: "Let's see who gets back faster."

We ran down the steep road. Our satchels were heavy and tended to pull us sideways. The noise of the factory was so loud that one preferred to shout rather than talk. We could not hear each other. I ran fast and felt hot, but I could not catch up with Ideen. His satchel was swinging in front of me. Although I knew that I was losing control of my feet, I let myself go. I rolled over, head first, and I fell flat. The operator came out of his little glass compartment and helped me stand up. My face was awash with blood and tears and my legs ached. A sleepy weakness ran through my body. I had difficulty in seeing Ideen who, happy and excited, picked up red, pretty fan blades.

Father kept hitting him with his belt while mother dressed my facial injuries. Father said: "For how much longer do you want to be naughty? Why are you so vicious?" And he kept beating him.

That night, mother could not stop my bleeding. Father twisted Ideen's ears and said: "You have broken his nose. Do you understand?"

Ideen said: "I haven't broken his nose. Don't blame me for things I didn't do…"

Father did not let him finish and boxed his ear hard. Ideen said: "I am sorry for him and his broken nose. But it isn't my fault."

Next day, father brought a doctor home, but to no avail. Even now that I am 40 years old, one side of my nose is still twice as large as the other.

He took out his pocketwatch, glanced at it and put it back. He was still in two minds about going or not going. He was afraid that it would be night before long. As was his habit, he brought the two sides of his overcoat together and then left them without doing up the buttons. He put his hand into the pocket of his overcoat and felt the ball of thick rope. A warm excitement covered his face and a sort of confidence flowed calmly through his veins. No. He had to finish the job without hesitation. Then he would be called a murderer. Who was it that uttered the word 'fratricide'? Mother, where are you now, to level false accusations, to share my guilt, to lighten my burden? But I swear to God that it will be good for him. He has been dead for years. Wherever he might be, in the Shoorabi teahouse or on the edge of the Salt Marsh, he smells of death. He is like a dry statue abandoned in his own past.

He looked at the people. Everybody was busy with their own problem. A gaunt old woman wanted to cross the street but was fixed there, motionless. A youngster was busy pushing two pieces of charcoal into the face of a big snowman in order to endow it with eyes. Some people were wearing nylon headscarves to protect themselves against snow. A woman wearing a black chador had so much snow on her head that she looked like Mount Damavand[3]. No doubt she was from a nearby village. Urhan walked on. A peculiar force dragged him towards the suburbs; more exactly, towards the Shoorabi teahouse. He walked so slowly and he was so absorbed in himself that he looked like someone who had nothing better to do, walking in the snow just for the sake of exercising.

I could not control myself. Besides, I didn't want to suffer silently as had always been my nature. I shouted: "You big lout. I have toiled for 12 years in this bloody place. What do you understand?"

He retorted: "Do you think I have nothing better to do? You expect me to be your apprentice?"

I said: "Even those bigger and more important than you should obey me, you, apprentice carpenter."

He waved his index finger as usual and said: "Some people are like you, some people are like me. It is a pity that I can't leave all this misery and go back to my carpentry. My conscience ..."

I interrupted him: "Don't talk about what you don't have."

He felt disarmed. He closed his eyes and sat down. I knew where best to hit in order to hurt him most. I said: "Father knew what kind of animal you were. It wasn't for nothing that he called you a coward."

He replied: "If you think you can make me quit by insulting me, you are very wrong. Because of what is in Father's will, I have a right to be here. I will not sell my share. Nor do I have enough money to buy the place."

I said: "You challenge me? I'll teach you a lesson." And I got up. I wanted to hit him hard and break one of his bones, but right at that moment, Esmayol came in. He closed the door and said: "You two are quarrelling again. What's the matter with both of you?"

I sat behind the desk. Esmayol said to me: "After all, he is older than you, isn't he?"

I banged on the desk with my fist and said: "An ass might be older than I am. Am I supposed to respect any such ass?"

Esmayol said: "After all, you are brothers."

I said: "I'll piss on such brotherhood." And then I saw Ideen leaving. I was feeling sorry for him but I could not make him understand that he should not have made any purchase without my permission. He had purchased four sacks of pistachio nuts. If he had waited a bit, I could have bought them five or even ten *toomans* cheaper per kilogram. Around mid-summer, it would be the time for purchases. But he did not understand these things.

In the evening we had another commotion in front of Mother. Mother said: "Alright, alright. See to your shares of the property and halve whatever you have: Two sets of scales, two of everything; it will be like having two separate shops, each of you to himself."

I kept quiet. That night I stayed awake, thinking about how best to deal with the matter. Mother had made every path of action impossible. She had said half and half, two sets of scales, two of everything.

But after such an outcome, would anyone pay any attention to me? Although our customers knew that I had 12 years of experience behind me, it was my brother they addressed straightaway. They thought I was the assistant. Worst of all were those disgusting women who had a crush on him as soon as they saw his nasty face. They entered the shop in their chadors and modestly veiled, but forgot about their modesty and their God as soon as they saw him: "What a pity that you haven't got married yet." They knew nothing of his sweetheart.

I said: "Is there anything proper about you associating with Armenian girls?"

He replied: "That's none of your business."

It was a depressing afternoon. I went to the cemetery, I sat at Father's grave and I wept. I said: "O, Father! What did you make me out of? And what did you use to create him? Why don't women look at me? Why do they scowl when they see me? Why is it that the most beautiful girl on earth has fallen in love with my brother? We have the same genes, don't we?" Father remained silent and motionless. He could no longer even cough. The ravens were sitting in a tree and a fierce wind lashed the dust into my eyes.

Symphony of the Dead

I said: "How are you going to administer the wedding vows? Aren't you supposed to be a Muslim?"

He said: "It's none of your business." And he filled the girl's handbag with pistachio nuts, saying: "You must now go and put on some kohl." When I looked at those golden eyes, begging for love, I felt like dying with desire. I could not sleep properly. I said to myself: "I swear to God that I'll kill you, brother."

Some time later, Mother would ask: "Where is my Ideen?" She was talking about the same person who used to wear a well-tailored jade-green suit with a tie, was clean-shaven and had a well-kept moustache. Mother looked at him with pride, smiled and said: "One is filled with admiration." And now she asked: "Where is my Ideen?" How could she not know where her Ideen was? He was either in the Shoorabi teahouse or behind the ruined walls of Akhavan Garden. Sometimes, he joined the porters at the end of the souk and cracked watermelon seeds with them. Or they cracked seeds while he recited news from World War II.

Mother said: "Wherever he is, go and find him."

But this time, there was no Mother. She was lying in peace, beside Father, under mounds of earth and snow in the town's old cemetery.

The street was cold and filthy. Fog and smoke were billowing over the town. Urhan turned back for a moment and looked behind him. It was as if all that smog was being pushed out of the nut-sellers' souk, moving to and fro and pouring out of the hall. For a brief moment, Urhan thought of going back and telling them to get rid of the fire and the smoke somehow. After all, although it was winter, they could buy a coal heater or install a chimney. He would be prepared to pay for it out of his own pocket. But he gave up the idea and walked on, moving away from the town. There was no more jostling, no bumping of shoulders, no wheelbarrow to hit his feet, no snowball aimed at his head. When confronted with a snowball, he always ducked but the snowball would invariably end up on the back of his neck.

There had been a heavy snowfall and it looked as if more snow was to come. Urhan dragged himself to the side of the carriageway so that he could perhaps find a taxi, a car or a horse-drawn carriage. But the snow had hit the town hard and brought everything to a standstill. There was no car and no other means of transport. There was only a police jeep passing through the snow with wheel-chains, leaving two parallel spirals behind it. What was he to do now? It would be a half-hour drive to the Shoorabi teahouse; but walking in this heavy snow he would have to continue until late in the night if be wanted to reach the teahouse. Would that not be better? In darkness he would suffer less and, besides, no-one's suspicions would be raised. But could he turn back? What if he kept going? No, he would get there in time. It wouldn't matter if he found himself in darkness or if the wolves tore him to shreds. To hell with life, to hell with everything! He had walked to the end of Sheikh Safi Street. He turned left and walked on. He heard the harsh, rusty voice of his asthmatic Mother in his ears all the time. What if he didn't find that bloody fool? No, He would certainly find him; and in the same teahouse. 'I'll find him Mother. I promise.' This time, he had made a pledge to himself, for the last time.

The further he moved from the town, the louder became the hubbub he imagined he could hear. But there was not a single soul moving in the snow. Nor did any old man slip and fall. He could no longer see any porters burning wood in braziers. Ahead of him, there was a wide, white wilderness that no creature dared to cross. The sky had dark-blue edges. A raven was perched on the branches of the last leafless tree of the town, chanting "snaw, snaw".

With the collar on his overcoat turned up, he began walking, like an old tortoise, along the snow-covered street. He moved forward with his usual slow pace. As always, he walked without haste. He knew the way very well, as he had followed the same route many times before and, every time, had found him in the Shoorabi teahouse. I said: "What are you doing here, you, good-for-nothing?"

Ideen replied: "Sir! I, too, have desires and long for a cup of tea."

"Shut up. You can drink your tea in the souk. You don't have to come here."

Ideen folded, neatly and meticulously, the newspaper he was holding and placed it in his pocket. He said: "I won't drink tea unless it is worth the urine I pass afterwards."

"To hell with you. I am fed up with you."

It was sunny, sheep were grazing on the hill opposite, and one could hear the clamour of the town from afar. With my hand, I indicated that he should get into the car. He said: "No." I said: "What the hell do you mean by 'no'?"

He said: "Let us walk, brother. I get a headache in the car, and I sweat."

I said: "That's not my concern. To hell with your problems." And I boxed his ear. I couldn't do anything else: I had to make him respect me and fear me. It wouldn't have been wise to leave him to his own devices in a hostile world. Abbas the teahouse keeper said: "He is, after all, a human being and besides, he is older than you." I boxed his ear once more. He crept into the car, sitting in the back seat. His hands were trembling and his mouth was foaming when we got to the souk. His eyes were pale. They made him lie down on the ground, in the souk. One of the porters – I think it was Esmayol – pulled out

Symphony of the Dead

his packing needle and traced a line on the bare floor, around Ideen's body. I said: "Why are you doing that, man?"

He explained: "I want his illness to remain on the ground and not rise."

I said: "Oh, yes, like my boil." I was reminded of the old fungal infection on my neck, a dried up boil as big as a large coin. We had drawn a circle round it with blue ink. Within two or three days, it had dried up and never reappeared.

Another porter washed Ideen's face and a third sat on his thighs. When they poured cold water on his head, he suddenly sat up, as if his deep sleep had been abruptly disturbed. He pulled out an old newspaper held in the belt holding up his trousers and began reading: "On the next day, they informed the prince that Mah-Banou was sorrowful, weak and pale because she was away from her prince and that she was in danger of losing her life. They told him: 'Oh, Prince! Come and behold the helpless ones.' He said: 'Ask the magic orange for advice on what I should do'. So they did. The magic orange opened up and the straw-clad girl, with celestial beauty, entranced the prince who fell in love with her. Mah-Banou said: 'I am no longer in danger. The stallion of love can only be harnessed on the pasture of love. This kingdom is worthy of those who are endowed with dazzling beauty, as my reign has come to an end'..."

The porters were mocking me with their eyes, as if it was I who was uttering such nonsense. I said: "Alright, alright. Be quiet. Go and crack your watermelon seeds."

He said: "Seeds? Seeds? For how long do you want me to crack seeds? Tell me brother: Why are there 24 hours in a day?" One could still see some foam at the corners of his lips. His clothes were soaked. He pulled another newspaper out of his trouser-leg and went to the end of the souk. He walked so proudly, as if he had defeated me in a game of wrestling. And I had no idea why there were 24 hours in a day. He thought about all these things. And all his pockets were filled with pieces of paper and newspapers. You could find a newspaper hanging on his belt as well. He held his newspapers upside down and recited news of the war in detail: "On the basis of these figures and considering the thousands of fatalities, Germany is submerged in defeat. Observers believe that only one person has remained alive in Germany: Hitler. But this is a lie. His mistress is alive too."

He did not read the newspapers. He only scanned the lines with his eyes. And he read with such an air of authority that those who did not know him thought that he was actually reading the news. But he just made it up. He did not offend anyone and was offended by no-one. For him, a bowl of broth with yoghurt sufficed for the whole day. They told him: "Sooji! Your broth is getting cold. Eat it up now and read afterwards."

"Let me read. What I have read so far is just the writing on the envelope. What would you say if I read the whole lot?"

Urhan walked on. He was in deep snow, up to his knees. The lower half of his overcoat was dragging on snow. What strange solitude! Father thought that one could be alone only when one was on his own, in his own shop. He didn't know that loneliness could be felt only in a crowd.

I said: "I have toiled for years, Father. Don't tar everybody with the same brush. I have carried these huge sacks of pistachio nuts on my back so many times, going down a staircase of 40 steps."

He said: "I just want to see both of you prosperous."

When Ideen completed secondary school and received his certificate, Mother said: "Come Urhan. We are celebrating Ideen's achievement. Come and have some cake and sweets."

I said: "Oh, for goodness sake! I am handling cake and sweets round the clock . Besides, what is so important about this? Has he conquered a kingdom?"

Mother said: "Well, why couldn't you have done the same?"

It was true that I had not been as successful. I had no reply. But Father came to my defence: "Urhan has attended school for eight years. He can read and write. That is sufficient." It was true that I could read and write quite well.

That year was the year of the ravens. God's black creatures were scattered all over in town. Mother found three or four cakes of soap every day. They had been carried away and dropped by ravens. Mother said: "Islam does not allow us to use them. After all, we don't know the unfortunate owners." But Father disagreed: "This is like manna from heaven. Wash on. Wash on."

Sheets, drying on the line, shone with whiteness. But traces of blue could also be perceived. Had it been raining, traces of blue would no doubt have been washed away. But our sheets were never completely white. A few traces of light blue were always there.

Ideen's bed was beside the window. He had placed his pot of geraniums on the windowsill. He had a glass of water beside him and had the habit of pouring the remainder of the water into the flowerpot.

I said: "Why shouldn't I be able to sleep beside the window?"

Mother said: "You can see the sky from where you are."

It was true. I could see the sky. Ravens flew about and perched themselves on the branches of pine trees and plane trees. The smoke rising from the fireplace in our room reached them. It was then that they chanted "snaw, snaw".

Symphony of the Dead

When he was quite a long way from town, his anxiety increased. For a moment, he thought: 'Shall I turn back? No.' Fresh snow had covered layers of old snow. Urhan turned back and looked. The town was submerged in mist and cold. It resembled an old newspaper that was full of words, voices, silence, dead people and living people, but was silent. It resembled those newspapers that Urhan had never had the time to read. He had left them behind and now he was anxious. He thought of his rudimentary education, his house that resembled a morgue and was only good enough to sleep in at night, a mad brother, and those who had been near and dear to him but who were now all in the graveyard. No wife, no child, no love. O, to hell with everything.

His fingers, deep in his pockets, were crying with cold. But his feet were numb and no longer felt the pain. He lifted his *papakha* and felt the top of his bald head with the palm of his hand. A shudder of cold ran over his warm head. He stopped for a moment and looked all around with intense concentration. Now that he could see nothing but the white, snowy curves of the hills, he felt the solitude more deeply.

At such moments of solitude, he had a better understanding of his brother's life. It was a strange feeling. During the current episode, of which no more than ten days had passed, he felt his brother's absence and somehow missed him. The mad Ideen, with whom he was now fed up, was a harmless person. He wouldn't know what to do with him if he found him. Nevertheless, he wanted to see him. Perhaps his presence at the end of the souk was a kind of assurance or encouragement. He thought: 'When I was sleeping in the room upstairs, I knew that there was another person sleeping in the basement, an educated but wasted person.'

He said: "The imbecile is the one who tears a banknote in half." He did not remember that in those days he was a noteworthy person, had a good appearance and was well dressed. A thousand pairs of eyes looked at him with admiration. He had struck up a friendship with the daughter of the Armenian coffee-seller. I don't know what sort of friendship it was, but every afternoon he loitered in front of the coffee shop. I said: "Do you really love her."

"Who?"

"Convert her to Islam and marry her. They say Armenian girls are really hot and passionate."

It was only a long time later that I learnt that he had been deeply in love. When he came back home in the afternoon, he kept himself busy reading books. After dark, he either wrote or read till midnight. I said: "Father, what if he marries her?"

Father replied: "Then he would drown himself in misery, like Ida. After all, they're twins."

I knew that Armenian girls were nymphomaniacs and I had no doubt that, one day, Ideen would make her pregnant. But I restrained myself and said nothing. He used to sprinkle himself with perfume, dress well, comb his hair neatly, wear a tie and go out. Father used to refer to his necktie as "the bridle of civilisation". But now, Ideen had forgotten everything and put all this behind him. Every other one of his teeth was missing. He was wearing worn-out, discoloured clothes and sitting down in an indolent mood at the end of the souk. His presence was a disaster, his absence a bigger disaster. All sorts of rumours flew about.

No. He didn't want it to happen in this harsh way. If, instead, he heard the news of his death all of a sudden, he would have him buried in a respectable manner, he could hold a memorial service for him straightaway, he would arrange a memorial service after seven days, after 40 days, after a year and, thereafter, on every anniversary of his death. On each one of these occasions, he would serve a memorial dinner to everybody in the town, to friends and strangers alike. He would stand at the entrance to the mosque, place a handkerchief on his eyes and cry loudly. He would shed enough tears to convince everybody that he loved Ideen.

What was he to do now? He took a step forward and was in snow up to his knees. He felt he was moving as fast as a lame mule. He was no longer as young as he used to be and could not be as frisky, as vicious, as a mule. He was 40 and he looked 50. He had a house, a shop at the nut-sellers' souk, an apricot orchard ... that was all. Father used to say: "When one makes one's fortune, one feels old at whatever age one is." And I used to reply: "No, Father. One feels manly and proud."

And now, there had been such a snowfall that it had immobilised not only him, but the entire town as well. The alleys were covered with snow and mud, water was overflowing from the gutters, and the nut-sellers' souk was quiet and mournful. The town looked dead under the snow.

The porters at the souk burnt wood in a brazier, sat around the fire and cracked watermelon seeds. The smoke rising from dry wood and moist wood billowed into the hall while Sooji read a newspaper. He wore a hat with flaps, turned the flaps down to cover his ears and fastened them under his chin. With a typically thin Tatar face, with a high stature and with beautiful black eyes, he wandered among the porters. My wife used to ask: "Where is Ideen?"

When Father was alive, Ideen wore a brown suit, trimmed his moustache neatly and held two books in his hands. He said: "I am not after your wealth Father. I am going to leave home."

Father said: "He will come back and beg. We'll see."

Both were stubborn. Father exerted moral pressure on him in particular. He said: "Why did you miss your prayers Ideen?"

"I was awake till late."

"Why, boy?"

"I was going through my lessons."

Father grumbled: "Prayer is sacrificed at the altar of your antics." His voice was as cold as a whip. He grumbled on: "We are on the eve of Friday. Do your ablutions. Recite a chapter from the Koran."

I ran quickly to the washroom, did my ablutions and recited my prayers eloquently in Father's room. Father asked: "Where is that unprincipled boy?"

Mother said: "He is in his own room."

Father was scowling. He was restless and could not sit down. He was moving about the room. He said: "Can you think of him being busy with something useful?"

Mother said: "I am sure he is praying."

"May he be punished for his faults. Can't he pray here?"

"Ideen doesn't like making a show of his piety."

I said: "Really? I thought it was the praying he didn't like."

Mother said, half in Turkish: "Has this got anything to do with you?"

She said this in such a fine way. Up to then, I had not heard anyone utter Azeri Turkish words with such eloquence. Mother told me: "After all, he is older than you. Behave yourself."

Mother was thin and nervous. She was easily angered. Very easily angered. She knew that Father was aware of everything and kept an eye on everything even when he was praying. She said: "When your Father says whatever nonsense he likes, what can I expect from you?"

Afterwards, I went to our room. Ideen was lying down on the bed, on his stomach, reading Balzac's *Le Père Goriot*. Father had never come into our room, but that night he did. He knocked a few times and entered. He asked: "What are you reading?"

Ideen jumped up, holding the book. He stood fully upright, his hands folded on his chest. I could clearly see the trembling of his hands. Father persisted: "I said 'what are you reading?'" He then frowned and walked around the room.

Ideen said: "I am reading *Le Père Goriot*."

Father asked, calmly: "What is Père Goriot?"

Ideen's index finger was still between the pages of the book. His other fingers were trembling. He said: "The life story of an old man."

Father asked: "Who is he?"
"Le Père Goriot."
I laughed. Father said: "Shut up". And, looking at Ideen, he said: "What is this old whatsisname?"
"He makes vermicelli."
"What?"
"Vermicelli."
"What?"
"European noodles."
Father said: "What are you?" Ideen was silent and Father kept looking around the room. He had a small stature. But with his round spectacles and their heavy frame, coupled with the wrinkles on his forehead, he was so awe-inspiring that one felt frozen stiff when one looked at him. Ideen, too, used to refer to his imposing personality. He used to say:
"One feels frozen stiff. I don't know why I'm scared of him. Aren't you afraid of him Urhan?"
And I used to reply:
"No. Father is Father. There is nothing to fear."
Ideen used to say these things when we loitered around the edge of the town, where women washed clothes in the open air.
He said: "Have you ever seen him laugh?"
"When he is in the shop, he jokes and laughs from morning till night."
"I like him but I fear him." He looked at the swallows flying overhead. He had no idea that these little, beautiful birds could bring disaster to human beings. When women had finished their washing and left, we, too, turned back towards the town. The women were carrying washed clothes on their heads and we looked at them casually, with total peace of mind, with no worries.
Father cast a glance at the other books on the shelf. Then, he turned back suddenly and said: "You, son-of-a-bitch! You go on reading nonsense, don't you?" He snatched the book from him and tore it in half down the spine. Then he tore off the pages until the floor was covered with paper. He tore the pages and scattered them about. At the same time, he shouted and roared. He said: "Don't bring such rubbish into my house." When he was leaving the room, he looked at Ideen's thin moustache that was now well established above his upper lip. He said: "What wounds do you want to inflict with this dagger of a moustache?"
I could clearly see the nervous twitch of Ideen's eyes. By way of habit, I kept rhythm by tapping on the door with my fingertips while I was looking at them. Father pointed at my hands which were behind me while creating that pleasant rhythm and grumbled: "That's enough."

Symphony of the Dead

That very night, Father assigned a separate room to Ideen. He said: "Right now. And don't argue."

Mother protested: "Why?"

"Because the rotten tooth should be pulled out and thrown away so that the healthy ones remain healthy."

Mother swept the basement reluctantly while saying: "It is bad luck to do this at night". Father said: "Sweep. Don't argue."

Mother placed a rug on the floor and we moved Ideen's bed, that very night. There was a staircase with seven steps leading from the courtyard down to his new room. The room was dark and damp and reeked of vinegar and the juice of sour, unripe grapes.

Father always advised: "When there are possibilities, one must make use of them." For that very reason, I immediately moved my bed and placed it next to the window. I looked at the sky and was fascinated by it. There appeared to be more stars than before. The smoke rising from the fireplace kept dancing in the air. And, no doubt, God's black creatures, the ravens, would perch themselves on tree tomorrow and chant: "Snaw, snaw."

That night, I dreamt of a garden with golden trees. Our alley had become wider. The electric fan factory had risen from the pit and was now at ground level while it sported a red tin-roof. And I reviewed my lessons. And, then, I was dead. Next morning, when I talked to Mother about my dream, she said: "You will have a long life, my boy."

The snow covering the wilderness had two layers. With every step, his boot went through the upper layer. But underneath, there was another layer that felt as hard as a rock. He felt as if he was walking with bare feet. He felt the pain deep in his body and, for this reason, he walked slowly and did not press his feet too hard. He had spent the whole morning looking for Ideen in town and had even searched the municipal garden and the old cemetery. Nevertheless, he did not feel tired. The only things that tormented him were his frozen feet. He shouted: "Sooji!" There was no echo. The sound was lost in snow. He walked on.

One day, Father had brought a few of Ideen's books to the shop. From early morning, he had been picking them up and going quickly through the pages. The more he read, the less he understood. He kept the books in the shop until the day Ayaz the policeman came in, saying:

"Djaber, you burnt a feather for me, so I came[4]."

"I had to talk to you about an important matter. Take a look at these books."

Ayaz the policeman picked up the three books, glanced at their titles and then held them in his hand, one by one, feeling their weight. He asked: "Where has he been?" He closed one of his eyes and waited for the answer. Father replied:

"Don't ask."

Ayaz said: "Let me see what is written here." He read the book titles aloud and with difficulty: "Odyssey". He looked at Father and asked again: "Where has he been?" He then read another book title: "Jardin d'Epi ... cure". He didn't read the third one. He asked: "Whose are they?"

"Ideen's."

"Your Ideen?"

Father looked worried: "Yes. My own Ideen."

"O, my God!"

"I wanted to make a good person of him, but I didn't succeed." He rubbed his hands together and asked: "Where is the Garden of Epicure?"

Ayaz replied: "Our misfortune is right here."

"Where?"

Ayaz replied: "These are bad times". He paused for a moment and then, putting his mouth close to Father's ear, he said: "Have you heard that the communists have laid a green garden and fascinated the young?" He placed the books in a big bag and then left in extreme anger, without eating his pistachio nuts. He said he was going to get rid of the books and added: "Let us keep a watchful eye on Ideen. We have to take care of him."

Father said: "May God always keep you for us."

At the doorstep, Ayaz turned back and said: "If my head rolls, it will be for friendship, brother."

Father said: "If I didn't have Ayaz, what would I do?"

He sat at the desk for a moment, lowered his head and then said: "Get moving Urhan."

"Where are we going?"

"We will call at home." He assigned some work to the assistants and told them to look after things. He donned his *papakha* and we set off. Father never went back home at that time of the day. It was ten o'clock in the morning and we walked fast. I had no idea about what he wanted to do. When we arrived at home, Father asked Ida: "Where is Ideen?"

Ida looked pale with fear. With her lips trembling, she said she didn't know. Father pushed her aside and went towards the basement. He stood at the top of the staircase and called me. I ran forward. He said: "Bring whatever book, notebook or piece of paper you find."

I went to the basement and collected the books I found on the shelf, the notebooks, the handwritten notes and the books under the bed. I took them all out and brought them to the edge of the pond, where Father was standing. With his finger, he pointed to a spot on the ground and I let whatever I was holding drop. Ida, standing at the kitchen window, was weeping helplessly. And Father was so angry that Mother dared not appear. She was no doubt eyeing us from somewhere. Father asked: "Is that all?"

"Yes."

Father sprinkled some paraffin and I struck a match. What flames! And what a dance performed by tormented pages! It looked like the death pangs of a strong man who had been stabbed. They stretched and bent, they turned golden, they turned brown, and then they turned black. Father gazed at the centre of the bonfire and said: "*Le Père Goriot*. Isn't this one *Le Père Goriot*, Urhan?"

I noticed that the book had just caught fire:

"Yes. It is."

"Had I not torn this one up?"

"He must have bought another one."

"Then I destroy it once more."

When the flames subsided, we washed off the ashes and left for the shop. But a black stain persisted on the square bricks covering the courtyard. It looked like a black beast, flattened by the back of a spade. Ida was standing behind the window and I had no idea what the future had in store. Father said: "Whatever had to be done has now been done, no matter what is to come."

In the evening, when Ideen noticed the black stain next to the pond, he stood there for a moment and, then, fearful and trembling, he headed for his basement room. That night, he didn't come to dinner. I was watching from upstairs. He went to his own room and switched the light off. I think he went to bed. At dinner, no-one wanted Ideen to be present.

From afar, he saw the green-hued Shoorabi and his heart started to pound. He had no idea what he would feel on seeing Ideen this time. The excitement of thinking about this encounter, coupled with the pain of his frostbitten feet, made him restless. A few steps ahead, he perceived the silent Salt Marsh, dead under snow. The stone bench at the edge of the Salt Marsh was also covered with snow. There was no Ideen.

He said: "I so much wish these migrant birds would fly close and come ashore."

"What shore?"

"Do you see these seagulls?" He was sitting on his stone bench, looking at the sky.

I said: "What seagulls?"

"The one that has a black circle round its neck is the bird of peace." With his eyes, he followed a line in the sky, his whole face beaming with a smile.

I had no time for this sort of thing and, besides, I had left the shop unsupervised. I said: "Alright. Get up and let's go."

He said: "It moves its wings with so much feeling. Do you see, Urhan?"

He bored me; and if I did not stop him, he would go on with his fantasies all night. I said: "We've had enough of this, you beast!"

He frowned and, looking at me, said: "I am no beast, Father. I am a human being."

"Yes. You are a human being. You are right. Now, get up."

He suddenly turned his head and looked at the Shoorabi: "How about getting into the water?"

"Look at the sun. It is setting. We have to get back before dark."

At that moment, I remembered those years when Father was alive and, every afternoon, we got into the water and had a swim, with nothing to worry about. Ideen used to say: "Look, Urhan. No animals, no insects. This water pushes back every useless thing. All those leaves and unwanted things are pushed out by those little waves." He played about in the water and kept talking. His black, smooth hair covered his forehead. With so much energy in the water, he swam a hundred metres back and forth every time. The water was salty and bitter and we constantly spat the taste out.

I said: "I'm beginning to feel cold. Look at the sun." I wanted us to get back home. But Ideen was too enthusiastic and could not leave the Shoorabi behind.

He turned back and saw the little adobe building that was the teahouse, overlooking the Shoorabi. He was sure that Ideen would be there now, sitting on the main bench, with his newspapers and scraps of paper scattered around him. He would have totally rotten teeth and he would utter words with difficulty. He thought: 'He is afraid of me, like a whipped dog, and will follow me like a sheep.'

I stood at the misted windows of the teahouse. It was autumn and a bitterly cold wind was blowing. I had a look and saw Ideen sitting, cross-legged, on the main bench reading a newspaper. He was reading seriously and attentively while he waved his index finger in the air. There was an empty tea-glass in front of him. When I opened the door, he was taken unawares and looked alarmed. I said: "What are you doing here, boy?"

He replied: "I have come to inform the people of the news, Father."

I clearly saw the trembling of his hands and I could read his feeling of unease on his face. I laughed and said: "I am Urhan."

"Don't try to trick me, Father."

"What have you come here for?"

"I was feeling so unhappy. I was longing to see Ida. I have no idea what has become of her son Sohrab. I was feeling really unhappy, Father." Then he suddenly narrowed his eyes and said: "Can you believe that Ida could have set herself on fire?"

I said: "Not every topic is suitable for talking about away from home. You shouldn't have come here."

Mashd Abbas, the teahouse keeper, said: "Oh, Urhan. When he wants to come here, let him do so. What is wrong with coming here? Why do you bother him?"

"Because I am the one who gets into trouble. He won't come back of his own accord. Every time he comes here, I have to come after him."

Ideen asked: "Where are we going now?"

"Mother keeps asking where her Ideen is. Get moving. You know she's not well. Why do you irritate her? Why do you irritate me?"

He said: "These pimps and bastards have finally succeeded in preventing our people from achieving national sovereignty. Do you understand, brother? Do you understand?"

"Yes, I do understand. Now get up and get moving."

We set off. Ideen was at least 30 at the time. His sideburns had turned white. Mother said: "Isn't it odd? Isn't it odd at his age?"

A bitterly cold wind was blowing outside. Until we got to the town, he talked so much and about so many things that I was filled with astonishment. I wondered when and how he had learnt so many things. He had a fantastic memory and knew many fascinating tales. But a moment later, he said: "Look, brother. They say that these snowy fields are full of partridges. If you had brought a sack with you, I could fill it up with a hundred partridges."

"But there is no snow now. Winter is a long time away."

"Oh yes, there is snow. Only you don't see it. There are plenty of partridges on the mountains."

"So what? What would you do with so many partridges?"

"I don't know." Then he stood still and looked at the mountains that were acquiring a tinge of violet with the sunset. I was losing patience and I felt very hungry. I said: "You're talking too much. Get moving or I'll hit you..."

No more words from him. He just followed me like a child. We left the teahouse behind us, mud-walled, gloomy.

It was dark and misty. He felt encouraged by the thought of getting himself warmed up at the teahouse. He moved towards the teahouse, rubbing his hands together. He wanted to pound the soil with his feet and blow his warm breath into the palms of his hands. But all that would be of no use. He had to get to the teahouse, enjoy the warmth near the samovar and have two glasses of hot tea in order to forget his feeling of weariness and cold. He stepped forward, getting stuck in snow with every step. He stood behind the door. Astonished, he murmured: "Oh, what is this?" The windowpanes were broken and snow had advanced to the centre of the teahouse. There was no samovar, no bench, no sign of life. Nothing! The teahouse looked like an abandoned mortuary in which vultures rest, attracted by the smell of death and staleness. The walls were covered with lines and curves drawn with charcoal. Above the platform at the end of the teahouse, the wall was blackened up to the ceiling. This was no doubt the remnant of a big fire. On the right, rubble from the collapsed ceiling was in a big pile. The skeleton of an animal could be seen at the top of the platform on which the samovar used to stand. One would think that beasts of prey had stood on top in order to eat the animal. Maybe in the middle of winter, a wolf has snatched that animal from in front of the eyes of its hungry cubs, brought it to the top of the platform, eaten the whole lot and even licked the bones so much that they looked as if they had been smoothed with a file.

Urhan looked around. No. There was no trace of vultures either. He turned back. What had he come here for? What was he going to do now? Suddenly he heard a sound. He listened carefully; something was moving. He listened more carefully. It was the sound of an animal. He walked about the teahouse, terrified, slowly. Now he clearly heard the sound of a horse. The stable's door opened up with a dry rasp and a gaunt old man appeared in the door. He was wearing a fur hat. The whole scene looked like an old painting. Urhan automatically took off his *papakha* and held it tightly with both hands. He felt as if something like a spirit moved up through his legs and his chest and, then, left his body through his head. His throat turned dry, his knees felt weak and his eyes gazed at the old man. He remained motionless until the old man made a move. He then felt his heart pounding. He asked: "Who are you?"

"This snow brings everybody to a halt."

Urhan took a step forward and said: "You must be very tough indeed." And he scanned the old man from head to toe. He was wearing a short overcoat. Black woollen leg-warmers covered his legs up to his knees.

The old man said: "I am obviously exhausted." And he stood aside.

Urhan entered the stable, stamping the floor with his feet at the entrance. Snow fell off his boots and his overcoat. He said: "Fire. Haven't you made any fire?" He looked all around him. It was dark and the air reeked of the smell of animals. He repeated: "Haven't you made any fire?"

The old man, stupefied, looked at him. He said: "What with?"

Symphony of the Dead

Urhan was trembling and his legs were aching. He felt the dampness that had penetrated his clothes. He was trying hard to concentrate. He said: "There was a teahouse here, wasn't there?"

The old man sat on a pack-saddle and said: "I don't know."

"Yes. There used to be a teahouse here. When Mashdi Abbas fell ill, they packed it up. Who was the owner of the building?"

Urhan looked around once more. Right at the end, two donkeys and a horse were huddling up to one another, with their faces in a nose-bag. The old man had taken off one of the donkeys' pack-saddles to sit on. He chain-smoked.

Urhan asked: "Are you going to town?"

With a harsh voice, the old man replied: "No."

"Where are you going then?"

"To Ram Asbi village."

"You are not going now, are you?"

"No. It will be dark soon. I'll wait till sunrise."

Urhan remained silent. He didn't want to be alone. And he feared that the old man might change his mind. He said: "In this season, the wolves have no mercy."

The old man lit a new cigarette with the end of his old one and said: "Wolves have no mercy at any time. At the neighbouring village they ate up three men in broad daylight." He got up, removed the pack-saddle from the other donkey and placed it in front of himself. Urhan, who had been walking around and stamping on the floor with his feet until that moment, sat down and looked outside. It was white and cold. He rubbed his hands, undid his boot-lace, took his boots off, removed his socks and wrapped his arms around his legs, clasping his hands. He said: "I am Urhan."

"Urhan? Which Urhan?"

"Sooji's brother."

The old man looked more carefully and said: "Fratricide?"

Urhan felt as if he had been stabbed in the back with a sharp, cold knife. But it was no use denying anything or shouting at the old man. He nodded. Then, pressing the fingertips of one hand with the other, he shouted "Ouch!" Addressing the old man again, he said:

"I am now a merchant of watermelon seeds."

"Watermelon seeds?"

"Yes. Nuts and seeds in general. It's really cold in here."

It was really cold. His joints felt as if they were snapping.

The old man said: "Take off your overcoat and wrap it round your legs and feet."

"No, no. I am very sensitive to cold I'll catch pneumonia."

He felt a pain all through his bones. He asked: "You don't have tea, do you?"

The old man was silent and kept smoking. Urhan said: "Is there nothing here which we can make a fire with?"

The old man kept quiet. He lit up yet another cigarette and crushed the old cigarette butt under his foot. Urhan said: "I am now almost Sooji's captive. You know him, don't you?"

"Chain him up."

Urhan could not warm his feet or even alleviate the pain in his bones. He moaned and said: "It has now been about 14 years that I've been stuck with him. How can I chain him? He's no child. He is 42 years old."

"Lock him up in a room and give him food and water. That's all you have to do."

"That's my intention if I find him. But our madman is like a bird. If you put him in a cage, he will die. Outside it, he flies away. He is not a violent lunatic. He's harmless. He was born just to torment me." He wanted to keep talking but he was not sure whether the old man was listening. He felt so degraded and downtrodden.

We gradually got used to the situation, both of us. Whenever he felt unhappy, he disappeared for two or three days and then came back. I would ask: "Where have you been, boy?"

"I went to pay my respects to my master."

"What gift have you brought back?"

"Nothing of much use could be found. All I brought back are these sunflower seeds and poor-quality apricots."

"Alright. Go into the souk. Don't hang around so much. Think of my reputation."

"Brother, two glasses of Mashdi Abbas's tea bring happiness and vigour. Do you understand?"

He filled his pockets with watermelon seeds and disappeared. His presence was of no importance to me, but his absence was most annoying. During the nights when he slept in the basement, I was upstairs. I was alone, but I knew there was someone down there. I knew that someone was breathing down there. And this was comforting; especially in a house filled with the smell of Father's jacket, damp with rain, the smell of asthmatic Mother, and also the smell of Ida. For two or three days, I put up with all these and I knew that he could come. Frowning, I asked him angrily:

"Where have you been, boy?"

"I went to Moscow."

"What for?"

"It was all war and fighting. In that freezing weather, fire was raging with huge flames."

"Did you fight too?"

He gazed at the people who passed by, outside the shop, slowly or in a hurry. He said: "Where do you think so many people get their spoons from?"

"Tell me about the war. How many did you kill? How many did you wound?"

"We have brought a woman prisoner of war with us. But she's turned out to be a whore. Her name is Martha. She is fairly good-looking. I think she is from Yugoslavia."

"Which side did you fight for?"

"I am finished brother." He looked sad. They were both silent, gazing at the wilderness outside.

It was as if both of them were expecting someone, or a group of people. Urhan asked: "Aren't you feeling cold?"

"I put up with it". He paused for a moment and then asked: "How have you come here?"

"On foot. Do you have any cigarettes?"

He felt as if cold was transforming itself into tear-like drops, rolling out of his eyes and over his cheeks. He suddenly yearned for a cigarette:

"Do you have a cigarette to spare?"

The old man opened his cigarette-box and held it in front of Urhan:

"It will stop you shivering."

The old man waited for Urhan to take a cigarette in the dim light. When he struck a match, he had a better view of Urhan's face and feet. His feet had turned very red indeed. He asked: "Have you come here just to look for Sooji?"

Urhan, moaning from his throbbing feet, nodded. The fact that he made the old man believe that he liked his brother gave Urhan satisfaction. But his heart was in turmoil. He had walked that route over and over again, in the cold and in the heat. He had frequently endangered himself in order to make Ideen come back. But, now, he had decisively made up his mind. He wanted to finish the job, whatever the cost. He exhaled the cigarette smoke intermittently, with anger and relief. He didn't know what brand of cigarette he was smoking, but the taste was horrible. He got up and closed the stable door. Through the gap in the broken door, he looked at the open country outside. He said: "We are stuck here. We are going to have to stay." The old man was silent. The open country outside was uniformly dark and covered with snow. He had never thought that he would have to stay. He asked: "Where has this brother of mine got to, then?" The old man kept quiet.

Father used to say: "It doesn't matter at all where he has gone."

I said: "One is not always the master of one's feelings. From morning till night, Mother keeps asking where her Ideen is. She wants to bring him back. She pays him a visit every now and then."

Father said: "She has no bloody right to do so. With whose permission does she pay him a visit?"

About a year had passed since Ideen had left home. He worked at a timber factory overlooking the river passing through the village of Ram Asbi. He had become thin and gaunt and he did not eat properly. But he had firmly made up his mind to be independent and never to set foot in his father's house. After that book burning, he had been deeply offended. He felt as if he himself had been set alight. And indeed he had been, he in the fire of Father's ire and Father in nature's.

The day after the book burning, the newspaper Aftab-e Sharq reported the incident thus: "At 12.30pm yesterday, there was suddenly such a reduction in sunlight that one would think a broad, stocky hand had eclipsed the sun's face." And we knew this sentence by heart.

That day, the sun was completely blocked out and day turned to night. Although Father had not had his lunch yet, he looked at his watch to make sure of the time. And although he saw the hands clearly, he thought there was something wrong with his eyesight. Astounded, he asked: "Is it nighttime already, Urhan?"

I didn't know what had happened. I said: "Oh, my God" and I ran out of my room. It was even darker now and, right at that time, I heard the siren that signalled the end of work at Lord's Electric Fan Factory. I was sure that it really was nighttime, as the factory had not closed during working hours even during the war. What was even more astonishing was that during the days following the occupation of Iran by Allied forces in 1941, when people would kill each other for a loaf of stale bread, the factory had continued to work. But now I heard the siren. People's tumult could be heard from streets and alleys. Some superstitious types were beating their copper pots and pans on their roofs creating a loud cacophony.

Father came to the courtyard and stood beside Mother and I. We gazed at the sun without protecting our eyes with our hands. Mother was weeping. Every now and then, she would find an excuse for missing Ida who lived in Abadan. Then she would weep.

Symphony of the Dead

The sun had turned into a blood-red disc and a black dust had filled the sky around it. That day, I saw Father scare for the first time. Darkness had spread everywhere and a horrifying din could be heard from the alley.

Mother recited a prayer in a barely audible voice and, at the same time, cried in a heart-rending manner. I, spellbound, kept looking at the sky that had, suddenly, been studded with numerous stars. There were more stars than I had seen on any night. I said: "Oh, my God."

Father interrupted his prayer and said: "This is an bad omen. This is a calamity that has descended on us. Do you know what this means?"

He held the palms of his hands towards us and, in a feverish manner, said: "Have we shed any blood?"

Mother said: "God forbid!"

Father said: "This is the result of our deeds; ours and our children's. Oh, God! Have mercy on us."

A moment later, the noise in the street subsided and the town was submerged in such darkness and silence that one would think that its inhabitants had been dead for years. It was as if there had never been a town there. Mother lit an oil lamp and placed it on a shelf. None of us dared to leave the room.

Mother said: "What about Ideen?"

Father said: "Let him be, wherever he is."

Mother was worried. Later on, when the smell of burnt food filled the house, she slapped her knees hard with her hands and said: "What disaster has fallen on me". Panicking, she ran towards the kitchen. Father, holding an oil lamp, followed her. At the kitchen door, he stood and said: "This is the result of our deeds. What have we done?" I saw his hands trembling and his face covered with tears. I took the oil lamp from him. Father said: "We are living on top of a mound of subversive books. Our own son has stored a pile of blasphemous books in the basement. He has become a poet too. I presume what he'll do next is pick up a musical instrument and become an amorous entertainer. I simply cannot put up with this state of affairs." At the same time, he rolled up his sleeves and said: "We must recite the Ayat prayer."

We went back to the room and recited our Ayat prayer.

It was dark for an hour and a half; and we shivered for an hour and a half. Then, it was like twilight, as if the sun was about to rise or had just set. Thereafter, the sun shone and we had daylight again.

With his head, Father signalled that I should follow him. We both went to the courtyard. Mother, standing on the veranda, was as puzzled as I was. She said: "Why aren't you going to the shop? Don't you know what you want to do?"

Faced with Father's silence and the smell of burning, Mother preferred to keep herself busy somewhere else, out of sight. Father said: "Throw the carpet and all the clothes out of the room."

I rolled up the carpet and brought it out. I placed Ideen's clothes on the veranda and was about to pull out his sheets and blankets when Father said: "Fire needs fuel." But Father did not know what there was in the room. Following the previous book burning, there were now books and notebooks galore all over the place: under the bed, on the shelf, up the staircase and in the corners of the room. Ideen composed poetry and had struck up a friendship with a few other poets. Father said: "Pour some paraffin down there."

I carried the paraffin can inside and poured paraffin over everything. For a moment, I wanted to drag the bed out, but Father, preventing me, said: "Strike a match." I did so.

When Mother left her room it was too late. Flames were rising from the basement door and window and something was burning with a frightening noise. Mother wanted to do something. She was waving her hands, but she was spellbound.

Father said: "It is the soul of the devil that's burning". And, indeed even the burning soul of the Devil could hardly have made so much noise and smoke. The heat could be felt on the far side of the pond and smoke billowed into the sky. Some of the neighbours knocked at the door to enquire about what had caused the smoke. Father explained: "We are making tomato puree."

I was scared that Ideen could have a heart attack as soon as he saw what had happened, but nothing happened to him. He came back home at sunset. The house was submerged in a mournful silence, as if someone had died and everyone was hiding the secret. Ideen placed the bundle of books he was carrying at the edge of the staircase and was about to wash his hands at the pond when he noticed that the cellar was dark and frighteningly black. The smell of burning was everywhere and could not go unnoticed. The three of us watched him from upstairs. Ideen moved towards his room but when he reached the staircase, he could not stand upright. His hands and legs were trembling and his whole body was shaking. He left the house without uttering a word or looking at anybody.

Father was silent. He had not guessed that this would be the outcome. He walked round the room and thought. Mother said: "Is this what you wanted?" And she started crying.

Father said: "What are you worried about? We have done this for his own good. Can't you see these are difficult times and that they arrest and imprison young people for the most trivial reasons?"

Symphony of the Dead

That night, Father suffered such debilitating diarrhoea that it drained all his strength, energy and willpower. He neither sat, nor stood up. Nor did he sleep. He kept going to the toilet and paced back and forth between the visits.

Mother repeated: "Is this what you wanted?"

Father replied: "Let a few day pass. Hunger will bring him back."

Mother retorted: "Either you find him and bring him back this very night or I will leave this house tomorrow."

Father said: "Is he not my child too? Do you think that I don't feel sorry for him? If you don't interfere, I hope to teach him a lesson and make a respectable man of him."

After that fire, Ideen was so offended that when Father and I went to see him a few days later, he did not show up. Mother kept insisting that Father should bring him back and Father and I would go to Ram Asbi village again and again. The workshop was situated on a kind of isthmus above the river. Workers were busy on top. One day, when Ideen was sawing a tree-trunk, Father swallowed his old pride, stood in front of him and said: "Forget the past, Ideen!"

Without raising his head, Ideen replied: "Forget me, Father."

And we went back home. Father was full of anger, vengeance and respect. From then onwards, he uttered Ideen's name in a particular tone. Ideen worked there for perhaps about a year. Mother enquired about him and I paid him a visit every now and then. But he would accept nothing. We took him food, books and clothing and he returned them untouched. He would refuse even Mother's offerings. Whenever we persisted, he would say: "My educational record, my books, and the poems that were my mine..." and he would burst into tears.

Gradually, he lost his characteristic *joie de vivre*. It was as if he himself had been burnt. He didn't look well. I had noticed that his black, simple shoes were split open on both sides. He always wore the same long overcoat and black trousers. He fixed one foot on the wood and sawed the timber, so vigorously that the timber would give off smoke and then separate into two pieces. He would wipe the sweat off his brow and select another piece of timber.

I stood near him, waiting for him to finish his work. Then, we set out together, heading for Shoorabi. He walked warily as his black shoes were split.

I said: "Aren't you paid wages Ideen?" He panicked, thinking that I wanted to borrow money. He said: "I have money, do you want some?" He was about to put his hand into his pocket and bring some money out when I said: "Why don't you buy yourself a pair of shoes?" He looked at his shoes and said: "It is neither raining nor snowing now. I have thought about it. Wait till autumn comes." From above the hills, he looked both at the Salt Marsh and at Shoorabi. He said: "I love Shoorabi."

On the far side, the Salt Marsh had a wave pattern and salty mud had dried hard. With each season the wave pattern appeared to have changed. He said: "It looks so much like the sea."

I said: "Yes." We were standing on top of the hills overlooking Shoorabi and a gentle breeze blew. Below, Shoorabi was stagnant and its reed beds could be seen in every direction. On one side of Shoorabi, between the hills and the water, tall reeds with sharp leaves had grown. Ideen looked at the scene with great attention and a sparkle in his eye. He said: "It looks like the United Nations building."

I asked: "Where?"

He pointed at the scene facing us.

I asked: "Why?"

He explained: "This reed bed reminds me of the flags of the United Nations."

In good old days, Father used to say: "Be happy with Shoorabi and don't underestimate its value. In a few years' time, this place will become another salt marsh, a swamp covered with bitter, useless salt." We had not reached the age of puberty yet. I would pick up the red bucket and Ideen the green one. Father would undress and jump into the water. In water, he appeared older. We, too, would undress and dive in. The sunshine was hot and the water tasted salty and bitter. I remember one day when fallen leaves moved away in large groups on the water surface. Father had stretched out both of his arms and we could see his almost bald head sticking out of water. He said: "Go further in and bring some sludge out."

The Russians used to pump the sludge out and carry it away in tankers. Father said: "This sludge is the best cure for rheumatism." He rubbed his body, jumped out of the water and lay down in the sunshine at the edge of Shoorabi. He had put one hairy, thin leg on top of the other and, resting on his elbows, looked all around him. He said: "Bring me some sludge before I begin to feel cold."

Ideen took a deep breath, opened his mouth and plunged into the water. Little bubbles filled the space where he had been. Then, he came up from the depths with a single push. Sludge filled half of his bucket. He said: "Take it." And he ran towards the water again. I took the bucket to Father who was resting his head on the ground and waiting for us. I looked back. Ideen swam on in the depths of the water. Father said: "Well done son. Rub it on my body. I am dying for it."

A gentle wind was blowing, agitating the reeds on the far side of Shoorabi into a dance. I took the sludge in handfuls and rubbed it on Father's skin. I started at his feet. Father said: "Think of me as a shoe. Give me a good polish."

He had turned quite black, looking like a statue sculpted out of tar. He stayed stretched out until the sludge dried up on his skin. As for us, we rubbed the sludge only on our legs and sat down waiting for the sludge to cake up. Then we jumped into the water and washed the sludge off.

Father said: "Collect some for Yousef too."

After that fall, Yousef had become a useless chunk of flesh, only eating and defecating from morning to night. He lay in a corner of the room downstairs. Motionless and speechless, he gazed at the door and chewed something all the time. The room stank with the smell of a dead animal and Mother was busy with washing his sheets in the courtyard all the time.

Ida used to say: "If you make him a little room in the courtyard, that would be a relief for all of us." But no-one paid her any attention.

Father was eating a cucumber to quench his thirst. It was a good summer and the sunshine was hot. The sludge on Father's body had dried up and big ants were crawling over his stomach. Father got up and went into the water to wash the sludge off. He said: "This is the proof that the medicine works ". All his skin had turned red. He said: "It is time to quench my thirst" and kept on eating cucumbers.

Urhan had forgotten that he had taken another cigarette from the old man and that he had lit it with the end of the first one. He puffed energetically and felt an excruciating pain in his legs and arms. He said: "What am I to do now." And he looked around. In that darkness, a monotonous chime could be heard, like the chimes of the Three-Star clock on Mother's shelf. He asked: "Where's that sound coming from?"

The old man replied: "Dripping water," and he pointed to a spot on the ceiling, above where the horses were resting. Urhan looked at the roof and remained silent. The old man said: "Don't worry. You'll find him." Urhan kept quiet. The old man continued: "He runs away, doesn't he?" Urhan looked at the floor and did not want to listen to him.

I asked: "Who did Ideen run away from, Father?"

"Run away as well. Go to hell. All of you."

"I don't want to run away. I am not the same as Ida or Ideen. It's Friday today. I want to go to Shoorabi with the guys."

"Who is going to see to the shop then?"

Mother said: "Let him go. He's not like Ida or Ideen, who are both quiet. Do you think you could be a match for this one?"

Father retorted: "They're all the same."

Mother picked up Father's pipe and put it on the shelf: "After all, this one has inherited his habits from you. You shouldn't smoke a pipe all day." She then placed her hands on her hips in a gesture of defiance and, standing in the middle of the room upstairs, addressed me with incomprehensible anger: "Go then. What are you waiting for?"

We left town in a bus with wooden bodywork. People in the town always remember that year as a bad one. There were 40 of us. Some of the guys were soldiers. We sang and clapped on the way. We first chanted the 'Flag' song and then 'With my Beloved on a Dark Winter's Night in the Desert'. While driving along the streets on the edge of town, we noticed a house on fire. Smoke and flames billowed out of the windows. The driver stopped and we all rushed out of the bus. The owner was an old man with white hair. He was hitting his head with both hands and he yelled and roared. He sometimes sat down and sometimes ran in front of his house. Then he turned back and, looking at the flames, resumed hitting his head. Some time later, we found out that he had no family. Nevertheless, at the time of the fire he was killing himself with rage and sorrow. Altogether, eight water hoses from locations far and near aimed at the house and black mud had covered the street. The flames were so wild that they left almost nothing of the house. The fire was extinguished when the roof collapsed.

I remembered that in the previous big fire, too, no-one could do anything at all to put it out. A raging fire swept through the bazaar and a column of black smoke rose into the sky. People, astounded and helpless, stared at the smoke. There was no electricity. Policemen on night duty in the bazaar fired their guns into the air and shouted for help. Some people ran about yelling. The stream running along the street had, unusually, no water in it that night. As far as the eye could see, people with lanterns in their hands filled the street and moved towards the bazaar. Father was trembling with fear. He was holding my hand, and Ideen's, firmly and he kept reciting prayers. He prayed to God, imploring him not to let the warm wind carry the flames as far as the nut-sellers' souk. Fire raged along the bazaar. It had become merciless. We were standing at the corner of the square, just looking, like everyone else.

That night, the bazaar kept burning until dawn. And the fire continued through to the following night. An entire row of shops, mostly confectioneries and one or two sugar storerooms, was burnt down. When the walls collapsed and ruined the livelihood of many people, the fire ended, all by itself. But black smoke hovered over the town for several days. The smoke was so dense that the wind could not shift it. On the following day, it rained. The rain tasted sweet and people placed pots and bowls outside so that the sweet-tasting rainwater would not be wasted. We noticed what was going on only when it had stopped raining. Our hair and clothes were sticky and our hands stuck to whatever we touched. Father licked his hands and remarked: "Sherbet."

For some time thereafter, taps gave out sherbet instead of water. I said: "I want water."

I panted with thirst. The sweet water could not quench it. Father said: "Drink the sherbet. Where are we going to get water from?"

"Get it from somewhere."

"What are you talking about? These days, even urine tastes sweet."

With the passage of time, water lost its sweetness, Ida set herself on fire, Father died, and Ideen, too, was overwhelmed by disaster. Only Mother and I were spared. Mother slept under a white sheet and snored. She snored all the time because she was suffering from asthma. In the middle of the night, I thought I was hearing the harsh sound of a hard surface being filed. Ideen leant his head against the wall, one could see the blood vessels of his temples and his neck pulsating fast and his eyelids twitching occasionally out of nervousness.

Mother said: "Tell me, my dear son: Who brought this misfortune upon you?"

Ideen said: "The fire of war was extinguished in the cold winter of Moscow."

He was right. All fires, with all the flames and the smoke they make, with all the death and damage that they cause, would eventually die down of their own accord. But all fires would die down amidst death and destruction. People still remember that there were 40 of us. Some of the guys were soldiers. When the fire died down, we got into the bus that had a wooden body and wooden seats and, along the bumpy road, shook us so severely that our entrails were about to burst out. When the bus headed off again, we saw the red fire-engines approaching and howling. But it was too late and what used to be a house was now a mound of rubble.

We set out again, singing and clapping. Once again, we sang 'The Flag'. At the edge of Shoorabi, all of us stood up shoulder to shoulder as we always had done. I counted: "one, two," ... and when I said "three", all of us dived into the water from the rocks with our clothes on. We swam as far as the reed beds and swam back. The water was cool and a gentle wind was blowing. Then we saw a boat approaching from the east. The only person on board was a man, with a white, dirty skullcap on his head, standing at the helm. He was paying attention both to us and to the harsh noise of the boat's engine. He asked: "Aren't you coming on board?"

We said: "Hurray" in unison and we clung to the boat's wooden body on every side. It smelt of lacquer and paint. With every movement, it creaked, as if it was going to disintegrate. The fact that Shoorabi now had a boat made us feel happy and we agreed that we should come back to this place every week. Hurray! But none of us had seen the boat until then. We didn't know who the owner was, when he had arrived at Shoorabi, or where he had come from. He was an elderly man who laughed but who, at the same time, looked worried, like people who sit behind the steering wheel of a car for the first time. He said: "I have four children. Life is dear." And he kept laughing and grinning widely.

When all of us had got out of the water and were on board, the boat left the shore behind with its engine purring. The boatman said: "Come every day." I said: "I'll come every day. Faster." It was my first boat ride and all my clothes were wet. The boat shook and rocked in a peculiar, frightening manner. When we reached the middle of Shoorabi, I felt the boat sinking. The guys shrieked and rushed to the door. The boat began submerging from the engine side and then flipped over. Now the boat was on top of us like a heavy tent and submerging further, upside down. We shouted and pulled ourselves upwards. Our heads were hit by the heavy body of the boat and we sank down again. I looked up. It was dark. We had to get away from under the boat. I drove away the sludge with my hands and tried to move away from the sludge. When I saw light, I pulled myself up. I realised the boatman was stuck in the sludge up to his waist. With eyes wide open with fear, he wanted to shout. He raised four fingers and I thought this must mean that he had purchased the boat for four thousand *toomans*. In my mind, I imagined telling him 'so long as you are alive and safe, to hell with the boat'. I struggled to pull myself up, but I felt as if someone was holding my trouser legs. I found the culprit underwater: It was the tall, useless, Jamshid who was, at the time, a soldier. He swallowed water and pulled me down. He was stuck in sludge up to his shoulders. The golden epaulettes of his uniform were shining. He pulled and I struggled. Suddenly, I thought of undoing my belt. I did so and freed myself.

At the time, I was 20 years old. I went back home wearing only my violet underpants. It had been a disastrous day. For a long time to come, I felt the taste of the salty, bitter water in my throat. People still remember that there had been 40 of us. As for the tall good-for-nothing Jamshid, his mother told me: "You have survived. But you will have a troubled life."

The driver of the tractor said: "Urhan is a favoured creation of God. Treasure him."

Mother said: "Come. I must show my gratitude to God for your survival."

Symphony of the Dead

She brought a large, new piece of cloth, stretched it from my toes to my head, and folded it over until it reached my heels. Then she cut the cloth and gave it to a beggar. It was an ominous time. There was mourning all over town and in every street. Divers from Astara, on the Caspian coast, searched the sludge at the bottom of Shoorabi for three days. They pulled out the wrecked hull of the boat, but they found no trace of the drowned youths.

The old man said: "Do you have a temperature?" He placed his hand on Urhan's forehead and said: "You are hot. But your temperature is normal. Take care." He lit two cigarettes, giving one to Urhan: "If we are not frozen by dawn, we'll never die."

"That's true."

"Why did you set out so late in the day when you knew night would fall soon?"

They could not see each other. Only the red-hot tips of their cigarettes, sometimes glowing prominently, could be seen circling in the air. Urhan said: "When Sooji is not at home, I feel dead with loneliness."

"I had heard your name before. Fratricide."

Urhan kept quiet, but the old man had now become eager to talk: "Did you kill your brother?"

"People say something of the sort." And he no longer wished to talk to the old man. He flattened his half-smoked cigarette under his boot and hung his head between his knees.

When I thought about it years later, I could remember that the tall, thin soldier we referred to as the long stick was Jamshid. He had clung to my trouser legs and wanted to drown me with himself. He was my friend and I don't know why he wanted to do this to me. One Friday afternoon, when the shop was closed, I went to the Akhavan Garden. It was a garden with no gates or walls. A few years later, the government got hold of it, planted new trees, felled the old pines and plane trees, laid lawns, installed a few slides, swings and see-saws for children, lit it up with electric lights, and called it the Municipal Park.

But, at the time, Akhavan Garden was the same old Akhavan Garden, with crumbling walls and the bricks stolen and with a mountain of rubbish which so many flies and mosquitoes inhabited. We were not 14 yet. We loitered around the periphery of the garden and looked at ice-cream sellers and wooden-flute makers. At sunset, ravens arrived in flocks and attacked the refuse of the rubbish dump. And we loitered and looked around. I scratched the ground with the heels of my shoes, as I wanted to make dust rise. Ideen said: "Why can't you stand still and behave yourself, kid?" And I continued to raise dust with the heels of my shoes. Then a blackened coin surfaced. I kicked it and shoved it away with the tip of my shoes. It rested in the shadow of a willow. Jamshid jumped forward and picked it up. We laughed.

He said: "Who wants this coin?"

We didn't want it. We had not suffered enough poverty to make us yearn for a blackened coin.

Jamshid said: "I think it's a two *rial* coin."

I said: "Why don't you put it into your pocket?"

"Bigger coins than this are all over the place in our house and no-one picks them up."

"Coins are not found all over the place in our house. But may God bless my father's business." Ideen looked at us, laughing. He liked my cheekiness and always said: "I like this. You're a cheeky guy."

Jamshid said: "No matter how wealthy you are, I don't think you can compete with us." He tossed the coin into the air and I caught it. I felt that it was thicker than a two-*rial* piece. I held it under the tap of the cement tank that was leaking all the time. I washed the coin but it wouldn't be cleaned easily. I rubbed it on the ground and held it again under water. Jamshid said: "We have three gardens. If you set out from one end of one of them in the morning, you will reach the other end in the evening." I was busy with the coin and noticed that it shined like gold. It was a gold Pahlavi coin. I held it between two fingers so that Jamshid and Ideen could see it. Ideen asked: "Is it gold?"

Jamshid said: "It was mine." He was very tall. He was also thin. He had a bent nose and a mouth that always looked as if it was ready to utter the word 'thou'. We used to call him 'Jamshid, the long stick'. He stepped forward like a giraffe and said: "I picked it up first."

I retorted: "You didn't have to pick it up."

"It was mine."

"What is yours is in your pants."

"I found it."

"You didn't have to find it."

We came to blows. Whatever spot I hit was bony. Ideen said: "It's not right to fight over money. Share it."

I said: "What for? I wouldn't even give him something as worthless as my balls." We went back home. In the evening, I saw Jamshid looking for our house near Lord's Electric Fan Factory. I asked: "What are you looking for, you long stick?"

"I wanted to say that you should give me the coin."

"What for?"

"Because we are poor people. My father died a few years ago. My mother works in the chocolate factory."

"Well. Sell your garden and spend the money."

"We can't. We have no garden."

I could not reach his face. So, I hit him on the stomach. When he bent down, I slapped his face. He was shocked and started crying. He said: "Why did you hit me?"

"Why did you lie to us, you, son-of-a-bitch?"

Some time later, he reappeared. From then onwards, he would come every now and then and we would take a walk around the town and further. He no longer talked about the coin. Thereafter, he became a soldier. And on that fateful Friday, we went to Shoorabi together. In a swimming competition in which 40 of us participated, he was the last one. Then, on that banger of a boat, he tried to climb over the cabin. And the divers of Astara were unable to find his body.

Jamshid was my only friend. When a memorial service was held for his late Uncle Ezzat, only 17 people had turned up. I was the eighteenth. A few minutes after I entered, the memorial service was wound up and no-one else came. I asked: "Why aren't your relatives and your clan turning up?'

"There is no-one else. These are all we have."

"What about neighbours?" And I noticed Ideen, sitting in a corner of the mosque. I said: "Look, Jamshid. My brother is here."

"Yes."

"Why didn't you hold the memorial service at the mosque in your own neighbourhood?"

"It was too big and it would cost a lot. And this place is far from anywhere."

Jamshid's uncle was a hawker. He had a cart out of which he sold baked beetroot and boiled broadbeans in winter and fresh fruit in summer. I had seen him quite often. Whenever Jamshid and I went somewhere together, we ate something at Uncle Ezzat's cart. He didn't charge us.

I asked: "Hasn't your Uncle Ezzat left a will?"

"A will?" He chuckled and said: "He didn't have enough money for his creditors to come after his estate."

"Who has he left his belonging to, then?"

"To no-one. His cart is no use to anybody. It will be ten years before his son is old enough. By then, his cart will have rotted under rain and snow."

* * *

The old man got up, opened the stable door and gazed at the sky. Cold air rushed in once again. It was sharp and debilitating. Urhan said: "Close it, close it." The old man closed the door quickly and with agility. He said: "It will snow again."

Urhan was feeling sleepy. He said: "How are we going to sleep?"

"I'll wait till dawn breaks. Then I'll set out again." He struck a match and looked everywhere. He struck another one and held it above the manger. He said: "Sleep here."

Urhan passed between the horses and donkeys, feeling some warmth in the middle of the ice-cold air. He said: "Strike a match again." The old man did so. Urhan looked at the manger. It was full of shingles and pebbles. He asked: "Here?"

"Yes. Sleep there. Don't worry."

He climbed into the manger and sat in the middle. He stretched out and said: "A blanket or something." He tried to look around in the dark. The old man laughed with a hollow sound. Urhan was now sitting cross-legged. He said: "What shall I cover myself with?"

"If you are not offended, there are two pack-saddles."

Urhan, shivering, buried his hands under his coat.

* * *

I said: "Are you going the same way as those who buy on credit?"

He had thought I would not see him if he turned his head away. He said: 'Hello, Urhan."

He had begun his national service. He had been given a haircut and his eyes seemed to be sinking into their sockets.

Ayaz the policeman used to say: "Jamshid has begun his national service. That's going to put some sense in him."

He wasn't a bad guy. I wonder where he appeared from, why he died so pointlessly and why he was my friend. When he waited outside our house with that tall frame, I asked myself why he was so patient. He leant one foot against the wall and waited for me to leave the house. I told him: "If you want me to come with you, you must wait for me to go to the bathhouse and come back."

He scratched his head and said, with a twisted mouth: "Bathhouse? Can't you go there some other time?"

"I haven't been to the bath for a week."

"How long is it going to take?"

"An hour. Maybe two hours."

"Alright. I'll wait. But for goodness sake, come back quickly."

Jamshid didn't know, or maybe he did know but didn't care, that when I went to the bathhouse, I wasted so much time surrounded by the hot steam, I washed myself so many times, I turned red, I drank water and I got feverishly hot. When I returned, the "long stick" would be still waiting for me, one foot leaning against the wall, exactly as when I left him.

Then I said: "Well, long stick, shall we go and see Martha?"

* * *

Urhan listened to the silence of the snow. He didn't know what was going to happen and whether he would find Ideen eventually. He was sure that Ideen was alive. He wanted to go all the way now that he had made up his mind. He wanted to finish the job and then, with no Ideen to worry about, deal with his own misery. He knew that he could easily tie him up and leave him in the snow without shedding his blood, without hitting him at all. He could tie him to this very doorframe. He could even make him fall from the top of the rock into the middle of Shoorabi so that his soul would quickly be drowned in eternal peace. After all, Father used to say: "The cooler the resting place of the dead, the less they suffer."

We poured water on Ida's grave. Mother was holding a bottle of rose water and was waiting for the scent to fill the air. Ideen said: "She suffered everything she shouldn't have suffered. Now it's too late." He was standing at the grave, looking at the sky. He was wearing his navy-blue suit that day. A fine scarf, hanging parallel to the flaps of his jacket, was visible down to where the jacket was buttoned up. Father, who was reciting something, looked up and glanced at him, furtively. Then he whispered in my ear: "Look at this big good-for-nothing." I whispered back: "What has that go to do with me?" Father shook his head: "No doubt he wants to go to Armenia at four o'clock in the afternoon." Ideen kept looking at the sky, as if he was following the slow descent of a paratrooper.

As children, we always wore clothes of the same colour and the same style. Mother would give us two large biscuits and say: "Go and play." We had been taught to hold each other's hands when we went anywhere together. Occasionally, Mother would send us away to buy buttons, gauze or other material. Sometimes we would go to the Lord's Electric Fan Factory. Ideen and I ran downhill towards the factory, hand in hand. The factory roared down there. The workers, wearing yellow uniforms, continually packed electric fans into cartons and placed them into small GMC trucks in the area in front of the factory. For as long as I was a schoolboy, we went to school together. We were naughtier than other kids. I pointed out the bullies among them to Ideen. Ideen would drag them to a wall and slap them three or four times. He would tell them: "Don't forget that Urhan is my brother." When I caught measles, he carried me home on his shoulders. But life was not always the same. We had good days and bad days. But as we grew up, it got worse.

Ideen said: "In this country, we are ruined before we are 30. You in a way, I in another way, Ida in yet another way."

I said: "The shop permit should be registered in my name, brother."

"Alright. Let it be registered in your name."

"The partner's consent should be formally registered. But we are brothers not partners." And I registered the business in my name. Ayaz the policeman said: "You are now ten steps ahead."

Mother said: "You had no right to do such a thing. Why do you make your Father turn in his grave? Whatever you have should belong to you two equally."

I could do nothing but leave the documents as they were. At night, when I looked at the sky out of my window, I thought I could hear Ideen blinking and thinking in the basement. As soon as I closed my eyes, I saw him with a big knife, about to cut my big, red watermelon into two halves. It was as if I was seeing him clearly in broad daylight. I remembered that I had carried sacks of pistachio nuts down 40 steps and up 40 steps. It was not fair as, at the same time, Ideen did nothing but go to school. It was I who had benefited the business with my labour. Father used to say: "The donkey is working and the pony is eating." No. It wasn't fair. I had toiled for so many years. I said: "Mother, couldn't I go to school and continue my studies?"

"Didn't I tell you so many times? You could have got on with your education if you had wanted to."

Life was hell. It was poisonous and bitter. I suffered fever at night and worked during the day. I said: "Oh God! Where is your justice? Half and half?" Out of my window, I looked at the smoke rising from my fireplace and floating towards the ravens. It wafted around the branches of the pine trees so that the ravens would remember to chant "snaw, snaw" when the morning came and the sun rose.

I am now sure that he is alive. He doesn't get ill either. But his teeth are all rotten and he can no longer eat bread and walnuts. He can't chew much else either. Most of his food is broth and soup. His appearance is like that of a decrepit old man; but he's restless. He's awake from dawn until late at night. I have no idea what he's looking for.

Symphony of the Dead

Father asked: "What are you looking for?"

"Myself."

At first, I thought he must have a twin spirit that irritated him. Sometimes I thought that *jinns* had taken over his soul. But it was none of these things. I discovered that it was he who irritated himself. As a result, he sank deeper and deeper. Everything about him was abnormal and upside-down. Even his falling in love had no resemblance to the type of love of normal people. He was deeply in love with an Armenian blonde called Sormeh. For years, he worked in a timber workshop and spent all his money on books. All the time he thought he was a poet.

Father asked: "What are you looking for?"

"Myself."

One couldn't expect more than this from a man who looked for himself and found madness. He was a harmless madman who, nevertheless, could not be tolerated. He wasted his time, from morning until night, among porters at the end of the souk. When night fell, he followed me home. Along the way, he said hello to everybody, asked them something, or counted the lampposts.

He said: "You see, brother? God has been stuffing the world with snow for two weeks." He looked at the sky through the hole in the dome of the souk and said: "He has stuffed us with so much snow that he is ashamed. That's why He now does it at night, when people are asleep."

The amount of snow was immeasurable. It was the same accursed snow that has turned me into a roaming wanderer. It was cloudy during the day and it snowed from nightfall until dawn, ceaselessly.

He said: "Am I not telling the truth, brother?"

I laughed: "You are free to say what you like."

He entered the shop, placed a handful of watermelon seeds in his pocket and sat on a sack that was full of nuts. He said: "Give me some money so I can go to the bathhouse, brother." I told one of the assistants to give him a two-*tooman* banknote. Ideen said: "Tell him to give me more, brother. I want to drink tea too."

"You can drink your tea here."

"The only tea worthy of the name is that of the Shoorabi teahouse."

He came closer and stood beside me. He was a bit tired and his voice sounded grumpy. He said: "I must pack up and go, brother. The situation is too chaotic and hopeless."

"I wish you well. Where are you heading for?"

"Zabol, or maybe Kabul."

"God be with you. Don't forget to bring me presents and souvenirs when you come back."

How was I to know that he would never come back?

When we returned from Villa Darreh he felt sick. Mother said: "Push your finger down your throat. Maybe you'll be able to vomit." He pushed his middle finger down his throat, but he couldn't vomit. Mother asked: "What have you eaten?"

"Kebabs and yogurt and the sort of things that all other people eat."

Mother asked me: "You have not been affected, have you?"

"No."

"Why is it then that Ideen is suffering like this?"

"I have no idea."

"Take him to the doctor."

He was feeling very poorly, more so than someone suffering from food poisoning would. I took him to Dr Nayadanov's surgery. We sat in the waiting room. He said: "I feel as if my head has become a coppersmith's workshop."

We could smell fried garlic from the floor above the surgery. I said: "Let's wait our turn."

"I have a stomach doing somersaults. I feel as if people are washing their clothes in my stomach."

"You must rest for a few days." My hands and feet were trembling and a funny feeling of lethargy had spread through my body. My heart was beating too fast. I said: "You're suffering from weak nerves."

"I feel as if somebody has attached live electrical wires to my legs."

In my mind, I imagined telling him: "In that case, you're finished." He held his head in his hands and rocked back and forth. He was restless. In fact, he had looked sad and tired since that morning. It was now our turn and we entered the surgery. Dr Nayadanov had grown fatter and was as fat then as I am now. He was sitting at his usual brown, wooden desk. He had a beard like that of professors, and rows of furrows on his forehead. He asked: "Which one of you is the patient?"

I pointed to Ideen and sat down.

"What is wrong with him?"

"He feels as if there is a coppersmith's workshop in his head, a washerwoman's tub in his stomach and electricity surging up his legs."

"Take him to the madhouse." But he then examined him and wrote out a prescription. We headed back home. Along the way, he repeated his usual sentences in answer to whatever I said. At home, he said: "Turn off the light over my head."

Symphony of the Dead

"I think you have a temperature."

He kept whispering something and nodding his head. He had difficulty opening his eyes, walked with big steps, swung his arms and could not find his way. He said: "Earthquake."

"Where?"

"I have recently discovered that when there is war in a country, earthquakes could be imminent. You ask why? It is obvious. You will understand later on, when the city goes up in smoke."

He sometimes composed poetry and said things that I had not heard from him before. Mother said: "What have you done to make him go mad? Have you lit him on the head or something?"

"Me?" Without wishing to do so, and against my better judgment, I went to the clairvoyant woman and brought her home. Nevertheless, I could not convince Mother that I was innocent. The clairvoyant said: "Give alms. If I talk more than I have, disaster will befall all of you."

Mother was extremely distressed. She was restless and there was nothing she could do. She said: "Perhaps someone else has done something to him."

The clairvoyant said: "Go and be grateful to God for the way he is now."

I said: "Why don't you ask Ideen himself, Mother? Do you really think someone has hit him on the head?"

The clairvoyant said: "The indications are that he has brought this upon himself."

Mother said: "I don't know." And she cried. She kept going downstairs and coming back upstairs, she opened a window and then closed it, several times. She didn't know what to do.

We took Ideen to bed. We made him lie down on my bed. He wouldn't fall asleep. So, we took him downstairs to his own empty, eerie room. But even there, he got up every now and then and kept babbling. Mother said: "Fetch another doctor."

Dr Shooshanik asked: "How long has he been like this?"

I explained: "He has been abnormal for a few days but today he is at his most abnormal."

Mother asked: "Where did you go? What did you eat?"

"We went to Villa Darreh, we had kebabs and we came back."

The doctor said: "It can't be poisoning. It's a sudden shock." He took a blood sample from Ideen for examination.

Ideen had fallen into a rage of rapid babbling. His lips moved so fast that we couldn't make head or tail of what he was saying. He wouldn't stay in one place either. Before leaving, the doctor made him sleep by injecting him with something strong. Mother regularly washed Ideen's feet with cold water and kept crying. She thought Ideen was suffering from fever. I was standing at the entrance to the room. She looked at me with such hatred that I felt dead.

She said: "You did what you wanted to do, didn't you?" She leant her head against the edge of Ideen's bed and wept profusely.

I so much wish she had lived longer so that she could see how I am suffering. If she could see that I was so desperate and helpless in the face of Ideen's problem that I had to chain him to the railings of the upper veranda, she would weep for me.

Second Movement

Symphony of the Dead

1

On the day Father bought the shop from his partner, he was very happy and made a great show of his happiness. He brought a fountain pen for his eldest son Yousef. The fountain pen leaked, Yousef's hands were blue with ink and the carpet was also stained with ink. Mother had to wash the carpet and Father said: "What a stupid boy!"

Yousef was a simpleton and anybody could easily deceive him. One could fool him by telling him a simple lie and, then, submerge his head in the pond if one wished to do so. He was too sensitive and easily excited. He had neither the power to raise objections nor the willpower to endure suffering. He always chose a corner to cry in and kept himself busy with something for hours on end, silently and with no need for anyone's company. He looked like someone suffering from diabetes. But he did not pass water often and he had no pain. He looked pale, sad and dejected. His eyes could not concentrate on anything. When he was called by name, he would turn back, gaze at the person for a moment and then say: "Yes?"

Father said: "To hell with your 'yes'. Why have you rubbed ink on your nose?"

"What?"

Father had bought Ideen a German magnifying glass so that he could keep himself busy and amuse himself with it and no longer steal lenses from other people's glasses. And what theft! A month before that, Grandfather had travelled from Oroumiyyeh[5] to Ardabil after an absence of six years. He had travelled with his sons and daughters, wishing to pay a visit to his other sons Djaber and Saber. Saber had become a registrar at the municipal offices and Father, with his characteristic perseverance, had managed to acquire a shop and trading office at the nut-sellers' souk. He had achieved this by selling his share of a vineyard and by toiling day and night.

When the missing lens of Grandfather's glasses was found in Ideen's schoolbag, it was already too late. Grandfather had returned to Oroumiyyeh barely finding his way as his glasses only had one lens. This was Grandfather's last visit to Ardabil. Father used to say over and over: "His visit to Ardabil was not a happy one."

Grandfather was a peculiar type of person and there were all sorts of stories about him. Father believed that he was too stubborn. Forty years before, Grandfather had sold stones to the Qajar[6] government and he had not been paid. The Shah had died and his son had ascended the throne. Grandfather had persevered, only to be told that times had changed and that he could not hope to get his money. Thereafter, Grandfather had pursued his claim for 39 years, making several futile journeys to Tehran and Tabriz. And all this trouble for a pathetic pittance! He was owed only 332 *rials*. And for this, he had quarrelled in government departments, written several petitions, and made numerous complaints without achieving anything. During the reign of Reza Shah, he had penned a lengthy petition. They had torn up his petition and he had drawn up another one. During World War II, he had nurtured the hope of regaining what was due to him, drawn up several letters, made numerous complaints and appealed to many people in authority. During his last visit to Ardabil, he carried all the relevant files in his brown briefcase and never ceased to talk about his 332 *rials*. Father wanted to give him 332 *rials* so that the matter would be closed. But Grandfather maintained that he was not after bribes to be silenced; his aim was to achieve what was rightfully his. He stayed with his Djaber for a few days and left Ardabil for Oroumiyyeh. Two years later, when he was on his deathbed, he told his children: "Don't let your rights be trampled on. Do you understand? This piece of advice is my only will and testament."

Father said: "With his last breath he was no doubt thinking of his glasses too." He wept and said: "His last visit to Ardabil was not a happy one."

When Ideen came back from school, Father reprimanded him: "You, son-of-a-bitch! What did you want to do with the lens of my Father's glasses?" Ideen, not knowing that the lens had been found in his schoolbag, swore that he knew nothing about it. Father was furious: "Don't lie to me." He then took Ideen to the courtyard, tied him to the pine tree with a length of rope and flogged his buttocks with a belt. Father continued until he himself was breathless. But it was no use. Ideen did not confess and his stubbornness made Father angrier. He continued beating him. Yousef, who was nine years old at the time, watched the scene from the upper veranda and cried very loudly.

Symphony of the Dead

Father said: "What are you braying for, you son of an ass?" Mother, suffering from asthma, had difficulty in coming to the rescue of her favourite son. His skin had already turned blue because of the flogging. Mother, scowling and extremely angry, confronted Father and, snatching the belt from him, shouted: "What has it got to do with you? Why are you beating my child?"

"He is my child too."

Mother said nothing more. She untied Ideen from the tree and took him away. The following day, Ideen, suffering from pains in his back and his legs, did not go to school. He stayed at home and turned Mother's life into hell.

On the day when Father bought his shop and office from his partner, he was so obviously happy. He bought Urhan, who was five years old at the time, a second-hand toy lorry that was made of iron and had 12 rubber tyres. Urhan attached a piece of string to his lorry and dragged it behind him in the court-yard. It made a loud noise. Ideen was always on the watch, waiting for Urhan to fall asleep or get distracted for a moment so that he could examine the lorry and find out where the noise was coming from. He would take the lorry to pieces and re-assemble it without discovering the source of the noise.

A few days later, he made a toy lorry with wood, bobbins, wire and some ink taken out of Yousef's fountain pen. It did not make a noise and its wheels did not move either. He went back to Urhan's lorry, dismantled it, re-assembled it and, again, he had no success in finding the source of the noise. Five years later, he completed his design. He procured some scrap metal, wood, tin boxes and other bits and pieces from Lord's Electric Fan Factory and made a lorry that looked like Urhan's. It made a noise and moved. Furthermore, its front lights lit up. But his efforts had led to the destruction of Urhan's lorry.

Father said: "Didn't I buy a magnifying glass for you, son of an ass? Why did you meddle with Urhan's lorry?"

Father was extremely happy. He moved about aimlessly: From downstairs to upstairs, from one end of the corridor to the other, then to the drawing room, then to another room. He would then, absent-mindedly, open the window and exchange greetings with neighbours, from the upper floor. He would go back downstairs and tell Mother: "If my children have the know-how and can be hard-working, they will be able, one day, to buy the shop at the corner of the souk and we'll be able to merge the two shops into one..." But no-one listened to what he said.

He had bought Ida an American rubber doll that would squeak when it was squeezed. The doll was held by Ida all the time. Ida caressed it, but this did not cause the doll to make even the slightest noise. The doll was a fat, black woman that scowled and squeaked when it was squeezed. The squeak was like the crying of a shrew. Ideen, after being beaten severely by Father, took the doll to his own room upstairs and pulled out the whistle with his teeth. He discovered that the squeaking function was caused by a little gadget. He held it between his teeth and blew into it. Repeated squeaks pleased him no end. Ida heard the constant noise of her doll. The noise was coming from the courtyard. When she looked out of the window, she saw Ideen who was apparently imitating her doll. She went to the courtyard for a closer inspection. But she didn't understand what was going on. She even looked at Ideen while she was standing right in front of him. She was still puzzled. Ideen said: "Squeeze me." Ida squeezed him and he squeaked, exactly like the doll. Ida went to her silent doll. But the more she cried the less she was able to draw anybody's attention to her problem. So, she decided to solve the problem on her own. When Ideen was fiddling with Yousef's fountain pen, she bit his ear so hard that he roared with pain.

Ida said: "Cry like my doll."

That night, Ideen was spared a second severe beating, as Father would not get into a rage for the sake of Ida. Father believed that girls should learn housework. He said that, later on, they would have their own children and would be dealing with real dolls. The following day was a Friday, a day of rest, and Ideen spent his time on experimenting with his magnifying glass, pieces of paper and sunlight. He gathered local children around him and, without using a match, set fire to their textbooks and notebooks. When they became concerned about what was going up in flames, it was already too late.

Ideen was not a well-behaved child. The devil was in his veins, his nerves and his ears. He was restless. He was the sort of child that would make life hell for other people. He moved about all the time and, like his twin Ida, was very energetic. He was the last one of us to go to bed and the first to get up. Mother was very kind to him and tried to keep him happy with toys, money and food. Father didn't know what to do with this "bastard" and felt helpless in the face of Ideen's rebellious nature. Without doing his studies or going through his lessons, he got top marks all the time and added to Father's astonishment. Father knew no remedy but beating and it was perhaps for this reason that he failed to control him. At the end of every confrontation, he found he was no match for this seven-year-old child. Father wanted peace and quiet. He returned from work exhausted and what he wished for was a quiet, sweet child to fill his time at home. Urhan was his favourite child. He joked and talked in a pleasant manner and, yet, he was as quiet as Yousef. He was too dependent on his parents and this very characteristic pleased Father. They put food into his mouth, he fell asleep on Father's knees and, unlike the naughty twins, all

Symphony of the Dead

he wanted was to sit on Father's knee and eat those easily chewed pistachio nuts. Father chewed the nuts and placed them in Urhan's mouth. This had become a habit for both of them.

Yousef's desire was to carry on eating ready-chewed pistachio nuts as he had done in the years gone by. But he was now content with seeing his own past in the little Urhan. Without bothering anybody or complaining about anything, he minded his own business and kept himself busy with doing something aimless until he fell asleep. Sometimes, he sat in a corner and gazed at the movements of the adults as they put up with the mischief of little children. Even if a child emptied a glass of water on to his shirt, pouring the water down his collar, he would not complain. He thought that this was his destiny and it had to happen this way. His greatest pastime was to spend time with the twins. He gave them his own food and did his best to be liked by them, unsuccessfully. Hand in hand, they went to a corner of the courtyard and arranged the pine cones in rows until something like a fairy tale castle was built.

Father said: "Yousef and Urhan have inherited my characteristics."

Even many years later, one cold winter's night when Father had stretched himself out with the quilt of the *korsi* pulled up to his chin, he worried about Ideen and said: "I wonder who Ideen acquired his characteristics from. The more I think about it, the less I can think of anyone in our clan resembling him, either in appearance or in behaviour."

Mother said: "You have sown the seeds and I have given birth."

"I wish I had not sown any seeds. I wish you had not given birth to him."

Father assumed an expression of innocence, narrowed his eyes and, with a sad voice, said: "It's as if he's not our child. He neither accepts money, nor has any needs, nor attaches any significance to his parents."

Many years later, Ideen, too, felt that he did not have much in common with the rest of the family. He had forgotten the excitement, the liveliness and the naughtiness of his childhood. Nothing was new or exciting to him. It was as if he had lived in this world once before and was now experiencing his second life. He felt that he even didn't look like any other member of the family. This similarity to Ida had waned with the passage of time. By the time he was 18, he was thin and already very tall. His hitherto handsome face acquired an air of sadness. Father's eyes were small, blue and almost devoid of eyelashes. Mother's, even when she used extra make-up to make them look like Ideen's slit eyes, had no "Mongolian" narrowness. Father was slight. He had remained tiny and looked like a dry raisin. His voice, by contrast, was so powerful. One wondered where this voice came from. It was cold and penetrating, like the authoritative voice of members of the security forces.

On his last trip, Grandfather had said: "Djaber was always noteworthy for his voice." And, switching to Azerbaijani Turkish: "His body was of no significance."

Mother was bony, delicate and frail, like a length of straw. She had beautiful black hair, usually done in pleats. Whenever the pleats were undone, her long hair waved downwards. Ideen, however, was broad-shouldered and tall. His thick eyebrows were almost linked. He had narrow eyes and smooth hair, partly covering his forehead. All this gave him an appearance different even to Ida's.

Father said: "Look at these little devils. They are gradually turning into lions."

Mother replied: "You know how children grow, don't you?"

"This brat will not have a natural death. He will bring a disaster on himself."

"May God never allow such a fate." Mother scowled and, with a reprimanding look, carried on: "How can you allow yourself to say such a thing, Djaber? Ideen is my favourite child. For me, he alone equals the rest of them put together." Mother praised Ideen's thinking, sleeping, naughtiness and even crying. She said: "Ideen's voice is like velvet."

Father carried Urhan in his arms and showed his son's clenched fists to everybody. Urhan's fists could not be forced open, especially when he was asleep. Father said: "Look at these hands. This boy will gather wealth and hold my business in his protective fists. He is my son. He is my Urhan."

Ideen paid no attention to such expressions of affection. Years later, when he was looking for ravens in the darkness of night, he remembered that the ravens sitting on the pine tree were never safe in his presence. He aimed at them with his catapult. Ida gradually learnt to look elsewhere for affection. She did not have the slightest share of the affection showered on her brother.

Ida was a perfect twin for Ideen. She mirrored Ideen perfectly. She was giggly, naughty and noisy. As soon as her parents were not around, she turned the house upside-down. She astounded her brothers and gained their obedience. Moreover, she was really beautiful, in a sense, too beautiful. For this very reason, Father was worried about her every now and then. He wanted Ida to be a dignified, silent and even backward girl. Ida was the exact opposite. By her charm, by her crying and even by making faces, she always got what she wanted. Father, who was always preoccupied with his business, would suddenly notice a development in his household. His children, and Ida in particular, grew very fast. With the passage of time, they gained in height, but none as much as Ida. Besides, she grew more beautiful.

Symphony of the Dead

As years went by, Father gradually suppressed Ida's rebellious, energetic nature. He confronted her excitement and her mental effervescence, transforming her into a docile, quiet girl. But he couldn't be a match for her on his own. He called on Mother's assistance, asking her to train Ida in the kitchen. He had stipulated that Mother should teach her everything she wanted to, from sewing to artificial flower-making, in the kitchen. Ida languished in the damp kitchen, getting used to the horrifying loneliness. She had no classmates, she did not leave home to do anything, and no guest would set foot in their home. Gradually, she was distanced from her brothers, turning into something of a stranger. No other member of the family was so introvert. She envied the big wheel of life that turned day and night and on which there was no place for her. She got used to silence. She had become so invisible and so silent that everybody had forgotten about her. It was as if she had been born to be alone. When she was 11, she started suffering from rheumatism in her joints for no apparent reason. Dr Shooshanik prescribed an injection of strong penicillin once a month. Thereafter, she went to the doctor's surgery once a month, accompanied by Ideen. Submissively, she lay on the doctor's couch for the injection and, afterwards, she limped back home. In the kitchen, she cooked alone, she ate alone, she did the washing up alone and slept alone. She resembled a housemaid who was an outsider and a leper. No-one ever asked: "Where is Ida?" apart from Ideen. Whenever Ideen asked where Ida was, Father would reply: "Is that any of your business?"

Years later, an introvert, patient, sad and broken girl left her father's house for her husband's. Her name was Ida.

2

One day in late August, about one month before the beginning of the new academic year, Father agreed, at Mother's persistent insistence, not to go to his shop so that he could accompany Yousef and Ideen to school for their enrolment. Mother was adamant that her children should enrol before any other pupil, believing that this would ensure that their names would come at the top of the daily register. Father was uneasy: "This is a hassle! By God, this is a hassle!"

Mother retorted: "Who is going to enrol them then?" She dressed the children quickly, combed their hair, cleaned their faces with a wet handkerchief and said: "Every father should visit his children's school at least once a year. Alright, you can't do it more often. But you should be able to manage once a year."

Father had already put his suit on. Nevertheless, he liked to grumble when he performed a task. As always, he punched one hand into the palm of his other and said angrily: "If I am not around ..." He donned his *papakha* and, going down the stairs, he asked: "What class am I supposed to enrol them for?"

In the alley, some people hurried towards the street. The shops had not opened yet. Unusually, the electric fan factory was silent. It appeared as if the daily work had not yet begun. Father, without uttering a word, felt that he should firmly hold his children's hands. When he was passing by the front of the electric fan factory, he glanced at the pit for a moment. He stood near the barbed wire fence that encircled the factory, kept the children behind him and said: "Where are all these people going?" He talked to himself in such a way that the children could not make anything of it.

Two large halls, with red tin roofs, lazily squatted among rows of poplars. Factory workers came out of the halls, holding shovels or iron bars. They

Symphony of the Dead

moved towards the street along a steep footpath. The factory was absolutely silent and the town, as Father put it, looked like the time when people living under Nimrod wanted to leave their homes and their livelihood and head for the open country.

In the street, there was a multitude of men holding sticks in their hands and carrying shovels on their shoulders. Some were armed. They had thin, gloomy faces and their eyes looked glazed. They passed through Safieddin Street, went around Shah Square and marched on along Shah Esmail Street. In absolute silence, they stood in front of the brick building of police headquarters. The headquarters, with the iron fence around it and flowerbeds adorned with dahlias and amaranths, looked like a private hospital more than what it really was. All the men sat on the ground. A sort of muted hubbub hovered over the crowd. There were so many men that Father could not tell where the crowd ended at the far side of the square. A dry wind was blowing, raising dust in its wake. Father held the children's hands and just watched. More men came to join those who had sat down. The new arrivals held their *papakhas* on their heads with one hand to prevent them from being blown away by the wind. In their other hand, they invariably held something. Father just managed to say: "When the wind finds its way below the rim of your *papakha*, it will blow it away." He held his children's hands more firmly and waited to see what was going on.

A man, his hand under the lapel of his jacket, was leaning against a wooden pole. Father asked him in, Azeri Turkish: "What's going on?"

The man said nothing and walked away quickly. Father said: "We must try to get back home, otherwise we'll be trapped by the crowd." But he had no clue as to the reason why so many people had assembled. In the past, he had seen unemployed men being taken to Tehran or other cities for road building or tunnel digging. He had even seen workers assembling in Ali Qapoo Square early in the morning or late in the afternoon. And now what puzzled Father was not why the crowd had assembled in front of the police headquarters, nor why some of the men carried guns nor why they were so silent. He was simply astonished by the fact that there was such a great number of men in Ardabil without him being aware of it. He asked an old man: "What's going on?"

"Nothing."

The scowling old man cast such a cold glance that Father lowered his head. Thereafter, he tried not to ask anybody anything. He began to walk fast along the street when he saw Ayaz the policeman with his huge figure and his moustache covering much of his face. As soon as he perceived Ayaz from a distance, he said: "That's him."

Ideen asked: "Who?"

"Don't talk. Come along."

Father ran thankfully towards Ayaz who was standing on top of a flight of steps, gazing at the crowd. Father wanted to step forward and embrace him. But Ayaz cast a menacing glance and twitched his moustache. He then said, between his teeth: "The situation is chaotic. Pretend you don't know me at all." He winked in a kind way. His moustache wriggled like a worm.

Father, pretending to be looking at the building opposite, stood next to Ayaz and asked: "What's going on?"

"Peace and quiet."

"Have we won or have we lost?"

With his big hands, Ayaz the policeman pushed the crowd away and said, between his teeth, "To hell with Germany, with Russia, with the bloody lot of them."

Father just managed to ask: "What are we to do Ayaz?"

"Get on with your life. That's all."

"I'm not worried, Ayaz."

The walls of Father's home were high and sturdy. The building, with its high arches, was secure from burglary. It resembled a castle whose architect had done his best to take every precaution. Even the windows were higher than usual and the cornice had been arranged in such a way that it would give no foothold to a would-be burglar. Moreover, the fact that Lord's Electric Fan Factory faced Father's home gave him peace of mind. He knew that even if the city were razed, the alley in which the factory was situated would be spared. Nevertheless, he said, in Azeri Turkish: "Hurry up children."

The muted din of the people, the whisperings, the irritating wind and the general feeling of insecurity that persisted for days caused prices to rise. Long queues formed in front of bakeries. Scuffles, and even murder, could not prevent people from gathering in front of bakeries' closed doors.

These were tasks that could not be performed by women or children. Only Father could stand in the bread queue from midnight and come back, with one or two loaves of bread at lunchtime the next day. Russian aircraft attacked all the time and paratroopers descended gently. People looked upward and shouted noisily: "Aeroplanes! Aeroplanes!"

Father was unhappy, as he had had to pay ten *toomans* for school fuel costs. Right at the square, he had gone to Anooshirvan the Just School and enrolled his sons. He now just wanted to get back home quickly and lock the door behind him. He kept telling Ideen: "Come along. What are you looking at?"

Yousef kept stumbling on something or skidding. His eyes were fixed on the first formation of Russian aircraft that flew over the town. Father, horrified, pulled the children behind him. They could not keep up. Besides, they wanted to watch the planes. The effort made Father sweat.

The innumerable men of Ardabil turned out to be no match for the invaders. On the same day, late in the afternoon, the army surrendered and the Russian troops poured into the town. They occupied every spot. As the day advanced, the town came to a standstill, the police headquarters fell, Narin Castle, which housed the garrison of Ardabil, the largest garrison in the whole province of Azerbaijan, surrendered. When night fell, paratroopers descended from Russian planes in clusters.

Father said: "Use sparingly whatever you have for the time being."

He had assembled the entire family in one room. He frequently looked out of the window to see if anything new had transpired. Ideen was trying to climb doors, windows or walls like a kitten. Father repeatedly drove him away from the window. He walked about the room and said: "This situation can't last forever. Dammit. This situation must come to an end no matter what."

Muted sounds could be heard in the distance. Every now and then, the firing of single shots could be heard from various spots in town. Urhan and Ida, horrified, were stuck to Mother. Ideen, however, had made Yousef clasp his hands so that he could place his foot on them and reach the windowsill. From up there, he related what was going on. He then grasped Yousef's hand and pulled him up. They saw three paratroopers descending slowly. The wind tended to move them slightly sideways.

Father said: "It is not a nice thing to say, but I think we've had it. We have been struck by disaster."

Yousef was fascinated by the spectacle of the paratroopers. His shaven head was held high. With his astonished eyes wide open, he gazed at the sky so eagerly. It was as if he wouldn't be able to see the paratroopers again if he blinked even once. He was spellbound and saliva flowed down from the corner of his lips. Ideen, however, gave Mother a running commentary, telling her where the paratroopers were at any moment, how many of them there were, what colour their outfit was, and in what direction the wind moved them. He explained that everything depended on chance. One of them might descend on the pine tree or right into the pond. Suddenly, Father noticed Ida and began to think of a secure place.

Mother said: "People are descending upon us even from the sky. Isn't this a bad omen?"

Ideen replied: "Of course not. Just the opposite, it's so beautiful."

Father said: "There are so many towns in this region. Of them all they have chosen Ardabil. This really is bad luck for us."

Ideen said: "If one of them falls on to the pine tree, he'll get caught between the branches."

Mother said: "I wonder what these infidels want from us."

Ideen continued: "On the first day, we won't give him any food. We'll let him swing up there so that he tastes the result of his mischief."

Ida followed up: "We'll pour water on him from an upstairs window."

Ideen agreed: "And, also, we'll light a fire under the tree." He rubbed his hands together and laughed with glee.

Ida said: "On the next day, we'll give him some bread."

Yousef disagreed: "Don't give him anything to eat. The sooner he dies, the better."

Ideen said: "No. We'll give him one piece of bread a day to keep him alive. We'll have to get our own back with him for some time to come."

Ida agreed: "Yes. We'll use a long stick to make him swing. Let him move to and fro."

Yousef said: "Okay. Don't give him any bread. But don't mistreat him too much either."

Ideen said: "Two more are coming down. I'm sure their uniforms, too, would turn out to be blue. They are drifting away with the wind."

From outside, one could hear soldiers marching past.

Mother said: "The world has come to an end, I'm sure of it." She turned up the lantern's wick, increasing the light before serving dinner.

Father began his narrative: "No. It is by no means the end of the world. It is Germany's work. Well, let her conquer and occupy. What is the difference between this king and that king? For people like us who want to win their daily bread and go back to bed at night, there is no difference between Hitler, Roosevelt or the Shah. They are all the same asses, only with differing pack-saddles. After all, what has bloody Stalin done for the Russians? He has ruled them with tyranny and, now, he is being punished for it. I swear to God that if I were Hitler's minister, the war would have a different outcome." He stood up with his back to Russia and, with his hands, made a gesture, as if pulling the rest of the world towards Moscow. He said: "The road to Russia passes through where we are. After we turn into a bridge, India and China can be conquered with little difficulty. It will be possible to occupy every country within an hour. Let him conquer. Whatever the outcome, it will be better than our present condition." Father became aware of Ida's presence and that of the other children and fell silent for a moment. He then shook his head and, with a deep sigh, said: "I am an Iranian. I feel sorry for my country. But the situation we are in is so dreadful that we would allow ourselves to be conquered and saved from misery."

Symphony of the Dead

When the gunfire was at its loudest, Ideen jumped out of the window, attempting to rush out of the house. But Father stopped him by giving him two heavy slaps across the face.

That night, the whole family had dreams about paratroopers and parachuting. Every one of us felt like descending from the sky, hanging from a green parachute, swinging, free. We felt as if we were empty inside and falling from mountain tops into deep valleys. Father woke up four times. Each time, he drank a sip of water and recited his sunset-prayer and night-prayer. He eventually missed his morning prayer. Dreaming about paratroopers had got on everyone's nerves. Our sleep was frequently interrupted. We woke up, drank a little water and tried to fall asleep again in order to catch up with the rest of the dream.

In the morning, fighting continued and Father was not able to go to work. He stayed at home and grumbled. On the one hand, he was bored and impatient as he had nothing to do and, on the other hand, he was worried. He started nit-picking. He twisted Ida's ear twice and whipped Ideen with a belt three times. He also gave Yousef, as he put it, a splendid slap on the face.

He said: "I can't manage four children. How is this madman going to manage the world?"

Mother asked: "What are we to do now?"

"They have been shitting on our country. No news. No radio. One wouldn't know what the hell one is supposed to do."

The aircraft passed over again and more paratroopers landed. Father looked out of the window and said: "We are finished."

Yousef, having been given a "splendid" slap on the face, had lodged himself on the upper veranda to watch the paratroopers from there. Ideen, however, was all over the place and provided us with frequent news. From the windows, he kept a watchful eye on everything and provided us with constant updates. He gave a detailed account of whatever happened around the house. At one stage, he said: "The radio! Radio transmission has restarted."

When Father listened to the radio, he learnt that the Russians had occupied all of northern Iran. He went to the nut-sellers' souk and secured the door of his shop with an extra padlock. It was then that he noticed that there was a shortage of bread. Shops were closed. Some people had broken the lock of a door and were looting the shop in broad daylight and in full view of passersby. Some people were beating others. The police had been disarmed. They were moving about without their uniforms and with nothing to do. The security chief of the police department, having been found stealing, had been beaten by the workers of Ali Qapi district. It was in the middle of this chaos that

Father learnt that he had to wait in the bread queue from night until morning. Law and order had broken down in the town.

On one of the following days, Father, standing in the queue, was really incredulous when he noticed Ayaz the policeman wearing civilian clothes, going down the street on his motorcycle. And how fat he looked in civilian clothes! Father left the queue quickly and rushed towards Ayaz. He pulled on the rear carrier of Ayaz's motorcycle and, still running, said: "Ayaz! Ayaz! I beg you. Do something for us."

Ayaz, taken unawares, dismounted and, with a deep frown, said: "You must not approach me. I'll call at your house in the evening. Go."

Late in the evening, when it was completely dark, Ayaz threw himself into our house and said: "I haven't got much time, Djaber. Our task is very difficult now. There are lots of burglaries and the Russians don't like us. That's why we move around in civilian clothes. Don't forget this: When you see me in the street, pretend that you don't know me at all."

Father said: "I'm begging you. What's the news?"

"The raven has flown away."

"Hitler?" And, as if he had understood Ayaz's allusion, he went on: "So the raven has flown away, has it?"

"Yes. Now Hitler exerts greater pressure. The Russians are pushing from one side. No doubt, the Germans, too, will emerge ..."

"Which raven are you talking about?" At this stage, Ideen intruded.

"The Shah has left the country." [7]

He was bending down over the staircase railing, keeping a watchful eye over Father and Ayaz in the dark.

Father exclaimed: "What are you doing there, you son of a goat?"

Ayaz burst into uncontrollable laughter. He said to Father: "Go on. Tell me what you wanted to tell me."

"Bread?"

"Four loaves a day. Will that be enough?"

"What would I do without you?"

"You can count on my friendship, Djaber." He left and closed the door behind him.

Father was overwhelmed by such generosity, such wonderful friendship and such profound kindness. He burst into tears. Or perhaps he was feeling helpless and fed up. He didn't know. Tears rolled down his face. Father was a weak man. Until those days, he had never suffered so much hardship.

The following day, Mother developed a severe headache. Father gave her lots of lime juice and salt, to no avail. She could not cook. She held her head in her hands and walked about all the time.

Father said: "At least sit somewhere. Or lie down."

"I can't."

"In that case, I am going to get dressed so that we go to the clairvoyant. Put your chador on. Let's go."

"What about the children?"

"The children? They are inside the house and the door will be locked."

"But we can't leave them alone, can we?"

"In that case, we will take these two troublesome ones with us. The other two can remain at home."

They set out with trepidation. The clairvoyant lived at the end of Lord's Factory Lane. After going round two corners, they would reach her house, which was near the coppice. They kept knocking at her door, but there was no response. Ideen, looking through the gap between the two flaps of the door, said: "They are inside. I wonder why they are not opening the door. I can see the clairvoyant herself. She is wearing a red dress. But she is not coming this way to open the door."

Mother stepped forward and looked through the gap. The door opened and Mother smiled with joy. They sat in the hallway. The clairvoyant insisted that they should sit in the room. Mother declined, saying that she most anxious about the children left at home.

The clairvoyant produced a big wooden spoon to the end of which a piece of string had been attached. She recited a eulogy to the Prophet Mohammad and said: "Well, Djaber, start."

Father said: "Saber."

The clairvoyant repeated "Saber, Saber, Saber" while turning the wooden spoon between her hands.

Father continued mentioning names: "Ojaq-ali."

"Ojaq-ali, Ojaq-ali, Ojaq-ali."

" Suleiman." Whenever Father uttered a name, he started going through his prayer beads anew. He started from the first bead and went through the rest of the beads quickly.

"Suleiman, Suleiman, Suleiman."

"Fatima."

The clairvoyant, kneeling, turned the spoon with a degree of care more suited to threading a needle: "Fatima, Fatima, Fatima."

Father said: "Have we left anyone from among the dead? Well, Solmaz."

The clairvoyant repeated: "Solmaz." And the spoon suddenly stopped.

Uttering the name "Solmaz" once again, she looked at Mother and said: "You see. It is your sister who is more useful to you than anyone else. May God bless her soul. Give alms in her honour and for further blessing of her soul. She expects that from you. May God bless her soul. Give dates and sugar-plums to the needy. Better still, give to charity in her memory from time to time."

Mother said: "Very well. Let's go."

The clairvoyant fetched some burning charcoal from her kitchen and sprinkled a handful of frankincense over it. When the smoke rose, Father praised the Prophet Mohammad and, turning his face towards the clairvoyant, said: "May God bless your deceased relatives." He gave her a five *tooman* banknote.

On the way back, no shop was open and nothing could be bought. Mother insisted on buying something so that she could give to charity. Father explained: "We are not living in normal times. You see that everything is closed."

"I am not asking anything from you for myself. Solmaz's soul is suffering. The Almighty will not be pleased, will He?"

Ideen asked: "Who was Solmaz?"

"She was my sister. She died young."

Ida was curious: "Why did she die young?" And she lent an attentive ear to the sound of a single shot in the distance.

Mother ruffled Ida's hair and, looking at her with tenderness, explained: "She fell ill."

Every now and then, when they encountered Russian soldiers on their way, they fell silent and quickened their steps inadvertently. The soldiers, holding their rifles tightly to their chests eyed every passer-by curiously and fastidiously. Ideen made faces at them and they laughed. Father told him off and was fed-up with him by the time they reached home.

The war brought much misery in its wake. People suffered from hunger. Young girls ran away from home. There were many burglaries and instances of hand-to-hand fighting. There were also instances of rape committed by the blue-eyed soldiers in the town. A few married women had been raped. A policeman had been lynched and dismembered. A girl had disappeared from Pir-Maadar district. A number of other young girls, who did not mind associating with the opposite sex, had left the town on the pretext that they feared being raped by Russian soldiers.

Years later, a 28-year-old woman who had lived in Ardabil, being the daughter of a rug merchant, surfaced in Tehran, changed her name to Ziba and

Symphony of the Dead

became a dancer in various restaurants. Before all of this, Father, haunted by his thoughts, fuelled by fear, shame and anxiety, had told Mother: "I wish you had not given birth to Ida."

Mother, feeling cold and rubbing her hands, asked: "What are we supposed to do?"

Father instructed: "If someone knocks at the door, don't open it."

This instruction was, however, of no use. One dusty afternoon, the door was knocked at so hard and with such persistence that Father had to hide Ida in the closet under the staircase before opening the door. Two Russian soldiers burst in. One was thin, tall and blue-eyed. The other one was slight and had a swarthy complexion. They were saying things in Russian, which Father could not understand. But it was clear that they were looking for someone. Father said: "You, infidels, what are you looking for?" He looked astounded and helpless, not knowing what was going on. He thought that the soldiers intended harming a member of his family. He was really frightened. He asked: "What has happened? What's going on?"

The soldiers, not understanding Turkish, just wanted to search every room. As soon as they saw Ideen, they pointed at him and wanted to take him away. Father said: "He is my son ... my ... my ... Ideen."

The soldiers had got hold of Ideen and were taking him away. Ideen was holding a dustpan with a hollow handle in his hand while being pulled by the soldiers. At that moment four more soldiers burst into the house. They forced us into a corner in the corridor. Their rifles aimed at Father.

Ideen, his eyes sparkling, listened to the soldiers attentively and looked happy. Mother cried. Father's hands were trembling. He said: "What has he done?"

The thin, blue-eyed soldier squatted on the floor, got hold of Ideen's arms and shook them violently. He said something in Russian. Ideen showed him the dustpan and said "dustpan".

Father asked: "What have you done? What do they want you for?"

Ideen said: "With this dustpan handle pointing at them, I said bang, bang." At the same time, he aimed the dustpan at the soldiers like a rifle.

The soldiers burst into laughter. They guffawed so much that they had tears in their eyes. One of them said something in Russian which sounded like "Nete Pele Qoni ... ." and left the house. Their commander, still laughing, came up with another incomprehensible utterance: "Khorosho-ni eznoni" and gave Ideen a fur hat to keep for himself. Many years later, when Ideen was mentally ill and could not tell the fur hat from Father's *papakha*, Urhan would wear the fur hat, do up his overcoat's buttons and go to the shop.

After the Russian soldiers had left the house, Father grasped Ideen's ear between his fingers and was about to pull him towards the courtyard when someone knocked at the door again. Father let go of Ideen's ear and said: "Has something happened again?" Frightened, he opened the door. It was Ayaz the policeman. Father said: "Hello Ayaz. Where are you these days?"

With a gesture from his shoulders as if he was passing through a dense crowd, he came into the house. He closed the door and said: "I have come just to inform you of the latest news and I must go. I have been able to get a newspaper. I thought you too should be told about what's going on."

"How did you get a newspaper?"

"Never mind." He sat on the steps. Father wanted to usher him into the drawing room upstairs as an honoured guest, but he refused. He said: "The shops in the centre of town have been open during the past few days. In this district, all shops must open tomorrow. Believe me, the town has been eerily quiet and lifeless. It resembles a city of the dead. I go to the souk every day to see what's going on. I'm worried that someone might have broken a lock, a door or something. We have no-one else around here to see to these things."

"You have been a real friend to me Ayaz. Read so that I, too, am informed."

Ayaz was sweating profusely. He pulled his newspaper out from inside his coat and held it in front of Father's eyes. Ideen ran forward to have a look. Ayaz told him: "Go and sit down over there. I will read and everybody can listen."

Ida, wearing a white chador and holding its edge between her teeth, was standing beside Mother at the kitchen door. Before Ayaz started to read, Father filled his pipe with tobacco and lit it. He sat right in front of Ayaz, face-to-face, and said: "Very well, read."

"They are turning the country upside down and destroying it. It is like the end of the world. Listen to this: 'How Iran was taken unawares. Frightening and heart-rending news is arriving from everywhere. It is reported that soon after midnight, British warships approached Khorramshahr and attacked the port with guns. They destroyed the Iranian warships at dawn. A number of marines and officers were killed.'"

Father looked at him with his mouth wide open in shock and astonishment. Ayaz looked back at Father for a moment and said: "You see, Djaber? What do we have by way of security forces? It is all sighs and hot air. One of these days you might hear that you have lost Ayaz."

"God forbid."

"Reza Shah has been brought to his knees despite his awe-inspiring greatness. I'll read it to you."

Symphony of the Dead

Ayaz resumed reading, inserting his own comments here and there: "The Commander of the Iranian Navy, Rear-Admiral Bayandor, (he was a tough guy, you know) was killed. British and Indian forces disembarked. A few minutes later, there was news of an aerial bombardment of Ahwaz. At the same time, there was frightening news from the north. There was news of Azerbaijan (they are talking about our place) being invaded and bombarded. Frontier regions are similarly affected. The news goes on like this: Garrisons are attacked, Soviet and British forces attack Iranian troops in the north, south and west and Iranian forces launch counter-attacks. People are struck with fear and foreign forces move forward quickly. Many families flee from towns and cities. The arrival of such news further saddened the Shah, minute by minute. He summoned the Soviet Minister Mr Smirnov (I have seen him myself on two occasions) and the British Minister Mr Bullard. At eleven o'clock in the morning, the diplomatic delegations of the two invading countries had a meeting with the Shah at Sa'dabad Palace. They talked for an hour with no result. Although little is known about their talks, it is understood that the Shah insisted that Soviet and British governments specify their requirements and undertook to order that all facilities be placed at their disposal so that the Allies are satisfied that their war materiel can pass through Iran. He also promised to reduce the number of German nationals in Iran and to give any other type of assurance required by the Allies so that they stop their invasion and withdraw their troops. The Shah's perseverance was of no use and his expectations were in vain. (You see, Djaber? A person of such greatness and glory persevered in his friendship and they refused.) His efforts were in vain. As pointed out before, this nightmarish scenario had been thought of several months ago. This meeting deeply saddened the Shah. He noticed that their plan went beyond demanding transit, which he had thought of as the last resort. Their attitude was truly based on their opposition to the Shah himself and on the fact that they saw him as a barrier to the realisation of their aims."

Ayaz continued: "Well, they could have simply told him that. He would have gone in peace as he has done now. Why did they launch an invasion?" He read further: "On the next day, the Shah decided to abdicate. He summoned the ministers to Sa'dabad Palace. They met him in the afternoon. He told them: 'I know that the reason behind their invasion and aggression is their disapproval of me. I deem it wise to abdicate and let the Crown Prince ascend the thrown so that I prevent disruption, destruction and the shedding of the blood of innocent people and soldiers who are being bombarded. Make your views known to me. I give you a few minutes to confer.' The Shah left the room and the ministers began their consultation. The Shah's words had deeply saddened the ministers. Three of them shed tears. They then decided to advise the Shah against abdication as, in their view, this would cause much disruption and disturbance in the country and would do more harm than good. They duly petitioned the Shah not to abdicate. The Allies, however, had posed a serious threat to Reza Shah. As Winston Churchill put it, on the morning of the 25th of Shahrivar[8], in the wake of the previous night's news and the advance of Soviet forces towards Tehran, the Shah was informed that Soviet forces had begun moving towards Tehran from Karaj and that the motive behind this movement was obvious. The Shah had no choice but to leave the capital and to abdicate. He summoned Mohammad-Ali Foroughi, who had been prime minister for less than a month, and conferred with him. He told him: 'From the very first day, I knew that the Allies' motive was their disapproval of me, but the government was of the opinion that my abdication would be detrimental to the country. Today, I have no choice but to abdicate. Today, Churchill says that when arms come into play, the law falls silent.' At 11:30 in the morning of the 25th of Shahrivar, Mr Foroughi told the Parliament: 'I must inform you of one of the most important developments ...'"

Father said: "Politics is nothing but a game for bastards. You told me so yourself, didn't you Ayaz?"

Ayaz, sobbing with emotion, took a handkerchief out of his pocket. He shed tears so profusely that Father started weeping too. A moment later, Ayaz left the house without saying good-bye. A deadly silence fell on the house.

Father who, until that moment, had been hanging his head, took a deep breath and said: "It's all about shedding innocent blood."

Ideen disagreed: "No. That isn't the case. Their aim is to occupy the country. That is why they have invaded on two fronts."

"Do you think you are wiser than I am, my child?"

"If their aim were to suck blood, they wouldn't go to war. They could simply use a few leeches."

"Just like you. You are sucking my life away with your stupid comments."

Mother intervened: "Come, night's about to fall. Let's go into the room. We'll wait and see what happens."

Everybody went into the sitting room, as was the practice on previous nights. Mother lit up the oil lamps and Father, rolling his sleeves up, said: "Well, children, follow me and do your ablutions. I want you to pray tonight."

Ida said: "I will say my prayers alone."

Father objected: "What for?" and he twisted Ida's ear.

"Because Ideen makes me laugh during prayer."

Symphony of the Dead

"Then you should try not to laugh. Besides, if Ideen disturbs our prayer, I'll chuck him out." He gave Ideen a little tap on the head.
Yousef asked: "Where?"
Father replied: "Outside. In the alley."
"What about the Russians?"
"Don't worry about this little troublesome guy."

3

One day there was a shortfall in the wages paid to the workers of Lord's Electric Fan Factory. The news quickly spread through town. The workers were disappointed and unhappy. They decided to stop work from Saturday. A few of them stopped working on the same day before the end of the shift. Mr Lord learnt that the factory was in danger of closing down because the supervisor had reduced the workers' wages.

Mr Lord acted quickly and made a speech inside the factory. He reprimanded the supervisor in the presence of the workers. He even insulted and threatened him. Thereafter, he ordered that a special bakery, catering for the workers, be set up within the factory so that, in defiance of the occupying Russians, Lord's Factory workers would not have to worry about their bread. He promised to provide the flour needed within two days. And so he did.

The bakery was a little room with a window. The workers did not have to wait in a queue. They just received their hot, freshly baked bread at the window, put a piece of cloth over it and went home. A multitude of hungry eyes, young and old, watched enviously. No-one knew where the flour came from, but come it did. And regularly. Some people said it was imported from Turkey. Others believed the source was the Iranian government. Ayaz the policeman, however, told Father he himself had seen that the flour bags were unloaded from a Russian lorry somewhere along the road to Nameen. Whatever the truth, the result was that the workers went to work, happy and lively, in the morning, worked twice as hard as before and, later in the afternoon, went back home carefree, carrying a bundle of bread.

Productivity was twice what it used to be. Some men of Ardabil who had previously refused to work in the British Lord's Factory and who would not reduce themselves to being "fed by Britain", rushed to register for work at the factory. Within just a few hours, from early morning until midday, the workforce, well under-capacity before then, was at full capacity. Mr Lord thus achieved what he had not been able to achieve for five years.

Now, to the people's astonishment and the Russians' disbelief, the factory worked constantly. Every day, GMC vans, carrying the electric fans along the steep road leading to the outside world proved the factory was working at full capacity. The workers assembled the components and the factory roared more than it ever had done. The workers' flour quota increased many times over and 'Lord's bread' was sold around town at exorbitant prices. Bread changed hands several times and, when it was stale, it was sold to Father at 30 times what the first person paid for it. It tasted good. It was white, without husks and odourless. Father said it was worth the price. He swore that it was worth even more than the inflated price.

Paratroopers kept landing and a macabre silence hung over the city. The only sounds that were heard were a muted hubbub and occasional sniper's fire.

Watching from the veranda, Yousef was absorbed in the descent of the paratroopers. He stayed on the veranda for hours on end. He felt neither thirsty nor hungry and didn't go anywhere. He stayed on the veranda round the clock. One day, he decided to fly. The decision was easy to implement. He went to Father's room, picked up Father's big, black umbrella, tied himself to the umbrella with a few pieces of rope and 'flew' from the rooftop. Thereafter, there was such a commotion around Djaber Urkhani's house that Mother was filled with disbelief. The crowd stretched from the house to well beyond Lord's Electric Fan Factory.

That was the event that Mother related to her other children for years to come. She told them that the reason for the suffering of their elder brother was that he had 'flown'. He had been transformed into a creature that was half man and half beast. He was neither dead nor alive. He had become just a chunk of flesh, or an animal that just devoured food all the time. The children readily believed what Mother told them. The only one who didn't believe was Ideen. Whenever he thought about his dumb brother, he fully realised that the entire war and the invasion, as far as their family was concerned, had but one conspicuous result: Yousef's metamorphosis.

Ideen always had a pale, distant image of Yousef in his mind. He recalled that, during the previous days and nights, Yousef must have been asleep all the time or that he may have been sitting in a corner and gazing at the sky. On one occasion, before the episode of trying to 'fly' with an umbrella, he had imitated swimming boy-scouts and dived into the pond from the upper floor veranda. Following this incident, Father intended to chuck him out of the house. But, later on, it would have been impossible to throw him out. He lay on a little mattress in a corner of a downstairs room, amid the strong stench of urine and faeces. Of all his senses, only his sense of sight still worked properly. He gazed at people or looked greedily at their hands or whatever they held.

He had one bone broken in his thigh and another one, in the other leg, at the knee. The bones had fused and the flesh had withered in such a way that his legs stretched out to the sides of the mattress, parallel to his arms. They resembled a duck's legs.

When Yousef's broken, ruined body was brought in on that day of fighting and shooting, Father, standing at the top of the staircase, shouted: "Take him to the cemetery."

Mother objected: "Why should we take him to the cemetery?"

"He isn't alive, is he?"

"Oh, yes. The poor thing is alive."

But Yousef neither talked nor moaned. He just munched a dusty piece of apple that he had found in the alley. From that moment on, they placed him in a corner of the room downstairs. The harder they tried, the less successful they were in finding a doctor. Father said: "He's not in pain. So, let him lie down for the time being. We will do something about him after the war."

Mother, putting Yousef in bed, said: "Look, Djaber. His legs are somehow wobbling."

"I don't think so."

After the passing of a few days, Yousef had lost all human characteristics. He had been transformed into an animal that just devoured food. He didn't hurt anybody. He didn't catch a cold, fall ill or make a noise. He just lay motionless in a corner of the room. He resembled a big stone in the middle of a river that would not be moved by any current or flood.

Mr Lord came to see him personally and expressed his sorrow at the plight of the family. He addressed Father as "honourable neighbour" and "honourable fellow citizen". He stipulated that five loaves of bread be delivered to our house every day. Aqa Farman, the messenger at Lord's Factory, delivered the loaves every afternoon.

Mother soaked little pieces of bread in a meat and vegetable stew and fed them to Yousef, one spoonful at a time, three times a day. She washed Yousef's hands and face, placed the bedpan under him and changed his sheets. The stench in the room was so strong that frankincense had to be burnt constantly. Gradually, Yousef ceased to be a brother and a son. He had become a food storage depot that was nothing but a nuisance. Dr Nayadanov had said: "He will never recover to become a normal human being."

Years later, whenever Ideen recalled his childhood, he realised that everything had changed from that moment on. He knew full well that the first child always paid for the younger children's mistakes or mishaps. He also knew that sole heirs were greedier for ownership. These were dreams or nightmares that proved real later on.

Father wanted to give Ideen a better education. But the more Ideen tried, the less he achieved success. His endeavours not only bore no fruit but, moreover, turned out to be detrimental. After Yousef's disaster, Ideen was now the eldest child and austerity began to be observed in his upbringing.

One day, Ideen, sweating profusely and with a face red from exertion, drank water from the tap in the alley and ran into the courtyard. Father was lying on a divan under the weeping willow. He was eating a melon. But he stopped for a moment to ask Ideen where he had been.

Ideen, panting, said: "In the alley." He was about to run towards the toilet when Father roared. He stood still.

"You play with these brats in the alley? Do you know who their parents are?"

"No." And he squirmed restlessly with the pressure of a full bladder.

"Play only in this courtyard. But don't break the windows. Go now."

Ideen ran to the toilet in the corner of the courtyard. His heart was beating hard and his chest was heaving. He was thinking about how to play in the courtyard and not break the windows. He was standing at the toilet hole, his heart beating fast. When he had relieved himself and calmed down, he suddenly noticed that he had entered the toilet without closing the door. He saw Father standing at the doorstep and looking angrily at him.

"You piss standing up, you son of an ass?"

Ideen felt dizzy and, in the middle of a feeling of calm and happiness, felt a sudden burning sensation at his waist. He quickly pulled his trousers up and stood up, stock still.

Father said: "Come here."

Ideen stepped forward. Father got hold of his ear and, slapping him continuously on the back of his neck, directed him to the divan under the weeping willow.

"You are not a dog, are you?"

Ideen lowered his head in shame and stood unmoving until Father said: "Get lost."

It seemed as if the heat had killed four gold fish in the pond. Ideen then noticed that his back was aching and his knees were trembling. In the midst of pain and fever, he realised that the fish had not died because of the heat. But he had no idea why they had died. For three days, he was unable to pass water. Mother kept feeding him with watermelons to alleviate his condition.

Father lost his control over Ideen day by day. He was rebellious and would not be tamed. Whenever he was locked up in the cellar, he kept himself so busy that he would not leave the place without lengthy persuasion. He would recite the contents of a book by heart and spell out words. For a while, his pocket money was denied him. As a result, he began to work at the dairy at Sarcheshmeh Square, where they made yoghurt. He stirred the big cauldron of milk and earned one *rial* per day as a wage. He spent his earnings on books and writing paper and, thus, further irritated Father. They would not buy him clothes. But he made do with his old ones. He was not seriously attached to anything in particular; but he knew very well that he hated selling watermelon seeds. He did not like living his father's life. He also disliked many of the things that other children of his age liked. Whenever he saw a girl dance, he felt sad. He didn't know why. But Father simply thought Ideen was the odd one out, opposing everything that was normal in his household. He sincerely believed this and swore by it. It was for this same reason that he continuously kept watch on Ideen.

There was a time when Father, with his slight body and his thinning hair, balding on both temples, carried Ideen on his shoulders and dipped him in the waters of Shoorabi. Ideen was frightened but when his feet touched the cool water, he was filled with excitement and happiness. He laughed and, pulling Father's ears, shouted: "Djaber!"

Mother had stretched her legs in the sunshine and cracked watermelon seeds on the warm banks of Shoorabi. She said: "Don't say Djaber. Say Father."

He said: "Father" and looked at Ida.

Father brought him down from his shoulders, hugged him and kissed him on the eyelids and neck. His moustache was flattened on the smooth skin of Ideen's face. Once again, Father dipped him in water and, then, put him down on the warm soil of the bank, telling him: "Go into the sun."

Mother quickly wrapped a chador around herself, held Ideen tightly and said: "Father loves you very much. You see?"

"No."

Mother also stroked Ida's hair. Ida was sitting on Urhan's shoulders and, smiling, looked enviously at Father and Ideen. Mother said: "He also loves Ida very much." She dried Ideen, seated him on her lap, put a mouthful of kebab in his mouth and dressed him quickly.

Symphony of the Dead

The green and blue Shoorabi looked more vast than usual in the sunshine. The town, lying beyond the hills on the other side of Shoorabi, could not be seen but one could hear its sounds. On the opposite bank of Shoorabi and in the middle of reed beds, Yousef was aiming at nightingales with his catapult.

Mother asked Ideen: "Why are you keeping your kebab in your mouth, my dear? Eat it."

Ideen's attention was entirely focused on Yousef and he was also fascinated by the reed bed. Years later, when he recalled these memories in his dejected, empty, cellar-like room, he visualised Father washing his face with soap at Shoorabi. It appeared to him as if Father washed his face with soap for a long time without closing his eyes. He asked: "Djaber, how is it that soapy water doesn't irritate your eyes?"

"Because God likes me and does not want my eyes to be irritated."

"Then why are my eyes irritated by soapy water?"

He recalled that everything looked so bright in the sunshine and, filled with joy by so much light and heat, he looked at Father who, 15 years later, was still looked upon as a kind-hearted father by Mother. She believed that no other father loved his children as much and that he was simply a bit austere.

Ideen wished to return to the water, to sit on Father's shoulders, to behave childishly and shriek. But Mother said he had been in the water for long enough. Father made faces at Ideen and laughed. He splashed some water on Ideen from where he was. He then said "Good-bye" and went under water. Ideen waited for Father to resurface but he didn't. He said "Father" again and looked at Ida who, like Ideen, looked worried. She held the corner of her little chador with her teeth to prevent it from falling off.

Mother laughed and said: "Oh, my God! Where is Father?" Ideen started crying and called "Father".

At this stage, Father resurfaced. He breathed out forcefully, splashed water on Ideen and laughed. Ideen, who had been crying, started to laugh and Mother wiped his tears away. Years later, whenever Ideen recalled the events of that day in full and without any omissions, he felt this recollection remained the first memory of his childhood. It was as if everything had started from that day. Father standing in the water with a smiling face, lathers his face and disappears under the water. But, in reality, Father was not like that. He was silent and austere and what he liked most was his work. He frowned a lot. Throughout his life Ideen always greeted Father out of fear. The sight of Father always gave him an incomprehensible fright. Years later, when he was 24 years old, he realised that Father was extremely proud. It was for the same reason that Ideen had gazed at him when he had got out of the water and wrapped a white towel round himself. Mother poured him some tea. He drank it on the spot while he was standing and then stretched himself out on the ground for a while, in the sunshine. On the other side, a herd of cows passed by on the hilltops, raising a lot of dust. Mother placed Father's *papakha* on Urhan's face to protect him from the dust. But Urhan woke up, pushed the hat aside and cried.

After this, a gentle breeze slapped the waters of Shoorabi against the reeds. Urhan laughed at the waves sent back by the reeds. A little further away, Yousef aimed at nightingales with his catapult. Ida smiled and chewed the corner of her chador. Father shouted at Yousef: "You, bad-mannered boy!"

The twins, Ideen and Ida, hand in hand, looked at a flock of birds circling in the sky above the Shoorabi's waters. The only visible sign of the town was a column of smoke. Once again, a herd of cows passed by. Father threw his melon peelings at a black cow that was the biggest in the herd and waited until the cow ate the peelings. When the sun began to set, Father said: "Let's get back." They went back home, as a wind had also begun to blow.

4

Mother was extremely frail and thin. She had large black eyes. Two similar pairs of eyes could be discerned in the twins. Her swollen cheeks sometimes looked red. Occasionally, when she applied kohl to her eyes and drew the black dye away from the corners of the eyes, she looked somewhat like a Mongolian woman. Two of her teeth were gold. Whenever she laughed, one could see the white row of upper teeth, with the golden teeth shining on both sides. But whenever she looked worried, with wrinkles on her forehead, she had the appearance of long-suffering women who knew a great deal but revealed little.

She said: "You think Father is your enemy. But you are wrong."

Ideen replied: "I know what you want to say. But his happiness is by no means my happiness." He looked at the branches of the pine tree. The wind moved them to and fro, causing them to shed their needles that looked so green as they settled on the ground.

Mother was sitting on the edge of the railing in such a way that she could lose her balance and fall over backwards or even be pushed by the wind at any moment. She said: "When you come back from school, you always go straight upstairs. You say you're doing your homework. But I know that you read other things as well. Well, you could spend some of your time helping Father."

Ideen, however, paid no attention to what Mother told him. He always had a book of poetry in one hand and he knew many poems by heart. He said: "I don't find this house a safe place to live in," and laughed. He made Mother laugh too. Mother continued: "You see that Urhan has been working in the shop for two years. He has both more money and commands more respect than you. Besides, he is livelier and jollier than you are. You are sad and despondent. Perhaps you don't remember, but when you were a child, you were extremely naughty. You were so noisy and wreaked havoc in this house. Don't you remember? You wouldn't stop being loud and noisy for a moment and you scurried about. But now...." And she fell silent.

The two long plaits of her hair hung from both sides of her head. She had the habit of pushing the plaits forward, undoing them and plaiting them again. She always undid the three strands and weaved them anew. She did this without looking at her hair. She weaved the plaits and then twisted them in her hand. She said: "The reason why I insist on your helping Father is that if you did so, everyone would immediately realise that you two are brothers. You are one; Urhan is the other. Ida will one day get married and leave this house, assuming that someone would want to marry her in spite her illness. And Yousef, on the other hand, is no proper human being. But the shares of you two are equal. Don't forget that you are even older than he is. I don't want you to lose what is rightfully yours."

"Alright. I will go and help Father, but only temporarily. I will do so only because it will make you and Father happy."

From the next day onwards, Ideen went to the shop late in the afternoon and came back home at night, accompanied by Father and Urhan. While in the shop, he saw to the clients' needs, collected what was owed to the shop, washed the floor, cleaned the windows, filled up depleted sacks of pistachio nuts and watermelon seeds and ensured they had the correct wooden price tags. He worked with such enthusiasm and diligence that, within two months, he had completely mastered the business. He could incorporate the contents of the daily bookkeeping into the overall annual ledger, sell the merchandise and perform additions and subtractions with an abacus.

Father kept a furtive, watchful eye on him all the time and sometimes tried, with indirect allusions, to convince him that that was what life was meant to be. Urhan, however, was not happy and could not easily accept the new situation. He suffered and felt jealous. He would have preferred Ideen to be absorbed in his studies and his books and nothing else.

One night, Urhan asked Ideen: "When are you going to study then?"

"Never. I don't do any homework. I simply listen while I'm in class."

Those days, although the war had ended, the city was still unsafe. Party members had broken all the windowpanes at the Lord's Electric Fan Factory. Mr Lord made two speeches during which he said that foreign powers did not want Iran to progress by industrial advancement and cared little for the dignity of the country. He went on to say that if security forces did not co-operate, he would have no option but to close down the factory and return to Britain. The closing down of a huge factory and the subsequent unemployment of so

Symphony of the Dead

many workers, especially in the years of progress, would cost the government dearly. Therefore, orders were issued.

In the morning of a day that saw the city being buried under an endless snowfall, two burley, moustachioed Party members were hanged in the middle of Ali Qapi Square, which was the main location where workers usually gathered. The disturbances duly subsided.

The news was given to Father by Ayaz the policeman. It was late in the evening and still snowing. Father, about to close the shop, was going through calculations with his abacus. He told Ayaz: "Have you forgotten that it's Thursday evening?"

Ayaz threw his hat on to the desk: "Don't ask. Don't expect me to be my usual self." He sat down on a sack of watermelon seeds.

"What's news?"

"Doom and gloom."

Ideen and Urhan hoped that Father would put his notebooks in the drawers and count the banknotes so that they could get back home early. But they could see Ayaz was stricken with fear. They guessed something was in the offing and could read its seriousness in Ayaz's face. Father would have been happy to give six kilograms of pistachio nuts and an equal amount of watermelon seeds in order to hear all the news. He said: "Go on Ayaz. Tell me." And he lent an attentive ear.

"The riots of the big moustachioed guys have been suppressed."

"Really?"

"Yes." He turned back and looked into the corridor: "Take care of yourself and your children. Party members may take retributions."

"But we……You are well aware that we….."

"You don't have any books or pamphlets issued by the Party, have you?"

"Not at all."

"Sometimes they might drop a clandestine pamphlet or something into your shop or your house. Or your children might bring such things from school." He glanced at Ideen and Urhan: "Listen to me children. Your father has been a respectable man all his life. For the sake of my honourable moustache, pay attention to what I am telling you in case any danger befalls you. It might one day…It is the sort of thing that can happen. Be careful."

Father said: "The younger one does not go to school. Only the eldest does. He doesn't listen to what I tell him."

Ayaz frowned and, with a mouth wider than ever, told Ideen: "What good has school brought you? Have you got nothing better to do? What territories are you going to conquer after finishing school?" And, facing Father, he said: "Get him out of school."

"I am of the same opinion. In these uncertain times, when we don't know which side is telling the truth…"

With a wave of his hand, Ayaz interrupted Father: "You must have heard of sham quarrels and fictitious battles. During the day, they beat each other up and, when the night falls, they eat their stew out of the same bowl like true pals. I, as a member of the Security Forces, am on both sides and keep a watchful eye on both sides. That means I am neutral."

"Excellent!" said Father. And looking meaningfully at Ideen, he made it clear to him that he wanted him to think and act along the same lines.

Thereafter, Father kept Ideen under constant surveillance. He inspected his books and every day told him to be careful. He tried to prevent Ideen from going to school, believing that his eldest son should follow in his father's footsteps.

That night, with a sheepskin coat on his shoulders, Father wandered all over the house like a character out of a cartoon. He walked back and forth. He said: "You must pay attention to what I say. Life is not a joke. What do you think you are going to achieve by studying? What do you think your salary will be after 30 years of studying?" He waved his finger in front of Ideen's face: "How much? You tell me." Ideen's silence further encouraged him: "One hundred *toomans*? One thousand *toomans*? You are not going to earn more than the Shah himself, are you? Whatever you are going to earn, I am going to pay you right now, on the condition that you give up your books and your studies and behave like a wise boy."

Mother agreed: "He is right Ideen." She was upstairs, washing Father's and Urhan's socks in the wash basin in the corridor.

Urhan was not happy about what was going on: "Why do you insist? Let him do what he likes. You are not supposed to force people, are you?"

Ida intervened: "What has it got to do with you?"

Mother continued: "She's right. You mind your own business." Whenever Father was in a talking mood, Mother fiddled and inadvertently clutched at something. She concluded: "Think hard, Ideen."

Father, in his sheepskin coat, was as awe-inspiring as he was whenever he sat on his sheepskin rug in the shop. Fatherly authority and pride flowed from his lips: "For whom and for what have I toiled for so many years? It goes without saying that I have gone through all my endeavours for the sake of you, my children, but only on the assumption and the condition that you would not tarnish my dignity or harm my interests. If people respect me, it is because of money. It is because I need answer to no-one. With the talent that you have, I want you to become a shopkeeper right from tomorrow. Do you understand Ideen? A shopkeeper." And he retired to his room.

Symphony of the Dead

Ideen had not been able to look Father in the face. He had heard Father while sitting on the steps. It was not that clear to Ideen himself whether he had been overcome by fear or shyness. Such power, such awe, emanated from Father's eyes and even from Father's spectacles that Ideen felt compelled to turn his head and cast an occasional glance at Father while he had his back to him. When Father left, Ideen felt that he should have said many things in reply. He would have liked Father to have been less austere and to content himself with Urhan's upbringing. But, when Father left the scene, such a silence fell on that sombre corridor that Ideen felt as if the clock on the wall had stopped and that he himself was swinging like the clock's pendulum.

Mother kept clutching the sock she was washing or, rather, she kept clutching a particular point of it. It was as if life was aimlessly turning around on itself. The monotonous sound of water flowing through the pipe made the monotony of repetition more pronounced. The water was cold and Mother's hands had turned bright red. Her hands had become as red as the red overcoat that they used to put on Ideen whenever they wanted to take him out of the house when he was a child.

Whenever Ideen remembered his little coat, he felt so sentimental. The red, well-tailored coat that had become too tight for him had been made of broadcloth, had four pockets and sported a hood that, when not on his head, fell back on to his shoulders. He used to tell Mother: "My coat is so beautiful Mum."

Whenever it was raining, or when it was cold, they dressed him in the red coat. This was the most beautiful piece of clothing he had ever had in his life. Sometimes he felt like hanging it in a spot that would allow him to see it when he went to bed. He felt as calm and relaxed in his red coat as Father felt proud when wearing his sheepskin coat.

On the day when Father was going to enrol him at school for the first time, he told him never to wear that coat again. Ideen cried. Father said: "Red coats are for girls." Ideen cried again and hugged his beloved coat tightly. Father pulled it out of his grasp: "Do you understand what I'm telling you?"

He said nothing in reply. He looked at Father who was irate. Father said: "If you want to wear it, tell me."

Ideen nodded.

"If you do, I won't enrol you."

Ideen cried again. On the stairs at the school, Father had firmly put one foot on the step, trying to convince his child: "If you want to go to school, never wear this again."

"Alright. I'll wear it only at home."

Father enrolled him at Anooshirvan the Just School. Thereafter, Ideen never saw the coat again. But he remembered that it was red and it was warm, unlike Mother's hands that were now so cold that, had she wanted to warm them up over the stove, she would have felt a sharp pain in her bones, making her grit her teeth and stare at the opposite wall. She might also be asking herself why Father was so bad-tempered and stubborn. Even if people around him dropped dead, he would not take his word back.

Mother said: "Father is concerned about you. He says you are so talented that you can embark on any job. Your talents should not be wasted. That is why he wants you near him. He doesn't want you to be a failure, does he?"

"I know that, Mother."

"Then why…" And a silence fell again, like Ida's silence.

He had bent his head forward and his hair, black and falling free, had covered his face. Not once did he raise his head to look at anyone, except when he cast a scolding eye at Urhan. And, now, he was as unhappy as his twin sister because he had, for hours on end, to turn his black hair into a barrier between himself and his life.

At the dinner table, Father said: "It seems you want to put up a fight. You hide yourself and you think that the whole world is centred on Ideen. You must have heard the parable of the ant that was being carried away by water and said the world was being submerged. This is unacceptable."

"Your opinion is worthy of respect in your own eyes, Father."

"Oh, really! It appears as if my child does not recognise me as worthy." Smirking, he faced Mother and continued: "One is tempted to break this boy's pride."

Mother intervened: "You two, don't push each other into an argument."

"Alright, alright. I will take a different approach." And turning his face towards Ideen, but looking at the tip of his own shoes, he said: "Listen son. Tomorrow, you won't go to school. You will come to the shop with me."

"I want to get on with my studies, Father."

"What will happen if you don't carry on with your studies?"

"I'll die."

"Then die!" And an icy silence fell upon the room.

Father had lost the battle. He was no match for his adolescent son and he didn't know what to do. He helped himself to some rice and said: "Eh! He is going to die!" He put some more rice on his plate, saying: "I don't give a damn." He then helped himself to a few spoonfuls of stew. He then ate a spoonful of yoghurt and said: "To hell with him. I'm alright; why should I bother?" He began having his dinner.

For a few seconds, no-one said anything. Then, Father resumed: "You see?

Your admirable son is going to die." After a few more spoonfuls: "I don't give a damn. A little wisp of a child defies me." And, suddenly, he shouted: "You should reply 'Yes, sir' to whatever I say. But, apparently, you don't like me; and that's why you don't want to become a shopkeeper. What's wrong with me?"

"I don't dislike you. All I want is to get on with my studies."

"What happens if you don't?"

"I'll die."

Father was enraged. He threw his spoon down and stood up. He began his familiar pacing, wearing his familiar sheepskin coat: "Do you see? Do you see how cheeky he has become?"

When Ida came into the room, she cast a glance at everyone and sat down beside Mother. Her hands were wet and the skin on her fingers looked old. Mother said: "Eat." She then looked at Ida's wet hands for a moment and said: "Dr Shooshanik has advised you not to put your hands in water so much. Eat."

"I'm not hungry."

Father shouted: "I don't give a damn if you're hungry or not. Get lost and go to bed."

Mother said: "Why are you angry with her?"

Father was looking out of the window. He was tired. He did not have much appetite either: "Because neither of them is well-behaved. Both have their own peculiarities. We make her the best food and she doesn't eat. Well, to hell with her. Let her suffer with her pain."

Ida left the room in silence. Father, facing Ideen, said: "If you want to go to school, I forbid you from setting foot in my shop."

Mother suggested: "But in the afternoons when…"

Father roared back: "There is no need for him. He is not allowed to enter the shop ever again. I don't need anyone's help. The shop will belong to Urhan."

Urhan ate his dinner enthusiastically. Father said: "As Ayaz puts it, there are two categories of people with whom you can't have an argument: The literate and the illiterate."

It was then that Ideen suddenly felt like touching Father. He longed just to get his fingertips near Father's hand or face. It had been years since he had last touched Father. He had not even had a chance to pass near Father. With his small stature, grey hair, dry lips and frowning face, leaning against the big cushion, he looked so awe-inspiring that no-one dared move in his presence. He looked so unfamiliar, so detached, that one dared only cast a furtive glance at the corner of his sheepskin coat. Ideen was always absorbed by the thought of how it was possible to put one's hand on Father's shoulder and stand next to him.

5

On a hot Friday afternoon in June, a black Mercedes, the likes of which no-one had ever seen in Ardabil, came from the direction of Lord's Electric Fan Factory and, raising a lot of dust in its wake, turned towards Father's house. It was moving fast and the neighbours were astounded by such speed and so much dust. When it parked in front of the house, the bewilderment was doubled. The reason was that, before then, no-one who was not known in the neighbourhood had arrived at Djaber Urkhani's house. In any case, even if a stranger did call, he would not arrive in such a posh car. The Russian silver that surrounded the lights and the mirrors and of which the bumpers were made glittered in the sunshine. The black bodywork was so clean and polished that it almost shone. The Mercedes emblem adorning the front of the bonnet dazzled the eyes. Neighbours, including mothers, pregnant women, boys, girls and even a blind old man had come out of their houses to find out which neighbour the occupants of this car had come to visit.

Father was having some watermelon in the courtyard while he lay in the shadow of the pine tree and the weeping willow. Ideen was reading a book in his room upstairs. Right at that moment, Urhan slapped Ida in the face as he thought that she was not fastidious enough in washing his socks and clothes. Mother, who was washing up, suddenly turned round and, with force and anger, smashed the bowl she was holding against the ground, exclaiming: "Why are you hitting her, you shameful boy?" Father shouted: "What was it that broke? What's going on over there?" It was at this very moment that they knocked at the door.

Ideen closed his book for a moment, listened with curiosity and then continued reading. He was reading *Crime and Punishment*. Ida was crying. Father, holding a segment of the watermelon in his hand and a little piece of it in his mouth, sat motionless. Urhan asked: "Who can it be?"

Mother, terrified, left the kitchen and, sobbing, said: "The Angel of Death."

Father opened the door himself. Aloof and without even sticking his head out of the car window, the man sitting in the driver's seat said: "Excuse me, which one of these houses is Mr Urkhani's?"

Father replied: "It is right here. Why?" He went down just one step from the threshold. He looked worried.

The man turned the engine off, closed the window, picked up his leather briefcase from the back seat, got out with a self-assured unhurriedness and locked the car doors. He now looked like a schoolboy struck by a strong wind disturbing his hair and throwing dust into his eyes. Neighbours, as well as passers-by who were around at the time, were all fixed to the spot like statues, without even blinking. They saw the man shaking hands with Father and entering the house. In the corridor, Father deliberately talked very loudly so that the female members of the household would know that a man who was not supposed to see them unveiled had entered the house. In such circumstances, they were not to appear unveiled or even to utter a word. The man looked at the house keenly, as if he had come to inspect the house on behalf of the city council or as if he wanted to buy it. He said: "How modern and ornate that plasterwork is. It has been cut in the Russian style. But, I must say Mr Urkhani, that the whole house has been built in the British style, with high eaves and symmetrical windows." He cast a glance into a room and, with a friendlier voice, said: "How beautiful! I congratulate you on your taste. This cornice formation shows that you have a delicate taste, Mr Urkhani." But the nauseating smell of the room made him frown. He asked: "The person sitting over there, is he related to you?"

"He is my son. But he is now in this miserable state. Ten or 12 years ago, during the Russian invasion…"

"And you, too, were wounded then." He was looking at Yousef who was munching something, in the manner of a cow chewing the cud.

"Not me. But my son, who wanted to imitate the Russian parachutists using my umbrella, brought this misery upon himself."

"Oh, I see!" He left the room, closed the door and continued: "Yes. I understand. In any case, you, too, were, in a sense, wounded. After all, this is your son that…"

Father wondered why this stranger had entered the house without being invited and why he was now walking towards the staircase. Nevertheless, he treated him with respect: "Do come upstairs please."

Symphony of the Dead

At the first bend of the staircase, the man suddenly stopped and said: "I am Abadani."

"Where did you say you were from?"

"I am from Tehran. But my name is Anooshirvan Abadani." He shook hands with Father once again, this time much more vigorously.

"You are welcome." And he ushered him into his own room upstairs. Abadani was wearing a navy-blue suit and a narrow, light-blue tie. The edges of his beard were lower than was customary and his moustache was not in a straight line but rather bent upwards at both ends. He was tall. While he was looking at the windows and the walls, he moved to the obvious focal point of the room and sat down right next to Father's sheepskin rug.

Father, who, impatiently, wanted to know who this man was, where he had come from, what he wanted and what he was going to talk about, sat on his knees, facing Abadani in the manner that he would face one of his debtors: "Well. Let's get to the point."

"So soon?" And he laughed.

"Well. I am listening."

"I don't know where to begin. But, not to worry. I must talk sooner or later. You know; my sister used to live in your neighbourhood until a couple of years ago. I obtained your address from her."

"Well?"

"Up to two or three months ago, I was studying in the United States. I have just recently come back to Iran. I have to put some order and rationality into my life. My sister has told me that your daughter is the noblest and the most beautiful girl in Iran."

Father felt uneasy. But he kept quiet and lowered his head.

Abadani resumed: "I wish to talk to your daughter, Miss Ida."

Father was taken aback. Hitherto no-one had dared name his daughter, let alone ask to talk to her: "What? Who on earth are you to…" His face had turned red and his hands were trembling.

"I did say I was Abadani."

Father stood up. He didn't know what to do. He was angry: "Yes, you are. But…"

With a soft voice, Abadani said: "I hope there is no misunderstanding. My intentions are honourable. I wish to get married. It is for this reason that…"

Father sat down again and lowered his head: "But this is not the way, sir." He had a voice devoid of feeling and wore a smile as cold as the winters of Ardabil: "You know that every town has its own…"

"You are right. I am well aware that customs and traditions must be observed. But I am a frank and straightforward type of person. And that is the reason why I have come to see you in person, rather than the more traditional custom of sending one of my female relatives. May I make just one request?"

"Please."

"If possible, I just wish to cast one glance at Miss Ida from a distance and then say my farewell."

Father rose again: "It is impossible." And he left the room. He noticed that both Mother and Ida, pale and wide-eyed, had been eavesdropping from the upper corridor. He took them by the hand and dragged them downstairs quickly. He took them to the kitchen and shut the door. He reprimanded them for having come upstairs without his permission. He consulted his wife about what to do. He then sent Ida downstairs to inspect the vinegars and the sour grape syrups, to find out whether the aubergine pickle was mature yet and to make sure that it had not gone mouldy. Mother asked: "How old is this chap? Where is he from? Why is he so impertinent?" Father knew nothing. He picked up a plate with slices of red, ripe watermelon and went back upstairs. Abadani was smoking his pipe. Father said: "Would you like some watermelon? Please have some."

Abadani was sitting cross-legged. He had a constant smile on his face and talked about various things: One will not appreciate the value of one's parents until one is a parent himself; the country is progressing but it has a very long way to go before it becomes comparable with America with its machinery, its skyscrapers and its marvellous bridges. He also talked about the Niagara Falls, powerful black people, slavery, oil, love, life and death. He expressed the opinion that Iranians would achieve everything if they worked hard and persevered. He asked why the temperature in Ardabil was always below freezing point in winter and why people were content with their simple houses and did not think about making their dwellings and their surroundings more beautiful.

Father, as if duty-bound not to leave any question unanswered, uttered a few words after each of Mr Abadani's narratives. He nervously played with his glasses. Abadani said: "I am an architect. I am working for a construction company." He ate a slice of watermelon and, taking advantage of Father's silence, said: "I wish to marry your very noble daughter. I even know that she has been suffering from rheumatism. I wish to cure her."

"I request you not to talk about these things. Please have some watermelon and leave."

Abadani had another slice of watermelon and got up: "Have I annoyed you with my remarks?"

"These things are not so simple. You are not buying a pair of shoes."

Symphony of the Dead

"In any case, I'll call again in a couple of months' time. If you change your mind..." At the same time, he shook hands with Father and continued: "I would be honoured to be counted as one of the sons of this family." And he left.

As he was getting into his car, he perceived a girl behind the window of a room on the lower floor. She had black hair and black eyes. She had pushed the curtain aside and, without blinking, just stared. Abadani felt a tremor in his heart. Ida, too, felt a tremor in her heart.

He reappeared the next month and left without having seen Ida. These visits continued for a total of 14 months. He brought a present for Ida every time: Cloth, clothes, shoes and, once, a braided gold necklace. One day, Father warned Abadani that he would complain to the police if his visits continued. Abadani retorted that he was not worried about that: He would be jailed for six months at the most and, afterwards, he would resume his periodic visits. Father felt helpless. He could not prevent Abadani from visiting the house. He conferred with Mother for hours without reaching any conclusion. He said it was impossible. He grumbled angrily: "That dandy tie-wearing man thinks that I'll be fooled by his car."

Mother remonstrated with him: "Don't turn your back on your daughter's good fortune. What do you want to become of her?"

"My decision is final. I will not allow this chap to marry even my daughter's corpse."

Ida, who had fallen in love with Abadani, kept her secret and dared not talk. She was rotting away in a corner of the house. She went on with her boring life, mechanically, like a deaf mute. She washed up, she cooked, she swept and whenever she felt much too lonely, she whispered a song. But, more than anything else, her aching joints had made her thin and miserable.

One day, when she was on her way home after visiting the tailor's, something peculiar happened. She was looking at the Electric Fan Factory, wishing she were not a girl so that she could, just for once, walk down to the factory, stand in front of the hall that was covered by a red tin-roof that looked like a sheepskin hat, shout, frighten and scatter the workers and quickly go back home. But she felt ashamed and went on her way in a dignified manner. At that very moment, she suddenly noticed that a car was slowly following her. She looked back. It was Abadani's. Ida felt that something rose from her body and flew away. She felt scared, her heartbeat quickened and she blushed. She moved aside so that the car could pass. But Abadani was getting out of the car. Ida began to run fast, as if she was running away from death itself. She kept looking backwards and almost fell a number of times.

Abadani got back into his car, drove forward and stopped a few steps ahead of Ida. He got out of the car and stood in front of Ida, blocking her way. He felt shattered under Ida's gaze that was overflowing with shame.

Ida was trembling. Her heart was beating so fast, as if it was about to break out of her chest. She felt a sudden, strong flush all over her face and her body. Her tongue was stuck to the roof of her mouth. The more she tried to look away, the less she was able to do so and her eyes met Abadani's again. He, too, did not know what to do. Hesitantly, he stretched out his arm. His hand held Ida's arm, covered with her black chador: "Miss Ida, you're avoiding me. Aren't you feeling well?"

Ida wished she could disappear into thin air or hide somewhere. She intensely wished that a magic siren signalling the end of the world would miraculously go off. She was in constant fear of being seen by Father. She said: "No. Don't touch me." And she screamed.

"My intentions are honourable."

Ida cried. As she was anxiously looking around, she saw her own house and ran. She felt as if the wind was pulling her into the depths of the factory. The house looked more distant and the repetitive, rhythmic noise of the factory felt like the noise of a hammer hitting a hard surface. As she was about to reach the house, she heard Abadani uttering words like "I'll come…that I shall stay…I am going…I can't see…".

That night, Ida was in a strange, disturbing state of health. Her body ached all over. She felt as if all her bones were shouting "pain, pain, pain" in unison. Dr Shooshanik was brought to her bedside. He gave her an injection. But, towards midnight, she developed a high fever, went into a state of delirium and began to talk gibberish. Mother transferred her bed to the large room downstairs and pulled a white sheet and a blanket over her. Father, frowning and wearing his usual horn-rimmed glasses, came into the room. His little head was covered with thinning hair. He held Ida's wrist to feel her pulse and find out whether she had a temperature. But Ida screamed and said:" Don't touch me."

Father was frightened and recoiled. But he must have exercised great self-restraint otherwise he would have slapped Ida. Afterwards, when Mother had cooled her face with a wet handkerchief, Ida realied that she was lying down in Father's presence. She felt ashamed, jumped up and crouched on the floor.

Father said: "Why are you behaving like this? Have you got a brain as small as a sparrow's in that head of yours?" He stood over her and placed his hand on her forehead while ordering: "Give her some *khakshir*." He then retired to his own room.

Symphony of the Dead

Mother said: "Why are you afraid of Father? Is he frightening, my girl?" As she was taking her back to her bed, she remembered the days when Ida was a sweet, little child. She kissed her and stretched the blanket over her shoulders. When Ideen entered the room, Mother grumbled: "Don't you think you should ask your sister how she's feeling?"

"Yes, yes. I came here earlier, but she was asleep."

"Alright. I'd now better go and see to your father's dinner."

Ideen sat on the edge of Ida's bed. For a moment, he looked at Ida whose eyes were closed. He called: "Ida."

Ida opened her eyes and smiled at her twin brother. Her lips had dried and cracked. Ideen said: "You look so beautiful today."

Ida laughed and moved her head sideways slightly. No-one had said such words to her before. She now longed to talk to Ideen. How good and kind-hearted Ideen was! She buried her hands in her hair and said: "You're joking."

"Believe me Ida. When your eyes were closed, you looked like Sleeping Beauty."

"And now?"

"Now, you look like Sleeping Beauty who has woken up and is no longer asleep."

Ida laughed again. Ideen said: "I have been wishing to talk to you for a long time. I don't think I like Father or Urhan. You, too, should not be like them. You're really grown up now. You should take your own decisions, whatever you think right. Fear nothing. Today, I saw you crying in front of the factory. But why were you frightened? I wish you had got into his car and talked to him. There is no doubt that Mr Abadani loves you and wishes to take you away from here. Well, I don't know whether you like him too or not. But don't be scared. You must face life's problems bravely and decisively, with no fear of consequences." And he fell silent. For a moment, the uncomfortable weight of silence was felt in the room.

Ida was in such severe pain that she bit her lip. Nevertheless, she laughed and, with a feverish groan, she said: "My dear brother." She slowly closed her eyes and, a moment later, she was asleep.

She dreamed of an angel that was the most beautiful of all angels. The angel was Ida herself. She was marooned somewhere, surrounded by rocks and there was no-one else around. Water was pouring down over the rocks and the air was pleasantly cool.

6

Ida, Ida, Ida. Who was Ida? She was the one family member about whom little was remembered by the others. Even Ideen, after the passing of many years, could hardly recall anything of Ida's childhood. No words, no noise, no presence. She had rotted in her damp, little room and, subsequently, had, in Father's words, got lost.

Her marriage took place during a very cold autumn, in Father's absence. The thin layer of snow in the streets and the alleys had turned to ice and a persistent rain fell noisily on the tin roofs and hit the windows. Father shut his shop for a whole week and went on a trip to Tabriz. He purchased a return ticket from a bus company in Ardabil and stubbornly kept to his plan. Mother had remonstrated with him not to miss his daughter's wedding, but he swore not to come back before "the two of them had got lost". He placed his prayer rug, his prayer book, his underwear and a towel in his little bag, put on his thick, black overcoat in which his thin body looked funny, donned his new *papakha* and left for Tabriz on the morning of the day on which Abadani's relatives were due to arrive from Tehran. Mother made him pass under the Koran and a mirror for good luck and said: "I wish you could show more tolerance."

"I dislike this chap and the way he tramples on our honour." He got into a two-horse carriage for his journey to the bus station. The horses pounded their hoofs on the ground in a hurry to get there soon. Just before departing, he stuck his head out of the carriage window and said: "Don't do anything that could lead to shame and dishonour. Go through with this as quietly as possible." The carriage took Father away as Mother poured water in its wake, to ensure a safe journey.

Ida kept herself busy, preparing her wedding dress with great enthusiasm. It was a white, long dress with tiny pleats at the cuffs, the waist and the collar designed to hide her thinness and to make her better suited to Abadani. The design was created by Abadani's three sisters and the sewing was done by Ida, assisted by two girls from the neighbourhood as well as her fellow apprentices from the tailor's where Ida had learnt the art of sewing.

Urhan, Mother and Neemtaj, the cleaner, did their best with the hard task of transferring Yousef to the small room downstairs. They cleaned and tidied the large room and opened its windows to let the air in. They also arranged good-quality Polish chairs, that they had hired, around the room. Ideen spent all his time with decorations. He adorned the door and the walls of the house with coloured paper and little flags. He decorated the simple, soulless alley with rows of coloured electric bulbs.

Abadani's relatives were also busy. His three sisters used old newspapers to clean and polish the windows and laid out the traditional wedding cloth in the large room on the upper floor. The wedding cloth was adorned with a large mirror and, in front of it, an ornate Egyptian Koran, two candelabras, two pieces of hide cut and finished in Czechoslovakia, a decorated loaf of *sangak* bread and a large wooden tray containing multi-coloured objects. Almonds and walnuts, covered with gold dust, were placed in golden baskets. They arranged and adorned the wedding spread so impeccably that Mother cried with joy.

They spent money liberally, as if they were scattering confetti. Orders were issued: "Anoosh, go and get fruit, sugar plums, sweets, cakes, bowls sculpted out of crystallised sugar…"

And he would run, speed away in his car and bring back twice as much as he had been asked to. Despite all this, the wedding reception did not have any resemblance to a wedding celebration. It was quiet and rather gloomy. It was mediocre. The reason was Father's instructions: "Go through with the wedding in such a way that it's in tune with the respectability of our family. It should be held quietly. Men should sit downstairs and women upstairs. If there is need for a dowry, here is the money. Let them buy whatever they want. But my advice is that you should give the money so that they buy what they want in Tehran."

The guests indulged in laughter and noise. The younger ones, in particular, wanted to give an air of jollity to the wedding celebration by way of jokes and merriment. They also had a vested interest: They didn't wish to have a boring night. Uncle Saber, trying to make the most of Father's absence, had brought a three-man orchestra with him. But, from the moment they arrived, they just kept eating oranges and biscuits. Children shouted, shrieked and ran about. Every now and then, one could hear the sound of a plate falling and breaking.

The deafening noise made Uncle Saber more intent on making the musicians start their performance.

The conductor, a slight old man with a sad face, meddled with his accordion. It appeared as if there was something wrong with his instrument. But, with a movement of his head, he signalled his readiness to his colleagues. The three of them started playing simultaneously and dominated the proceedings. They played a few supposedly jolly and noisy pieces that, in reality, sounded most gloomy.

The tunes had a fast, jolly rhythm and the younger guests hoped to start dancing. But, somehow, a wave of sadness and gloom emanated from the notes. At the same time, Mother came out of the kitchen and asked Uncle Saber not to allow music and dancing as Father would raise hell if he were informed of such things. But Uncle Saber paid her no attention. He intended to make the evening an occasion of happiness and merrymaking.

Mother remonstrated: "Uncle Saber! For God's sake, please stop this." But he still paid her no attention. At this point, Mother clutched the corner of Uncle Saber's jacket and begged him to stop. He suddenly came out of his excited mood and ordered the musicians to stop.

Once again, an air of boredom fell upon the wedding reception. A moment later, however, the guests started being noisy. They joked and used the tables as drums, keeping rhythm with the tapping of their fingers. Once again, Uncle Saber got what he wanted. His cheeks flushed red from the heat of the stoves. He kept telling Mother: "You see? You can't stop people from being happy."

Urhan was sitting on the widow sill at an upstairs window. Wearing his milk-white suit, he looked fatter and shorter than usual. Mother wouldn't leave the kitchen. She kept sending out tea, cakes, sweets and fruit to be offered to the guests by girls from neighbouring houses and by the bridegroom's sisters. Ideen was standing at the entrance to the large room which had been dedicated to the wedding ceremony and where the wedding cloth lay on the floor. He was looking at Ida whose lips looked so red and whose eyes so large and so black. When her eyes met Ideen's, she felt a mixture of shame and loneliness. Ideen felt that this was all a dream and that he was weightless.

Abadani was wearing a black suede suit and a well-tailored black waistcoat. With his shirt of white lace and his maroon tie, he looked like a European prince, exactly like those whose photographs Ideen had seen in foreign magazines. Now, he was holding the hand of a beautiful bride who cooked delicious meals, did the washing up impeccably, was not demanding and was occasionally beaten by Father or Urhan.

When the vow of matrimony was pronounced by the officiating clergyman,

Symphony of the Dead

Abadani took a step forward and shook Ida's hand, saying: "Now that Ida is officially my wife, I can say that I am married to the most beautiful woman in the world." He laughed and, then, kissed Ideen on the face and thanked him. Ideen, in his turn, kissed his sister on the face and whispered in her ear: "Go, Ida. Go and never set foot in this hell again." Ida trembled, but feigned a smile and moved away. Arm in arm with the bridegroom, she walked to her chair and sat down. Subsequently, a group of girls from the neighbourhood performed a Turkish dance. They monopolised the centre of the room and Ida could no longer see Ideen.

Ideen went down the stairs to sit on the stone bench at the door, outside the house. He wanted to sit under the oil lamps and listen to the rainfall. His ostensible aim was to welcome the visitors in his capacity as the bride's elder brother, as custom demanded in the absence of the bride's father. But the truth of the matter was that he did not like the unbridled noise and jollity and, more significantly, he always felt sad whenever he saw a girl dancing. He sat on the stone bench, smiling and nodding at the visitors and greeting and welcoming them, whether he knew them or not. Ayaz the policeman was due to come and stand guard at the door. But for some unknown reason, he didn't turn up.

The rain intensified and a wind began to blow. Then there was thunder and lightning and such a severe hailstorm that the little coloured electric bulbs, arranged in strings, broke one after the other. The power cable swung in the high wind. The alley was now almost completely dark. The guests were making less noise because they were having dinner. Out of darkness, there came a distant sad voice. Ideen sensed that somebody was crying and set out to find the source of the voice. His clothes were soaked and he felt dizzy. At the bend in the alley, right opposite Lord's Electric Fan Factory and in a place that looked like a little square, there was a dark, narrow passageway. The sad voice came out of there. It was a sad voice accompanied by a troubadour's tune. Ideen entered the passageway and stood in the vestibule of a very old house. The Turkish song was sung so beautifully and with such feeling that Ideen could not help weeping. The song went like this:

Do you see those mountains covered by mist?
And that hunter who has placed his arrow in his bow?
May my life be sacrificed for men of honour and chivalry in this land,
For those for whom taking of life and giving of life are equally sweet.
The flowerbud thought of the nightingale.
It felt pity and fell in love with the object of its desire.
The master looked at the wings and the feathers of his pigeon and said:

*Oh, my pigeon! Do me a favour, as you have a heart as vast as
  the Sea of Oman.*
I said: Oh, poet! Behold the life of the master.
Those who are wise never mount other people's horses.

The newly weds stayed in the house for three days. On a Friday morning, they departed amidst scenes of the neighbours' emotional farewell, the smoke of frankincense and the blood of a sheep that had been sacrificed in the traditional manner for them at the doorstep. Ida asked Ideen not to leave her alone but to come and visit her when he had completed his studies. Father, who had arrived back from Tabriz the day before, was so angry that he remained in the untidy room upstairs. He would not come down, even for a moment. Abadani went upstairs to see him: "I so much wish you had been present at our wedding, Father."

"Don't call me Father." He spoke with spite and anger.

"Don't be angry with me, Father."

Father moved to the window in the corridor, stood with his back to Abadani and Ida and, with a trembling voice, said: "You have stolen our honour."

Abadani tried to bring calm to the situation: "You are our respected elder. Don't say such a thing. Don't let us leave your house with unpleasant memories."

"I am not a man who goes back on his word. I have nothing to say to you."

Mother scratched her face and ran forward: "Djaber!"

"I am frank and truthful even with my brother, never mind with you."

Mother pleaded with him: "For God's sake, stop this Djaber."

Abadani intervened: "In any case, Ida is your daughter and she expects you to be kind and considerate. You have been negligent enough towards her."

"We did whatever we could for her."

"You thought too little of her, Father."

"How can Ida look into my eyes now?"

"Has she committed any offence, my dear Father?" Abadani now spoke with anger in his voice.

"She has committed something worse than an offence." Father was even angrier than Abadani. Nevertheless, he changed his tone and said calmly: "You made her defy me. She was not like that. You kept calling so many times and fooling the womenfolk so that what should not have happened did happen. In any case, this is her own choice and she should…" He did not complete his sentence. He sounded as if he was about to burst into tears. He then said: "Goodbye". And retired to his room.

7

On the day when Mr Lord, the owner and manager of Lord's Electric Fan Factory, died, the factory did not stop. It trundled on, making its monotonous noise and sounding its siren at the beginning and the end of the working day. In the dusty, unpaved area, at the bottom of that vast 'pit', the workers stood in a line. Each of them had a flower in his hand, to be thrown on to the coffin as it moved off. An Iranian and a British flag had been knotted together on the coffin. A photograph of Mr Lord had been attached to the front of the coffin.

As a sign of respect, Father did not open his shop that day. Accompanied by Ideen and Urhan, he walked down to the entrance of the factory. A big crowd, military as well as civilian, had gathered. The men had doffed their *papakhas*, holding them in front of them. The women were watching the scene from above, beyond the barbed wire fences. In front of Djaber Urkhani's house, a big crowd was waiting impatiently. The police force was controlling the situation. Its members were in full uniform, complete with shoulder sashes and white boots. Some were standing still, holding their rifles in front of them as a sign of respect. Others performed patrol duties and wandered around.

Father, leading the line of businessmen and shopkeepers, was standing next to Ayaz the policeman. Ayaz signalled to him with a movement of his head and Father, in his capacity as a respected, honourable neighbour, placed a bunch of flowers on the coffin and stood aside. Subsequently, the workers threw their own flowers on to the coffin. In accordance with Mr Lord's wishes, they did not stop work. They appointed a number of representatives to accompany the coffin to the town's old cemetery.

The coffin was not carried on the pall bearers' shoulders. A special guard, wearing light blue uniforms, moved in front of the crowd and took the handles of the wooden coffin that was black and shiny. A number of workers chanted *Laa Elaaha Ella Allah* in unison, but a warrant officer silenced them. At the same moment, an army band began playing a funereal march. The crowd was astonishingly silent.

Mr Lord was an Englishman who spoke Turkish most fluently. On the occasions of Christmas and Easter, he always appeared in front of the factory with a very tall sheepskin hat, a black coat and a white shirt with a lace collar and gave presents to every child in the neighbourhood: An illustrated English book with the letters of the alphabet appearing in various shapes and forms, a box of chocolates, a brooch of diamanté in the form of a peacock or a notebook with the logo of the Lord's Electric Fan Factory on its cover.

Sometimes, Mr Lord appeared in the neighbourhood and had personal conversations with residents and, in particular, with Father who was regarded as an honest, honourable neighbour. He talked about the past and the present and about his own country. Father offered him pistachio nuts and he ate them. Eventually, he would talk about his electric fans. Father had great respect for Mr Lord and was a good listener in conversations. The reason was that Mr Lord had conferred on him a medal that honoured him as an honourable neighbour and fellow townsman at one of the annual celebrations on the anniversary of the opening of the factory. This celebration was held every year in the Town Hall. Prominent merchants and townsmen of good standing as well as local dignitaries, attended these celebrations. They had fruit, cake and dinner and watched artistic performances. At the end of Mr Lord's speech, they applauded and Mr Lord gave medals of honour and honesty to three of them.

The hall was filled with guests. Strings of little, coloured electric bulbs, fluorescent lighting and strong floodlights created a bright atmosphere. The columns of the hall were adorned with Iranian and British flags in turn. There were four chairs around every table, which was decorated with blue and red, or orange and white, flowers. People said Mr Lord imported the flowers from abroad but they wondered how, as the flowers were so fresh. It was as if they had just been picked. The stage was drowning in flowers. A rostrum, on which a portrait of the Shah of Iran was pasted, was in front of the stage. From the beginning till the end of the evening, the guests talked, ate, drank, clapped and made merry. Foreign alcoholic drinks, tea, coffee, ice-cream and fruit juices were in plentiful supply and they all bore the logo of the Lord's Factory. On such occasions, Father only drank tea and chatted with Ayaz the policeman who, out of respect for Father, refrained from having alcoholic drinks in his presence.

Symphony of the Dead

Mr Lord, wearing a black coat, a white, frilly shirt and a very tall sheepskin hat, would appear behind the rostrum. The crowd applauded and Mr Lord, beaming with a broad smile, nodded in appreciation. With a wave of his hand, he asked them to be silent again and said: "My honourable fellow townspeople! You, the cream of the town, who have accepted my invitation and taken the trouble of coming here, have really honoured me. You have surely done so out of concern for the destiny of your homeland and out of your desire to pay your respects. Why have I left my own country? For once, ask yourselves why Mr Lord tries so hard. I have covered Iran with Lord's electric fans."

After his speech, Mr Lord invited his honourable fellow townsmen on to the stage: The Head of the Police who had managed to end the riots of the big, moustachioed men, the farmer who had mechanised his farm, the seamstress who trained half the girls in the town, the benevolent man who, after the fire in the bazaar of Ardabil, declined any compensation and whose only request was that the amount of two hundred-odd *toomans* entrusted to him by an old woman and lost in the fire be paid to her (this man was considered to be a perfect example of an honest, honourable human being), the policeman who had tried harder than his colleagues in ensuring law and order in the town with a combination of pragmatism, meticulousness and perseverance, and Djaber Urkhani, a thin, slight man, wearing round glasses and a brown sheepskin hat, with a stubble of grey beard and a brilliant record in the business of nuts and seeds in the town. He was feted as: "Djaber Urkhani, the honourable neighbour, the honourable citizen, the honourable businessman." The gathered guests clapped for him, Ayaz the policeman placed a garland of flowers around his neck and Mr Lord shook hands with him.

Mr Lord's demise, apart from causing sorrow in the neighbourhood and among the workers, was cause for some propaganda. On returning from the ceremonies of funeral and burial, workers' representatives voluntarily worked until seven o'clock in the evening. The fans were made and the vans carried them out of the factory on that uphill road. The fans manufactured on that day, however, were different: Each carried a sticker with the words 'Mr Lord has passed away. Let us remember him with respect'.

After the War, and, more particularly, after Mr Lord's death, nearly every house in the city was sprinkled with insecticides and pesticides. People decided to get rid of insects and other harmful pests by embarking upon an extensive fumigation programme. An American chemical and pharmaceutical firm, called Boycott, opened an office in Ardabil and undertook an advertising campaign. People rushed to buy its products. The supply was exhausted and people had to lodge applications and wait their turn. The insecticide was sold in one-litre, sealed containers together with a pump. On each container, there was a photograph of a blonde girl holding a big flywhisk with which she drove the mice away, out of her window. The important thing was the advertising motto: 'After War, insecticides and pesticides make life bearable'.

A few months later, Boycott Company opened a factory in a corner of the city and advertised for workers and office employees. The business flourished; pumps and insecticide could be seen all over the city and its surrounds. Grocers and greengrocers also sold Boycott's products and banks stuck its adverts in their windows. The pharmaceutical company decided to go into the toy business from then onwards. It started producing balloons, dolls, balls, human and animal figurines, brainteasers and games as well as many kinds of imitation jewellery. The factory made the biggest balloon ever, in the shape of an elephant, and let it float above the city. It made a toy cat with whiskers so heavy that its neck was about to break. The cat had a somewhat human face and appeared to be wearing glasses. The Boycott factory also produced a fan that, when switched on, flew around the room. Another of its products was a toy clergyman that peed in the sunshine or in hot weather. It also made a ball that, bouncing off the ground, would shoot a long way into the air and then explode. Yet another curiosity that it offered for sale was a book that, on being opened, would shoot a penis into one's face.

Subsequently, Boycott turned into the biggest client for sunflower seeds in the city. As a result, Father's business flourished. Later on, the firm also diversified into agriculture and cattle farming. The diversification did not end there: Banking, manufacture of machinery, printing, painting and decorating, electrical goods and oil all followed. With every new branch, a new subsidiary sprang up under the overall control of Boycott Company. Every building was treated with insecticides and pesticides before being put to use.

Father, too, had his house treated. One day, he took the whole family away from town and housed them in a tent overnight. The reason was that the pesticide was so concentrated and so powerful that it could, so far, count two women, a young girl and an old man among its victims. In accordance with the manufacturers' instructions, people had to refrain from going into their dwellings for a period of 24 hours after treatment with insecticide or pesticide.

While they were in the tent, Mother suddenly remembered Yousef. Apparently, no-one had thought of him when evacuating the house. Mother asked Father to let him be brought to the tent. Father, too, was worried and shed tears for Yousef. But, considering that pest-control workers, wearing masks, had sprinkled pesticide on every part of the house, not even sparing

Symphony of the Dead

cracks between bricks, spaces between doors and walls, openings in wardrobes and even cracks in the walls, what could Father or anyone else do?

That night, they stayed awake until dawn and shed tears for Yousef. When they were going back to the house the next day, they were all certain that they would be confronted with Yousef's swollen corpse. Father opened the door of the little room on the lower floor with trepidation. Yousef was sitting in his usual corner, with his usual dejected and astonished look. The only difference was that he now had company: A few dead mice, a dead cat and hundreds of crickets, fleas and cockroaches scattered on the floor, all laid low by the pesticide. Father quickly opened the window and rushed towards Yousef. He was astounded to find him alive and, moreover, eating something.

Mother had no doubt that he had eaten the dead pests.

8

Following Ida's departure, Father often became difficult and had become quarrelsome. With the smallest of excuses, he would shout and quarrel. He often criticised the food, had lost his appetite, was impatient and smoked his pipe all the time. When he returned from the shop, he would immediately go to his room upstairs. He would have his dinner, say his prayers and start a quarrel for some reason or other. He would then throw a cloak over his shoulders and go out. He would walk down the alley, lit up by light from the lampposts, come back and go to bed. During those nights, Father noticed a strange phenomenon. Every evening, at seven o'clock, Ayaz the policeman, riding his bicycle fitted with an auxiliary engine, rode northwards and rode back towards his house at exactly ten o'clock. Father was highly intrigued and bemused. On a number of occasions he had even asked Ayaz where he was going. Ayaz had explained that he went on a night patrol. Father praised his diligence and no longer had any doubts that the late Mr Lord had been right in naming Ayaz as an example of an honest, honourable official. From then on, Father did whatever course he was set on only after consulting Ayaz, without any hesitation as to the advisability of what was being done. Whenever there was a heated argument, Father would say: "Go away and mind your own business. As Ayaz puts it, you can't argue with two kinds of people: 'The literate and the illiterate.'"

Ideen felt that all this commotion was because of him. He did not wish to work in Father's shop and become, like him, an honest, respectable shopkeeper. What he wanted was to write, to read and be absorbed in his world of books and poetry. When they changed his room and he had to live in the basement, like an exile, he showed no reaction. He let himself be made fun of. He let Father call him a lout and a coward. Even when his writings and his books were set on fire next to the pond, he fell even more in love with his work and became determined to acquire again what he had lost.

Ideen had become accustomed to seeing Father frown. Sometimes he clearly noticed that when Father passed him, he pretended not to see him. Mother, however, was fed up. She could hardly put up with the situation. She complained all the time and quarrelled with Father about the twins: "That was the way you treated Ida and you treat Ideen just the same. Is he not your son? Why do you talk nonsense and why do you insult him?"

Father, however, was the same stubborn father: "I only want him to behave properly and follow the right path in life."

"You insult him in whatever way you can and yet you expect him to become a shopkeeper? You expect him to give up his books and work for you? That little lizard, too, follows your example and utters the most disrespectful words."

"Who?"

"Urhan." She paused for a moment and then she said: "He has no right. He has no right."

"What's he been saying?"

"Yesterday, he called him a coward. He doesn't call him by his name. Instead, he calls him a *mirza* or a lout. He calls him whatever he has learnt from you." And she burst into tears.

Father laughed: "He uses the right words, doesn't he? A coward is a coward."

"You have no right to insult my child with such words."

"He is my child too."

"You have made clowns of yourselves for the sake of your possessions, for the sake of a few worthless coins."

Father roared: "You deserve what you get. That should teach you not to keep defending him."

Mother shouted: "It's you who deserve what you get. You shouldn't have contributed to his birth in the first place." And a heavy slap landed on her face.

A few seconds later, Mother, shedding tears and wearing her black chador, went towards Ideen's room. She called him from the top of the staircase: "Ideen!"

Ideen stuck his head out of his basement room: "Oh, Mother!" He had not seen Mother in such a state before.

"Get dressed and let's go out." There was anguish and torment in her voice.

"Where to?" He quickly put on his usual long overcoat and ran upstairs. Mother was waiting outside for him. She walked ahead of Ideen and kept her distance. She didn't want her eyes to meet Ideen's. It was a Friday afternoon in October and there were few people in the street. Every now and then the wind swept through and raised the dust in the street and the passers-by had to close their eyes to shield them. The shops were closed and the only other people around were a number of idle youths loitering at a corner of the square. They walked through Shah Safi Street, passed the nut-sellers' souk and walked on. At the Shah Square, there was a row of horse-drawn carriages waiting for fares. Ideen asked: "Where are we going, Mother."

"The cemetery." And she moved towards a white carriage that was the first in line. She said: "Get in". She got in herself and pulled the canopy over their heads.

The carriage-driver asked: "Where you going?"

Mother replied: "The cemetery."

"Which one?"

"The old one."

The old carriage-driver was wearing a blue uniform complete with a hat, belt and a white shoulder sash. He got in and shook the reins. The carriage moved off slowly. It passed Akhavan Garden and turned towards Sarcheshmeh. In Pir Maadar district, a few shops were open. Mother said: "Let's not forget to buy some cheese sweetmeats." When there were passing a grocer's, Mother told the carriage-driver to stop for a moment so she could buy something. She got off, bought some sugarplums and got in again. The carriage set off towards the cemetery.

Mother sat beside her father's grave. She then placed her head on the tomb and cried. Ideen had never before seen Mother shed tears so profusely.

The cemetery was crowded. Here and there, a group of people were bending over a grave. Children ran about. The wind raised dust and howled between trees. A few steps ahead, hawkers were selling sugarplums, dates and cheese sweetmeats. Ideen got up, bought a kilogram of dates and offered them to the other people visiting the cemetery. When he returned to Mother, he found her in a strange state of consternation.

Her eyes were fixed on a distant point. She was not actually looking at anything or even blinking. She had the air of a model who was sitting for a portrait painter. She was deeply absorbed in her own thoughts. She was silent. She was so detached, as if covered by a thick fog.

Ideen faked an air of calm. With his hands in his pockets, he approached Mother:

"Aren't we going back?"

"Yes, we are." She got up, took a deep breath, lowered her head and began to talk. She said she was fed up and could no longer cope with the situation. She said that, after 25 years of marriage, Father had raised his hand to her and insulted her dead relatives. She said she was trapped and that she could do nothing to get out of the trap.

Ideen commiserated with her: "I am nearly 20 years old and I have yet to see Father smile."

It was crowded outside the cemetery. One after another, horse-drawn carriages took passengers who were going back to the town, aboard. Some visitors went back on foot, moving in single file along the street that led to the town centre. Old, poor women followed the visitors like scroungers, pestering them with their persistent begging. A few crippled beggars were here and there, sitting on the ground. The wall around the cemetery was in a lamentable state of disrepair and had fallen down in a few places.

Mother said: "I know how I should behave from now on." She now walked quickly and her heart was overflowing with sorrow and anger. She continued: "For a lifetime, we have suffered in silence. He treated us so cruelly during Ida's wedding. The little girl was ill and he treated her like dirt on the threshold of her married life. Despite this, we remained meek, gentle and silent. He now forbids me from going to Tehran to see Ida, I..." She left her sentence hanging.

Ideen said: "Don't forget that you yourself made it possible for him to think too much of himself". He had been waiting for an opportunity to say such a thing. For a moment, he thought it would be wise not to continue on the same tack. But Mother's silence encouraged him and he picked up from where he had left off: "What did he do for his brothers who bowed to him and gave him a swollen head? For the past few years he has forbidden Uncle Saber from entering the house. The last time I saw my elder relatives was many years ago. It was when grandfather and our aunts came to see us. It is as if we have no relatives at all. Haven't you got relatives yourself, Mother? Where are they now?"

"They are in Rezaiyyeh. But when he doesn't allow me to go, how can I see them? I am a woman and cannot travel as I like. And considering your father's behaviour, they dare not come either." They walked to a horse-drawn carriage and got in. Mother said: "Shah Safi."

Ideen was furious and wished to condense all his sorrows and disappointments into one sentence. But it was not possible and time was short. Recalling past problems would mean reviving numerous nightmares of his own and, moreover, remind Mother of them. He merely reiterated: "You yourself have encouraged him and given him a swollen head. It will now be extremely difficult to pull him down from his high horse."

The carriage moved slowly forward, more slowly than the one that had taken them to the cemetery. The carriage-driver gazed at the reins and looked as if he had been hypnotised. He was too exhausted to raise his whip to the horse. It was getting dark and the wind howled.

Mother said: "The more I think about it, the more I'm convinced that the only thing we can do is put up with him."

"What shall we do?"

Mother was taken off guard, she had not expected to be consulted in this way. But she quickly pulled herself together and said: "You, for example, can go and help him in the shop in the morning or in the afternoon. All he grumbles about now is that his eldest son has distanced himself from him."

"His eldest son is Yousef. What have I done wrong?"

"You should consider Yousef dead for all intents and purposes. Yousef is not a proper human being. You know that very well. What is wrong with clinging to a ready-made life and a ready-made job and thinking about your well-being? Who has he worked for for so many years? Only for Urhan?"

"I don't want to repeat and imitate my father's life. You knew very well, Mother, that I attend Nasser Delkhoon's poetry class. He is due to submit my poems to a magazine so that they can print them. And you expect me to become a mere seller of watermelon seeds?"

Mother looked at Ideen. He looked pale. For this reason, she adopted a playful tone and said: "I don't know what you want to do. But I know that all of you are stubborn. You've inherited your grandfather's characteristics. This is true about you, about Ida, about Urhan, as well as about your father. Even the miserable Yousef was stubborn and inflexible in that he insisted on remaining stupid." She then related, once again, the story of their grandfather's selling of stones.

The carriage stopped at the entrance to Lord's Alley and they got off. Mother paid the carriage-driver and headed for the house, saying, "And nothing more about your grandfather. Do you understand?"

Ideen was following Mother and walked more slowly. Mother turned back: "Only remember this: That if you don't get your share of the shop, the garden and the house, you will have been deprived of your rights. You don't understand these things now because you're too young. Life has many twists and turns. You have not suffered yet, and, because of that, you don't appreciate the value of a good life. Urhan, by contrast, already has everything. What I'm saying is that you should be whatever he is."

Ideen had remained quiet. When he was knocking at the door, he saw Ayaz the policeman who was riding towards the northern end of the street on his motorised bike. He looked at Ayaz and nodded.

Mother said: "Did you see?"

"What?"

"It was Ayaz the policeman. The poor man goes on his patrol duty at this time of night."

"Yes, I saw him."

As they were going into the house, Mother said: "After visiting a cemetery, one feels relieved and happy."

9

THE RED POEM BY IDEEN URKHANI

On the mountain pass, on a long day, in the beginning
the angry men of our tribe
stood for a moment
at the bend of the mountain
mounted their horses
with eyes devouring the entire valley.
The sun shone with such ferocity
that the warm lassitude of the earth climbed their legs.
They all slid and rolled down the rocks.
And without tying their horses to dried up trees,
they slept,
exhausted,
intoxicated with the sweetness of sleep
with their hats covering their faces.
The girls wearing red asked:
"Do these men not hear the neighing of their horses?
If they do, why do they not wake up?"
A high wind blew
and dishevelled the girls wearing red.

Ayaz repeatedly stabbed the newspaper with his fingertip and said: "Read it carefully, Djaber."

Father read the poem once more, looked at Ayaz and asked: "Is this really the work of our Ideen?"

"Do you think it isn't?" He narrowed his eyes, stared at Father and said: "He has called his poem 'The Red Poem'. Do you understand what this means? Besides, can this kind of rubbish be called poetry, for goodness sake?"

"What is to be done, Ayaz?"

"He should be stopped."

"I for one, am no match for him."

Ayaz bent over the desk, brought his head closer to Father's and said: "Were it not for people's idle talk, I would lock him up for a couple of months."

"He has been led astray by bad company. He must have been going somewhere, the sort of place where one is indoctrinated and instructed." Father was clearly worried about Ideen.

"I'm aware of that. And I already know that he goes to meet a guy called Master Delkhoon[9]. He's a crazy, philosophising type of man."

"I wish we could do something against this crazy guy."

"I must think about this."

A few days later, during an evening when a full moon had lit up everything, three members of the Security Forces pushed their way into Master Nasser Delkhoon's house. He was arrested, accused of leading the brave, young men of Ardabil astray, and sent to Tehran under guard.

Ideen's achievement after three years of continuous training was the transformation that he had undergone. Young people regarded him with a combination of hope and respect. He had composed a number of quatrains and couplets as well as many other pieces of poetry that could, perhaps, be numbered in the hundreds. His poetry was composed in Turkish. Some people thought that he had plagiarised them. A teacher, who was also a scout master, had said: "If you scour the surroundings of Ardabil, you will find many such hidden books."

Ideen, however, paid no attention at all to such rumours and devoted all his time to reading and writing. He did this with great attention and fastidiousness. He transformed everything into poetry. Whenever he wanted to strengthen his argument, he would quote a couplet. Within a short time anyone who knew him noticed that he was overflowing with poetry. Gradually, he developed his own particular style and his own manner of eating, sleeping, reading books, conversing and general behaviour. His fame spread all over the city, to the extent that, although he was no more than 22 years old, many girls and women were attracted to him. People were puzzled by the fact that this handsome young man, who was attractive as well as sensitive, had no woman in his life. Even Mother was aware of this and talked about it to a widow called Foroozan, telling her: "As soon as you talk to him about women, he says he prefers not to be tied down."

Foroozan was not sure that this was the case: "Who says there's no woman in his life?"

"Is there one? If there is, I do so wish to find out about his taste."

"It's very easy to find out. Leave it to me."

"Please go ahead. I'd be so grateful to you. Let's see if you can play the detective."

So it was that Foroozan got the chance to approach Ideen, get into his room, talk to him and invite him to her house.

When Ideen entered her room one summer's day, Foroozan closed the door, trapped him against the wall right next to the door and, trembling hysterically and feeling feverish, tore off Ideen's shirt, telling him: "Don't you like being with me?" And she wrapped herself round him like a serpent.

Ideen, however, lived in a world of his own. It appeared as if there was not much in common between him and other young people of his age. The more he was indifferent to them, the more they wished to be with him. They followed him in the streets, in bookshops and in Akhavan Garden. Foroozan who was burning with her love for him told Mother one day: "Your son must have a magic spell to attract everybody. But he is indifferent to them."

Mother replied: "It depends who we mean by 'them'."

"He doesn't even return a 'hello'."

"That's because he's shy."

Foroozan was an employee of the National Bank of Iran. She was a native of Tabriz and had stayed on in Ardabil after her husband's death. She lived on the opposite side of the street in an apartment on the upper floor. There was only one thing she liked in life; and that was make-up and cosmetics. It was rumoured that she spent all her pay on buying cosmetics and similar products. She used such strong perfumes that people almost fainted.

Mother was worried and felt that Foroozan's fixation on Ideen would be dangerous to him. One night, Mother dreamed that there was a fire and that Ideen and Foroozan were 'washing' themselves in the flames. The next day, when Foroozan came to see Mother late in the afternoon, Mother said something to her that kept her away from the house forever.

There was another girl who lived near Master Delkhoon's. She passed in front of Lord's Electric Fan Factory a number of times every day, hoping to see Ideen. But whenever she did see Ideen, she turned pale, simply cast a glance and went away.

There were other girls and women as well. But Ideen was first and foremost in love with poetry. He also had profound respect for his master and mentor.

Master Nasser Delkhoon had taught Ideen the metres and other technicalities of classical Persian poetry. He believed that Ideen had freed himself from the constraints of rhythmic poetry and would attain high esteem in the realm of Persian literature, although he himself had not been able to become a celebrity despite his vast knowledge of philosophy, literature and mysticism. He was a tall, thin, middle-aged man. He lived the life of an ascetic, very frugally. He had long hair, a bony face and a stubbly beard. He looked somewhat like a portrait of Hallaaj[10] that had been placed over the entrance to the dervish monastery called Sheikh Safi-od-din e Ardabili[11]. He had a soft voice and lived in a room in the district of Pir Shams-od-din. He was a good calligrapher and was a man of fine tastes. He occasionally played the sitar. Although books, notebooks, pieces of paper and inkpots were scattered all over his room, he managed to find a spot for his three-wick oil stove over which he made tea for his pupils. He was free from any temptations of fame, money or high position. He recited old poetry but composed modern poems. He revered the poet Nima Yooshij[12].

No-one knew anything about him. People did not know where he had come from, where he had been born or why he lived alone. But it was rumoured he had studied Arabic literature in France and that, for many years, he had been in love with a girl suffering from a severe illness and that, after the girl's death, he had found solace in poetry and chosen to live the life of a recluse.

Following the disappearance of Master Nasser Delkhoon, his circle of disciples was wound up, his disciples scattered and, thereafter, no-one knew anything about what had become of him or where he had gone.

10

Ida asked: "Why are you so thin?"
She had changed completely. She had put on some weight. She was no longer suffering from pain in her bones and her joints. She could speak English fluently. The childish air of fear and sorrow that used to characterise her was no longer present. She was wearing very fine clothes. She had brought Ideen and Urhan two pairs of foreign-made jeans. She said everyone in Abadan wore these type of trousers. She said they socialised with many British and French people in Abadan and that people like Mr Lord were numerous there. Mother told her on many occasions that she had intended to travel to Abadan to visit her and that she had always been in her mind at the dinner table, in the kitchen and, particularly, during the night. Mother added: "But you know how Father is, don't you? He never allowed me to travel to Abadan to see you. What can I do? A woman has no choice but to obey her husband."

She wanted Ida to know that she had a special place in the heart of her family. For this reason, she tried to keep her happy in a number of ways all the time. She bought a toy gun for Sohrab, Ida's son. A spark appeared at the end of the barrel when the trigger was pulled. Father grumbled: "Are you a fool? Do you expect a little child to appreciate a sparking gun?"

Every year, Ida paid a 15-day visit to the parental home. This was her third annual visit. Mother had made a shirt for Sohrab and knitted a pullover for him. She would not let Ida wash Sohrab's dirty linen or underwear and took care of that herself. Ida tried to look happy and lively. She was no longer silent, as she had been for years. Nevertheless, one could perceive an incomprehensible sorrow in her eyes. Especially so whenever Father came back from work, tired, frowning and in bad mood as usual. Ida did nothing but occupy herself with Sohrab, feed him, help him to walk and comb his hair.

Symphony of the Dead

Occasionally, whenever possible, she would cast a furtive eye at Father.

Father sometimes asked: "How are your bones and joints?"

"It is now about a year that I've been without pain. But I must have a strong penicillin injection every month. There are many foreign doctors in Abadan."

That evening, when Ida went into her brothers' room, she noticed that there was only one bed. She asked: "What's happened, Mother?"

Mother explained that Father became belligerent one night and subsequently made changes to the allocation of rooms. She told Ida nothing of the truth of the matter, as she did not want her to be unhappy. She had not deemed it wise to write anything about the episode in her letters to her either. Ida then asked where Ideen slept at night and Mother had to tell her.

Ida nervously fiddled with the button at her collar so much that it fell off. She said her brother was being tormented to death. She noted that Ideen had lost weight, that his eyes always looked tired and that he looked as if he was suffering from a severe illness. Mother explained that Ideen was on the right track to emerging as a great poet but that he had been feeling sad since his mentor had disappeared. She added that life had become really tough and gloomy.

Ida decided to clean Ideen's room, to make net curtains for the only window in the room, to clean up the walls and to transform the room, so that it would no longer look a mess. She asked him: "Why have you become so thin?"

As Ida's husband had not arrived, Ideen carried Sohrab in his arms and took him out to buy him something. Mr Abadani had vowed that he would never again set foot in that house but would merely accompany Ida and Sohrab to Ida's parental home, to return again in 15 days' time to take them back home. During Ida's stay, Sohrab missed his father and kept asking where he was. Ida cleaned the windows, fixed the curtains and, with wicker, made lampshades for Sohrab. Her hands looked as red as baked beetroots and she did not have enough time to comb her hair.

Again and again, Ideen took Sohrab for a walk in his arms and strolled along the nearby alleyways. He showed him the Electric Fan Factory and bought him rooster lollipops. By the time they came back home in the afternoon, Sohrab was fast asleep, with his hand under Ideen's collar. Ideen would then put him to bed. Ideen himself had no appetite for dinner. He would retire to his room in the basement, lie down on his bed, and go to sleep under the red blanket that Ida had brought him from Chahbahar. Around midnight, when everyone else was asleep, he would switch the light on, pick up his book from under the bed and start reading. Alternatively, he would write things in his notebook.

One night, during Ida's stay, Ideen heard the gentle sound of Mother's slippers. He listened more carefully. It was no doubt Mother who intended to come into his room and make sure that everything was alright. But when he looked up, he saw Father in the doorway. He was wearing his sheepskin coat, looking at everything in anger and muttering: "How strange! How strange!"

It was cold. The smell of vinegar and the sour grape juice that had been stored in the basement, combined with the odour of an Aladdin paraffin heater, was irritating. Ideen pulled himself together and sat up in bed. He kept looking at Father's feet to see whether he would enter the room or not. Father, wearing Mother's slippers, was standing motionless. Ideen was at a loss about what to do. His hands were trembling, causing the pages of the book to shake, making a peculiar noise. He tried to avoid trembling, with no success. Father came down the stairs slowly, looked around, took a deep breath and began shaking his head. His lips had turned dry and purple and Ideen feared he would do something out of anger. Father broke the deathly silence: "For the time being, he has contracted poetic diarrhoea. God only knows when he's going to be cured of it." He went away.

Ida asked: "Why have you become so thin?"

Once again, Ideen carried Sohrab in his arms and took him out. He bought him rooster lollipops and clockwork cars. He carried him through the alleyways and down the hill to the gates of Lord's Electric Fan Factory. During Ida's stay, Ideen kept himself well occupied with Sohrab.

Ida asked: "Would you like to have a child like this?"

"How?"

Ida, pushing a lock of hair behind her ear with her fingertips, said: "I have found you a good girl."

"I have other plans."

She was delighted and asked with enthusiasm: "What are your plans?" She kept sewing pleats in the net curtains without turning her eyes from Ideen.

"I want to quit this way of life altogether and find my own life. You know, Ida, that I was happy with Master Delkhoon and thought that, now that I had him, there was no need to go to university. But now that they got rid of him, I intend to go to Tehran, rent a room and pursue my studies. Master Delkhoon thought a lot of me and was sure of my future prospects. I also felt confident with his support."

Two days later, Abadani came back and took Ida and Sohrab away with him. But the more they insisted, the less he was inclined to set foot in the house. As before, he waited outside and even declined to accept an offer of tea while he was waiting. On the day he arrived, in the afternoon, he had taken

Mother, Ideen and Ida in his car for a drive round the town. He had told them that he and Ida intended to remain in Abadan for five years but that they were not yet decided about where to settle afterwards. He had told Ideen that he could move to Abadan, learn English and stay with them. But Ideen had replied that the provinces offered little chance of advancement. He maintained that the whole country had been destroyed and sacrificed at the altar of Tehran and that, therefore, the wise thing was to settle in Tehran and to begin whatever one wanted to do from there.

Ideen looked sad and absent-minded. His eyes conveyed a strange state of mind. Ida said: "It seems as if you have fallen in love."

Mother said: "If he gets married, I will provide them with a separate living arrangement so that they can live in comfort and privacy."

Abadani advised: "Now that he wishes to embark on university education, I plead with you not to prevent him."

Ideen said: "Although one can get uselessly old in this house, I'll wait until I'm quite ready. Eventually, I'll get to university with one great leap. When one is alone in a town like this, one develops negative attitudes and pessimistic ideas too."

Abadani agreed: "I understand, I understand." He talked about the time when he was studying in the United States. He referred to the fact that, at the time, he had been on his own. He said he greatly admired ambitious young men and swore that Ideen would one day be a great man as he was wiser and more knowledgeable than other people of his age. That night, Mr Abadani stayed in a hotel and, the next morning, he departed for Abadan with Ida and Sohrab.

From the next day, Mother was alone once again and silence settled on the house. Time passed slowly. Mother regretted the fact that she had forgotten to buy special soap, made in Maragheh, for Ida. She was also unhappy because Sohrab's trousers had been left behind. She prayed to God for a safe journey for Ida and her new family.

Life in the house was always monotonous and quiet. One felt tired and also felt someone was missing. There was no guest, no noise, no celebration and no mourning. Only occasionally, one could hear the noise of a raven from among the branches of the pine tree. Father allowed no-one to enter the house: It was his sanctuary. If his friends wanted to meet him, they did so in the shop. He would entertain them with a plateful of watermelon seeds or with tea ordered from the teahouse in the souk. Even Uncle Saber did not call at the house. Similarly, no member of the household ever called on Uncle Saber. Father said: "A drunkard who interferes in the problems of my children has no right to set foot in my house. Besides, if he had not deprived me of my money back then, I would now own half of the souk."

Mother said: "It's not possible to break with one's close relatives forever, is it? Do you have it in you say to your brother: 'See you on Resurrection Day?'"

"I piss on this so-called brotherhood. If I happen to see him, I shall treat him to some juicy swearing so he realises who he's dealing with. I know that he provokes Ideen to misbehave. He tells him to lead the life of a clown instead of taking up business like his father. What sort of a job is poetry? Especially considering the sort of cock and bull stuff that this lout of a son composes?"

Ideen occasionally met Uncle Saber in front of the Kolbeh Choobi wine house. On such occasions, Uncle Saber was either arriving or leaving. He was always drunk. On one occasion, he had pulled a wad of banknotes out of his pocket, telling Ideen: "Take it, Ideen, take it. Take as much as you like. I know you get no money from your father. He is, after all, my own brother and I know him very well. He gives you no pocket money because he wants you to be subservient and obedient. For how many years have you been wearing these checked trousers and this worn out coat? When do you want to enjoy yourself like a young man, then? Remember, dear nephew, that you must free yourself from your dreary lifestyle. Go and follow your studies. I will support you like a roaring lion." He was still holding the wad of banknotes in the palm of his hand: "Please take it, dear nephew. I insist."

"I don't need it, my dear uncle."

"I don't want you to be shy or formal with me. Take at least some of it." He turned his head and looked away. His substantial double chin, reddish in colour, protruded conspicuously from out of his white collar. Ideen felt like helping Uncle Saber by loosening the knot of his necktie. He said: "Thank you, dear uncle."

"Don't offend me with your refusal. I have turned my head away so that you can take as much as you like."

"I am grateful to you for just thinking of me and being concerned about me." With a movement of his own hand, he pushed Uncle Saber's away. Uncle Saber put the money back into his pocket and said: "At least come inside and let's have two more glasses."

"I don't drink, uncle."

"Okay, another time. But always remember that you have a bright future ahead of you. I'm very optimistic about your future." He took hold of Ideen's shoulder, squeezed it and said: "Do you want to go to university?"

"Yes, dear uncle."

"Which one?"

Symphony of the Dead

"As I have told you before, I wish to enter Tehran University. If I can't, then wherever I am accepted."

"Tehran University is very good. Shiraz University is not bad either. Shiraz itself is the city of the poets Hafez and Sa'adi[13] and its Khollar wine is second to none." With both of his hands, he held Ideen's right hand and shook it so enthusiastically that his double chin began to wobble. He continued: "God be with you. We didn't achieve anything in life. You must study so that you do better. I've got high hopes for you. By the way, when you pack up and are ready to go, come and see me. I want to write you a cheque so that you don't have to worry for at least a couple of years."

At the dinner table, Ideen said that he had met Uncle Saber. Father stared at him for a moment and said: "Who told you to do that, you silly ass?"

"Uncle Saber wants to pay for my education for a couple of years."

"The stupid man is talking sheer nonsense. He himself is destitute and has no money for his day-to-day living. If he is telling the truth, why is he living in a rented house? Father then changed his tone and asked, very softly: "Well, what decision have you arrived at, you happy prince?"

"I am preparing myself for university."

"To achieve what? What are you after? Tell me so that I can give it to you."

"Not everybody should become a shopkeeper like you, Father. Not everybody should inherit their job from their father. There are so many jobs, so many thoughts…"

"Don't argue with me. Either you come with me or you leave."

"I have spent a lot of time thinking, Father. It's not fair now to confront me like this."

Mother said: "In this day and age, only money brings respectability and acceptance. But you…"

Father resumed his tirade: "Let him follow his own desires, in which case he should stay away from me."

"I had no intention of doing otherwise."

Father shouted: "You see how shameless he is?" He got up and started walking about the room. He said: "That was my last word. From now on, we have no responsibilities to each other. This is an ultimatum, Ideen." He continued walking about the room for a few more seconds and, then, resumed: "What are you looking for?"

"I am looking for myself."

"In that case, get lost."

11

On that warm spring day, at half past twelve, there was suddenly such a decrease in sunlight that one felt as if an invisible hand had covered the face of the sun. It was suddenly as dark as it would have been at sunset. Father who had come back home for lunch glanced at his watch in that untimely twilight. Although he could clearly see the hands on the face of his watch, he thought his eyes were deceiving him. Astonished, he asked: "Is it nighttime, Urhan?"

Urhan rushed out of his room and screamed: "Oh, my God!"

It was getting darker. At the same time, the siren of Lord's Electric Fan Factory went off. That convinced Father that night had arrived or that, alternatively, he was still mentally in the previous night, thinking about what Ayaz the policeman had told him and that exhaustion had disoriented him in time and space.

On the previous day, Ideen's poem 'Days and Moments' had been printed in the *Ettela'at* newspaper. It was preceded by an editor's foreword, the wording of which made Father even angrier. It read: "Ideen Urkhani may not be a well-known figure for the people as a whole, but his name is quite familiar to the prominent poets and other literary personalities of this country. Being a native of Azerbaijan and the son of an ordinary shopkeeper, he studied for three years under the late Master Delkhoon and adheres to the modernist trend in Persian poetry. With printing his poem 'Days and Moments', the Editorial Board of the newspaper expresses its desire to get to know him better and to ensure his continued co-operation. For this purpose, he is invited, for a Monday or Wednesday, to…"

Father read the poem and understood nothing of it. But he was worried lest Ideen go to Tehran and there would follow what should not be allowed to happen. In those years, going to Tehran meant never to return. In front of the bus company's terminus, there was always a crowd of passengers about to travel to Tehran, Tabriz or somewhere else. Every passenger was seen off by their own crowd and the parting was so sad and distressing. Father was thinking that if Ideen moved to Tehran, that big, unknown city, nothing would remain of the family. Ayaz used to say that the poets of Tehran had poisonous minds, that they were all left-wingers and moustachioed adherents of revolutionary tendencies. With these nightmarish thoughts in his head, Father, sitting on his sheepskin rug in the room upstairs, had gazed at Ideen and said: "What do you intend to cut with the edge of your moustache, you, *mirza*?"

Ideen had retorted: "What would you have said if you had seen Master Nasser Delkhoon's moustache, Father?"

And Father had repeated Ayaz's sentence word for word: "Always remember where they hanged the moustachioed guys."

Mother had objected: "What has that got to do with us? What's the matter with you two? Listen to me Djaber! Do we always need some sort of misery to stop us from looking for a reason to quarrel?"

"What's poetry got to do with us?"

Ayaz said: "There was a time when one's child was regarded as one's property. Nader Shah ordered his troublesome son to be blinded. But, now, brother, you are not the master of your own life. Look at this lout." With his finger, he was pointing at the tall, good-for-nothing Jamshid. He was passing in front of the shop right at that moment. Father looked carefully to see him properly. Ayaz resumed: "Either they develop into a fellow like this who, at night, takes Martha the prostitute to the waste grounds outside town or they become a poet like your son. Not everybody follows the example of Urhan."

At that moment, Urhan was standing at the doorway. He called Jamshid and, then, he stepped aside to let him in. He said: "Jamshid, were you passing by without acknowledging us, like someone who buys on credit?"

Jamshid said 'Hello' and stood at the desk, next to Ayaz. He had shaved his head and looked thinner than usual. He said: "I have become a soldier now. My hands are empty but..."

Father asked: "How much does he owe?"

Urhan replied: "His debt has reached one hundred and ten *toomans*."

Father said: "If he stops his debauchery, I'll reduce his debt by ten *toomans*."

Ayaz showed some kindness: "But he is a well-behaved boy. He's now doing his national service. By the time he returns from the barracks, he will have become quite a respectable human being." He jokingly gave Jamshid a pat on his head and said: "Go."

Father said: "I wish Ideen would also do his national service and become a proper human being."

Ayaz shook his head: "Just wait. Just wait."

Father opened the newspaper again. But the more he read the poem, the less he understood it. He read a few words of the poem aloud, the words conveying the concept of blood, revolution and revenge or, as Ayaz put it, "red words". There was a reference to a town where all the inhabitants had died and were petrified. The poem also referred to Balokhloo river along the banks of which trees had been replaced by gallows. The more Father read, the less he could work out where Balokhloo river was. Was it the Balokhloo river that they knew? Urhan, while seeing to a customer, laughed and said: "Cock and bull masquerading as poetry." But Father was in no laughing mood. He was too angry for laughter. Danger was growing and spreading its roots right at his doorstep. The sapling of danger was growing into a tree.

Ayaz, who was standing up at that moment, sat down. He sat right next to Father and said: "You know what, Djaber? Yesterday, I was in my courtyard when I heard someone calling me. I raised my head and saw the Head of Ardabil Police who had opened his window and was looking at me. I saluted him and said 'Yes, sir.' He said 'Come upstairs.' So I did; and I entered his room. He said: 'Ayaz! We have few people like you.' I said: 'I am overwhelmed and embarrassed, colonel.' You know, Djaber, he calls me by my first name in the same way that you do. Let me tell you that I had lunch with the colonel yesterday. That bastard is a man of honour, and friendly."

Father exclaimed: "Really?"

"Indeed. Nevertheless, there is nothing I can do. Master Delkhoon was a left-winger. He also had a big moustache that identified him as a source of trouble. We sent him to Tehran under guard. But what am I to do with this boy?"

"You are Ayaz the policeman and you are asking me what to do?"

"To tell you the truth, for the sake of preserving the respectability of your family, I want you to allow me to make arrangements for two policemen to raid your house this evening."

"What for?"

"So that they can arrest him. I myself will arrange for his delicate posterior to be struck with a whip a dozen times. We'll keep him locked up for a couple of months so that he forgets about poetry altogether. I have told you many times that there are two categories of people you can't argue with: The literate and the illiterate. Never forget this."

"Give me a day or two. I want to give him an ultimatum."

Symphony of the Dead

"You do know, Djaber, that I have no personal interests. It is only your honour that…"

Father got up, stretched up on to his tiptoes and kissed Ayaz on the cheek: "You have been like a father to me, Ayaz."

Ayaz wept with emotion. While Father was thinking of Ayaz, his good friend who wept for the sake of friendship, there was a deafening noise of copperware being beaten from the rooftops[14] as well as general uproar. Groups of people moved about the alley aimlessly. Someone shouted: "The sun." Father went to the veranda. He saw Mother and Urhan in the courtyard. They were gazing up at the sky. He asked: "What's going on?"

Mother was crying. Every now and then, she found an excuse for reminding herself of Ida, who lived in Abadan, and for crying. She said: "Tragedy, tragedy, tragedy."

It was at this moment that Father noticed the sky. He looked up and saw the sun that looked like a blood-red disc, with a black halo surrounding it. A hubbub could be heard from afar. It sounded like someone moaning or shrieking. Father trembled with fear. For the first time in his life, he felt afraid of being alone. The house was submerged in absolute darkness. It was as if the world was no longer something that could be believed in. In that darkness, Father just managed to hang his *papakha* somewhere. He then rushed down the stairs.

Mother was whispering a prayer and crying at the same time. Her crying sounded like a very sad tune. Urhan was sitting at the edge of the pond. Numerous stars appeared in the sky. There were more stars in the sky than anyone had ever seen at night.

Father stood beside Mother and said: "Tragedy has befallen us. Do you know what this means?" He showed the palms of his hands and, with a feverish voice, he asked: "Have we shed anyone's blood?"

Mother cried. And Father said: "This is the response to our foul deeds, ours and our children's. Oh God! Spare us punishment."

A moment later, the street fell quiet and the town was submerged in such darkness and such silence that one could be forgiven for thinking that its inhabitants had been dead for years. The darkness persisted for about an hour and a half. The sound of someone crying could be heard from afar. It sounded like the wailing of a woman who had been trapped under rubble. Even Yousef howled and wanted to move away from his usual place. It seemed as if an earthquake was imminent.

Father recited the special Ayat prayer. Later, when it looked like twilight, he went out into the courtyard without talking to anyone. He stood at the door of the basement room, kicked it open and, at the exact moment the sun reappeared, he set fire to the room, all the furniture and all the books that were inside. He walked on the black stain that had, for many months, spread itself like a black spider next to the pond, saying: "This is the spirit of the devil that is burning."

At sunset, before it turned dark again, Ideen came home. A sad silence had fallen over the house. It was as if a family member had died and the walls were hiding the secret of that death.

Years later, whenever Ideen recalled those days, he would tell Mother: "It was very bleak indeed."

The air reeked of smoke and the smell of burning objects. As if he knew what had happened, Ideen went to the courtyard very calmly and approached the 'crypt'. When he confronted that blinding blackness, he felt weightless. He could not believe what he saw and was trembling with anger. He went down the stairs towards the basement. There was only blackness, only nothingness. Black water covered the floor. The smell was that of ruin and death, that of primitive people and that of bestiality. It was as if a human being had been burnt alive and their ashes had been rubbed on to the walls and the doors. The room was full of ashes and half-burnt wood. The books and the poems had gone up in smoke. There was nothing on which Ideen could sit for even a moment. Briefly, he thought of picking up a stone, shattering all the windows in the house and shouting: "If I don't set your whole house on fire, I'm not your son."

Years later, Mother said: "Since that day of hell, we have not had a moment of happiness. On that day, even Yousef howled."

12

In the autumn of that same year, Ideen went to Ram Asbi and started work at the timber factory there. He had rented a little room from a cattle farmer in Ram Asbi. The room's door opened on to the stable. There was much noise and the cows mooed from nightfall until dawn. Nevertheless, Ideen felt content because during his lifetime, he had gone through days and nights much worse than that. He remembered the days when he was hungry, had no money and the more he thought, the less he succeeded in finding a way to improve his life. In those days, his morale was very low. He thought people were moving about aimlessly. Everything was unnatural, colours were not real and time passed slowly. Morning led monotonously to afternoon and afternoon to night.

He managed to get through the first week by using up whatever he had with him. For the following two days, help came by returning the only book he had brought with him. He returned to the bookshop and got a refund. From morning to evening, he somehow passed the time: Akhavan Gardens, Public Library, or the shores of Shoorabi. By nightfall, however, all the sorrows and suffering came back to him. He tried to think of the poems he had composed, but he could not remember even one word of them. It was as if the books and the poems that had gone up in smoke in that fire in the basement, had also gone up in smoke in his mind.

One night, he slept behind the wall of Anooshirvan School on the edge of the wastelands. When he woke up in the morning, he saw women carrying baskets full of clothes, walking towards the river outside town. Ideen, feeling ashamed, walked away in the opposite direction without thinking of his own dirty clothes. One night, he slept in Akhavan Gardens. But he was disturbed by the howling of the jackals. So, he climbed a tree and lodged himself between some branches. During the following days and nights, he felt helpless because of sleeplessness, nightmares and exhaustion. He would not beg. So he wondered how he was going to get something to eat. He could not sleep next to the walls. So where was he going to sleep?

One day he was unconsciously drawn towards Kolbeh Choobi wine house. He saw Uncle Saber and greeted him. Ideen was hungry and Uncle Saber ordered him some beans. He said: "I heard you've left home."

Ideen turned pale. He asked: "Who told you?"

"I am well informed." He added: "Life has become very difficult, my dear nephew."

"You are right. I must go now."

"In any case, I have high hopes for your future." And he walked away, staggering, along a side alley that went downhill.

Loneliness and the sad feeling of being a stranger were torturing Ideen. He was a stranger in the centre of a familiar city. Oh, how lonely life can be! One feels like a small piece of straw in a high wind. He was often tempted to go back home or, at least, to pass along their alley. But he overcame the temptation and put up with the agony. He had learnt many things from Master Delkhoon. He had witnessed the Master's loneliness. Now he felt it. Master Delkhoon carved patterns on wood and engraved picture frames. As soon as he had earned enough money to support his frugal existence, he devoted the rest of his time to poetry. He would say: "I have completed my poem 'Courier' or issue the instruction: "Compose the poem 'Girls in Red'." Thinking about the master filled him with enthusiasm. But what could he do while he did not even have a single *real* in his pocket? Work.

That afternoon, Ideen went to the reading room. The man in charge knew Ideen because he had been a schoolmaster before his retirement. He was short, thin and red-haired. He had a pockmarked face and big ears. From before his retirement, when he had not yet been hard of hearing, he had been known as the Listening Seyyed[15]. Now, he did not hear properly when people talked to him. And when they shouted to make themselves heard, he would say: "Not so loud! Do you think I'm deaf?" Ideen arrived at the brick building and went up the stairs. He asked Listening Seyyed to let him have a look at the newspapers of the past few days so that he might find a job. While he was going through the newspapers, Listening Seyyed asked him what sort of job he would like. Ideen replied that he was looking for a job that would suit him well. At that moment, he suddenly saw a notice of condolence that was most strange indeed. He read it again and again. The elusive words danced in front of his eyes and disappeared. It was a notice of condolence addressed to all people in the realm of art and literature. It talked about a great loss. It offered condolences to "the venerable family" of Master Delkhoon. But what family? Master Delkhoon had no-one. Maybe he had an old mother. And probably he had been married with children. But Master Delkhoon had not been an ordinary man. In a letter to him, Nima Youshij had said: "Master Delkhoon has become like the Prophet Ezra. Why does he not get out of his cocoon?" Master Shahriar[16], having come on a trip to Ardabil, had stayed with Master Delkhoon for one night and had told him: "We have stayed in Tehran and are surrounded by so many people. Come and have a look at our suffering, Delkhoon."

Ideen folded the newspaper and left without saying good-bye. He did not know where to go. He was filled with the feeling of aimlessness and despair. He looked around the square and, then, began walking along the street. That night, he was sadder than ever. He missed not only Master Delkhoon but also Mother, Ida and even Father. Nevertheless, an inner force made him run away to a place of refuge, to somewhere away from the town, away from people.

He missed the old woman who used to see Mother. Mother gave her bread, an oil lamp and, sometimes, lumps of sugar. Her arms and legs were partially paralysed and one could see poverty in her appearance. She lived in a ramshackle shop facing Dr Shooshanik's surgery. One afternoon, she fell over a flaming brazier and that was the end of her life. Ideen missed the old woman he had known. It was rumoured that she had been the daughter of a tribal chief and that she had left the countryside to go to town to buy things for her wedding. Once in town, she had become paralysed and could no longer go back to the countryside.

In a ruined souk outside the town, known as the Lepers' Souk, old people, young people, addicts and the hungriest of people mingled and the most dejected and downtrodden of children howled and shouted. Ideen stopped there for a moment. Then, with much of his strength gone and with a feeling of fatigue and loneliness, he headed for Foroozan's house. Only that woman could perhaps do something for him. Or, if she could not, she could at least let him stay overnight. Foroozan's house was directly opposite Ideen's former home and if he were seen going to her house, that would be the end of her honour and good name. Nevertheless, he set out. He arrived at his former alley. The Electric Fan Factory, dark and silent, lay down there, at the bottom of the slope. His family house, with its high walls, looked like a house that had been abandoned and deserted for years. The light from Foroozan's window lit up the surroundings.

Ideen stood at a corner with trepidation. He picked up a pebble, threw it at Foroozan's window and hid in the shadow of a wall. He threw another pebble at the window. And another. Foroozan opened the window and looked out, puzzled.

Ideen took a step forward and said: "It is me. It's Ideen."

Foroozan, overwhelmed with joy, said: "Hello." She panicked and did not know exactly what to do. She said: "Wait."

With a heavy make-up and with eyes that laughed, she opened the door. She was panting. She repeatedly said: "Hello."

"Hello." And he entered. He suddenly remembered Master Delkhoon who had told him: "Women of this type ensnare you. Be with them, but don't get trapped."

That night felt as long as a thousand nights. While he was having dinner, while he emptied cups of tea one after the other and even when he was about to go to bed, he was filled with anxiety. It was as if someone was waiting for him. He did not feel sleepy. He felt like rushing out of the house immediately, running and going to some unknown place. But his ultimate destination was Tehran. He wanted to complete his university education and fulfil all his desires, at any cost. But, at the same time, he did not want to depend on anyone.

Foroozan said: "Go to bed."

"I will. Soon."

"The day your house caught fire, I knocked at the door. Your mother opened the door. She was crying and hitting her head with her hands. I asked what had happened and saw that the house was on fire. She said 'These infidels have set fire to my child's room. They have not spared even that damp dungeon of a room'."

Ideen was silent. As he lay down, he blinked and was in a pensive mood.

Foroozan asked: "What do you want to do now?"

"I'm going away."

"Where to?"

"Tehran."

Foroozan stood up. The faint moonlight, coming through the window, lit her face and she appeared more beautiful than usual. She seemed to be surrounded by a blue mist. She said: "I will be happy to come with you. Stay here for a while. I will get myself transferred to Tehran. Then you can go to the university and get on with your studies free of any worries. But you don't accept, do you?" She looked eagerly at Ideen, as if she wanted to swallow him up with her eyes. She continued: "Whatever I spend, you will give it back to me afterwards. Treat it as a loan."

"No. I told you before."

"Very well. What can I do with a difficult guy like you? You don't like working in the bank. And you don't want to be employed by the Ministry of Education either. But at our own bank, I know many people who would be able to find you a good job."

"That is exactly why I have come to see you."

"Haven't you come to see me for my own sake then?" She held Ideen's nose between her fingers and said: "What can I do with a guy like you?"

"Oh, Foroozan! For the sake of whoever you like, find me a well-paid job tomorrow."

"I don't know what sort of job you'd like."

"Whatever job. It doesn't matter."

"I know an Armenian who has an account with our bank. He comes from Erevan in Soviet Armenia. He is called Mr Mirzayan. I'll talk to him tomorrow. He has a big factory and I think he pays well."

"Where is his factory?"

"It is a timber factory in Ram Asbi."

The next day, Ideen began to work as a labourer. His job was to saw timber and he was paid wages on a daily basis. His perks were three meals a day and a small room where he could sleep. Late every afternoon, he could study in the municipal reading room. His daily wages amounted to two hundred *toomans* a month. Because Mr Mirzayan liked Ideen's character, he promised to help him so that he could save some money quickly. In that way, Ideen would be able, after a year or two of work and study, to pack up his belongings and head for Tehran.

Whenever Ideen went to town, he paid a visit to Foroozan. Alternately, Foroozan sometimes came to Ram Asbi and stayed overnight. Later, Urhan too paid an occasional visit to Ideen. He informed Ideen of life at home and of the fact that Mother was worried and unhappy. Ideen told Urhan that he had no intention of going back home but that Urhan could come and visit him in Ram Asbi if he wanted to. Urhan continued doing so occasionally.

One day, Father paid Ideen a visit and asked him to forget about the past. Ideen replied that it would be better if Father forgot him. He added that he did not need anything.

Winter arrived. A heavy snow fell and covered Ardabil, Ram Asbi and all the surrounding villages with a white blanket. Schools were closed and roads were blocked. But the timber business was still thriving. The factory was situated in an opening in the mountain. In other words, it was situated in a gorge through which a river, with clear water, passed. On the left, timbers had been arranged under a natural 'roof' beneath the mountain's ridge. On the right, there was the covered workshop of the factory, the open front of which had been screened with a tarpaulin. Inside, there were electric saws, lathes and planers with which a number of workers, as well as master carpenters, worked. It was only Ideen who cut timber out in the open. As he was never in a good mood nor in a talkative mood, he had not been able to develop a close relationship with other workers. He wore a pair of blue, woollen gloves and, from morning to night, marked the pieces of wood and cut bigger pieces into smaller ones.

One morning, the factory owner summoned him. Ideen went to the wooden hut of Mr Mirzayan, stood at the doorstep and greeted him.

Mr Mirzayan was sitting at his desk. He said: "Come in, my boy." Ideen entered.

"Sit down."

Ideen sat down and looked at Mr Mirzayan. He was a big man. He had a few strands of silvery hair stretching down one side of his head. His clothes were very clean. He was slightly cross-eyed.

"Why do you work like this, my boy?"

"How do I work, Mr Mirzayan?"

Mr Mirzayan had an Armenian accent. He had cheerful looks and appeared to have just taken a bath. If one looked carefully at his face, one could see the veins. He said: "I have seen you cutting timber from morning to late afternoon. And I am told that you read books till late at night. Is that right?"

"Yes, Mr Mirzayan. I am a contract worker."

"I know. But I am asking why are you killing yourself."

"I told you on the first day that my plan was to earn enough money to finance myself for four or five years' stay in Tehran."

Mr Mirzayan laughed, shook his head and said: "Even if a machine works like this, it will be dead within a year." He got up from his chair and stood at the window that faced the snow-covered countryside. He said: "Would you like me to mediate between you and your father…"

Ideen interrupted him: "Please don't, Mr Mirzayan." It sounded as if he was begging him not to intervene.

"From what I've heard, I can say that your differences are insignificant. It is possible for me to talk to your father so that he provides you with facilities to pursue your studies. I do know your father a little. I don't think he will refuse my request."

"It seems that I am a source of inconvenience to you and that is why you somehow want to get rid of me."

Mr Mirzayan turned back: "No. No. It is not like that at all. All I want is your comfort and success. I have three sons. They are all in America. It is for their sake that I work hard. For this reason, it is hard for me to see a young man, as young as my own son Sarkis, killing himself like this so that he can study later."

"I have given up everything and care for nothing. I don't want anyone to help me."

"You are a wise, intelligent boy. I think you should think and behave a bit more logically."

"If someone sets everything you have on fire, how would you react?"

"I concede that you have every right to be angry. And your ideas are praiseworthy and beautiful. But there are other ways for you to fulfil your wishes."

"This is the most beautiful way."

"Do you feel satisfied as you are?"

"Yes, very."

Mr Mirzayan shook his head, came closer to Ideen and put his hand on his shoulder: "Yesterday, when you were cutting timber, three policemen came in. Didn't you see them?"

"Yes, I did."

"They came here and asked which one of the workers was Ideen Urkhani. I asked them why they wanted to see you. They said you should be doing your national service and, besides, they had a warrant. I told them they were a week late as you had left this place last week."

Ideen looked worried and astounded: "National service?"

"Yes. You should know that these days they move about the countryside and press gang young people. But I wonder why I don't want them to take you and turn you into a soldier. These days, you have to be more careful."

"Yes, Mr Mirzayan."

"I don't want trouble either for myself or for you. If they come for you a second time, there will be nothing I can do."

"I understand, Mr Mirzayan."

At that moment, they noticed five gendarmes coming towards the factory. They walked along the country lane that had, in fact, disappeared under snow. They were in snow up to their knees and were trying hard to reach the factory. Mr Mirzayan said: "You see? They are coming again."

Ideen saw the gendarmes and noticed that one of them was actually Ayaz the policeman. He was struggling to move forward through the snow. Panicking and frightened, Ideen looked around and said: "I'll go and hide in the timbers. I'll go and hide in the middle of the timber."

Mr Mirzayan said: "Hide for the time being. I'll think about your problem later."

13

It was Thursday evening. It was snowing. It had begun to snow the previous night and it continued to snow until the following Monday. The road was white with snow. The city lights twinkled from afar. Ideen, wearing his overcoat, carrying an axe on his shoulder and a small suitcase in his hand, approached the city. The suitcase contained his books and his clothes. His mind was full of disturbing thoughts. He felt the thoughts were pressing against his temples.

He could not believe that Father, out of vengefulness, could have masterminded such foul conspiracies. The gendarmes had remained at the timber workshop until late afternoon. They were so sure of having come to the right spot that they no longer talked to anybody. They had lodged themselves at various locations and smoked cigarettes while waiting for their catch. Ayaz the policeman had told Mr Mirzayan: "Apart from the fact that he is a soldier who is a draft dodger, he is a dangerous man. He has leftist ideas." As they were leaving the place, Ayaz had added that he knew that one of the workers had either hidden him or helped him to escape but that he would catch him at any cost. Ayaz had continued: "There is also a warrant out for his arrest. If you have harboured him, you will be in real trouble, Mr Mirzayan."

With his thoughts very disoriented and his heart full of distress and sorrow, Ideen entered town at the Tabarqapoosi Gate. It was still snowing and the street had disappeared under snow. There were snowdrifts piled up in the middle of the street, mostly formed by masses of snow having fallen from rooftops. Only a winding route, formed by the movement of horse-drawn carriages, had remained along the street. No doubt, that would also be covered by snow and completely disappear by the next morning.

There was a danger of somebody recognising him along the way. Or, worse

than that, Ayaz the policeman might coincidentally be around and see him. He had pledged to himself that, in such an eventuality, he would slash his wrists and, thus, free himself from all this misery. However, it was too cold and snowing too hard for anybody to dare come out of their house. He walked to the end of Pahlavi Avenue and arrived at Gazoran district. A few seconds later, he reached Armanestan district and turned into Armanestan Alley. He felt someone was following him. Without looking back, he knocked at the green door that was right at the end of the blind alley. He knocked again and again. He went back to the entrance of the blind alley and, there, in the light coming from a lamppost, he saw the nameplate 'Fantasy Bathhouse'. This bathhouse was Armenian-owned and did not resemble other bathhouses in any way. A few seconds later, he heard footsteps and the door opened. A very short woman appeared at the doorstep. She was wearing a white headscarf as well as a few pullovers and jackets of various colours. Before she asked anything, Ideen said that he had come from the timber factory. The woman asked: "Yadeen?"
"Yes. Ideen."
"Come in please." The woman stood aside so that Ideen could enter. It was an old house with very high walls and with arched windows that had wooden frames. The windowpanes were covered with white or pink net curtains. In the middle of the courtyard there was a round pond that was frozen over. On two sides of the pond, there were rectangular flowerbeds that, parallel to one another, went alongside the building on both sides.

He suddenly noticed a beautiful, white building. It was the church, situated on the left-hand side of the courtyard and separated by a very low wall. The woman said: "Why are you standing there, my dear? Come in." She directed him into the courtyard.

In front of the building, there was a hexagonal veranda with three pillars that supported the domed arch. There were staircases, leading to the main door of the building, on both sides of the veranda. The woman said: "Shake the snow off your clothes."

Ideen stamped on the ground a few times and brushed the snow off his shoulders. The woman was holding the door open, waiting for Ideen to take his shoes off and come inside. There was a large entrance hall with a rectangular table in the middle. At the other end of the hall, there was a fire below a mantelpiece heating the whole hall.

An old woman was sitting at the table. She was knitting something. Mr Mirzayan and another man were sitting near the fire. At the other side of the table, a blonde woman, about 30 years old, was playing chess with a man on the opposite side of the table. Ideen greeted them.

Mr Mirzayan said: "You didn't encounter any difficulty. Did you?"

"No." Ideen was standing still, not knowing what to do.

Mr Mirzayan said: "Come here and warm yourself." He got up and shook hands with Ideen. He then directed him to the fire, saying: "Don't be shy, my boy. There are no strangers among us." He then introduced everybody: "My brother Sooren, my niece Sormeh, my nephew Michael who is leaving for Erevan tomorrow. And this lady is Madam Yevgineh, Sormeh's grandmother." Ideen shook hands with all of them and sat on a chair near the fire.

Sooren said: "Your hands are frozen. Warm them up well."

Ideen was so eager for heat that it looked as if he were about to devour the fire. He really enjoyed the heat of the red, dancing flames.

Mr Mirzayan said: "Mr Ideen Urkhani has completed his secondary school education and acquired his diploma in the field of science. He is also a poet."

Michael, busy playing chess, said: "Well done, well done" and moved his bishop.

Mr Mirzayan continued: "He is the son of a famous nut merchant. But he has encountered difficulties and been obliged to start from square one. For a long while I have noticed him working so hard and so enthusiastically at the factory. Are you listening Sormeh? He is the man I always talked about."

Sormeh said: "Yes, dear uncle." And she continued playing chess.

Mr Mirzayan, laughing, continued: "A tall beautiful woman had assured me of his good conduct. Whenever I go to the bank, she asks about him. In what way is she related to you, Ideen?"

"She is our neighbour."

Sormeh turned back and, looking at Ideen, asked: "Have you had dinner?"

Mr Mirzayan said: "I am sure he hasn't. What are you doing, Sormeh?"

Sormeh got up and left the room.

Sooren said: "I didn't quite understand your story. The other night, Galoost gave me an account but I was too drunk and didn't follow what he said."

When Sormeh entered the room again, Ideen, sitting politely with his hands folded over his chest, was relating his story in detail. There was a tone of anger in his voice, but he related everything calmly and objectively, as if he were relating someone else's life story.

Sormeh, while looking at Ideen furtively, uttered some words in Armenian. She spoke again in Armenian and Ideen could make nothing of what she said. For a moment, he felt he was so insignificant in front of that girl. With his dark, long overcoat, with his trousers made of broadcloth and the smell of wood that emanated from his body, he felt so ashamed.

The girl sat down and continued her game of chess. Occasionally, she looked furtively at Ideen, without turning her head. Her glance was fixed and persistent, from a position of pride, like the glance cast at someone to be pitied.

Sooren, who spoke Persian with an Armenian accent more pronounced than that of his brother's, said: "These are strange times we are living in."

Michael asked: "Weren't you helped at all by that lady who was your neighbour?"

Ideen replied: "I refused her offer of help."

Mr Mirzayan intervened: "Ideen is in a situation that does not allow him to deal with these problems. I strongly believe he has the same character that my own son Sarkis has."

Sooren said: "It really is shameful. Do they think they are dealing with a slave?"

Mr Mirzayan said: "You are a strong, persistent fellow. Don't worry. You'll achieve whatever you want to."

Ideen said: "The more they oppose me, the more I struggle."

Mr Mirzayan said: "I don't want to say I am your saviour. I don't want to look for trouble either. But I wonder why I like you. As I said before, I will help you. But I have no idea for how long they intend to hunt you down. Will your father ever give this up and leave you in peace?"

"One day, my father will notice that I have left this town."

"My plan is to hide you for a couple of years. But can you put up with this state of affairs?"

"Yes." And he looked at Madam Yevgineh who was deeply absorbed in knitting something purple.

At that moment, the young woman came in with a tray of food. She placed the tray on the table and left the room. Mr Mirzayan said: "If you feel warm enough, come and have dinner. And take it easy."

Sooren said: "Yes, he's right. Cheer up and don't worry."

Mr Mirzayan said: "We haven't prepared a formal dinner; just something simple to fend off hunger."

Ideen said: "Thank you. I don't want to be a burden." He looked at Sormeh. She nodded, to indicate some acknowledgement to his words.

Sooren said: "Your father is a bad-tempered man. Nevertheless, I never thought he could be so cruel."

The girl kept looking at Ideen. He wondered how he was going to eat dinner under that gaze. He was shy and hesitant, but Sooren, Yevgineh and Mr Mirzayan insisted so much that he sat at the table and picked up his spoon with a trembling hand.

Mr Mirzayan said something in Armenian and everybody looked at Ideen. Yevgineh said: "But what about your mother? Didn't she oppose your father?" And she continued knitting.

"You know these things better. A woman is a woman. And men like my father…" He fell silent, not knowing what adjective to employ in order to describe his father.

After dinner, Michael said: "Would you be kind enough to recite one of your poems? I want to recite it to my friends when I go to Erevan."

Ideen blushed and looked troubled: "It is not something that would be worthy of you."

Michael said: "You are too humble."

Sormeh smiled so beautifully and gazed at Ideen so intensely that he felt a tremor in his heart. Never before had he felt so astounded by the beauty of anyone or anything. And never before had anyone succeeded in affecting him in such a manner. He said: "I don't know which one to recite."

Sormeh said: "All of them." And she laughed. And she laughed again.

Ideen closed his eyes while visualising Sormeh. He tried to concentrate. After staying silent for a moment, he said: "The truth of the matter is that I don't know all my poems by heart."

"Recite whatever you remember," said Mr Mirzayan.

"Recite," repeated Sormeh in a serious tone.

So, Ideen began his recitation:

"Oh, you, who are always free, unbridled; oh, you, who reside in an orchard of red pomegranates;

Oh, you, who bring forth red, flaming love, springtime brings forth your scent.

The blood of a beggar like me is but a worthless gift, in the tradition that began with Hallaj.

The long chain of love continues unbroken even as far as the gallows.

Oh, you, a cloud that rains the sorrow of love; oh, you, a girl armed with the cutlass of love,

I am a sitar and you the plectrum; play me, wound me tonight; rain on me tonight.

As I am separated from you, I have closed my lips; I resemble one of a multitude of corpses.

I am entangled in the purgatory that is our time; and I am in fear of an uncertain end.

Alas! My heart is in mourning as I am separated from my beloved.

How can it break free from the jail that is my body? For how long can it

survive fasting? For how long can it refuse the nourishment of love and endure the absence of love?
The nightingale knows not on whose rooftop it lands.
He who is free from the sorrow of love imagines me as free and not benighted.
As soon as heartless foes or insincere friends touch me with the wounding plectrum,
I begin to groan like the delicate harp.
Tonight, my rebellious, wavering beloved has conquered my flaming heart.
I am now but a dormant volcano, a cold mountain.
Woe betide the broken-hearted and the nameless, fameless lovers.
Woe betide those who are abandoned along the way, who are just happy to remain in ruins.
Set my house on fire; hit my body with a lethal blow,
Scatter my ashes over every chalice of wine. I want my body destroyed like that of a man of courage.
A flag is a reminder of memories as it waves over rooftops.
It is the manifestation of a hidden love, a love that has grown old, that has mellowed with the passage of time."

Everybody clapped for him. Even Madam Yevgineh stopped knitting and began to clap. Ideen's hands trembled as they rested on the table. And Sormeh was looking at him so intently, as if she was about to be photographed.

Mr Mirzayan said: "Well done, well done. You are a poet worthy of praise, my boy."

Sormeh asked: "Who have you composed this poem for?"

"I don't know. I just composed it." And he shrugged his shoulders.

Sooren said: "We are living in a peculiar age. It was beautiful."

Michael was of a slightly different opinion: "Yes. But we should note that it is not quite mature yet."

Mr Mirzayan was persistent: "Oh, Michael! In all fairness, it was a jolly good poem, wasn't it?" Turning his head towards Ideen, he asked: "Where did you learn to compose such poems?"

"I learnt it from Master Nasser Delkhoon."

"Mr Mirzayan opened his eyes wider in shock and astonishment: "Delkhoon? You frighten me, boy. It looks as if you are looking for trouble or seeking martyrdom, like Delkhoon himself."

Sooren said: "I know him. He used to come to my shop to buy tea and coffee. He was a thin man and his hair was like that of a woman. But he also had a big, thick moustache. I wondered whether he was a dervish or a communist. But, in any case, he was a peculiar type of person. One day, we heard that they had done away with him."

Michael said: "Recite another poem."

"Unfortunately I don't know any by heart." He looked disturbed and, with a hoarse voice, he repeated: "Unfortunately I don't remember any by heart."

Michael asked: "Don't you compose modern poetry?"

"Yes. And I am a follower of the style of Nima Yooshij. But I can't recall any of my own."

Sormeh asked: "Haven't you written them down?"

"Yes. But my father set fire to all of them."

Michael said: "He is really gifted. I hope you become a great poet." And he resumed his game of chess.

Sormeh said: "Check." She paused for a moment and she repeated: "Check. You were checked an hour ago."

Michael apologised: "Oh, I'm sorry. I should have paid attention. I was distracted."

Sooren told Ideen: "If you were not in trouble, I would take you to my own shop and teach you how to grind coffee. We would earn our daily bread together and enjoy ourselves." He poured some wine for Ideen.

Sormeh said: "Check, again."

Mr Mirzayan said: "He can neither resurface nor leave town. He should take up a job in a safe place until, in future… I don't know what is going to happen."

"It doesn't matter where I take up a job. What matters is that I don't want to depend on anybody. I want to work."

"The more I try, the less I can think of anywhere as a safe haven. The only place I can think of is the church basement. That's the place I thought of as soon as the problem arose."

Sormeh frowned and almost shouted: "Oh, uncle! It is so dark there that it would be miserable."

Mr Mirzayan persisted: "We will do some electrical wiring and turn the place into a workshop. It would make no difference to Ideen. He would be able to work there and to sleep there. He would be able to continue until his situation becomes clearer."

"No, Uncle. It is not a proper place at all. It is infested with mice and cockroaches."

Ideen himself was not unhappy about the idea: "I am even prepared to live in a cave in order to attain my objectives. My father wants to bring me down to my knees, but…" He fell silent.

Mr Mirzayan resumed: "Yes. He himself should make the place tidy. We will give him the means to turn the place into a workshop and to start some simple work. What types of work can you do?"

"Master Delkhoon made frames sometimes. I, too, can do that."

Mr Mirzayan was overjoyed: "That's very good. It will be frame-making then." He laughed with pleasure and drank up his wine in one gulp.

"I like wood. I like working with wood."

"I know what he wants. First thing tomorrow, I'll fetch all the material needed for frame-making: One hundred bundles of wood, vices, nails, hammer, glue, workbench… He will be able to make quite a number of frames from morning till evening. He will earn good wages. At night, he will be able to sit down to his books and his studies. Great men have endured much hardship. There have been prophets who worked as shepherds. There have also been prophets who worked as carpenters."

Sormeh said: "Checkmate." She got up and stood beside the table.

Ideen asked: "When am I supposed to start?"

"Tomorrow morning."

Next morning, Mr Mirzayan took Ideen to his new workplace before going to his own factory. He told him: "It is no longer possible to take risks. They have warned us; and you could be in trouble too. I know it is going to be difficult. But you should resist and be prepared to work. In any case, this place is better than either jail or the barracks. I won't let you feel lonely. I'll get you books and newspapers. In exchange, I expect you to be patient. You know that this place is a church. People come here and if they see you… well, you know, this is a small town."

It had been snowing. They were in snow up to their knees while they walked. Ideen said: "You are my guardian angel."

"No. That's not true. We are conducting business together and I must support you." He pointed at the church and said: "It's over there."

The staircase leading to the basement was right next to the church wall.

"Let's go downstairs." Mr Mirzayan led the way while talking to Ideen with a harsh voice: "One must always work and be creative. Otherwise, one would rot from inside. Being unemployed is worse than being alone. A man with no work would feel lonely even in a crowd."

He opened a dark grey, wooden door. The old hinges made a dry, horrifying noise. Some days later, Ideen learnt that the former resident had been the church attendant and that he had died there. He had come from Baku. He had been a man with red hair, always wearing a shirt with a starched collar. One day, during the war, they forgot about him. When they went to see him two days later, they found his cold body.

It was like a big warehouse. In one corner, large, earthenware Russian jars lay in a row. A few steps from the jars, there were a number of wooden boxes. In the middle, four pillars supported the domed arches. Ideen counted the arches. There were nine of them. At one extremity of the warehouse, there was a little room, the entrance to which was covered by a curtain.

Mr Mirzayan said: "What's good about this place is that it's warm in winter and cool in summer." With two of his fingers, he pulled the curtain open. But, before entering the room, he pulled the curtain sharply and wrenched it away in one movement, throwing it away into a corner. Inside the room, there was a bed, a desk and a chair. Everything was basic, mediocre and small, like in a jail. And everything was worn out and falling apart. The walls were of brick, with gaps filled with a type of blue cement. It was very gloomy indeed.

It did not look like a place that would ever be clean and tidy. But, within a few days, it had turned into a workshop in which one would love to work. The workbench was directly beneath the skylight in the roof and, so, was lit by gentle natural light. Frame-making equipment had been placed in a box fixed to the pillar on the right hand side. There were saws, hammers, tongs and pincers. A wood-burning stove, made with tin sheets, warmed the workshop. They hung a blue curtain at the entrance to the little room, put in electrical wiring and changed the bed. They also provided a chest of drawers. Ideen put his books in the upper drawers and his clothes in the lower ones.

During the first few days of his work, Ideen made 30 picture frames a day. After he became more skilled with wood and could perfectly join two pieces at an angle of 90 degrees, the output increased to 50 a day. Every morning, Mr Mirzayan took the frames to his big shop. Thereafter, Galoost Woodwork Shop did a thriving business, supplying customers with ornate picture frames. Mr Mirzayan paid one *tooman* to Ideen for each picture frame and provided him with equipment and raw materials. A woman servant brought food to Ideen three times a day. Before sunset everyday, the little skylight in the roof, or the *putshka* as Sormeh called it, opened and her face appeared, framed by the skylight. She smiled, said hello and dropped down the previous day's newspaper before leaving.

From then onwards, Ideen worked all day in anticipation of that sweet moment. All his exhaustion faded away as soon as Sormeh opened the skylight. This fleeting meeting washed away Ideen's exhaustion. It gave Ideen a heartbeat as tumultuous as a rough sea, it slowed down the passage of time and

Symphony of the Dead

filled Ideen with a secret love and enthusiasm. Weeks and months passed by. Ideen forgot about his family. He also completely forgot about his poetry. He became thinner and thinner.

His daily life was summarised as a working day with a fleeting glimpse at its culmination: A glimpse of two honey-coloured eyes.

14

Springtime arrived with its lukewarm sun. The snowdrifts melted away. The skylight offered more light inside. Twice a day, someone meticulously washed the area and the thick windowpanes. Sometimes, a few drops of water landed near Ideen's workbench. Work went on at Galoost Frame-Making Factory. In a corner of the workshop, there were rows of simple frames, engraved frames and frames of various colours: gold, brown, black...

No-one knew where Mr Mirzayan obtained those delicate, ornate frames or who made them. One day, a shopkeeper asked: "Where is the factory, Mr Mirzayan?" He replied: "Do you think these frames are made in Ardabil?" Indeed, they had been crafted with such skill and such delicacy that they did not look as if they had been made in Iran at all, let alone in Ardabil. Nevertheless, they were quite cheap and all over the town, perhaps in every house, one or two of the frames embellished the portraits of the deceased or paintings of landscapes. Even Urhan had purchased one of them. He had hung it on the wall facing the kitchen door. It framed a picture of Imam Ali[17] sitting on his celestial prayer rug and holding his double-edged sword. He was flanked by Imam Hassan, clad in green, on his right and by Imam Hussein, clad in red, on his left. Angels had opened up umbrellas over them. From behind them, beams of light emanating from the very beginning of divine creation shone on the eternity spread before them.

One day, a letter was dropped into the house of Ideen's family. It did not bear the sender's address. In the letter, Ideen informed his family that he was safe and well. He said he had no feelings towards the house or his family but that, sometimes, he missed Mother and Ida. He had asked how little Sohrab was and whether Ida had continued to pay occasional visits. Ideen had added that he would be prepared to sign an official document in a notary's office in order to confirm that he had no claims against the family, provided Father would refrain from hounding him and, instead, would allow him to pursue his life in his own little corner. He had also asked why human beings provoked so many disputes and were so distant from each other, why people were so lonely, why... why...

Mother's asthma had intensified. She had no idea where Ideen was but she knew that he was lonely. She was sure of this and kept saying to herself: "May I die and not see you lonely." Every now and then she sat in a corner and cried. But the more she cried, the less she felt relieved. She felt that neither of her twins had much to look forward to in life. Ida was living in Abadan and contacted her family only very rarely and only by way of brief telegrams. She informed them that she and her child were safe and sound. She appeared to have become more and more distanced from her family. Indeed she lived in a far-away city. Ideen, however, who lived in the same town as his family, had disappeared into thin air. The more they searched for him, the less they had any clue as to his whereabouts. Mother sent Urhan to Ram Asbi timber factory repeatedly, but to no avail. Once, she herself went to enquire at the factory and came back empty-handed. She appealed to Mr Mirzayan, tried to bribe Aqa Rezvan and went to see the wife of Ayaz the policeman to ask her to mediate. She also visited the reading room. All her efforts were in vain.

One day, she visited the Church of St Mary and, afterwards, went to see Galoost Mirzayan. She met old Madam Yevgineh, as well as Sormeh and Sooren. She talked to every one of them, she cried and she told them how miserable, worried and heartbroken she was. They told her that not only had they no news of Ideen but that they did not know him at all. Mother said that her son was a poet and, therefore, the fact that he was not known to them was rather strange. They replied that they had heard his name but did not know him personally. What was to be done?

When Mother arrived back home, she thought back and was sure that she had seen Sormeh somewhere before. She had looked familiar to her. It was as if there had been clues to Ideen's identity in the girl's face. Perhaps there had been a scent of Ideen. Or perhaps there had been clues, such as the trembling of the girl's hands or a sparkle in her eyes whenever Mother had uttered Ideen's name.

The next day, Mother went to the Church of St Mary once again. She saw the girl holding a hosepipe, washing the floor, watering the flowers and, occasionally, drenching the nightingales. Mother sat on the steps of the church building and asked: "What's your name, my dear?"

"Sormelina."

"What a beautiful name. You look so much like my Ideen and my Ida." She cried again while she gazed at the girl and noted her particular gestures and movements. In the evening, she went back home, tired, miserable and sad.

Mother's anxiety had affected Father too. As hard and impenetrable as he appeared, he had, nevertheless, been shaken. Father summoned the help of Ayaz the policeman. They searched the town in so far as it was possible. They scoured nearby villages, barracks, hospitals and cemeteries. The only clue they were able to obtain was that he had left Ram Asbi two years before and had not gone back there. No-one knew what had become of Ideen. No-one.

Mr Mirzayan had his profits from Ideen's frame-making at stake. Besides, he had given his word of honour that he would not betray Ideen and that he would protect him. He was, therefore, adamant in claiming that he had dismissed Ideen after the gendarmes had come to arrest him. The gendarmes had threatened that he would pay dearly if he were found to be Ideen's accomplice.

"Where is he then?" asked Ida.

Mother had no answer to Ida's question. On the second last day of Ida's visit, Mr Abadani arrived to take his wife and son back home. He, too, joined the search for Ideen and, together, they made enquiries all over town. Ida left without seeing Ideen. During her 15-day visit, whenever Sohrab remembered his uncle, Mother held him in her arms and cried loudly.

Domestic life had become hard and bitter. Mother had lost all patience and Father shouted for no reason. The delicious, varied meals that Mother used to prepare were no more. Mother was ill all the time. Urhan behaved like a proud conqueror, controlling all the affairs of the house as well as the shop. He had taken charge of buying, selling and other matters. Yousef, however, howled in his dim, little room. He scratched the plaster on the walls with his fingernails, removed pieces of it and ate them. He ate the mixture of mud and straw used in the pointing of the brickwork. He could not pull the bricks out, so he howled. The stench of his room had filled the whole house. Every now and then, Father shouted: "Oh, God! Take this one away from us."

The relationship between Mother and Father had turned cold and meaningless. They exchanged a few words only if they had to. Then they went on with their miserable lives separately, each absorbed in their own sorrow. Every now and then, Mother said: "You made my child homeless and turned him into a tramp."

Foroozan asked: "Has he really disappeared? Is there really no news of him?"

Urhan said: "He has no doubt moved to Tehran to pursue his studies."

Symphony of the Dead

Father rejected everybody's theory. He even rejected his own theories and had become highly confused. He would say: "One can't make anything of this. He had no proper faith, he could do no job, and he wouldn't listen to me either. It's a pity that so much talent was wasted. It's a real pity. There was a time when, as a child, he wouldn't even let me peel a cucumber for him. He insisted on doing it himself. But I don't know what's going on now. If he's moved to Tehran, that would be the end of it. I have to forget about him. Ayaz says he might have left the country…"

Mother retorted: "To hell with that Ayaz." She was feverish with longing for her son and had no news of him. In times to come, when relating these things to Ideen, she would shed so many tears that Ideen, too, would cry.

Ideen, however, offended and unaware of what was going on in his absence, had no intention of going back home or even contacting his family. In times to come, whenever Mother talked to him about that episode, he would simply take a deep breath and say: "What could be done?" From sunrise to sunset, he made frames, carved wood and read books and newspapers. He, too, burnt in the fire of a one-sided love. He eagerly waited for sunset and for Sormeh to open the little skylight in the roof, or, as she put it, the *putshka*, and to call "Mr Ideen!" She would drop a book or a newspaper down and leave. No conversation, no interaction, not even a smile. The passage of time had made him less troubled by his crazy decision. He found solace in work with the hope that, one day, Sormeh would love him.

Expectation slowed the passage of time and turned it into something like the thick, heavy slabs of glass on which church visitors set foot and that were washed in the afternoon, with drops of water landing in front of Ideen's workbench. He, who had waited all day, looked at Sormeh's face lit by the dim light of the workshop's electric bulb. He was spellbound, his heart beat faster and his mouth felt dry. He longed to talk to her but didn't know what he wanted to say. Any word could be the wrong one, frightening Sormeh away and making it impossible for him to see her again. He could not, or perhaps he would not, believe that her aloof behaviour, her flirtatiousness and sheer indifference were in her nature and that she was a person who never ate and who was anywhere she wanted to be: Sitting on the veranda, on the ceramic vase adorning the shelf, amidst the leaves of a tree and even in the midst of fierce flames.

He had fallen in love with her but he did not want to admit it, not even to himself. He had lost all courage. The monotony and pressure of work and lack of sunlight had turned him pale, thin and old. He had turned into a timid, cowed individual whose heart began to beat faster as soon as he heard a noise. His face looked like a surface covered by a layer of mercury. It had turned wrinkled and old. His hard work was neverending. He made 50 frames a day and placed his earnings in a drawer. But he had no idea why he was making frames, why he was saving money or for how long he was going to stay there. A combination of love and horror consumed him from inside like a canker. He was in love with someone he hardly knew and was horrified by people whom he knew well. And now he did not want to know what he was living for. Not even once did he ask Mr Mirzayan for how long he was going to stay in that damp, dim basement. But he had great respect for him and he was, in any case, happy with the great number of frames he made and engraved. He was also happy with the arrival of sunset and the opening of the *putshka*.

The *putshka* opened and a wave of blonde, flowing hair rushed inside. In the middle of it, there was a serious, dignified unsmiling face. It betrayed anger. She remained quiet for a moment and then said: "Mr Ideen."

"Yes."

"Open the door. I want to come inside."

A cold torpor spread through his body. He turned pale and, with trembling hands, he opened the bolt. He said to himself: "Oh, my God! What am I going to say to Sooren and to Mr Mirzayan?" Sormeh entered the workshop. She stood in the middle of the workshop with her sparkling eyes, narrow eyebrows and prominent cheekbones. She was wearing a bright green blouse. Oh, how long her neck looked and how fast her heart was beating! Did her heart always beat as fast as that? Had she been running? Did she always run? If not, why was her heart beating so fast? Would she be upset if she were looked at? Oh, how beautiful she was!

Nothing was being seen. Time had stopped. There, parched soil stretched as far as the horizon and had no colour. Flowers had dried up. No wind blew. Their scalps prickled. A fluid weightlessness was about to burst under a intense pressure. It was neither day nor night. When was it then? And why was something constantly beating?

"Your heart."

Suddenly, Ideen returned to his senses. He was standing in front of Sormeh. He thought he was dreaming.

"Are you trembling?"

He just managed to say: "For God's sake, please leave this place."

"Where must I go?" She had a voice as soft as velvet. Besides, it had a sheen; it was rich. Its reverberation rubbed against eyelids as well as against the earlobes. Ideen feared her. He feared scandal. He feared lest the girl be punished for not being a virgin by being beaten with a cane. Besides, he was worried about himself. He feared being thrown dishonourably out of this place. He feared becoming infamous all over the town for being disloyal, for biting the hand that had fed him. He didn't know what to do. He said: "If someone sees you in this place, it would be a disaster for both of us."

"Why? Why would it be a disaster?"

Ideen was highly irritated by the fact that she did not appear to understand these things. He felt his knees were buckling. He collapsed on the ground like a telescope. Once again, he pleaded with her: "For God's sake, leave this place." He was remonstrating. He was begging. He felt he was about to cry.

Paying no attention to his words, Sormeh walked around the workshop and said: "Fear, my dear, is akin to death." She then said, with a commanding voice: "I go wherever I see fit." She was holding a book and two newspapers. She placed them on Ideen's workbench, cast a glance at the skylight and sat at the workbench. She picked up two small nails and, with a peculiar meticulousness, began hammering them into the worktop. She held the tools in her hands and tried to complete a half-finished frame. But she was not able to do it.

"Please allow me to show you. That's not the right way to do it."

"I know what to do. I don't need any help." She continued: "This is not a suitable environment. You look pale and, with this long beard and strange hair, you frighten people."

"So what. What else can I do?"

She retorted sharply: "One can do anything."

"It is now nearly two years since I was last visited by someone. Apart from Mr Mirzayan, that is."

"You are very cowardly. I have come to this place, but you don't attach ay importance to my presence."

"Today is a great day for me, my lady." Ideen felt that an untimely heat wave had washed over his face and ears. He added: "I am now used to this existence."

While playing with the tools, Sormeh said: "My father, too, visited you once or twice."

"Yes. Your father is a sociable person."

"What about me?"

"You are a hurricane."

"And, before anything else, I destroy myself. Is that not so?"

"No. A hurricane is never destroyed."

"I am a woman."

"A disturbance."

"These things are all feelings and sentiments, not reality."

"My only reality is bitterness."

"Most of life is bitterness and disappointment."
"Why should you of all people, say that?"
"Well. That's how it is."
"I like this skylight very much."
"*Putshka*? Why do you like it?" She cast a glance at the skylight and laughed with great joy.
"Because you open it every day and, for one moment..." He fell silent.
Sormeh laughed again. She laughed in such a way that it made Ideen feel he had said something childish.
Sormeh resumed: "Why should it matter to you?"
"Because it will make me happy."
"Is that all?"
"Yes. That's all."
"Oh, I see!" She caressed a pair of pliers and put it aside. She then picked up the hammer and asked: "Have you loved anyone before?"
"No."
"As for me, I got married many years ago. Three months after the marriage, my husband was involved in an accident." She raised her head, looked at Ideen and added: "And he died."
"I didn't know that."
"Fortunately, we had no children."
"Did you love him?"
"Not at all."
"Why did you get married?"
"I don't know."
"What made you come to see me today?"
"I don't know. I just felt like coming to see you."
"That has made me very happy."
"That's good." She was now leaning the palms of her hands against the workbench, trying to get up from behind it in order to make her way out. With every movement, she gave a turning and twisting movement to her hair. She then walked towards Ideen's little room. She stood in front of the entrance, pulled the curtain back with her finger and entered the room. Ideen wondered whether to stand still or to go in after her. He stood up and waited for a few seconds. By the time he decided to pull the curtain back again and go in, Sormeh was coming out. She said: "Pay some attention to your appearance, shave your beard and trim your hair. Come out occasionally so that the sun shines on you." As she talked, she went up the stairs. And she left.
Ideen remembered Sormeh's gypsy-like appearance and her habit of letting

her hair flow and fall freely and occasionally wearing a scarf round her neck and over her head. He also remembered her habit of dressing herself in purple sometimes and in violet at other times. He recalled that she was sometimes kind and sometimes abrupt. In short, a lasting impression of this gypsy-like girl had turned Ideen to stone, sitting at the edge of his bed and feeling as hard as stone itself. That night, he recalled Mother and Ida and remembered the staircase of the paternal house. He missed the basement room out of which raging flames had risen. He also recalled the tall, good-for-nothing Jamshid who had been such a nice boy. He recalled that whenever the very tall boy called at their house, he would lean one leg against the wall and wait patiently for Urhan.

Through the course of that night, he recalled everything and everyone. His mind filled up and emptied again. He had no idea as to why Sormeh had called and what she had been up to. She had said: "I am very lonely. Just think of it. I have been lonely for years."

Her presence had filled the whole place. Besides, she had been too broadminded and too bohemian from Ideen's point of view. She had been warm and friendly, noisy and flirtatious. Now that she had left, it was as if she had taken time itself with her. She had left a strange memory in Ideen's mind. It was a memory of troublemaking or the bitter taste of waking up after a sweet dream just before getting up in the morning.

She had asked: "If I ask you to recite a poem, would you do so?"

"Do you really have to make fun of me?"

"Oh, no! I have no such intention. I just want to hear a poem. If you don't want to recite one, I am not going to push you."

A few days later, while Ideen was sanding the frames in preparation for a layer of paint, someone knocked twice. Ideen opened the door and Sormeh entered. She said hello. She behaved like someone who knew both the place and Ideen very well. She did not look curious. She was holding a mirror, a piece of white cloth and a pair of scissors. She walked towards the chair and, with a wave of her hand, invited Ideen to sit down. She asked: "Have you looked at yourself in a mirror recently?"

"No." He gazed at her. And he felt ashamed of gazing at her. Nevertheless, he felt like looking at her constantly, albeit furtively.

She stood the mirror on the workbench, pulled the chair back and said: "Very well then. Come and have a look."

Ideen sat on the chair. Sormeh wrapped the length of white cloth round his neck and began. Without uttering a single word, she trimmed his hair with astonishing meticulousness and with motherly attention. She trimmed his beard and his moustache. Ideen, looking in the mirror, noticed that she moved and twisted her hand so quickly. He was worried that she might cut one of her fingers with a sudden movement of the scissors.

Sormeh said: "Last year your mother called at our house. Twice."

"My mother?" He turned back.

"Don't move, or you might find one of your ears in the scissors."

"What did she want?"

"She was looking for you. She had traced your trail from the timber factory and she was pretty sure that you were here."

"What a strong instinct! What a strong premonition!"

"Yes. And she loves you so much." As Ideen was silent, Sormeh continued: "She said I had a strong similarity to Ideen and Ida. Your eyes, however, are like those of the Tatars. Besides, I am blonde."

"I can swear that she was not inspired by similarity. I am sure she must have observed signs and indications leading her to the idea that I must be here."

"Maybe yes, maybe no."

"What do you mean by 'maybe yes, maybe no'."

Sormeh, now laughing, said: "I mean she must have sensed the feeling I have for you."

"Do you have any feelings towards me?"

"Why do you move so much? Of course I have."

With a peculiar calm, Ideen said: "Your love has grown old, has mellowed, in me, my lady."

"Like wine, I suppose."

"Manners and a sense of duty meant that I had no right to love you."

"Why?" She stopped trimming Ideen's hair. She leant on her elbows against the workbench and stared directly at him.

"I won't be offended if they throw me out of here. But I fear being hated by your father."

"It's not your fault. The truth of the matter is that they brought you up as a timid, cowardly boy. They have killed off all your courage. Look at yourself in the mirror and see how old and worn out you've become."

"Do you really think I don't need kindness?"

Sormeh resumed her hairdressing: "Every human being is in need of kindness." She opened a parting in the middle of Ideen's hair. She then combed his hair and said: "Look. You now resemble Jesus Christ. The only thing you now need is to take a bath."

Ideen looked into the mirror. He had no resemblance to Jesus Christ. He had much more similarity to a lean man of Tatar tribes, with tidy hair. While he

Symphony of the Dead

was being taken care of by Sormeh, the more he tried to control his excitement, the less successful he was. He said: "I always warm the water here and wash myself."

"We have a bathroom at home. From now onwards, you may use our bathroom if you wish."

Ideen shook the apron off and went to his frames. Sormeh said: "I like seeing you working." She moved about the workshop. She then sat on her heels and started sanding a frame. "You shouldn't dirty your hands."

"Why are you always frowning?"

"I don't know. I wonder at that myself."

"You're always in a pensive mood. You look like a worried millionaire who has just been told that his ships have sunk."

"I am looking for myself in the distant past. In the past, we had things that we no longer have."

"For example?"

"I don't know."

"From now on, I am going to come here every day." Before leaving, she entered Ideen's little room, sat on the bed for a few seconds, went through the pages of a couple of books and said: "Are you Joseph the Carpenter?"

"Miss Sormeh!"

"Sormelina."

"Miss Sormelina, would you give me permission to love you?"

Sormeh stood up, smiled and softly touched her upper lip with her tongue and said: "Oh, do you have to ask that question?"

Ideen kissed her with complete abandon. He took possession of her as a conqueror would an already demarcated territory.

15

Every Sunday, Armenians coming from the town or from the outskirts, visited the church in groups, prayed, proffered their donations and had lunch in the pleasant church garden that was adorned with trees and flowers. In the afternoon, they went back home. The church building had an outer layer of red bricks and two rows of double-glazed windows. In the middle, right in front of the entrance, were two very tall columns, in the baroque style, that were as high as the ceiling. Pigeons had made nests near the tops of the columns. There was a memorial plinth in the middle of the garden. It bore the statue of an old saint raising his hands in prayer. There were little flowerbeds around the building.

The clock above the entrance had stopped years ago. The old wooden door creaked and moaned when it was opened or closed. From the former army of servants, guards and caretakers, only a small lady had stayed on. She took care of everything to be done at the church and even at Galoost Mirzayan's house.

On Sundays, hawkers intermingled with pious visitors. They offered their goods around the church, along Armanestan Alley and all over Gazoran district, turning that quiet neighbourhood into a marketplace. The neighbourhood got crowded with paper boys, baked beetroot sellers, boiled broadbean sellers, itinerant greengrocers, clothes sellers, soapmakers from nearby villages, unscrupulous toy sellers who sold toys to children at exorbitant prices, roaming barbers who served cinnamon tea to their customers while they cut their hair and candle sellers who hoped to earn enough for a year out of the non-Muslims. At the entrance to the alley, carriage-men dozed off while waiting for fares.

Apart from Sundays, there were other special occasions. Whenever an Armenian died or got married, the neighbourhood became crowded again. On such occasions, Galoost Mirzayan sent a carriage to bring the priest to the church and ordered Sormeh to prepare a soft meal, suitable for old people, for the priest. On occasions such as these, he did not go to work. He also asked Sooren to stay on and serve tea and coffee to the guests.

Late in the afternoon of one such day, a warm, pleasant Thursday, Sooren went to the workshop to have coffee with Ideen and to talk to him. Madam Yevgineh had told him that Sormeh regularly visited the place. And now, he wanted to find out what kind of a man Ideen was, how he thought, and what his plans for the future were.

Ideen told him that he planned to leave the place in a few days' time. He added that he had not yet told anyone but that he could no longer put up with the situation.

Sooren was taken aback: "You want to go? Where to?"

"Tehran."

"What for?"

"To study. To live. To do as other people do."

"Considering the fact that they have a warrant for your arrest, that you are a fugitive and that, in short, you are in an awkward situation, I don't think this would be a wise idea."

"Maybe not. But four years of my life have been wasted in the factory, in the workshop and in this basement. It is as if four years of my life have been cut off with a pair of scissors and thrown away. Now, I want to go and find out what there is out there. I have suffered a lot, Mr Sooren. My educational certificates have been burnt. My poems and my writings have been burnt. It is as if my past has been cut away from me. I have become impatient. In any case, I can't stay here forever and I have to go some time."

Sooren looked embarrassed and worried. This could be read in his face and his movements. He dropped the nails on the worktop and picked them up again, placed them in the box, took them out and dropped them again. He arranged the picture frames one on top of another and, inadvertently, stretched his hand to pick up the hammer. He looked really nervous. He said: "You are right. I know what you're going through, although I have been in worse situations than yours. My life, too, went up in smoke. My wife died. So did my child Daniel when he was just one year old. The war scattered us. From all that liveliness, all that happiness, only Sormeh has been left to me. And she is not much better off either. Maybe she hasn't told you. But her marriage ended in tragedy. Three months after she got married, her husband died. With the passage of time, she lost her high spirits and her *joie de vivre*. Many of her cousins wished to marry her but she was not interested. We couldn't force her into marriage, could we? So, she remained a widow. Now, she has become too fastidious and is suspicious of all men. I can't send her to Erevan; but I don't want her to stay here either. I have, however, switched off from everything while my hollow life goes on day after day. *C'est la vie.* You see that we are in no better a situation than you are. But we can't fight with destiny."

"You're right. You, too, have suffered. But what am I to do? The way things are going, I might stay in this damp basement and make frames until the end of my life without knowing what to do with my earnings and without any social life. What have I been born into this world for?"

"Why have you made up your mind so suddenly then?"

"I have thought about it a lot. I have had a lot of time to think. And now…"

"You are young. You are living in your own country. You are wise and educated. Why should it be like this?"

"This is the destiny bequeathed to me by my father."

From this point on, the two were talking as one. Both of them complained. And both of them were disheartened, exhausted and sad. When leaving, Sooren said: "Think a bit more on it. There may be other ways."

Late at night, when all noise had subsided, Sormeh descended the staircase, knocked and entered. During the day, she had been too preoccupied with various things and had not been able to pay a visit to Ideen. Now, she looked horrified and disturbed. She placed the newspaper she had brought with her on the workbench and entered Ideen's little room. She sat on the bed and gazed at Ideen with the gaze of a person who was witnessing the falling of a plane from the sky. Moments passed in silence.

Ideen broke the silence: "It looks as if you are very tired."

"You intend going away?"

"Your dad told you?"

"Yes."

"Yes."

"Why had you not told me then?"

"I wish I had not told Mr Sooren either."

"Is that all?"

Ideen remained silent. He had never seen Sormeh so troubled.

Sormeh resumed the conversation: "What is going to become of me then?"

"I am no good for you, Sormeh. Believe me."

"Why do you suddenly behave like this?"

"I am even tired of myself. I have lost my patience. I am rotting from within."

"What about me?"

"I don't know."

"Ideen!"

Ideen looked at her. Sormeh had fallen silent. For a few moments, they looked into each other's eyes. Then Sormeh, trembling and hardly in control of herself, said: "All those beautiful words..." And she stared at the floor.

"All those words expressed my true feelings. My sentiment is still the same. But I must go away before I allow myself to be held down by you. I must kill the enthusiasm. I must behead the love in my heart."

Sormeh's tears rolled down her cheeks and now she spoke calmly: "Loving you is not an easy task."

"Believe me, Sormeh. I am no good for you."

"Don't say such a thing."

"I am not a cruel man, Sormeh. Here, I feel each day is as long as a thousand days. Were it for the sake of my own heart, for the sake of my love for you, I would stay. But I also want to be a poet. I must reawaken my enthusiasm for poetry. I have fallen behind in everything."

"At least let me come with you."

"Where?"

"Wherever you're going."

"That wouldn't be wise. How can I take you to a city where I know no-one and make you wander about aimlessly?"

"You unfair man!" She burst into tears and left the place, sobbing.

That night, Ideen dreamed of himself as Jesus Christ, with a crown of thorns on his head and a cross on his back. He was being taken to a desert in order to be crucified. Someone whipped him and said: "Faster, faster!" He could not carry the heavy cross. His feet had lost their strength and his heart felt like it had stopped beating. In the distance, a woman who looked like Ida was chanting a litany for him while crying. The wind howled.

When reading his newspaper the next day, he had forgotten about his dream. He had had his lunch and was now going through the pages of the national daily *Ettela'at* from the 7th of September. On page 3, he noticed a bold headline: "Woman sets herself on fire in Abadan". Under the headline, the news item read: "Watched by the tearful, astonished eyes of her son, the woman, Ida Urkhani, poured paraffin on herself and set herself on fire. She burnt to death. There was no-one around who could save her. When the police arrived..."

Third Movement

Symphony of the Dead

There was blinding lightning and roaring thunder. Large drops of rain followed. The echo of the thunder reverberated over the city and died down. He looked at the dark cloud overhead, dragged himself to Dorostkar's, the watchmaker, and took refuge under the arch of the doorway. He stood there with his hands in his pockets and a smile on his face. The smile made him look sadder than he was.

He said to himself: "The big poppy burst in the sky, it scattered petals of cold drops, the blossoms raining down..." The more he tried, the less he could remember the rest of the poem. He cast another glance at the sky and, then, at the closed door of Sooren's coffee shop. He felt weak inside. He felt that something heavy was pressing on his heart. He pulled a cigarette out of the pocket of his jacket and struck a match. Since summer, he had become a smoker. The severe downpour made it difficult for him to light his cigarette. He cupped the match in his hands and, this time, he was successful and took a drag on the cigarette. He gritted his teeth and thought of the way I walked. He eyed the crowd quickly. No-one walked like me. His eyes were not even attracted to the schoolgirls going home after school, wearing their navy blue uniforms and white socks, holding their books under their arms and walking with such gaiety and such gangly movements that they looked as if they were dancing in the rain. They were also wearing pink ribbons in their hair. One of them had a big bun of black hair. But none of those girls walked like me.

I walked fast and my hands went back and forth. My big steps resembled the jumping of galloping horses. While I walked, my hair floated up, showing the back of my neck. That is why he thought I was jumping. He did not know why he was troubled. He was simply troubled. He looked at the sky. It was raining hard and the rain washed away the mud and the sludge that were the remains of the melting ice on the ground. The trees were about to break out in buds. I walked fast.

He had said: "I suppose you'll now get your legs in a twist and fall."
I had said: "Morellooo?" But my real intention had been to purse my lips. I wanted to sit on the swing in that big garden that was full of trees and flowers. I wanted to swing. I asked: "Would you like to eat some cherries?"
He replied: "No." He sat at the edge of the pond. He was wearing a jade-green suit and a light blue shirt.
I said: "Don't get dusty."
"It doesn't matter." And he gazed at my going to and fro on the swing.
I said: "*Lava*?" And I laughed, bending my head to one side.
He said: "*Lava*."
"*Inch peses*?"
And now, the more he tried, the less he could recall that word. He tried even harder. It was no use. He looked at the closed door of the coffee shop and stood still, waiting for the rain to stop. His left hand and three fingers of his right hand were in his trouser pockets. He puffed at his cigarette all the time. Someone greeted him. He did not hear. He really did not hear. He was thinking about me.
It started to rain and I was no longer swinging. There were so many little, concentric waves on the pond's surface. The fish jumped up to take air bubbles in. He said: "I feel the rain is falling for my sake." He looked askance at me in such a way that I felt obliged to say, once again, "Morellooo."
He said: "And you, too, have become so beautiful for my sake."
"I have done nothing to make myself beautiful. I haven't used any make-up. Nothing. I have simply taken a bath."
"Do you always take a bath?"
"Don't be cheeky."
We went into the building. When we were at the bottom of the staircase, he held my hand. I could hear his heart beating faster, as if through his hand. We went upstairs. The room had white net curtains. I opened all the curtains wide, so that we could watch the rain fall.
He said: "The trees, too, are full of buds for my sake." With a fingertip, he pushed aside a few strands of hair that were covering his forehead. With a trembling voice, he said: "But I don't know for what purpose I continue to live."
No-one could decipher what could be read in his eyes. I had realised this at our very first meeting. On that evening, when he first entered our life, he was a man in a ragged cloak, with an axe over his shoulder. He took big steps. He would halve a thick log with a single blow of the axe. With each blow, he moaned "Eh!" But he had been brought up in such a way that his behaviour

was distinct from that of others. He considered the world to be more serious than other people thought. That night, I thought it was fear that had given him these characteristics. But, with the passage of time, I realised that I had been wrong. I realised that to understand him was easier than smelling a flower. For this, it would be enough just to see him. The only thing I did not know was whether his mother loved him as much as I did. Could anybody understand how pleasant it was to love him, that to love him would guide one to the realm of eternity? One would feel filled to such an extent that one would not wish to think of anything else, would not wish to have a trembling heart for anyone else and would never hesitate. No. His long overcoat, his hand-knitted sweater and his old sheepskin hat merely constituted his superficial appearance. When these were taken off, one's sun rose.

He always smelled of wood and varnish. For a whole year, I had been familiar with that smell from the *putshka*. Whenever I opened that skylight in order to drop the newspaper in, I smelled wood and varnish and was filled with pleasure.

Suddenly, silence reigned over his mind. There was only emptiness and weightlessness. Ideen's eyes had lost the ability to focus. People who ran, a black umbrella, the nameplate of Sooren's coffee shop... He saw all these things. A horrifying silence filled the space hitherto occupied by all the people in his mind. He could no longer remember whom he had been thinking about. Only the vague remnants of a sweet memory irritated him. As soon as he was about to find the entirety of that sweet memory, Ida had arrived. And there was nothing he could do about it. In his mind, Ida laughed and, shaded by the trees, kindled the fire in order to brew tea for Father. Her son, Sohrab, was in Ideen's arms. And Ideen, leaning against a tree, gently bounced the child, reading his book at the same time.

Father asked: "What are you reading Ideen?"

"I am memorising poems."

Mother had grated a melon for Ideen. He had added a spoonful of sugar. Little pieces of ice shone on the grated melon. Father exclaimed: "What about Urhan?"

Mother explained: "He is sitting idle. Well, he can come and help himself to some melon."

"And what does Ideen do? Does he lay golden eggs all the time?"

"You are all golden eggs, thank God!"

"I am not attaching any importance to a melon. What I mean is that you should not discriminate between your children."

"In the same way that you don't, I suppose."

The seeds of hatred had been sown for years and there was no need to sow any more. And the children had to learn.

I followed his thoughts and overcame him again. But I did not mean to tease him. He himself did not want me to leave him alone. He wanted me to say: "Like a flower bed, hair is in need of constant grooming." And I did say that. My fingers moved and wriggled through his hair. I felt hot. I said: "But I don't know how to do it properly."

"It is not important, madam. It is kind enough of you to help me in this way."

"Don't you feel bored?"

"What with?"

"With this workshop. With the fact that you have lived alone for a year and a half."

"I am accustomed to this life." He closed his eyes and gave me a chance to tidy his hair in silence. Gradually, I discovered that he liked me to play with his hair. He had not told me. I had to find out for myself that he liked me to caress his face. He tried to get up from the chair a number of times: "Don't you sleep? Aren't you going to bed?"

"No. I want to watch you when you're asleep."

He would sleep with amazing calm and ease. He would just let his face slip between my hands and he would fall asleep like that. One morning, months after Ida's death, I was still sitting and caressing his soft hair when he woke up. He got up, knelt in front of me, kissed my hand and wept. He said: "It is for the sake of these very things that I can't detach myself from you."

Ida's death had been a severe blow to him. He felt sad and lonely. He could not sleep at night. He had nightmares. He often went into a trance and talked nonsense. He cried for no reason. He said: "Her neighbours have said that that night, Abadani had thrown Ida out of the house. What for? No-one knows. The newspapers had mentioned no reason. And the bloke himself packed up and left for America. My guess is that Ida must have been in an difficult situation. She would have felt ashamed of going back to Ardabil and she could not go anywhere else either. Well, she brought this calamity upon herself…"

I had gone out of his mind and my place had been taken by Ida. She was standing somewhere, gnawing at her fingernails.

Father had told Ida: "The dowry I am giving you is much below the dignity of a person of my status, but a girl who chooses the wrong destiny instead of going the right way can expect nothing better." This had been very similar to what he had told Ideen years before: "You don't deserve a woollen suit. I'll buy you a cotton one so that you are no longer disobedient." Ideen never put on his new cotton suit. He had said: "I'll keep my old clothes clean and keep wearing them."

There was no letup in the thunder and the downpour. Water had collected in puddles and whenever cars passed through them, they splashed muddy water on the passers-by. People had taken refuge under doorway arches and there were not many of them around. Mother frequently insisted that he should get married. She kept saying: "Do you want me to arrange a marriage between you and the daughter of your Uncle Nasser?"

He had retorted: "You say strange things Mother!" And he had thought of me.

Mother insisted: "Come and have a look at her photo. See for yourself how beautiful she has become."

"Oh, Mother! I myself am a burden on this household and you want to get Nasser's daughter here too? All the way from Urmia? What for?"

"Whatever you wish." She fell silent and Ideen thought of me again.

And, now, I was in his mind once more, with a purple shirt that had long sleeves and a buttoned collar completely covering the neck, with a skirt covering the legs to below the knees and with black shoes. That is the way he liked to see me. Whenever he looked at me, he persisted and would not take his eyes off me. He wanted me to move about in front of his eyes, to bring tea, to arrange the books on the shelves, to throw a piece of wood into the fire and to keep talking while doing various things. I was happy with these moments. I talked, I pulled the curtains closed, I pulled the curtains apart again and I was all the time thinking of doing something in front of his eyes. He liked me to move about in his presence. I only found out about this later on. The time always passed very quickly and I was always afraid lest he want to leave.

I said: "I will live in whatever way you want me to. I would do whatever you tell me to do. You tell me to die and I'll drop dead."

He was sitting silently on the chair. He just stared. I said: "You are my supreme commander."

He laughed and got up. He took a few steps towards the window and I thought he wanted to go back home. But he went back to the chair and sat down again. I wanted to tell him something that would reassure him of my profound love for him. I said: "You are my Jesus Christ." I knelt in front of his chair, made the sign of the cross, clasped my hands together and lowered my head in respect. He kissed my forehead. I always longed to see him. I always feared that he might not come and asked myself what I was to do if he really didn't. I told him that love should be accepted in its entirety, not only in the body, but in the soul as well. It should be sought, furthermore, in the air, in mirrors, in dreams and in breathing. One should feel it enter the lungs and grow in size. I realised these things only when he failed to visit our house for a month. Those were the days after Ida had died and he had returned to the paternal house after four years.

One day, I was sitting in front of the church and looking at the flowerbeds. On that day, the flowerbeds and the walls of the church were being visited by so many blue and yellow butterflies. On that day, if someone told me that I had grown a pair of wings on my shoulders, I would not have been surprised as I was indeed ready to turn into a different creature. Ideen arrived at four o'clock in the afternoon. He looked older and sadder than usual. He looked worn out and sorrowful, exactly like a person who was entering a cemetery.

I was about to shriek with joy. But, without paying any attention to him, I went to our own building, quickly went up the stairs, lifted the corner of the net curtain of an upstairs window and looked at him. He appeared to wander in weightlessness, like a stranger. He could not believe that I had paid no attention to him. He stood for a few moments in front of the church, right where I had been sitting. Then he walked on the shingles in the church courtyard. After this, I saw him leaving the church courtyard quickly. My heart was beating fast and my hands and legs were trembling. I did not know what to do. I opened the window and called him: "Ideen!"

He could not tell the direction of the voice. I felt, once more, that he was floating in weightlessness. I said to myself: "Oh, my God! What a foolish thing I've done."

He turned back and looked around, puzzled and confused. I opened the window fully and said, excitedly: "Hello."

He smiled and said: "Where are you then?"

I said: "Wait." And I ran out of the building. I added: "You want to see my uncle, no doubt."

"No. I have come to see you."

I said: "I was cross with you and had intended to break up with you for the time being." His face acquired an unhappy expression. I offered him my condolences on Ida's death and wished forgiveness for her soul.

"You can't imagine, Sormeh. You can't imagine what a great sister I've lost."

We walked and talked until nightfall. We went round the church and our own building several times. He talked to me about his father, about his mother, about Urhan and about many things that he had neglected or had not known about during the four years of his absence. Whenever he talked about Ida, I wished to cry for her.

Symphony of the Dead

After he left, I could not sleep at all that night. It wasn't that I had gone mad with the memory of him. No, it wasn't like that. On the contrary, I felt that even the memory of him was running away from me. Everything was running away from me. Even the furniture and the utensils were running away out of the windows. The walls retreated. I had been left alone with the memory of him. They had agreed that he should go to his father's shop during the day and be free in the evening. His father had embraced him, had cried and said: "What have I got if I haven't got my children?"

It was now raining and Ideen was looking at the overflowing brook that carried the water forward and, further on, forced its water out, spreading it over the street. Father had died about a year ago. The image of Father on his deathbed had remained in his mind like a sacred icon. At the moment when Father, suffering from heart disease, was about to die on a white, clean bed, he had said: "Ideen, Urhan, I want you to love each other. Life is worth nothing." That day, Ideen had held Father's hand. He had seen Father snoring constantly with closed eyes, unable even to wipe his own saliva. Mother kept wiping it off with her handkerchief. Father's skin gradually turned yellow. With great difficulty, he uttered words that sounded very strange to Ideen: "God has drawn a line in the middle of the wheat field. Everybody's share is separate, but connected." When he could no longer breathe easily, he had said: "Well now, a caravan behind and a caravan in front…"

Ideen never forgot the sacredness of that moment. On that day, he was closer to Father than ever before. He had poured water, blessed from having been mixed with the dust gathered from holy shrines, down Father's throat while reciting the sura of Al-Hamd, eulogy to Allah, from the Koran. If I had been present at the scene, I would have made the sign of the cross.

After Father's death, Mother's asthma had intensified. She squatted sadly in a corner of the corridor and stared into the courtyard. Ravens arrived and flew away en masse and she just kept staring. She was worried about Ideen all the time. She told Ideen: "If you wish, I'll write to your Uncle Nasser and tell him to bring his daughter here so that you can see her."

Ideen replied: "Don't even talk about it." He was in no mood to hear such words. He didn't want to forget me. When he got up in the morning, he had thought of me, as he had every morning. He felt a great sorrow pressing against his heart. He pictured me all the time. I had a different shape every time. Sometimes, my image was so pale and vague that he felt he was looking at me through thick fog. I said: "I am still drunk with last night's memory. You are such a strong wine."

I longed to know how he was feeling. When he kissed me, he didn't close his eyes. He wanted to observe the effect of the kiss on my face. He had been naughty: Had he simply asked me, I would have told him what I felt.

He said: "You smell so nice."

"I place a few jasmine flowers inside my collar."

His breath smelt of wind, smelt of rain. It was cool. His mouth smelt of wood. And I suddenly felt myself in flames in his arms.

On the previous day, he had asked: "Would you give me permission to love you, Miss Sormelina?"

My reply had been: "Oh, do you have to ask?" And I had said to myself: 'There is no need for permission to love, is there?' Subsequently, I had found it necessary to say that, years before, when I had been 16 years old, I had got married to an army lieutenant from Baku. After three months, he went on a journey to Russia and I was informed that he had been killed in a car accident. In due course, I easily forgot about him. For some time, I was frightened when imagining his blue eyes. But, gradually, I got accustomed to isolation and learnt to live within my own cocoon, like my grandmother, Madam Yevgineh. But I had to rescue myself somehow. It took me a year and a half to approach Ideen. I had lived with his memory every day. It was rather odd that whenever his eyes caught mine, he fell silent as a statue. He looked frightened and isolated. He preferred to be alone in the church basement and whenever I asked him to be a guest when we entertained other guests at home, he had replied that he was not ready for such functions.

My father said: "It is New Year's Eve and, besides, there is snow and frost. How can you be so unkind and not invite him?"

Uncle explained: "Well, today I called on him three times and, every time, I invited him to have dinner with us tonight. He replied: 'I am not ready for this, Mr Mirzayan. I am sorry'."

I said: "In that case, I am going to invite him." I went to the church courtyard. It was cold and I was in snow up to my knees. With my hand, I wiped the snow that had gathered on the skylight. I opened the skylight and I saw that he had lit a fire in a brazier. He was reading a book at the workbench. I called him: "Mr Ideen."

He raised his head and said: "Hello." He got up. I think he was afraid.

I said: "Come up quickly so that we can go and have dinner."

"If Mr Mirzayan would not feel offended, I wish to stay here."

"But everybody is waiting for you. Why don't you want to come?" I was feeling really cold, to the extent that I was gritting my teeth.

"With this untidy appearance... I don't know what to do."

"My father and my uncle will be offended." I was gritting my teeth hard now.

"You will catch a cold. Please go. I'll follow in a moment." He did come. I am pretty sure that he had washed his hands and his face in the pond as I could detect a thin layer of ice on his beard.

Uncle said: "What's the matter my boy? You're not upset with us, I hope."

He was sitting in front of the fireplace. Water dripped from his chin. He said: "I didn't want to make a nuisance of myself." At that very moment, I brought him a glass of tea. I said "Happy New Year" and I laughed.

Father and Uncle were both drunk and guffawed. Ideen listened to them and, occasionally, smiled. I felt that when one was alone, the sorrow of the whole world sought refuge in one's mind. He would feel so alienated from other people that he would never again be able to approach them. One sees that in the midst of so many people, one is really alone and has no-one in this world. That night, I wished to share my happiness with him. I wished to halve my happiness like an apple so that he could pick up whichever half he fancied. Perhaps he knew these things but did not reveal this to me. He did not betray even the slightest sign of his feelings. Only occasionally, his gaze felt so heavy on my eyes or on my hair. But as soon as I turned my head towards him, his gaze had flown away like a frightened sparrow.

I said: "The world is like a centrifuge. The faster it turns, the more likely it is that we'll be thrown off."

He replied: "Yes. It turns so fast that one feels dizzy and lonely."

"What are we to do then? What's the right course of action?"

"Silence and persistence."

"When you're in love with someone, you feel lonelier because you can talk about your feelings only to that person." I wanted to observe his reaction when he heard these words. But he replied with his customary seriousness and meticulousness: "I have not experienced such things or been through such stages yet."

Father, who was laughing at Uncle's words, said: "Offer fruit to the guests, Sormeh."

I placed two oranges on a plate and handed it to Ideen. I said: "And if that person happens to be the one who encourages you to be silent, your loneliness would be complete."

"It can't be any different."

That night, we talked to each other until it was almost dawn. But I could still not find out whether he had any feelings towards me.

I asked: "May I pour you some wine?"

"No, thank you."

"Are you being formal and too polite?"

"No. I don't drink."

The fact that he did not drink made me happy. Nevertheless, I was curious and wished to know whether, when drunk, he would be as cautious. I said: "Well, what were we saying?"

"I don't know." He now opened up his clasped hands and I noticed that there were a few wounds on them. I looked more carefully and I noticed that the skin on his hands had cracked in a few places.

I asked: "Do you need hand lotion?"

"Not now. I'll ask you for some later on."

Uncle Galoost, who had eaten too much, said: "If you are bored, we can play cards."

I asked Ideen: "Would you like to play cards?"

"I don't know how to."

Father and Uncle Galoost had fallen asleep on their armchairs and we were still talking. But I had still learnt nothing of his inner soul. The next day, before dawn, I took him into the church. I prayed in front of the altar. I prayed to God to make him love me.

The rain stopped and the clouds broke up. Intense, beautiful sunshine shone over the town. People who had taken refuge under door arches dispersed while looking at the sky. Everybody went about their business. Ideen began to walk towards the shop. A sound, like that of a church bell, reverberated in his head. I was wearing a white dress and he a navy-blue suit. Suddenly, a cyclist knocked him sideways. He managed to stay on his feet and to avoid falling into the open gutter. He held on to a tree trunk to keep his balance and he turned back. I had passed him before he had been knocked by the cyclist. The butcher came out of his shop and said: "Go after him. What if you had fallen into the water?"

Ideen shrugged his shoulders in a sign of indifference. He turned into Sheikh Safi Street. There was a hat shop on the corner. Behind its window, an old moustachioed man, wearing a hat, was gazing at the world outside. Ideen thought he was a statue. He looked more carefully and, this time, the man blinked. In the middle of the afternoon crowd, Ideen tried hard to get quickly to the shop.

He thought of me again.

I said: "Oh, you don't have to thank me. I haven't done anything for you."

He said: "I didn't want to be a nuisance." He wanted to add a few words to what he had said. Maybe he did not find any more words.

I said: "I have a peculiar pattern of behaviour. If I observe someone in the street who is not able to pull his trousers up, I feel like taking a step forward

Symphony of the Dead

and pulling his trousers up for him. If I notice that the door to a house has been left open, I close it. In the morning, I wake everybody up at home, I make them breakfast and help them to get ready to go to work."

He said: "It's about two years since I last saw myself in the mirror."

I said to myself: "I am still drunk with last night's memory. You are such a strong wine." I said to him: "I used to work in Father's coffee shop. I ground and brewed coffee and I washed the cups. Later on, it wasn't possible to stay in Father's shop any longer."

He had remained motionless and spellbound with his hammer in his hand. I said: "Get on with your work." He sat at his workbench and gazed at me while I walked about. I said: "You know what? If you wear a suit, you'll become a gentleman."

"You mean I'm not a gentleman now?"

"Oh, you are. You are very much a gentleman."

"If I manage to get out of here, I'll certainly order myself a suit."

"Do you know that that overcoat doesn't suit you at all?"

"No. No-one had told me that before. The thing is that I've got used to it."

"I suggest you wear a navy-blue suit, a blue shirt and a narrow, red tie. Then you'll become a gentleman. What I mean is that you'll be more handsome."

"I wish I could get out and have a walk around the town."

"There's no need to order a suit made to measure. A new shop has been opened that sells readymade suits. There are suits there that would fit you."

"Really?"

He was so loveable, simple and dignified. That night, grandmother grumbled that I was not letting him sleep. I got up frequently, went to the window, looked into the courtyard, at the trees and at faraway buildings that looked like ghosts in the dim light of the midnight moon. They looked somewhat like chess pieces. The trees had conic heads like pawns on a chessboard. They gazed at me unashamedly, making me feel ashamed. I would cast a glance at the sleepiness and oblivion of the town and go back to my bed. Considering the fact that my heart had trembled for him at first sight, why had I waited for such a long time before paying him a visit? And now, I didn't know what I could do for him. We were both lonely but we dared not speak the truth. It is quite possible that were it not for Uncle Galoost's idea, I would never have dared go to the basement and get acquainted with him. I had spent a whole night with him on the New Year's Eve, but I had found out nothing about him. Uncle Galoost told me that the profit from Ideen's work was as much as one-third of that of the whole of his huge factory. He was so happy that he interrupted the smoking of his pipe and began to sing: "Oh, you, starry sky. Oh, you, starry sky!" He gave his voice the character of that of an opera singer. I said to myself: "May God curse you!" And I made the sign of the cross.

That evening, I walked with Father in the courtyard and asked him: "Does Uncle Galoost have the right to exploit this poor man so much?"

Father looked at me with astonishment and said: "I am happy to see that you have been happy, energetic and rather misbehaved for some time. I know why. I have had no enjoyment in my life. The war displaced us, your mother contracted typhus and died in agony and we lost whatever we had, as you no doubt remember. But I am saying these things so that you realise that if we have stayed here and if I haven't thought of your future, the reason is that I have raised my hands in surrender. I have lost the game. I owe you something because I have ruined your life too. There was a time when I wished you to get a kick-start for a good life, to get married early. But now, I am broken-hearted and I've got used to a monotonous life. I don't know what Ideen's feelings towards you are. I understand your feelings but I don't know what sort of a man he is. In any case, the fact is that he is a Muslim and you are Armenian Christian. So, be careful."

"I am not unhappy with my life. But when I see how severely Uncle Galoost exploits this poor man, I feel sad for him. Did you see his hands on New Year's Eve?"

"Yes I did. I have also paid him a visit a couple of times. He is a broken-hearted but dignified boy. It might be a good idea if you talk to him. His knowledge of literature is good. He knows some French too. And he is a disciplined man."

"When I take a newspaper to him late in the afternoon, he opens his mouth like a fish on the pond's surface at feeding time."

The next day, I went to him with a copy of the daily *Ettela'at* and a copy of Dostoyevsky's *The House of the Dead*. Instead of dropping them down from the skylight, I went down the stairs. When he opened the door, he turned pale and stared at me.

I said: "Your heart."

"Young lady, haven't you thought of what would happen if they see you in here?"

"Nothing will happen."

"For goodness sake, leave this place. This is not proper."

"Why not?" And I went straight to his workbench and sat on his chair. I handled the tools. I inspected the saw for no reason. His pair of pliers had red handles and looked like a nightingale's mouth when it was opened and closed. I picked up the tiny nails out of their box and hammered two of them into the workbench. I picked up a clamp and asked: "What are these things used for?"

"I hold the picture frames together with these things."

I picked up a half-finished picture frame and, clumsily, smashed it into pieces using a nail and a hammer.

He said: "This is not the way. Allow me to show you how."

"I know what to do. I don't need instructions."

He was trembling, his eyes flitted nervously and he was simply stranded in the middle of the workshop with the weary appearance of someone who appeared to be suffering from a fever. I got up and walked about. I had not been in that basement for years. Now, it smelled nice and no longer frightened me. A picture hung on the central column of the workshop. It had an ornate, carved frame. Around the frame, little fish in bas-relief curved and had their heads in each other's bellies. I asked: "Is that a picture of your father?"

"The father of all poets."

"Nima Yooshij?"

"Yes. He died last year."

I looked at the portrait again. It was that of an old man who was passing his thin fingers through his hair and gazing at the floor. I said: "You are growing old in this place. And you look so pale. Why don't you think of a remedy?"

"Remedy for what?"

"Come outside. Breathe the fresh air. Enjoy the sunshine."

"But if someone happens to see me…"

"You're a big coward."

"I have to be careful about so many things."

"Why are you shivering? Are you feeling cold?"

"You know. Because Mr Mirzayan has supported me, I don't want to do anything that could put him in an embarrassing situation and put myself in a shameful one."

"Shameful? Why? Have you done anything wrong?"

"The reason is that you are here."

I was getting angry: "You feel ashamed in your relationship with Uncle Galoost just because I'm here?"

"Well. What would he think if he finds out that you have been in here?"

"Oh, he has no right to interfere with such things. If you are embarrassed, I won't come here again."

"In that case, I will go to town and give myself up to the police."

"To what end?"

"So that you can get rid of me."

I laughed. He laughed too. He said: "I am grateful to you for the newspapers and the books that you bring me."

"Have you noticed that there is no difference in the content of newspapers?"

"You have no doubt been feeling bored and that's why you've come here."

"No. On the contrary, I am quite busy."

"If so, then why for such a long time…"

I suddenly turned back and gazed into his eyes. He appeared offended. My lack of attention, my being aloof, had shattered him. I said: "Yes; but you too never invited me to come and see your workshop."

"It is, in fact, your own workshop." He laughed. But his eyes betrayed his anxiety.

"We don't live like other people. We have been brought up with more freedom than you have. I have spent 13 years of my life in Erevan. My mother died in the war. Later on, we moved here and stayed on with Uncle Galoost." I kept on talking and went on to tell him that I had been married, that I had lost my husband three months after the marriage and that, for years, I had been simply seeing to domestic chores.

He said: "You don't look like someone who has suffered so much. Not at all."

"And you don't look like someone who has been created to suffer as much as you do."

"What can be done?"

"All sorts of things can be done. I have come here. But you are attaching no importance to my presence."

"It is a great day for me, my lady."

I sensed that his face had turned red. It had a glow.

Someone called: "Ideen."

He turned back. It was Urhan. He was standing in front of the nut-sellers' souk, laughing at him. He asked: "Where were you going?"

He replied: "I wasn't going anywhere in particular. I was with Mother. Then I felt bored." When they entered the shop together, he saw Esmayol coming towards him. Esmayol laughed and said: "You've got a letter Mr Ideen."

Ideen picked up the letter, put a five *tooman* banknote in Esmayol's hand and sat at the desk. The envelope had the seal of Tehran Literary Society on it. He was not in a reading mood. He put the envelope in the pocket of his jacket and looked at the shop across the road. Its *zanbouri* lamps had been lit.

Urhan was replenishing the sacks of nuts, arranging packets in order of size next to the scales and chewing on something. He asked, in Azeri Turkish: "What's news?"

Symphony of the Dead

"Nothing"

Urhan, looking at him askance, said: "I don't think you have no news at all."

Ideen kept quiet. He didn't want to get into an exchange of words with Urhan that could lead to a quarrel.

Urhan asked: "Aren't you feeling well?"

"I'm alright."

"You haven't been suffering from insomnia, have you?" He shifted the sacks of nuts. He also arranged the measuring pans neatly, placing one inside another, and placed the whole lot next to the scales. While he was pumping the *zanbouri* lamp, he said: "You have also abandoned your books, haven't you?" He pumped again and resumed talking: "And, at last, she left you and went away?"

"Don't interfere in my business."

"Where did she go?"

Ideen felt that the more relevant questions would be where Ideen himself had gone and why Ida had burnt herself to death. Oh, how talkative Urhan was! Ideen hid his face in his hands and gave no more replies. The more he tried to be friendly with Urhan, the less he could do so. He did not hate him but he was unhappy with him and felt offended. He had told him several times: "Don't dismiss brotherhood for the sake of money and possessions." Urhan had replied: "I piss on this kind of brotherhood." Was it possible to answer him without further inflaming this hostility? He had once told me: "I'll keep quiet and persist in my silence until I bring him to his knees."

After Ida's death, I went to see him every day at four o'clock in the afternoon. We would walk about the town and come home. Uncle Galoost had left the upper floor to us. He himself would leave the house at four o'clock in the afternoon in order to go to Armanestan district. There, he would loiter in front of the church before knocking at the church door. But there was no-one there to open the door for him. He repeated this futile passage between house and church for several months. Where was I? It was my absence that made him go home alone, creep into the basement, occasionally read a book and, for the rest of the time, lie on the bed and just blink.

Early in springtime, when, following a long winter, the first sunshine of the spring had warmed the town, Ideen went to the shop one morning. He found the door shut and locked. He asked the porters for the whereabouts of Urhan. No-one had a clue. He walked to and fro in the hall for some time and went back home. Mother knew nothing either, apart from the fact that Urhan had slipped out of the house before sunrise.

Ideen asked: "Why did he leave without telling anybody?"

Mother retorted: "Haven't you got a key to the shop?"

"No." He went back to the shop and decided to call a locksmith to have the locks opened. Just before midday, when the locksmith, surrounded by the porters, was filing a lock, Urhan arrived and asked: "What are you doing?"

"We are cutting the locks," explained Ideen. He showed him the lock that had been cut. Another lock had been filed half way.

"Why are you cutting the locks? I have a key."

"Oh, brother! When you are going away, leave the key behind."

"I am not authorised to hand over the key to anyone."

Ideen shouted: "You have no bloody right to act or talk like this." He slapped Urhan on the face.

Urhan, shaking with anger, shouted: "You parasitic lout!"

They pulled at each other's collars and a serious scuffle broke out. The porters intervened but not early enough. Urhan, lifted by Ideen, was shaking his limbs in the air in a struggle to free himself. His belt and his collar had been gripped by Ideen. His legs kicked aimlessly in the air. The porters, making a lot of noise, eventually brought him down.

That day, the brothers did not open the shop. In the evening, Mother said: "Father must be turning in his grave. You have gone down the road of hostility and vengefulness. Father gave you so much advice, so much guidance. But you have closed your eyes and you only think of yourselves."

Urhan said: "He has put a new lock on and put the key in his pocket."

Ideen retorted: "Now it is my turn to be the keyholder for a while."

"I see! How about me ceding the shop to you altogether? Shall I pack up and go?"

"There is no need to hand the shop over to me. I own the shop. You own the shop too. But own it like a respectable human being."

"Who gave you the right to slap me in the face?"

"I did it so that you behave yourself and stop insulting me. You should think about what you're going to say before saying it. You should understand your limits and not cross them." Turning to Mother, he continued: "All the time, he makes fun of me and makes snide remarks. And he is so persistent in his hostile behaviour. Well, I am busy with the shop, the accounts, the customers, I can't…"

Mother intervened: "Look, Urhan. I swear to God that I'll teach you a hard lesson. I'll come and stand there personally and order a partition to be built in the middle of the shop."

Urhan was uncompromising: "I have toiled for 14 years. I'll not allow anybody who has just arrived to…"

Symphony of the Dead

Mother shouted: "That's enough. Shut your mouth. There is no need for you to tell me about your hard work. Remember this: Whatever we have belongs to you and Ideen in equal shares. Half of it is yours and the other half is Ideen's."

Urhan would not give up: "He is wasting his time in the shop."

Ideen burst out: "That is none of anybody's business. I decide for myself."

Mother said: "I don't understand why our life has turned sour like this. Who caused this disintegration? What will people say? You two should understand that you can't go on fighting all the time."

Ideen said: "Who taught Urhan to call me names such as lout, *mirza* and dishonourable? Has Father left me no dignity? Am I not the elder brother?"

Mother cried. She then felt unwell. The two brothers called a doctor. By the time Mother felt better, it was late at night. With great difficulty, they made her eat something. Mother asked Urhan to kiss Ideen on the face. The brothers embraced and kissed each other.

Urhan said: "We will not go to the shop tomorrow either. We will have a day out at Veela Darreh. We may have exhausted ourselves."

Mother agreed: "Very well. Go there, get some fresh air, and go back to work renewed." But it was raining the next day. Having a day out at Veela Darreh was postponed for a month.

He raised his head from the desk, lit a cigarette and thought of me again. He recalled the day when we went to Nameen in a four-horse carriage. On that day, Uncle Galoost was to be present at the baptism of four newborn babies. We returned to Ardabil late in the afternoon of the same day. When we were approaching Ardabil, Uncle Galoost told the carriage driver to stop. We got off. Uncle bought some honey and we walked around the gardens of that area. Both on the way out and on the way back, Ideen watched the wastelands on both sides of the road almost all the time. But he sometimes cast a furtive glance at me too. Whenever our eyes met, he felt shy. His hair had turned white with the dust rising from the dirt road. Later on, when Uncle wanted to buy some honey, we walked for a while. Ideen gave me a poppy, all the petals of which had fallen off by the time we got back home. Madam Yevgineh asked me: "What is it you are holding?"

"It was a flower."

"Who gave it to you?"

"A dear person."

She made the sign of the cross and looked worried. She said: "This is not a good sign. Keep away from this person."

"Oh, no. Why?"

"Because he will make you fall apart into petals like this flower." She stopped knitting.

"Don't be afraid. Throw these superstitions away."

She went back to her knitting. A few seconds later, she said: "I know that your father and your uncle don't interfere with your life. But how can you two get married?"

"My first husband was chosen for me by Father and by Uncle Galoost. But everybody agrees that this time, I should decide for myself. Besides, Father likes Ideen even more than I do."

Father had a special respect for Ideen. He sometimes took chocolates and coffee to him. They played chess and sometimes drank together. Father always called him "Mr Ideen." And Ideen called Father "Monsieur Sooren", unlike other people who referred to him as either Monsieur or Sooren. Whenever Father entered the room, Ideen stood up in respect.

Father said: "I like Mr Ideen more than any of you does."

But I can never believe that anybody could love Ideen as much as I did. And, yet, my grandmother never believed that I could get married to Ideen. She would say: "I have not seen a good sign. I fear that he might break you down into petals."

Whenever I related these things to Ideen, he laughed. And I would say: "You have broken me down into petals."

He said: "I want to see you with a hat all the time."

"Yes, sir!"

I always wore a pink, green or blue hat, the same colour as that of my dress. I let my hair hang down from the brim of my hat. On that day, I was wearing a purple dress with a high collar that covered my neck. I had done up the buttons on the sleeves. And I was wearing a purple hat. Father commented: "Like a lady." And he told Ideen: "I am looking forward to your freedom."

The following day, I bought a navy-blue suit for Ideen and told him to come upstairs in the evening, wearing that suit.

"You have been too kind."

"You might not like it."

"How is that possible? How can I dislike a present that my wife has bought for me?"

I laughed and said: "Oh! Does that mean you are my husband?"

He gazed at the smoke from his own cigarette. He was feeling sad and was about to cry. He missed me. He recalled that many years ago, when his father was about to depart for his Hajj, his grand pilgrimage to Mecca, they had gathered at the bus station to say farewell. Father had first slapped him lightly on the face, then kissed him. He had told Mother: "In this way, they will not forget me."

He turned his head back. The customers had left and Urhan was standing there, about to say: "It's four o'clock now."

The clock's cuckoo chanted four times.

Urhan said: "Why have you become like this, Ideen? You are thinking all the time. You are never yourself."

Ideen said: "I don't know. I am going out." And he set off.

Urhan asked: "Where to?" He did not wait for an answer and added: "If it is fine tomorrow, we will go to Veela Darreh."

Where? Armenia. He had composed a poem especially for me. I always recited it to the tune of the song 'The Dawn Bird' when I was busy doing something. He said: "It is a pity that I am no longer in that special mood, otherwise I would compose a new poem for you everyday."

He had likened me to a sky with 40 suns and himself to a moonless night. He had likened me to a lush tree, with many branches and numerous leaves that would shade people from intense sunshine and himself to a tree with rotten roots. He had likened me to the snow-covered Mount Sabalaan[18] and himself to ruins that had never had any visitors, to ruins always in the darkness of night. And, now, even worse than ruins.

He thought he had embarrassed me by what he had said. I frowned. He said: "It's unbecoming of you to frown."

I laughed. And I said: "Laugh."

He said: "This rain is also falling down for my sake. But I myself have no idea what I'm living for."

"And when you come here just for one day after a long time, do you have to say these things?"

"Think of your future, Sormeh. I am no good for you."

I was trembling with anger. I said: "In that case, go. Go!"

"Where to?"

"Get out of my life." And I cried.

"I am not afraid of marriage. What I fear is that you, too, might become fed up and desperate like Ida. I was looking for something that I had lost. But I am gradually turning into a person who simply thinks about thinking. Now, thinking has become my habit, my objective. All the time, I want to sit down and to think, no matter what my hands are doing."

"Be strong. It's true that they ruined your life. But it's also true that, after Ida's death, you've practically hanged yourself. You've still not stopped this self-destruction."

"Whatever I do, it would make no difference now. I've just let myself be carried away by floodwaters. You don't know what's going on in my heart."

But I did know what was going on in his heart. He had become a person who had cut himself off from his own future and his present and who had clung to his past. He had become despondent. He liked being alone more than anything else. Between confrontation and avoidance, he always chose avoidance. In the beginning, I thought that he only avoided me. Whenever he didn't turn up, I asked myself whether I had done something wrong and whether I was being justly punished. Why was he indifferent towards me? I was beginning to lose my self-confidence. I felt that I had been thrown away from the turning wheel of the world. I said to myself: "Sormelina is dead."

But, later on, I noticed that that was in his nature and his behaviour had nothing to do with me. I knew that he loved me. I did see that in his behaviour. Or I tried to find something in his behaviour that betrayed his love for me. He would travel from the other side of the town just to see me. He would sit facing me and talk for hours. He recalled his past and his sorrows. He told me about a tall, thin young man called Jamshid who had drowned in Shoorabi, about a little old woman who had fallen on to a brazier and whose heart had burnt, and about Master Nasser Delkhoon who had so easily surrendered to death. He also recalled his childhood and the day Ida told him: "Come with me so that I can see the Electric Fan Factory." He had never accompanied Ida and Ida had never seen the damned factory.

I let him shout whenever he felt angry. And what was all that anger about? It was about a policeman called Ayaz who had two wives and, at night, left the house where his first wife lived to go to the other wife. People thought that he went on his night patrol and referred to him as an honest, hard-working policeman. It was about a Polish woman called Martha who had taken promiscuity to the extremes and who slept with men even under bridges. But, first and foremost, he was unhappy with Urhan who made snide remarks all the time. The gentler Ideen tried to be, the more venomous Urhan became. Ideen said: "One day, I will extract the poison from him."

In the afternoons, I would go to their shop. This had become a habit for me. I had to go there and fetch him. I told him: "The night you receive the news that Sormelina is dead, make love till dawn."

"To whom?"

"To whoever you fancy. To whatever type of woman. Even to Martha."

"You too, making snide remarks, Sormeh?"

We were right in front of my father's coffee shop. I stopped for a moment.

Symphony of the Dead

I said: "You know something?" We went inside, had coffee and went back home. My father said: "Mr Ideen, check. And mate."

Ideen said: "Come earlier."

We set out. I locked my arm into his and said: "Well, recite the poem 'Days and Moments' while we are on our way."

"While I am on the way, if my memory helps me, I'll recite the poem 'Days and Moments'." Whenever he closed his eyes, I smiled, nodded and looked at him. But he couldn't close his eyes. The pavement was crowded with wheelbarrows, jostling people and, worst of all, running children. He would have preferred to walk in a desert, or anywhere devoid of people, so that he could walk with his eyes closed. He wondered why he was always in need of someone to be kind to him. He also wondered why he wanted me to always be in his mind. But he did know that whenever he woke up in the morning, I was in his mind, I loved him, and I was not there.

He was afraid of going to sleep at night because he sometimes dreamt of me and when he woke up, I had flown away. He was afraid of sleeping as he knew that he would suddenly wake up, sit up, look around and then, like little children who have just lost a parent, start crying in that cold room with walls of cement. He cried with a great burden of envy on his heart and a peculiar sorrow in his mind. He turned pale and his hands trembled. At this stage, Mother would come to him, make him take some crystallised sugar dissolved in hot water, talk to him and insist that he should move to another room. But he would reply: "I'll stay right here."

He said: "Why do I think about these things? I will recite the poem 'Days and Moments' if I can remember it." The poem was in Turkish and had a fine rhythm. After crossing Sarcheshmeh crossroads, he remembered the poem and began to recite:

"I know well that life is but a stage.
I know that well.
But I want you to know
that not everybody
has been created for petty plays."

He tried hard. But he could remember only bits and pieces of the remainder with difficulty:

"Think of the days full of sorrow.
Think of the days..."

He could not continue. Only the finale had stayed on relatively well in his memory:

"Remember
that days and moments never come back.
Think of time; think of the cruel ambush that time is going to unleash.
We will have a long, hard winter ahead of us,
a winter that no-one will forget.
What else can I say
but to remind you not to forget your winter clothes?"

I clapped my hands. We were now in Armanestan Alley and the church was in front of us. There was no-one else in the alley. I looked back. No, there was not a soul. While I continued to clap, I kissed him. I said: "I have kissed you in front of the House of God." And I added: "You are my Jesus Christ." My sound now reverberated in his mind a few times. And I said again: "You are my Jesus Christ."

When he arrived at the door, he turned back. He tried hard to remember how he had come all this way and where from. But the more he tried, the less he remembered. He only noticed that he had arrived. He opened the door without a sound. Unlike other men, who would somehow declare their arrival or their presence, he went into the basement quietly. The room, with its dark cement walls, had no ornament apart from a family portrait. Father was sitting on a chair. Mother was standing behind him, wearing her usual white chador with a floral pattern. She was thin, as she always had been. Ideen was standing on her left and Urhan on her right. Behind everybody, half of Ida's face could be seen. She had dressed herself neatly in her black chador. Oh, how beautifully she had sewn the curtains and the net curtains! And how beautifully she pleated them! She would then ask: "Is it good? Do you like them, Uncle Ideen?" She pretended to be her son, Sohrab.

He went into his room, closed the door, drew the curtains and lit a cigarette. He lay on the bed and tried to think, first of me, then of Ida. But he couldn't. They all approached together and went away together. His mind became crowded and then, suddenly, it was as empty as a dry desert with not a soul in it. When he was outside, or when he read a book, he could easily think of anyone he wished – of me, of Ida, of Mother. He could even think of Jamshid who had drowned in Shoorabi and whose soul had tortured him, Mother and even Urhan for years. Mother said: "All the time, I think someone is knocking at the door. I fear that when I open the door, I may see Jamshid standing there and saying: "Hello, Mother. Please call Urhan."

"Urhan is not at home."

"Call Ideen then."

Mother said: "I dread that he might come to see one of you and I might not see you again, as, sometimes, the dead come back to the world of the living and take one of the living with them."

Urhan replied: "Whenever he comes, tell him Yousef is around. Perhaps he will take him away and allow us to live in peace."

Mother retorted: "Has this got anything to do with you?"

Ideen intervened: "A foot that roams about too much is more likely to bump into a stone. So be careful, Urhan."

He then felt that his temples were stretching, pressing against his skull. He also felt that his hands were trembling. He had recalled Ida. He wondered why he thought, all the time, that he had witnessed the self-immolation of his sister. He clearly saw the flames rising from every part of Ida's body. It was late at night and there was no-one in the street. Not even the dogs were around. Only their distant barking could be heard. Sohrab was sitting in front of the closed door of the house, shouting and shrieking. Ida was burning and running. Nevertheless, she managed to turn her head towards Sohrab every now and then to make sure that he was not falling into the open gutter or being mauled by dogs. Then, the door opened and Mr Abadani ran outside. But it was too late. A pile of charred flesh was all that was left of Ida.

He then recalled that Abadani, weeping, dishevelled and wearing black, had followed the body to Ardabil. He would not dare surface. Afterwards, he picked up his son Sohrab and left for America. A year later, he wrote a letter, addressing Father, Mother, Ideen and Urhan, in which he apologised to them and said that he would repay his moral debt to Ida's legacy, that is, to Sohrab. He wrote that he would devote all his life to Sohrab and would never return to Iran. But no-one ever found out what had befallen Ida that had driven her to self-immolation. Even newspapers printed nothing in this regard.

He lit another cigarette. A few seconds later, the door opened and Mother came into the room. She asked: "Why aren't you coming upstairs."

"I'm not feeling well."

"What's happened? Have you and Urhan quarrelled again?"

"No, Mother. It is just that I am not in a good mood."

"What has happened then? Tell me."

"I suddenly thought of Ida."

"Yes. Ida. My poor Little Ida."

"What went wrong? Why did that happen?"

"I wish I knew. I wish I knew what she was suffering. But whatever it was, it was because of Abadani. Towards the end, they did not get on well with each other."

They both fell silent for a few seconds. Ideen was gazing at the ceiling but could not focus on anything. Mother sat on a step. She said: "This room is so gloomy. Even a healthy person would fall ill in here. Why don't you want to go back to your previous room?"

"I didn't like it there."

"Would you like me to make the big room ready for you?"

"No, no, Mother. I'll stay right here."

"Why have you become like this then?"

Ideen wished to be alone and to think of me. He was angry with himself as he could not stay anywhere away from home for any length of time. He said: "I have become like what, Mother?" He moaned as he breathed.

"All you do is think from dawn till dusk. You are introverted all the time. Shouldn't I know what you think about? Wouldn't you like me to write to your Uncle Nasser so that he can help you find some order in your life?"

"For God's sake, Mother, please don't talk about this again."

"You're destroying yourself."

"I can't make any decisions right now." He puffed vigorously on his cigarette and crushed the butt against the ashtray that was on his chest.

"I presume you want to think of Sormeh to the end of your life and, to your way of thinking, remain faithful to her."

Ideen was wary of saying "yes" because, in that case, Mother would have started giving him advice. She would have said: "Don't think of the dead." For that reason, he kept quiet. He was looking for me in his crowded mind. When Mother talked, he could think of me. He could remember me walking and on a swing. He could remember that rainy night and the Norooz new year celebration when I had made wet grain germinate on a plate. He said: "It hasn't been your practice to celebrate Norooz, has it?" And I replied: "From now on, it will be. And don't forget the Norooz present." He asked: "What would you like as a present?" I said: "Kiss me again." He kissed me. I said "Morellooo" and I laughed.

Mother had started walking about the room. She took two or three steps, reached a corner of the room, looked at the untidy pile of books there, turned back and looked at Ideen. Then she started moving back and forth again. She said: "Do you know that when you torture yourself like this, you also torment her soul."

"Sormeh is not dead, Mother."

"I am not telling you to forget her. No. Love her if you so wish. Think of her. But think of yourself a little as well. Look." She sat on the edge of the bed and continued talking: "Urhan is an avaricious, money-loving sort of fellow. Like your late father, he only thinks about the business. He thinks about his nuts and seeds all the time. He would be so happy if you were not around so that he could own everything on his own. But I want both of you to have a decent, regular life from now on. I don't want either you or Urhan to be the loser. But you are treating your life like child's play. I am so ill. And I worry about what could happen to you if I drop dead. For so many years, I quarrelled with your father for your sake and, now, I have to suffer at the hands of that monster of a son. Why? Because you don't want to defend yourself and protect your rights. As soon as you hear the slightest unkind word, you withdraw. Why?"

Ideen lit another cigarette and kept staring at the ceiling. I was lost in a big melee in his mind. Everybody was lost. The more he tried to remember what I had told him in Armenian, the less he could. The room was filled with smoke. Mother opened the curtain and opened the door: "For my sake, try not to think about the past."

He sat up and looked outside. The ravens sitting on the severed branches of the pine trees were so still that it seemed time had gone back to many years ago, drying up and standing still at a certain point in time. Ideen was 14 years old. He had his brown school bag with him. He was sitting on the steps of the downstairs passageway. He was eating bread with something. Then he went to the shop. Father would not ask how or when he studied. But he knew that Ideen studied well. His only concern was to make Ideen interested in the shop and the business. He had said: "Keep yourself busy with some work all the time. The body should get used to this."

During school holidays, Ideen worked in the shop. He washed the floor, blocked mouse holes with cement and plaster, re-arranged price tags or attended to customers. Urhan, having lodged himself under Father's desk, used wood and nails to make miniature boxes and chairs. Occasionally, Father bent down to see what was going on under his desk and saw Urhan nailing two pieces of wood together. He asked: "What are you doing, my boy?"

"I'm making a nest."

"For whom?"

"For the birds."

"Why don't you work, my boy?"

Urhan used his hammer to drive a nail into a piece of wood and said: "Is this not work?"

Father laughed, picked up a handful of pistachio nuts and stretched his hand below the desk. Urhan brought his little box forward so that Father could fill it with the pistachio nuts. Ideen was eyeing the whole scene from the other side of the shop. Father was well aware that he was watching. In the evening of the same day, he had told Mother: "He is so proud. Although he works well and studies well, he is full of pride. One feels tempted to break his pride."

Mother said: "Why do you smoke so much? You never used to smoke, did you?"

Ideen replied: "I don't know." And he lit his cigarette. He tried to remember the day when I had told him: "Oh, no. Who am I to teach you what to do? I only wish to see you tidy and well-dressed."

He said: "Tonight, I intend to ask your father's permission to marry you."

I replied: "We are not worthy of you."

"You are everything in my life."

"We will get married twice: Once in the church and once in the Marriage Registry."

"What flowers would you like?"

"Why?"

"I wish to give you a bouquet of flowers."

I liked all flowers. I also liked all combinations of flowers.

He puffed vigorously at his cigarette and said "what a pity" to himself. He then looked at Mother. He wanted to pay attention to Mother for a few seconds in order to say something or hear something. But he again remembered my pale face and my constant feeling of nausea. Then, the blackness of my eyes got bigger and bigger until it covered my entire face. He could recall almost nothing in that blackness. The only thing he could recall was Ida. But, by the time she could make an appearance, she had been reduced to a crumpled pile in the middle of the flames.

He lowered his head and looked down. Again, he saw my eyes and, then, my face that was the colour of quince blossoms. He also saw my ears and their lobes. He recalled that he always tickled my earlobes with his tongue and this made me feel uncomfortable. He picked up a pencil and said: "Let me reproduce the beauty spot on your lip." I had a little black beauty spot above the right hand corner of my upper lip. With his pencil, he made me another one on the left hand side. It was painful, but I didn't say anything. I let him make the artificial beauty spot darker and more pronounced. I looked in the mirror and I laughed.

He said: "It doesn't look good at all. Wipe it off. Let me wipe it off."

"Leave it for a while."

"No. It was my fault. I should have known that beautiful things cannot be reproduced."

"Please don't make fun of me."

"Don't you trust me?"

Symphony of the Dead

At the same instant, an image of Mother appeared in his mind. Her chador had fallen on to her shoulders and she was sitting on the bottom step of the staircase leading to the basement room. She was silent.

He puffed at his spent cigarette for the last time and tried hard to remember. I did not appear in his mind, except in the form of a white piece of cloth covering what he called a delicate body. Now, a swollen corpse that had turned blue was lying on the mosaic floor of the hospital in front of his eyes. He had said: "It would have been so good if man could struggle against death."

"How?"

"In a way that would show that he doesn't want to die. A real struggle."

"That's impossible. Death is not the same every time. Each time, it acquires a new shape."

In his mind, he wanted me to say: "You are dreaming." I did say: "You are dreaming." He threw his cigarette butt away and he moistened his fingertips with his tongue. He noticed that Mother was looking at him.

He said: "The world is hollow and worthless. It's worth nothing."

I said: "Say nice things. The world is not worthless. The only thing is that it is so difficult to live like a true, worthy human being."

He said: "Yes." And he wanted me to say "No. The world is not worthless. It is not a difficult place either. You are dreaming." And I did say: "The world is not worthless. It is not a difficult place either. You are dreaming." I said this slowly and word for word. Then I laughed. He wished to see me sitting on the swing and laughing. I did sit on the swing and I did laugh. The wind was playing with my hair. I asked: "Aren't you going to swing?"

"No."

He was sitting at the edge of the pond. He was wearing jade-green clothes. There was mist and it was about to rain. I said: "*Lava*?"

He answered: "*Lava.*"

Mother said whatever she wanted to say. As always, she returned to cooking and washing up. Ideen tried to think of Father. It seemed to be only yesterday when Father, with his slight body, came back home from the shop and went up the stairs slowly and with difficulty while he was still wearing his dark grey overcoat and his black *papakha*. But despite his imposing presence and his awe-inspiring character, he suddenly disappeared from Ideen's mind and turned into a few bones under the ground, in the town's old cemetery. No matter whom he thought about, the result was the same. The image suddenly flew away and gave way to something else. Even my pale face would not stand still for a moment in his mind and, as a result, he could not look at me properly in his mind. In times gone by, he could think for hours about whatever or whoever he remembered. He could construct the image, talk to it and destroy it. But during the past month, and, especially, during the past few days, whatever could happen to him had done so. Therefore, he thought of Father and, then, of his own childhood. He visualised himself, as a child, diving into the pond from the upper floor veranda and he recalled Father, wanting to throw his child out of the house. In his mind, he also visualised the childhood of his dejected, hallucinating brother. He saw the Russian aircraft and the blue-clad parachutists descending, softly and slowly, from the sky. Perhaps they were descending just to destroy that ten-year-old child. Father disappeared. He then reappeared wearing different clothes. He so much wished he could say all these things to Mother. Eating and sleeping were not all that there was to life all the time. There were also delicate, subtle things he could not tell Mother about.

Father asked: "Why didn't you become the top pupil of your class?"

"Well, I am second from the top."

"Can't you be the first?"

"Yes, I can."

"Then become the first." He was concocting some sort of old potion for his own backache and his children's aching legs. He pounded pistachio nuts, hazelnuts, walnuts and almonds in a mortar, dissolved the mixture in milk and drank two glasses of the solution, one after the other. Ideen remembered this vividly, as if it had happened just yesterday. Father called his children: "Come and drink it." He gave a glass each to Ideen, Ida and Urhan. Urhan, sitting on Father's lap, peed on the spot. Father said: "Where did this child inherit his habits from?" He was angry. He went outside, washed his legs and changed his trousers. He then sat down where he had been sitting before. Mother was making trousers for the children on her sewing machine and Ida was busy doing her homework and writing her exercises. Mother said: "He has inherited his habits from you. His peeing, I don't know."

Father grumbled: "Alright. Now get up and get him changed. A big six-year-old child still peeing in his trousers..."

The furnace-like heater snored in a corner of the room, sending smoke towards the sky. Father told Ideen: "If you succeed in becoming the top pupil in your class, I'll buy you a bicycle."

That year, Ideen studied day and night. The Ministry of Education gave his photograph to the newspapers and they printed it. Father had placed the photograph, cut from the newspaper, under the glass sheet covering his desk. He proudly showed it to his customers, saying: "You see? It says Ideen Urkhani, with the average mark of 20 out of 20."

But Father did not buy Ideen a bicycle that year or any other year.

He raised his head. Mother had gone. A sharp stench, resulting from chain-smoking, had remained in his moustache. He had no idea why he had come back home. He got up in order to go to the shop. Mother called him from the kitchen window: "Where are you going?"

"To the shop."

"It's night already. Urhan will be back home at any moment. I am about to serve dinner."

He went back to the basement. Amidst the silence of early evening, the chanting of the muezzin and the monotonous purring of the electric fan factory could be heard. It sounded like a meaningless snore. This was the night shift. One felt that the factory, lying at the bottom of that pit, wanted to go further down and bury itself. But it had been lying there for years. It neither disappeared under ground nor rose up. The only thing that happened all the time was that the GMC vans carried the electric fans up the slope and away.

He lay down on the bed and looked at the ceiling. He liked the *putshka* more than he liked me. But later on, after I began visiting him, his views and his feelings changed. He asked: "How old are you?"

I replied: "What's your guess? How old would you like me to be?"

"Twenty-two."

"I am not that young."

"How old are you then?"

"I am three years older than you are."

"How old am I?"

I gave him the correct answer. He was delighted. He was really pleased. He asked: "How do you know?"

"A raven informed me." And I laughed. He was delighted. I laughed again, whole-heartedly. He was thoroughly delighted. His delight had no end. He wanted me to carry on laughing. But I said: "The Jesus Christ of the Tatar tribe."

And now, I was lost in the ceiling of his room. He closed his eyes. He wanted me to laugh in the way I had laughed on that day. I did laugh. Then, Ida was standing in my place. A black chador fully covered her face. She said: "My dear brother, I would rather die than see you unhappy. What are you unhappy about? Would you like to come to Abadan and stay with us?"

"No Ida. I am going. I must leave this town before I perish and die."

"Why?"

But his wish was never fulfilled. He never saw Ida to tell her: "They burnt my books, my writings, my poems. Do you understand, Ida? They burnt my beloved poems."

Ida said: "I would rather die than see you in such distress."
Ideen asked: "Who have you come with?"
"I have come on my own."
"On your own? Where is Sohrab? Where is Abadani?"
Ida ran, burnt and ran again. In whatever direction she ran, she burnt. She shrieked and she melted in the middle of the flames. Her child cried at the doorstep. Then, they dug her grave under a cypress tree, at a spot that was less overcrowded with graves than other locations in the cemetery. They buried her.

Again, I arrived on the scene. I said: "You're a real pain in the neck. What am I to do about you?"
He replied: "Oh, say it. Keep saying it."
I said, in a staccato voice: "What…am…I…to…do?" He vividly remembered that I used to open up my right hand like the petals of a blossoming flower and say: "What am I to do?"
He said: "Sit down right here so that I can look at you."
I objected: "Oh, you are so irritating. You're killing me."
He said: "Let's go. Everybody's waiting."
We set out. A number of our neighbours were waiting for us at the entrance to the church. When we arrived, everyone clapped. We entered the church and stood in front of the altar. The priest conducted the wedding vows.

The next day, we went to an Islamic marriage registry. Grandmother, Father and Uncle Galoost were there too. A man wearing a white turban was sitting at the desk and inspecting the certificates of identity. He asked me: "Excuse me. Are you a Christian?"
"Yes."
"What about the bridegroom? He is a Muslim, I hope."
Ideen replied: "Yes. I am a Muslim."
"This can't be done, can it? I can't administer the vow of matrimony."
I asked: "What are we to do then?"
"Become a Muslim."
"Okay. I become a Muslim."
"In that case, say 'Ashhado a'llaa elaaha ella'laah.'". I did. He then said: "Say 'Ashhado ana Mohammadan Rasoul ol'laah'." I did. He went on to say: "Say 'Ashhado ana Aliyyan vali ol'laah'." I did. He said: "Congratulations. May this be auspicious for you." He then administered the marriage vows.

The entrance door to the house could be heard being opened and closed. A few seconds later, Mother said: "Dinner is ready."

He went to the room upstairs and sat at the table. Urhan asked: "Are you feeling better?"

"I am better."

"You must rest. If there is sunshine tomorrow, we will go to Veela Darreh together to get some fresh air. I think it will do you good."

Ideen said: "I am too devastated to benefit from such things, brother."

Mother said: "Eat."

He ate two or three mouthfuls and went back to the basement. On his way down, he heard Urhan saying: "Early in the morning. Very early in the morning."

He said: "Very well." And he crept into his room. Again, he lay on the bed. He saw me lying on a cold, tiled floor with a white piece of cloth covering my body. He struggled to convince me not to come to him in that condition. But, again, I appeared to him in the same condition. He lay down and I arrived.

They carried us round the town in a two-horse carriage. Father shook hands with both of us and kissed us. Thereafter, Uncle Galoost, too, shook hands with us and kissed us. We then went to our own room.

He said: "I am looking for myself in the past. We used to have things that we no longer have."

There was no-one there to reply to him. He said "Sormelina" so that I would say "My dear".

Madam Yevgineh said: "I was dreaming of you last night."

I asked: "What was I doing?"

"It was a good omen. I dreamed that Mr Ideen had adorned your ears with a pair of beautiful filigree earrings."

I told Ideen that I was pregnant and, on the same day, he bought me a pair of filigree earrings. He hung them on my ears with his own hands. He then stood aside and looked at me in such a way that the only thing I could do was to put my head on his chest.

We then went on a trip. There was no-one at home and I was seven months into my pregnancy. I said: "This is your child. Do you want a boy or a girl?"

"A girl."

We set out the next day.

The doctor, wearing his white coat and his small black-rimmed spectacles, came forward: "Please."

Ideen squatted down, removed the white cloth from my face and gazed at the face. He looked very carefully. The forehead and the area under the eyes looked bruised and blue. The face was swollen and yellow and, at the periphery, somewhat blue. The hair was wet and untidy.

The doctor said: "This is the only corpse that has been delivered to us during this period."

His heart beat fast and his hands trembled. He said: "It is not this one, doctor. Believe me, this is the one. But I am sure that it is not this one."

It was now exactly seven months that Sooren's coffee shop had been closed and the church bell had been silent. He said: "Where are you then, Sormelina?" He had scoured all places: hospitals, the Police Headquarters, the mortuary and all the other places where I could have been.

I opened up my left hand that had a ring with a turquoise stone on the middle finger. I passed my fingers through his hair and said: "My darling, my darling."

He said: "Where are you?" And he cried.

I said: "My darling."

He stretched his hand above his head and switched the light off. Despite the darkness, he saw me passing my fingers through his hair. He wanted me to say "My darling."

I said: "My darling, my darling."

Fourth Movement

Abbas Maroufi

Symphony of the Dead

If Esmayol were not around, who else would call me Sooji? Urhan, too, calls me Sooji. He also calls me the big imbecile. He says: "What are you doing here, big imbecile?" I fancy some tea. Oh, my brother! Think of life. Think of the days of sorrow. An icicle had formed at the tip of my nose. I said "Bang" and the suspended icicle broke. Brother, I have vowed to God to make an endowment of one candle and two chandeliers if God protects you from catching a cold. One on this side, one on the other side. Is that you brother? Well, tell me. I want nothing of..."

I was in a big town. It had big houses with vast, bright and cheerful gardens, like the gardens of princes. Sormelina said: "Would you like to see my parents?" I answered: "Can't I skip that?" She replied: "No. You must see them."

We went into the biggest room of the house. Sormelina was sitting there. We had arrived in a horse-drawn carriage. Akhavan Garden was covered with frost. It had big rocks in it. It looked like a mountain range. Sormelina's mother was tall, but she could not walk. She had grown out of the soil, like a tree. Her sap had oozed out of her branches.

The chains have left their impression on my hands. There were a thousand people there and a thousand chains. A thousand ravens were sitting on branches, gazing at *Mirza* Ideen Urkhani. I change my voice and I talk like Russian soldiers. Brother! It is time to pack up. Destruction and desolation have broken their bounds. When did they break their bounds? It is the fault of the alleys. Do you see? No, you don't see. Do you see? All the alleys twist and turn like a maze. That one is Mr Lord. He is walking along a cobbled alley. He then descends. His feet are on the sky above the paving and his head is writhing on the ground. It is as if his photo has been printed on water.

After I set out in the morning, I'll pick up as many pieces of wood as I can find. We will burn them in a brazier. Don't make so much smoke, Esmayol. Very well, Mr Urhan. Oh. I am suffocating.

I said: "Get out of the water." He said: "You fool, I am suffocating from the smoke." I said: "Well, don't smoke." He slapped my face, on both cheeks. Big imbecile. What business of mine is this? When my hands are not tied up, I read a newspaper or a letter. I used to scale these very railings. Not me. Yousef used to scale the railings. He used to dive into the pond. Father said: "You, son of a bitch! You should be ashamed of yourself. Instead of doing this, go and burn the kids' books using your magnifying glass. Who extinguished the war? The one who was looking for love. He filled the pond with…"

I wish I could become Hitler for one day. I would decree that whatever people have does not belong to them; they belong to God. And we represent God. Divine glory applies to us as well. We have books too. They are on their way. Whenever you gave me an old sheepskin hat, I wore it on my head and went to the closed coffee shop. I said: "Monsieur, *lava*?" "*Lava*.". Germany, too, had made good progress. Father said if he were Hitler's secretary, the outcome of the war would be different. I said: "Father, the light in the room upstairs has gone off." What did Father say? He said: "Change the bulb." Where was it? In the room upstairs. Not this one. The one in which the cats have given birth to their kittens.

Have you got newly arrived old magazines, sir? What about today's, with a picture of Hitler? Sormelina wouldn't let go of my hand. Her father was there too. Her father's voice had frozen. Sormeh's father was Sormeh's father but he wasn't Monsieur Sooren. He was a bad-tempered man, one of those men who wear striped, brown suits and who look like small letters of the French alphabet.

According to the latest news, a new country has been discovered in the southern hemisphere. It is called Boorani. They have even signed an oil contract with them. Every day, a great number of ships bring chairs and carry the oil away. They have put their fingerprints on to the contract. Its ambassador wants to come here. He has said he intends to arrive on a trip and find out whether he can get himself cured in the waters of the Shoorabi. He is suffering from rheumatism. Ida, too, had rheumatism. She died. What did Mother suffer from? She suffered from asthma. She died. This person has got rheumatism. The pain starts at his waist and goes into his legs. It turns round again, goes back to his waist and ends up in his shoulders. He is just stuck on all fours. I said: "Where is this Boorani, brother? I have looked hard for it on my map but I have not found it. I don't remember having heard its name in my geography lessons at school." Urhan said: " I think it's over there." I said: "What? I thought it was over here." He laughs his heart out. Again, we look for it on the map but we don't find it. Instead, we discover a new land. It borders Boorani on the north side. One side of it is desert. It borders the sea on the south side. What we haven't accounted for is the left side. On the left, there is an expanse of land covered with trees. It is an apricot orchard but nobody owns it. They intend to arrive and conquer it. The fate of this orchard will be decided by the outcome of the war. My brother Urhan says if the heirs put their fingerprints on it, it will be all over. I said: "Tell me, brother. Why are there 24 hours in a day?"

I said: "Tell me, brother. Isn't this Christopher Columbus of ours dead yet?" He asked: "Why?" I said: "He roams about and discovers new lands. Why doesn't he come here to discover our place?" I then went on to shout: "Mr Christopher Columbus! Why don't you come to discover us?" Chris-dom-Koloft, Chris-dom-Koloft. One is reminded of the mammoths. But I am not a human being, am I? It is for this reason that I don't think of the mammoths. I think of the dinosaurs instead. I then think of my own *Dayee* Nasser who is from the generation of speechless sheep.

My brother Nasser is a meek, harmless man. He is living alone in that alien town. Do you want me to arrange a marriage between you and his daughter? No, Mother. I swear to my ancestors, I am not telling a lie, my brother. You should be ashamed of yourself, you big imbecile! Alright, I will be ashamed of myself. As soon as I see him, my limbs begin trembling and I forget what I intended to say. Well, he has managed to get himself into our circle. What business is that of mine?

We are frail, delicate people. We resemble smoke. Father said I should behave like a civilised child. What shape or form is a civilised child? If you want to know to whom the book originally belonged, read the footnotes. Mr Lord closes his factory on Sundays. Mr Lord has passed away. Let us remember him with respect. Oh, Father! I know that, one day, the breeze generated by Lord's electric fans will blow all of us away.

He was breathing his last. What a harsh snoring sound came out of his throat! I wonder how he had breathed his first. The town was in total chaos. If I become prime minister, I will give all my cabinet posts to women. Then, I will go to Moscow and become a political refugee, as we no longer have any country to talk about. Don't laugh so much, Ayaz. Are you Uncle Saber? Your hair is now threadbare. What happened to your hope then? I'll stay in that basement. Eventually, one day…

I kissed you in front of the House of God. I kissed you in front of the House of God. The dead can lie down and sleep in whatever way they wish. What a good idea to enter the drainpipe from the outlet and come out on the rooftop. Tall and good for nothing, like Jamshid? No. What business is it of mine? Let them chain my hands and feet. It is for my own good, no doubt.

The town was big. Sormelina's house was like a museum. A number of people were entangled with each other. Half of their bodies were rotten because of leprosy. Each looked like a rock torn apart, like a tree chopped here and there, like chewing gum. They were twisted and entangled with each other, like small letters of the French alphabet. The second letter had no head. In place of the head, there was a big, dried-up wound on its neck. Like chewing gum, like a tree chopped here and there.

Sormelina said: "This is my uncle." She showed me a person who looked like a small letter of the French alphabet. But he was very big. They were all big. Their sap was oozing out of them, like the sap of cut trees. I wished to touch them, but I had become very heavy. I wished to get myself some bread with fresh herbs.

I wished to open a police station and employ a few policemen. I would then appoint Ayaz as the head of the security police. I would send them on patrols. I would pay them one *tooman* for each patrol. This would be the best job in this chaotic situation. But Urhan wouldn't let me even talk about the scheme. Were it not for his opposition to the plan, we ourselves would constitute a platoon of soldiers. How far is Auschwitz from here? If we set out in the morning, we would be there late in the afternoon at the latest. We would get rid of that bloke and turn his furnaces into brick-kilns. And we would give one of the kilns to Urhan so that he could roast his watermelon seeds in there.

He said: "Use your finger." I did, but I couldn't vomit. He said: "Press your fingertip there." I did. "Press." "I will." I did. I placed my fingerprint on one hundred pages. I first did it for the title deed of the apricot orchard. Then the shop. Then the house. I said: "Brother, let the title deed of this basement remain in my name." He said: "I leave the basement to you. I leave the pine trees to you. I leave the ravens to you." I said; "I don't want any ravens. I don't want any swallows. I want some tea." "Okay, go and have some." "Okay, I'll go and have some." He reappears: "Big imbecile!" Well, my brother, sometimes I am a human being too."

Mother said: "I wonder why the taste of everything has changed. Even this sugar plum, my favourite, no longer has its usual taste." Urhan said: "You see, Mother, you have become paranoid. You are so pessimistic towards everything. Okay, I am a bad guy. But what about your sugar plums?" Go away, you, dishonourable rogue. Who was a dishonourable rogue? Well, what business is that of mine?

It was Hitler's mistress who caused his death. If Sormeh wants to irritate me, I might commit suicide. You look like a wreck now. I said: "Who will harvest a kiss from the rose of your lips?" "You." Oh, Mother! From now on, I

Symphony of the Dead

won't let you feel sorry for the dead. Who shall I feel sorry for then? Play me a melody in the *Mahoor* style so that I can cry. Oh, porters! Forward! In single file! Start: Left, right, left, right. They are now beneath those innocent, speechless sacks that have had their mouths sewn up. But the pistachio nuts? Oh, their mouths are wide open. Urhan's desk has got legs. It walks. It walks beautifully. Like this. I can't walk as well. Like this: Plod plod, plod plod. All tables and desks have legs. They can't be stopped. They take away whoever sits at them. Father was awe-inspiring. He said the sludge of Shoorabi cured every disease, especially rheumatism, exactly like opium. The difference is that although opium cures 70 diseases, it brings you a disease that has no cure.

Your brain is not working. Whose brain is not working? Mine? My mind makes bricks, from morning till night, in the brick-kiln. When it comes back to the room at night, it falls on the bed like a corpse. It lies down on its stomach and thinks for hours on end. And at the end of it all, it still wouldn't find out how old it is. He asked: "What time is it, sir?" I replied: "Last week, it was five o'clock." Listen, gentlemen. This country needs bread queues. There is nothing wrong with letting prostitutes earn their bread. You will even earn God's blessing. But does your honour allow you to sleep beside a prostitute at night? I spit on any dishonour.

It has now been long time since I last recognised you. How is that possible? I am me. Have you heard about the herald of the *hajjis*' caravan? The only thing that was lacking was someone to wound himself with a cutlass in mourning. One would feel one was about to burst under the pressure of sorrow and weeping. The only thing that has been allocated to us as our destiny is tears and lamentation. Our hearts are dying for a wedding reception. What was the name of his mistress? All Germans had died. The only one who had stayed alive was Hitler. Alone, he fought from morning till night and slept with his mistress from night till morning. It was that very woman who caused his death. Oh, I so wish that the world would stop suddenly, that everybody would freeze, that everybody would turn into an upright, lifeless nail stuck motionless in wood. Oh, peace be upon every nail! Don't blaspheme with your "peace be upon it". What shall I say, Father? Just say "nail, nail."

When you press your fingertip against the pupil of your eye, every tree turns into two trees, my two legs turn into four legs, there's an earthquake and Urhan gets drunk. It's possible to shake the whole world vigorously just with one finger. I had better go and stand in front of the mirror, take myself near the mirror and say, with a bad voice, bastard, bastard. I should say, with a voice rising from the depth of my throat: You bastard! You illegitimate child! Come forward so that I legitimise you. I summon legitimacy from the sky. The war:

You two on that side, we on this side. You turn so that we turn. When was it that we of Iran were called the Bridge of Victory?[19]

Remember, gentlemen, the fire of war was extinguished with the cold of Moscow. Apart from this, the important point is that the romanticists will come to power again. Don't ask me why. Ask your hearts. You see, brother? Father used to say: "A mischievous son resembles a sixth finger. If they cut it off, they will suffer pain. If they don't cut it off, it will be superfluous and ugly." Fullstop, next line. So, we duly wrote and arrived at the beginning of the next line. We were not around during the reign of Reza Shah to eat rationed bread. We used to present a red coupon and receive a loaf of black bread. Now, you can eat thick, white, good quality *barbari* bread. It's full of vitamins. Well, it wasn't Reza Shah's fault, was it? It was war, my friend. It was war. Oh, stop it and shut up. Tell me then, who created the university? Who built the roads? Who built the railways? And the National Bank? Shut up my friend. You aristocrats have a sumptuous dinner only on Thursday nights. But we, poor people, have great dinner on the eve of every Norooz.

I said: "Tell me, brother, who was a dishonourable rogue?" he said: "Don't say such things again. Go and repent. Go and rinse your mouth out so that it becomes clean and doesn't churn out such dirty talk." I have rinsed my mouth so many times that I feel like a colander. Listen my brother, people have done their shopping. They did it in the year of Father's death. You should change your job. Selling clothes is no good. The people I have seen will have sufficient clothes for a long time to come. They have got everything, from sheepskin hats to shoes. Look. A vest, one or two shirts, add a pullover. Also, a jacket, a pair of trousers, a waistcoat and an overcoat. Even if you fire a cannon, they won't care. They are all thick-skinned and resilient. When they are wearing their clothes, you won't be able to cut their thick necks even with an axe. Go and think of some other job. Go away, get lost and don't talk nonsense. Alright, I'll go away.

Are you Sormelina? Why don't you say hello then? They felled that beautiful plane tree and put a donkey's head in its place. I myself am such an ass. I wonder why I don't go to the Shoorabi teahouse to have two glasses of tea and to read a newspaper to the pilgrims. One on this side, one on the other side. What are you doing here, you, big imbecile? No, my brother. I want to avoid any situation that could cause you not to ever forgive me. He has a prisoner. You understand, don't you? Six months in the basement. And he blocks the windows with mud. Well, I'll make for the sea of the salt desert. It will be both for tourism and for commerce. When one goes to a seaport, one does not come back empty-handed. Buying and selling. Giving and getting. And what excellent merchandise. All brand new and profitable.

Symphony of the Dead

Sormeh says let us go. Her brother, too, was with us. Did she have a brother? Her father was a frowning sort of man. We set out. Vapour rose from the noses of the horses that pulled the carriage. We went to a little house. The streets sloped downward. They were cobbled and their surfaces looked like lead. The house had a high wall and a room. There was a samovar in a corner of the room. Sormeh lay on the bed. She said: "Touch me". I was afraid of touching her. It would have been sinful.

She took her socks off. Skin had been grafted to her ankles. She said: "I have grafted oranges to Seville oranges. The grafting may be successful; or maybe not. My father has done the grafting."

I realised that she had contracted leprosy. She said: "Touch me". I felt frightened. She said: "Sleep with me". I felt very frightened. I was about to start crying. She said: "Come and touch me". I said no. Her father said: "On what part of your body do you want me to do a grafting, my son?" I said: "You are all lepers." The town was the colour of lead. There was steam in the air. The streets were cobbled. It was sunset. Everybody had a leper in his house. They wore socks. Father's suit was striped, brown and navy blue. I shook the chains. I shook them. I said: "Why like this? What do you want to do with a man like me whose hands and feet are tied up?" There was no-one around. The ravens that had been sitting on this tree flew away. Did I cry?

Our column, eight abreast, moved forward. It was snowing. Father said: "If I were Hitler's adviser, the outcome of the war would be different." I said: "Father, the light in the room upstairs has gone off." "Change the bulb, my son." I said: "Where?" He said: "Forward to Moscow." He had grown a Hitler-style moustache. It suited him so well. A swastika was hanging over his stomach. He said: "Forward to the cold of Moscow!" A fire had burnt down everything. The grass was burning. Smoke was rising from treetops. A girl was using a stick to get her skirt down from the tip of burnt branches. I said "Sormeh!" She said: "It is me. It is Ida." She was Sormeh and Ida at the same time. An icicle had formed at the tip of my nose. I said "bang". The icicle broke. Drink Turkish coffee. Don't sleep. Revise your lessons. Write: The Barmaki Dynasty[20]. We wrote 'The Barmaki Dynasty'. I got up and moved about to find out how many marks I had been awarded for my orthography. I said: "Oh, brother. Do you have to tie me up?" But I didn't actually utter those words. I only said them to myself. What business is it of mine?

Oh, Uncle Saber! What has become of your hope? Oh, Ideen, you are all my hope. Would you like to drink with me? Urhan asked: "Would you want me to chain you?" Oh, brother, the days are the same, but the times have changed. Would you believe that Ida has set herself on fire? Where is the world of the dead? It is in the subsoil. Forward to the subsoil! Forward to the basement! What about these newspapers? When Mother sees the impression of the chains on my hands, she begins to cry for no reason at all. Have you got newly arrived old magazines, sir? Go away, you, stupid nuisance. A car had strayed on to the pavement. Progress from Lord's fan making industry. Tell me then, who built the Palace of Justice? Who built the railways? Were it not for the Germans, what would we have? I shouted: "Brother! Brother!" "What is it? Aren't you asleep yet?" "No. The light in this basement has gone off." He changed the bulb. One gets lit up. One gets enlightened. Oh, my dear uncle, turn the switch on so that you get enlightened. For goodness sake, don't beat me, brother. God has already beaten me. He clasps his hands behind him and walks. He gazes at the stars. I said: "A lazy person becomes either an astronomer or a star expert." Shut up.

The aforementioned person was a high-ranking SS officer. He escaped after Hitler was defeated. The Polish Liberation army is looking for the aforementioned person day and night. I pray to God that he is not captured by these atheists. If he is captured by them, they will cut him to pieces. War is war, isn't it? You hit your opponent with your fist and he hits you back twice with his fist. You always get one blow more than your enemy gets from you. This is the law of nature. It is a pity that our Mr Lord passed away. Otherwise, he would bring his electric fans to the seaport, give them to the Portuguese and, in return, get pencils and chalk from them. Believe me, our kids do not have chalk to write with on the blackboard. We always cut every pencil in half so that more pupils could share them. Sir, you are the Head of the Education Department, so I am complaining to you. We have no chalk. We have no paper. Well, buy some, gentlemen. It makes no sense to say that you haven't got them. They stick so much paper on walls and doors. Well, they can give the paper to the children. There was a piece of paper, with the heading 'NOTICE', on the lamppost. Honest partner needed. Address: Shah Ismail Avenue, Qarahsu Alley, next to the Brick Workshop, Haqiqat Balloon Factory. I got myself there at midday. I said: "It is I." "Who are you?" "An honest partner." "Very well. I provide the capital. You provide the labour." I started on the same day. By the time night had fallen, I had made 145 balloons and burst them. He said: "Why have you done this, boy?" I said: "When you blow into them, they always explode with your last puff. Always remember to tie the inlet with a piece of string just before your last puff." He slapped me. On this side.

Whenever I have indigestion, I chew a handful of wild rue or some other herb. I also drink a glass of water. Then I see people shrunk to no bigger than an open hand. They walk about in the alleys and climb walls and doors. One

Symphony of the Dead

of them was making his way into our neighbour's house through the drains. I was about to get hold of his wrist in order to stop him. But I said to myself: "What has this got to do with me?" But Hitler acts cleverly. He ordered Germans to eat wild rue. Subsequently, he shrank to a size no bigger than an open hand and he made his escape. They say he is roaming about in the province of Sistan and Baluchestan in south-eastern Iran. He is wearing Baluchi tribal costumes, has grown a handlebar moustache and has become a true Zaboli, looking like any other male inhabitant of Zabol. May God damn the father of every adulterer! I had better go to Sistan and Baluchestan and find him. One on this side, one on that side. What are you doing here, you, big imbecile?

To my dear friend Mr Shah: Where was that ruined hall? What tune does he play? He is a young man in love who has got nothing from his youth, just like me. Whoever arrives slaps me. He was an officer in the regiment. He was walking with his wife. I said: "*Uz ishidi.*" He slapped my face straightaway. I cried. I cried my heart out. Oh, my God, you have so many stars and, despite that, you have never told off *Mirza* Ideen, not even as much as telling him to coax his chickens back into the chicken coop. And, yet, look at this officer brother of ours who has only three stars on his epaulettes and is arrogant enough to slap me so hard.

Ardabil is colder at night. Regarding that, a person who is chained inevitably wets himself and what he is lying on. I wet myself three times: Three cheers to the health of my brother! Let me press my finger against the pupil of my eye. Undo my chains brother. Undo them. They are killing me. By the glory of God, if you tie up even an elephant with these chains, it will be over.

"Don't talk nonsense. Take it with tea."

First Movement

2

It was about midnight when he dreamed that his mother was coming towards him. She was wailing. Urhan stood aside and said: "No, no." Mother shouted: "I will disown you. I will sell the house, the shop and the apricot orchard and I will give the proceeds to Ida." Urhan walked over dried stinging nettle leaves and said: "You are saying strange things, Mother. You are dead. Ida is dead." Then, Mother disappeared and a wind began to blow, shaking the yellowed leaves of the plane tree. Ideen kept sticking his head out of the basement to find out what was going on. His index finger was between two pages of his book but he had hidden his hand behind the wall. He asked: "What's going on?" Urhan laughed and said: "Oh, there you are. I was looking for you." Yousef ate bread, ate dried mud and stared with his eyes wide open. Urhan held the iron handrailing of the staircase and counted. He went up 21 steps.

The drawing room had been adorned with pink muslin curtains. The wind made the curtains fly into the room. In the middle of the room, there was a set of luxury armchairs made of expensive brown material. The armchairs had been arranged around a Kashan carpet. In the middle of the carpet, there was a table made of patterned tiles. At the top of each leg of the table, the head of a wild goat had been sculpted. But the vase in the middle of the table was empty. The black, vast opening of the vase appeared to be about to devour everything. A black wind drove the curtains to the middle of the room and a cold, whip-like breeze tended to crack one's skin. Next to the window, a half-naked woman was standing in the midst of the billowing curtains. The curtains were her sole cover. She turned back and looked at Urhan. She was chewing gum. She said: "Two handsome children." She tried to cover her tall figure with the curtains but the wind would not let her. She looked rather thin and pale. Her blonde hair was in curls. She had the same appearance that she used to have whenever she got out of her bath, with the same dignified, slow movements.

Urhan asked: "Are you Azar?"

The woman said: "Azar has flown from this world." She laughed.

Urhan said: "Come." He was full of desire, anger and vindictiveness. A suppressed desire made him very impatient. He said: "I must talk to you."

A black wind drove the curtains to the middle of the room. Urhan rearranged his *papakha* on his head and gazed at the woman's naked body. Father said: "Very well." He got up from his armchair, knocked on the table-top with his knuckles and said: "Eight thousand *toomans*."

Mother exclaimed: "Eight thousand *toomans*?" She raised her eyebrows, each to a different height.

Father said: "How much did you have in mind then, woman?"

Mother laughed and her gold teeth showed. She asked: "Is it not made in Qom?"

Father said: "No. It is made in Finland."

Urhan put his hand into his waistcoat pocket and stood in front of Father: "Let it come out of my account. I want these armchairs."

Mother said: "What?" She sat on one of the armchairs, forgetting to cover her thin, white knees. She leant her left leg, or perhaps her right leg, against the edge of the table and let her arms hang from the two arms of the chair on which she was sitting. She then moved her head slightly backwards so that she could cover all the armchairs with her eyes. She had difficulty breathing. Her breathing sounded like a rough snore. She was suffering from asthma. She said: "Very well. In that case, get an armchair like one of these for Ideen as well."

Urhan said: "Ideen? He's not around, is he?"

Mother said: "He's in the basement."

Urhan explained: "No, Mother. He is not there. It is now two or three years since he left this house."

Mother said: "He'll come back one day. I am trying to bring him back. He will need a set of armchairs like these."

Urhan, lounging on one of the armchairs, said: "If you manage to find them, buy a set for me too."

Father said: "Out of the question."

The wind lifted the curtains and made the chandeliers jingle. Azar could no longer be seen. The memory of her figure tormented Urhan. He had become restless. The clink-clank of a two-horse carriage could be heard from the alley.

Symphony of the Dead

The horses' hooves got stuck in mud every now and then. The cold was bitterly cruel. Urhan said: "Close those windows, Azar." Somebody closed the windows. But the cold was not from outside. He said: "Also put a blanket on me." He turned back. There was no-one in the room and Urhan ground his teeth severely because of the extreme cold.

He rolled over. The cold sides of the manger hurt the skin on his face. He raised his head. It was dark. And, now, Mother was lying under tons of earth and snow. He asked: "Where are you?"

There was no-one around. The old man had taken the pack-saddles and the horses and mules. What was his name? He was a native of the village of Ram Asbi or maybe some other place. It would be quite easy to teach him a lesson he would never forget. The bastard! It would be possible to get rid of him by spending just two thousand *toomans*. He shouted: "Where are you, old man?" No. There was no-one around. The only sound that could be heard was the howling of wolves. Water dripped from the roof.

He had a headache. He got out of the manger and, surrounded by darkness, managed to get himself to the door. The snowdrifts had advanced as far as the middle of the stables. But it was no longer snowing. When had it snowed? How much more snow was to be endured? A dazzling whiteness irritated the eyes.

He looked at the sky. He found no sign of light. Whatever he feared during his childhood had come to pass. He saw a coffin carried by four white-clad, pale, stupefied people. They came forward harmlessly. They moved so slowly that they appeared to be almost stationary. Their gaze, expressionless and from the depth of their eye sockets, was concentrated on him. He held on to the door-frame in order not to fall over. The only thing that could comfort him was to shout, but no sound would come out of his mouth. He wished to scream until doomsday, continuously, without any respite.

The cold had stayed on and settled in the dark space of the stable. If he could walk in snow, he would no doubt feel less cold. He could push the snow aside, dig the earth and go down into the warm earth beneath the snow. He could thus move into the region where the soil breathed. He could breathe warm air in and he could then breathe out, letting his warm breath slide over the snow. His body was too lax and too heavy to allow him run with his imagination. He took a step backward and, in that darkness, pounded his feet on the ground. He did it again. He waved his hands and arms in the air, put his sheepskin hat in a corner, undid the buttons on his overcoat and began worrying again. He had to stop his shivering somehow. All his life he had tried not to suffer from heat, cold or hunger. All his life he had tried hard to attain honour and credibility and never to let his spirit die. He had endeavoured to go to the shop every morning wearing the same overcoat and the same sheepskin hat that he was wearing now, to have his lunch, go back home, lie down on his bed for a couple of hours in his room on the upper floor and go back to the shop in the afternoon. He always wished that, on his way back home in the evening, he could walk in a different manner from that of other people. He wished to walk in a such a dignified way that when people said hello to him, he could greet them in reply without looking at them. But now that it was ordained that he should die, he did not want to die in these circumstances. He wished to die surrounded by his family members, all crying loudly in deep sorrow, and he wished to have enough time to divide the estate among the beneficiaries: My dear Uncle, I want you and your brother to come to terms amicably over owning it jointly. But you must take care of it. It should be irrigated regularly and its wall should not be allowed to fall to pieces. Some bastards stole some of its bricks a few months ago. You should take care of the big mulberry tree that has a hole in its trunk. You should not let it die. I like that tree. As for the house, my maternal aunts and my maternal uncle should come to an agreement. The furniture shall belong to my paternal aunt. She is old. She may transfer it to her children. But the shop! What shall I say? What can I say? I have dedicated all my life to the shop, every day, from morning till night. I have sacrificed my youth for the sake of the shop. I could still take a wife but I am single. You know that, don't you? Now wait a while and don't do anything. I'll think about the shop.

He could divide the remainder of his estate among a number of people in order to boost his popularity so that he would be mourned even by the flying birds. That doctor had better go. This doctor had better come. Doctors of Tehran, doctors of Germany, doctors of Israel. They can cure people by placing their hands on them. Ideen used to say: "They say that whatever they touch, it turns to ashes. That's why they've made a mess of the whole world." They should come to his bedside, take his pulse and listen to his heart. What disease was he going to die from? Whatever. Say diabetes or cancer. Not cancer. It's a horrible disease that leads to a horrible death. He had heard from someone that fat people died either of hypertension or of a heart attack. If he had been able to keep himself to Ideen's weight, he would now be a thin, swarthy, Tatar-looking man who would die of a stomach ulcer at worst. No. No. Foreign doctors would cure him just with an injection. And he could go to the shop again, give orders to the assistants, buy the shop at the corner of the hall and remove the partition between the two shops. He could order Martha the beggar to leave the step at the corner of the hall and sit a bit further away.

Symphony of the Dead

He could change the nameplate of the shop. He could order a new nameplate saying, in very large letters, 'Urhan's Nuts and Dried Fruit Emporium'. He could install powerful lights and employ a dozen apprentices. There would be wheelbarrows and everything. There would be a vast clientele and a noisy, lively atmosphere. But this time, with a walking stick. That, in itself, would be an attraction. It bestows awe and grandeur. When one limps along, people don't just casually say hello. They follow you and ask questions on the state of your health: "Have you tried Dr Aftandalian, Mr Urhan?" "I wanted to come and pay my respects yesterday. I wish to have a word with you." "Say it, my dear. Say it." "Dr Shooshanik is not bad either. He could revive a dead man." "My dear boy, your father was a close friend of mine. May God bless his soul. Why do you look so old so early in life?" "It is out of sorrow for my brother." "Well. Well, the Russian Dr Nayadanov…" "He's dead." Let them die. Let them all drop dead. How much torment can one expect from life?

I said: "My dear Ideen, listen to me. You have turned 40. You should not frequent this type of teahouse any longer." He kept turning up right here, as if his life depended on this teahouse. But they no longer paid any attention to him. They no longer listened to him when he read his newspaper to them. They got bored and they would not even serve him a glass of tea. He was unhappy about their behaviour. Nevertheless, he kept coming. I said: "Whenever you want tea, drink it in the souk. It will be on me."

"I drink the sort of tea that would be worth pissing out afterwards."

It is now about two years since he last came here. It was autumn and there was a light rain. I was not around but I took a taxi in order to go to him. He was sitting outside the teahouse and his legs were red with cold. He said: "I'm freezing."

"Why don't you go inside?"

"Mashd Abbas is no more." He brought his hands out from under his jacket and said: "There is a caravan behind and a caravan in front."

While Mashd Abbas was still around he took Ideen inside, poured him some tea, listened to him and, at lunchtime, served him a stew. Mashd Abbas used to come to the shop occasionally. Whenever he did, I gave him pistachio nuts and watermelon seeds as a sign of appreciation for his kindness to Ideen. But two years ago, after Mashd Abbas had become old and bedridden, a Turk from Tabriz rented the teahouse. To hell with him. He has made a mess of the place. He was bad-tempered and unfriendly. I told him: "Oh, brother! Why don't you let our Sooji come inside?"

"We are busy. We are in no mood for this sort of thing."

"But he's harmless, isn't he?"

"I told you. I have a headache. I am in no mood for this."
We turned back. Ideen said: "Let's go on foot, brother."
I exclaimed: "In this rain?"

I took him to the shop in a car. He was unwell. He had turned pale and he felt dizzy. His limbs trembled and some foam had formed at the corner of his mouth. He sat on the step at the shop. I gave him a glass of tea. He moaned and swore until the afternoon. He said: "The adulterer thinks I am the hero Amir Arsalan[21]. Oh, you bastards! Go home quickly. The prime minister is finished. Think of the sad days when you will curse yourselves for having surrendered. Think of the days of sorrow. Think of the days when not even a thousand curses will bring back a moment of the past. Hey, Esmayol! Give me another recent newspaper so that I can tell you what it's all about. But I'm fed up with my poor health."

I felt embarrassed and ashamed as so many eyes stared at me. When were going back home in the evening, I said: "From now on, you are not allowed to go to the Shoorabi teahouse." He followed me silently. He was not feeling well. I continued: "If you go there once more, I will be angry and I will have to come to some other decision for you." He kept quiet. He looked at the people who held plastic bags over their heads and who ran about in the rain. The rain fell obliquely. I was holding an umbrella and Ideen could not keep himself under it. He was soaked. I said: "You go all this long way to Shoorabi. What for? To drink tea? I have told you so many times not to go there. Well, don't go there then." I shouted in order for him to take notice of what I said. He kept walking in silence. He looked sad and dejected. He did not respond. The shops had turned their lights off. Only the lights of cars appeared and disappeared as they sped past. We had arrived at the doorstep. I said: "Get inside." He lowered his head and went in. I followed him. I locked the door and asked: "Are you having dinner?"

With a movement of his head, he signalled that he was not going to have dinner. He went to the basement. His room was cold and dark. I asked: "Would you like me to put the heater on?" Again, he lowered his head to indicate that he did not want me to do so. He crept under his quilt and gazed at the opposite wall. I said: "I swear by God that if you go there once more, I will lock you up in this very room." He raised his head and looked at the little window. He knew what I wanted to say. I said: "I will block the window. Or I will chain you to the railings of the upstairs veranda." He had kept quiet and I noticed that he was crying. I said: "A grown-up like you, aren't you ashamed?" And I shouted: "If this is repeated once more, I'll never forgive you."

When I perceived that, despite his big body and the pride he used to have,

Symphony of the Dead

he had become obedient to me, I was filled with joy. All his life, he had wanted to know more than I did so that he could show off his knowledge to me. He wanted to go to university, gain a higher education and achieve high positions. But, after all, I had grown up in the marketplace, among the wolves. I said to myself that he would swallow his pride when he can't save money in order to go to the university. He was a proud man who wouldn't look at me when he talked to me. He gazed at some distant point. He paid no attention to me and would keep his secrets to himself. But, after all, I was his brother, next in line in the order of birth. This went on until that defeat brought him down to earth. He no longer wore his brown or his navy-blue suit in my presence. He reverted to his previous characteristics, when they piled lengths of timber in front of him, like grass in front of a sheep, and he sawed as he sweated. He went back to his previous clothes: Trousers made of broadcloth, a pullover knitted by mother and a threadbare overcoat. He became the mad Sooji.

From that night on, he never visited the teahouse again. For some time, he was attracted to the salt marsh. He would go there and sit on a big stone that he himself had carried there and was shaped like some sort of a chair. He gazed at the wave patterns of salty mud while the wind moved the strands of his smooth, black hair like pages of a book.

I said: "Get up, you, beast. What are you looking for in this wilderness?"

"Don't talk to me like that. After all, I am two years older than you."

"Yes. You're right. But, now, get up and get moving."

"Let me wait until these seagulls get to the shore."

Oh, that really made me mad. I exclaimed: "Seagulls?"

"Come and sit here." He moved aside to make room for me. I sat beside him. He pointed at a point in the sky and said: "You see? Do you see how beautifully they move their wings? The one that is flying alone is the bird of peace. I like it very much."

He had assumed a serious, composed air. He continued: "Excellent! Excellent! What a beautiful sound they make. They fill one with joy."

"Look. I've left the shop unattended. I am a busy man."

"You mean you don't want us to wait until the cargo ship arrives? I want to find out what we export and what we import. After all, we are living in this country."

I held his hand and took him back. I said to myself: "Winter is approaching. This is a weight that must be held by a chain to the veranda railings."

The cold was killing him. Not simply the kind of cold that makes the teeth chatter and the fingers ache. It was the kind of cold that turned the skin blue, made the blood around the fingernails clot, gave a stabbing pain in the bones and even made the heart ache. He rushed out of the stable. The howling of the wolves would not leave him in peace. He had not moved at all overnight and he now felt frozen. By sheer force of habit, he put his hand into his waistcoat pocket in order to take his watch out. But the watch was not there. He searched all his pockets. Trouser pockets, front, back, jacket, waistcoat... No, it was not to be found. He remembered that he had touched it as he was about to fall asleep in the manger. But, now, it appeared as if it had been severed completely from its chain. Who was the old man, the one who uttered the word 'fratricide'? Oh, the decrepit old man. He turned his head. Back, front... No, there was no trace of him. There were not even any footprints. Whoever he was, he had taken the watch with him. He asked himself: "What time of night is it now?" And, in a low voice, he answered himself: "Around midnight".

He set out with the intention of walking towards town. But he did not know which direction to follow. He did not know from what direction he had come. He tried to work it out, but with no success. His old body was shivering as he set out.

It was all snow and cold. With every step, he found himself in snow up to his knees. When had the sky put this load down? Had the whole sky fallen?

When we buried mother, it was as if the sky had settled on my shoulders. I was now on my own with two disabled men. Father's inheritance. They had put a stinking chunk of flesh in the corner of the room on the lower floor and they had called it Yousef. His only duty was to eat and to defecate. Nimtaj came to our house occasionally, did the washing up and washed our clothes, cooked or swept. I told her to take care of Yousef and I paid her good money. But she, too, rejected us and paid no more visits. I went to look for her. And that was difficult in the winding alleys of Houzabad district. I looked around until midday and I eventually found her. She was washing her child's bottom at the pond and the child screamed incessantly. I said: "Why don't you come to us any longer, Nimtaj?"

"You, sir? Here?"

"I will pay you more. The house is stinking. Please come."

"I can't take care of that animal, sir. He has put me off eating. No food goes down my throat."

Once again, Father was revived in front of my eyes: "Is this animal still alive?"

Mother replied: "Yes, he is still alive."

"When is he going to die?" And he went upstairs. Father had developed such severe dysentery on that day that he had lost all his vigour, willpower and dignity.

Symphony of the Dead

Mother replied: "When God wills."
Father concluded: "His death would be a blessing, a great blessing."

I turned back. There was no longer any other course of action open to me. I hired a taxi and took him outside the town at around sunset. When we were near nothing but wilderness filled with mountains and valleys and with not even a bird in sight, I told the driver: "Pull over." He braked and asked: "Here?" I said: "Yes." I pulled Yousef out of the car. He was heavy and his legs stuck to his torso like the two wings of a chicken. I carried him on my back through the heart of the wilderness. I walked on and on. When I could no longer breathe, I put him down. He was munching something, or ruminating, as I liked to say. Apparently, he had not finished eating his bread yet. I sat down and waited for him to have his last supper.

I then put him in a pit. I wanted to cover him with earth but I felt pity. I untied my belt and coiled it round his neck. I pulled the belt. I pulled again. And again. He did not move and made no noise. He kept munching and gazed at me with his eyes wide open. I diverted my attention away from him and pulled on the belt until I felt breathless. But Yousef would not suffocate. He had no intention of dying. He had acquired the resilience of a dog. I took my little knife out of my pocket and cut the veins of his wrists. I sat beside him with the intention of waiting until no more blood was left in his body. But almost no blood flowed at all. A thick, sticky liquid slid down his forearms in drops and dried up a few seconds later. I pushed his head to one side and cut the artery in his neck. Again, just a black liquid came out drop by drop and dried up. Night was about to fall and his blood would not flow out. Or if it did, it did so very slowly indeed. I thought of cutting him to pieces but my pocket knife was too small and could not cut his flesh. I stabbed him in the heart a number of times, but to no avail. Yousef remained as he was. He munched, stared and did not move.

It was getting dark. I was filled with horror. I just put him into a smaller pit that was a little bit further away and I started covering him with earth. How could I have guessed that it would end like this? I threw all the earth around the hole down on to him: on his body, on his face, on his legs. And I stamped the earth with my boots to compress it. I knew that he would be suffering and I stopped for a moment. I felt pity. I pushed away the earth that was covering his face and I saw him eating earth. Without blinking, he kept voraciously eating the earth. I wanted to push all the earth away and to take him back but he was too heavy and, besides, I could not reach his legs with my hands. My hand could not find anywhere to lean on and the more I bent down, the less I could find a way of freeing him. The weight of that stinking body was making me breathless. I said: "Oh God! Help me." I said: "Why is it that I encounter difficulty and cannot finish what I'm doing?" Again, Father was revived in front of my eyes with all his innate magnificence. I said: "Look, Father! Look and see what misery I have led myself into."

And now, Father, do you see what quagmire I have led myself into? This is your inheritance.

Father said: "His death would be a blessing."

"Which one do you mean, Father?"

Mother said: "It is not possible to quarrel with God. He will take him away when He sees fit."

Father said: "When, then? I am ill. I have a pain in my heart."

Mother retorted: "Has this got anything to do with you? He's just lying harmlessly down in that corner, eating and defecating."

"Whenever I look at him, I get fed up with life. I wonder why he doesn't contract a deadly disease so that, at least, he is relieved of his misery."

I straightened Yousef out with a few kicks. I said: "Oh, Father, you will be responsible for this sin." He was still buried up to his neck. I said: "Whatever will be, will be." I looked around. I picked up a very big stone and stood above his head. I lifted the stone with both hands and pounded it against his head with such ferocity that I felt something subsiding beneath my hands. His brain had squirted out from the left corner of his head and he still stared, with his eyes wide open. Using my hands, I covered his corpse completely with a mound of earth, to a height of one metre. I ran back to town. I looked back every now and then while I ran.

Cold and snow. With every step, he was up to his knees in snow. Where is this town then? Where are you going? Wait. Suddenly, he heard a voice from behind: "Hey, you! Fratricide!"

He turned back. Not a soul.

I have told him a hundred times not to go anywhere without telling me first, neither the teahouse, nor the salt marsh, nor the cemetery. Yes, the cemetery. Everything we have is down there: Father, Mother, Ida and poor Uncle Saber. Even Ideen can rest next to Ida if he doesn't get himself lost in the middle of mountains or deserts. They were born together and they can go to the eternal life together. But he just went off to this or that place without telling me. At the cemetery, he would sit beside Mother's grave cross-legged, like Indian yogis, and just look at the grave. He looked in such a way that one would think he wanted to torment Mother's soul. His silence no doubt irritated Mother. I said: "What are you doing here, you, big imbecile?"

"I have decided to build a beautiful wooden fence around it."

Symphony of the Dead

"Why don't you let me know when you disappear?" And I slapped him. "When you come with me to the souk in the morning, you must come back home with me in the evening. That's final."

He fell silent and crept into the basement. Late at night, he came out and said: "Brother, allow me to go the hall nearby."

"The hall nearby? What for?"

"Somebody is playing a beautiful tune. Do you remember Ida's wedding reception?"

"Go to bed, you lout. You talk too much."

"But you don't know what tune or what instrument is being played, do you? It's been many years that I wished to go and listen, but I don't have much time, do I?"

"Go to bed. It's late at night now and I can't…"

He insisted. He sat down, got up again and argued with me. He would not give up. I shouted: "Go to bed, you mad man! You don't leave me in peace even at midnight, do you?" I pushed him out of the room and slammed the door behind him.

But he occasionally did visit that dark, narrow hall. One night, he had fallen asleep while sitting there. It was midnight and no sound could be heard. I had looked for him in many places and I was so tired that I could not even talk. I said: "Get up. Let's go."

"Do you hear, brother? Do you hear how beautifully he plays? And, yet, his instrument has not even been tuned properly."

"You should be ashamed of yourself, you big imbecile. You don't stop this nonsense even at midnight, do you?"

"Let me think of Ida. You should not want me to forget her."

I held his hand and pulled him out of the hall. It was filled with the smell of damp. It was a narrow, dark place. Its walls were crumbling and nobody lived there. It was rumoured that a carpet merchant had bought the place and intended to build a big house on the site. It took a few months for the ground to be levelled. Subsequently, a white, four-storey house was built on the site. It had opaque, patterned window panes and its doors were always shut.

When I was going to the shop in the morning, I saw him wandering in the alley, going back and forth. I asked: "What are you looking for, boy?"

"There was a hall here, wasn't there?"

"Well, it isn't there now. So let's go to the shop." And I moved off.

He followed me, saying: "You can't imagine how beautifully he played. He had such a sad voice when he sang Turkish love songs."

The heavy snowfall of midnight had covered the old layers of snow and, now, it imposed its vast, undulating, ocean-like covering on the earth. Is this winter ever going to end? Why is it always winter here? Why is the temperature always below freezing? Why is the sun never shining? Oh, Mother! Come and see what your favourite son has done to me.

He turned back and looked everywhere. There was only sky and snow. The mountains were dazzling white and the earth had been so degraded that any piece of cloud, anywhere, deposited a winter load of snow on it before moving off. And there was no let-up. He pressed his boot against the ground. It was hard and frozen. He wished the earth would open up at some point and swallow him. He suddenly said: "Ouch!"

Father brought builders in. They chiselled away the surface of the black, damp wall of the basement room and replastered it. They installed a pretty door and an attractive window and painted them blue. They also installed a shelf on one side of the room. It was transformed into a nice, tidy room. Nevertheless, it still smelled of burnt things as well as vinegar and sour grape juice. In the afternoons, Mother went out to buy various bits and pieces for the refurbished room. A new brown, wooden bookcase was brought in and placed in a corner of the room. There was also a new bed with a pink bedspread. After we had laid out the carpet, Mother said: "Now, go and get him the books that you burnt."

Father said: "I don't know what books they were, do you, Urhan?"

I said: "No. I didn't look at all their titles. The only ones I remember were *Le Père Goriot*, *Les Miserables* and *The Odyssey*. I don't remember the rest."

Father retorted: "Well, he can come and read my books."

Mother objected: "Ideen will want his own books."

"Alright. I will give him money so that he can go and buy them."

Everything was in order. So Mother said: "Now, go and bring him back."

In the afternoon, Father and I headed for Ram Asbi. On the way, we saw Shoorabi with its reed beds. Dried leaves were crushed under our feet. The salt marsh was on our left and looked as it always had done. Father said: "Once upon a time, the salt marsh had been like Shoorabi. Gradually, its water evaporated and its salt remained." He just wanted to say something so that he could cover up having being brought to his knees. He said something in anger and then changed his words, or the subject. He told cock-and-bull stories, changed topics frequently and, then, suddenly fell silent. When we reached Ram Asbi, he cast a glance at the ramshackle houses and at the mounds of dung that had been deposited beside the walls to dry out and he shook his head in disgust. In order to get to the other side, we had to roll our trousers up and walk across the river. Father said: "This isn't a suitable place for any respectable human being to live, is it?"

We climbed a steep goat-track in the rocks and stood in front of the sawmill. The sunshine was hazy and weak and a cool breeze blew. The weak, barely living flies of the end of the season stuck stubbornly to our skins. A row of donkeys with loads of wheat passed by in front of us and we heard the incessant sound of wood being sawed. Father sat in the shade and lit his pipe. A few seconds later, he said: "Let's go and find out what this big lout has to say for himself." He got up and walked off.

I said: "I don't think he is going to come back."

"He will."

The factory was situated in the middle of a gorge between two mountains and a river flowed past down below. On the other side, two workers were placing planks beside the rocks. A few other workers were sawing timber right in front of the factory. The one in front was Ideen. Father stood in front of him, gazing at him with a peculiar frown. But Ideen's mind was miles away. He was not aware of our presence. But he suddenly raised his head and said: "Hello." He appeared to be at a loss for words. He looked dumbstruck for a moment and then looked down.

Father said: "Forget about the past and…"

"Forget about me, Father." With his face betraying a peculiar sadness, he went into the sawmill.

Father was frozen on the spot. His eyes moved up and down aimlessly. His hands remained raised in the air. He turned back in such a way that his eyes would not meet mine. He had accepted the fact that he had to turn back. He had never been defeated in his life. On that day, I realised the meaning of bitterness.

Urhan said: "Hey!"

He had forgotten to pick up his *papakha*. He had the habit of turning back to pick up some or other forgotten object, as there was always something that he forgot. But he had never forgotten to pick up his *papakha*. This was the first time. He turned back. He could hear the howling of the wolves. He quickened his steps and arrived back at the stable. The wolves' howling was like a raging flame that turned and twisted in all directions and made one's limbs tremble. What could he do? He stood in front of the door, undid his trouser buttons and pissed. By way of joking with himself, he raised one leg like a dog and laughed in agony. He then shook his body severely, leant his heavy body against the door and threw his body against it with one great movement. The door stood firm like a stone wall. He repeated the action a few times. The hinges had rusted. With a dry, creak, they returned the door back to its original position after each of his efforts. The wolves' howling got nearer.

Eventually, the door opened. He picked up his *papakha* from the ground, put it on his head and walked to the manger. He sat down there and noticed that the old man had left his cigarettes and his matches behind. In a loud voice, he said: "Cigarettes in exchange for the watch." Mother used to say: "Support each other like two friends. Then you'll see your situation improving day by day. Don't let Father be bothered."

I said: "Mother, one has got to be like a wolf to be able to continue his business in this bazaar. This brother of mine pities other people more than he pities himself."

Father was ill. He was breathing his last. Following Ida's death, Father was never the same again. He had become a bad-tempered man whose overcoat began to become too big, and still bigger, for him from one day to the next. He just went to the shop in the morning and came back home in the evening. The twins had worn him down. Especially during the three or four years following Ideen's disappearance from home, he gradually lost his normal characteristics. And following Ida's death, we all sensed that Father's back had been broken. Towards the end, he did visit the shop every now and then until he became bedridden. We placed his bed under the window in the room on the upper floor. We brought a doctor to his bedside every day. We had the problem of running the business, seeing to the customers' accounts and records and taking care of bedridden Father. That was a lethal combination that was making us absolutely desperate. Father neither died nor lived. Nevertheless, despite all these concerns, I said: "Ideen and I had better set out for Gavmish Goli."

Mother agreed: "Yes, go. You are both tired. It would be a good idea."

Ideen hesitated: "While Father is in this condition?"

I said: "There is nothing you or I can do, is there?"

We set out. Shoorabi was on our way. When we reached Sar Ain, we noticed that other people were also going there. They were still coming as late as nine o'clock in the evening. Around midnight, they gradually packed up and left and the place got less crowded. During summer nights, when people felt feverish because of the heat, that place remained cool. One could see *zanbouri* lamps hanging from doors and walls. Their bright light and their constant hissing were a nuisance. A number of cripples were making their way towards the hot water springs. People who walked with walking sticks, as well as those who could not walk, had formed a queue at the entrance to the 'General' hot water springs. That place was the most crowded. It was rumoured that, during the war, a British general who had been crippled had cured himself and that, now, he stood upright in the British Army and issued commands, like a lion. Some people were coming back

Symphony of the Dead

with towels over their shoulders, hats on their heads, shawls round their waists or wearing gowns.

The teahouses were crowded with customers. So were the modest restaurants that served sheep's tripe and head. There were many hawkers selling their wares at every bend and every corner of the narrow, winding street. Things worth no more than half a rial were sold for five rials. There was no order and no control. Whoever wanted to earn some easy money could pick up some rubbish or other and bring it to Sar Ain. An old, wrinkled barber shaved men's beards in quick succession and charged ten rials a head. In town, the rate for having a haircut as well as a shave was five rials. But here, the bloke charged ten rials just for a shave. He had also placed a beautiful vase with honeysuckle flowers on his worktop, with a notice reading 'For sale'. I asked how much it was and I noticed that each of its three flowers was of a different colour: Red, blue, yellow.

He said: "One thousand rials."

"What a crook!"

Ideen was silent all the time. He neither talked nor laughed. And he was not interested in anything. We had not brought towels or swimming trunks with us. Nevertheless, when we got off the wooden seat in the old bus in which we had travelled, we immediately made for the hot water springs of Gavmish Goli. The air in that place was different from that of any other place. Great clouds of vapour rose from the hot water. The crippled and the disabled had crowded the pool. I bought two bottles of morello cherry juice and two cigarettes. I lit up both and gave one to Ideen: "Smoke it."

"I don't smoke."

"Neither do I. But this is the sort of place where smoking would be pleasant." He was not interested in anything and was not a good companion. He looked at the people suffering in the polluted hot water and who insisted on staying there. I asked: "What do you want to do next?"

"I don't care."

"What I mean is what job do you intend to take up? Now that Father is about to die, what are your plans?"

"Have we come here to talk about that sort of stuff?"

"We have to talk about these things sooner or later."

"Well, for the time being, I'm working in the shop."

"But you don't like our work. You don't want to be a shopkeeper. Why then…"

"I have no choice. I have to stick around for the sake of both Father and Mother."

But he had no business flair. Whenever sacks of pistachio nuts and watermelon seeds arrived at the warehouse and we swept the warehouse floor the following day, he just stared with his mouth wide open. The only thing I could do was to tell him to block the mouse holes with chalk. And he did so. I no longer wished to lose money because of him. Every crook who had dealings with us had spotted him as the partner who could easily be taken in. He had once purchased three sacks of walnuts. When we opened them, we noticed that the walnuts were infested with worms. I asked: "How much did we pay for these worms, Father."

Father looked at Ideen, shook his head and said: "Take them away and eat them yourself."

I followed up: "Yes. Make a dish of *fesenjan* with them and eat it."

Father was furious. His lips were pursed and looked purple. We carried the walnuts home in the evening. The next day, Mother spread them out in the sunshine. They covered the entire courtyard and the worms danced and wriggled in the pleasant heat of the sun. Father told him to go and become the Minister for Economic Affairs. And I told him: "Ideen, go and find out if there are any more of these walnuts?"

"What for?"

"Buy some more and bring them home so that we can spread them on the rooftop."

By the time we headed back, I think it was past midnight. At Sar Ain garage, passengers rushed towards a bus. A European woman was standing at a corner. I said: "She's up to something." But he paid no attention. I said: "Shall we take her to a quiet corner and deal with her as we should?"

"No."

"She's up to something."

"How do you know?"

I knew. Every now and then, the woman turned back, opened up her chador and then wrapped it firmly round her again. Her eyes were laughing. I said: "Hey!" She turned back. I winked. She frowned. I said: "Look!" She turned back and, this time, smiled. She then got into the bus with an old woman who was accompanying her. We, too, rushed forward and got in. There was not enough room to sit, so we stood. I was right next to her and I didn't want her to look at Ideen all the time. When the bus moved off, the lights inside were turned off and I could no longer see her golden hair or her face bearing lavish make-up. I wonder why my feelings had completely surrendered to her. Never before had I been so attracted to anyone. That night, a girl smiled at me for the first time and stole my heart. I told Ideen that I had to find out, that very night, where she lived. He asked why and I replied I didn't know. But I did know. I really wish we had not made that visit to Sar Ain. I really wish my heart had not been stolen by her.

He lit up another cigarette. He shook his legs and arms. He pounded his boots on the ground. He could hear the wolves howling behind the walls. He didn't know what to do. He had heard from someone that wolves were afraid of fire. He struck a match and looked for something with which he could make a fire. There was a mound of wet straw next to the manger. That was no good for making fire. No. Oh, God! This is not fair. What is to be done then? He got inspiration from the peasants of Ram Asbi who gathered pieces of dried dung and made a fire with them. He put a few pieces of dung together and, with great difficulty, managed to start a fire. It had a pungent smell. The flames moved slowly among chunks of dung and made a peculiar noise. The howling of the wolves was now so loud that it seemed to come from within the stable. Urhan looked around. There was no-one. He could roar with no inhibition and blow into the fire. The weak flames persisted for a moment and then subsided. He gathered all his strength and blew into the fire. Flames rose a little once again. Urhan sat on the ground and held his hands over the fire. He took his shoes off and held his feet near the fire. The fire had been revived and its smoke burnt Urhan's eyes. He could, at the same time, smell the sort of yogurt that was made in rural areas.

I said: "Why do you leave the house without my permission? Was our Mother not a woman?"

She was chewing gum and looked at the back of her hands, with their attractive curve. And what a warm body she had! She said: "What have I got to do with your mother? I have to visit my family."

"Do you lack anything in this house?" I provided everything, more than she wanted. Nevertheless, keeping her in the house was a difficult job. She was like a flammable liquid. She said: "What is there in your life to make me happy? During the day, you go to the shop. At night, all you think about is your nuts and your melon seeds."

Later on, I realised that all women were the same, without exception. Father used to say: "Women should not be tolerated." He meant Mother. And he meant Ida. He showed them the kitchen door and said: "If you can make a good job of that place, you will be good women."

Now he was hungry. His eyes felt as if they wanted to pop out of their sockets. He always had the habit of putting a handful of nuts or melon seeds in his pocket so that he could pick at them every now and again. But, this time, he had forgotten to do so. The smell of burnt dung filled the stable. The heat of the fire had revitalised him to some extent. He now wished to go back. He would go back. He had no doubt he would. He could set out after warming his hands and feet a little. He would arrive at sunrise, go to the room upstairs and rest next to the *korsi*. He would then sleep until midday or even until evening. He would skip the shop. Suspending business for just one day would be alright. But after all this torment, he would not hesitate a moment longer. He would teach Ideen such a severe lesson that, once in the Eternal World, he would go and talk to Mother about what had happened. After all, how long would it take to kill a clumsy person? He would be finished within half an hour.

I waited for Ayaz the policeman to reappear. One morning, he did come. He was no longer in his effervescent mood. I said: "I want to divorce her."

"So soon?"

"She is infertile."

"Well, that would serve her right."

How long could I wait? I wanted to find a very chaste girl. Ayaz said I should not divorce Azar before finding the girl of my choice. He said: "Sell your house only after you have bought another one."

"She lives in her own world."

"Well, you haven't married someone from within your own family. So, you shouldn't be upset about it."

"I found her at Sar Ain garage. I did not know her family."

"What is brought with the wind will be gone with the wind."

On my way back home, I felt strong and confident. I talked to myself about her clothes and her cooking. I could still sense the delicious taste of mother's cooking. I talked to myself about the fact that she was not properly dressed, often wearing a sleeveless dress. She did not cover her face in Ideen's presence. When I saw her in front of me, I said: "Pull a chador over your head at least in front of this big imbecile."

"Don't you understand? This miserable man is even more childlike than a child."

"I am tired of this life."

"What are you looking for this time?"

"A child."

She cooked me a Tabrizi meatloaf and gazed at me while I was eating. I said; "You have inherited your faults from your younger aunt. She is sterile too, like my Uncle Saber."

"It is not my fault, is it? It's God's will."

"No matter whose will it is, I want an heir."

Symphony of the Dead

"They give out children at the orphanage. One day, I will go there and pick up a pretty one. There are beautiful little children there. Even the kids born during the war are quite good. There are girls among them ready for marriage."

"It must be my own child."

She was fed up. She said: "Do you want me to arrange something with the woman who washes our clothes?"

"No. I don't want a washerwoman's child."

"After she gives birth, we will bring the baby to our own house and raise it. It will be your child too."

There was no end to our arguments. At about the same time, a new doctor had come to town. His surgery was at a corner of Shah Square. She said he could perform miracles. She had heard that with a single dose of his medicine, any woman would be able to give birth to one child every year. Later on, I found out that these things had been fed to her by the slut who lived in the house facing ours, and who was good only at using make-up.

I took her to the doctor. I wish I hadn't. And I wish I had not been so preoccupied with the idea of a child. I was not looking for excuses either. But that vast courtyard had nothing in it: No bicycle, no ball and no noise of a child to keep me busy or to dive into the pond from the upper veranda so that I would be forced to whip him. No. When we collected the results of all the tests, we found out that it was I who was sterile. But my desire for an offspring was still in my head: An offspring who would shout, who would pull my hair, who would climb all over me, who would break my neighbour's window and who would cause me yet another headache every day.

He felt he was talking too loudly. He lit up another cigarette, took his shoes away from the hot ashes and put them on, got up, shook the dust off his trousers, stamped with his shoes on the dying fire and stood in front of the door. The only things that could be seen were snow and a sky completely obscured by cloud. The thought of this town made him feel nauseous. This was a town with a temperature that was always below freezing. There was always snow and a cold, whip-like wind. Even one's tears would freeze here.

He was right there. I said: "What are you doing here, you big imbecile?"

He had drunk half his glass of Turkish tea. He read aloud from an old newspaper. He was holding it upside down. I lent an ear to find out what he was reading. He was talking about the war. As soon as he noticed me, he said: "Brother, the fire of war was extinguished in the cold of Moscow." It was green outside and the sun shone incessantly. Two rams were having a playful contest with their horns beside a tree. They took a few steps backwards and then, ran forward quickly before banging their heads and locking horns. Ideen occasionally raised his head and said: "Well done." When the rams had raised a lot of dust, he came out of the teahouse and, without paying any attention to me, applauded. He then took a few goose steps to and fro and laughed. Subsequently, he walked toward a number of people who were sitting in a row in the sunshine beside the wall of the teahouse. They were smoking their pipes while they laughed at him. He stood in front of them and said: "If you want to discover the identity of a book's author, read the footnotes."

They laughed and he said: "I wish I could become the leader of these people for one day, just one day, like Hitler. I would then frown and say: 'Things people own do not belong to them. They belong to God. I am God's representative and divine glory applies to me as well. I have a book too. It will be available soon.'"

The younger ones laughed and threw clods at him. I said: "Aren't I talking to you? What are you doing here?" As if he had just seen me, his laughter froze on his face. But, in the presence of so many people, he tried to laugh again. He then said: "Sir, I am like other people. I have feelings too."

I slapped him three times, on both sides of his face, and said: "You are bloody wrong to behave like this."

"You mean I shouldn't be tempted to have tea?"

"Drink it where I told you to. Don't let me have to come running after you."

Mashd Abbas, the teahouse keeper, noisily washed a saucer and a glass, submerged them in water for a final rinse and poured me a glass of clear tea. He said: "At last, you felt like paying us a visit. Please have some tea."

"Thank you." I looked at Ideen who had innocently bundled himself against the wall, holding his head in both hands. I said: "Don't read these newspapers so much."

He murmured a song with a warm voice. Mashd Abbas said: "If I am not wrong, we must be about a month into spring, because he starts to sing when he sees the swallows."

My heart beat faster with apprehension. I feared lest he start talking and inadvertently tell everything. But he submerged further day by day. It was as if he was stuck in a swamp.

Mashd Abbas said: "Allow me to bring you a chair."

"I don't want one." But I did want one. I was getting on. I was overweight and not very energetic. I was well into my 37th year. Yes, Those were the days. Now, my legs, enduring the weight of my torso, sometimes buckled and had pins and needles. I sat on an iron chair that had been painted blue. I could see the whiteness of the salt marsh in the distance. Mashd Abbas brought me a table as well. He said: "Only Sooji can bring us the blessing of your presence. Were it not for him, you wouldn't pay us a visit."

Ideen was sitting on the ground, leaning against the wall. His eyes appeared to be fixed on a point far, far away. I got up and took his hand: "If you are not drinking tea, let's go."

I no longer had any need to drag him after me. He just came along, rubbing shoulders with me. I said: "You shouldn't have come here. You've been around here for three days. Doesn't it occur to you that I am alone in that dreary house?"

"Well, this is how human beings are."

When we reached town, it was late afternoon and the streets had been sprinkled with water. Policemen were on the beat in pairs, porters were eating watermelon on their wheelbarrows, barbers gave haircuts for ten rials a head and children, as soon as they saw Ideen, shouted: "Sooji! Mad Sooji!" Sometimes, somebody shouted from behind a wall: "Dinosaur!"

I knew that pupils at Safavi Secondary School were good at this sort of thing.

The wolves rubbed their snouts against the ground and stood in a circle. They then surrounded the stable and jumped up and down so that Urhan would come out. He said: "Well, this is how human beings are. Sooji, Sooji, mad man." He shouted: "Sooji!" But the wolves became further agitated when they heard his voice. He squatted on the stable floor and pulled the tail of his overcoat over his legs.

It seemed just yesterday when Mother shouted from the depths of her throat, with grating breath, felt breathless, turned pale, held her hand against the wall for support, slowly knelt on the floor and, finally, lay down. That bitter life passed quickly and, suddenly, I noticed that 14 years of my life had been totally wasted. It had been barren and useless. It felt like wasting a whole lifetime. While Mother was around, one could be sure that the *korsi* in the room upstairs would be warm and cosy, that the smoke rising from the heater would wind round the snow-covered branches of the pine tree and that the samovar would be full of boiling water, although Urhan was not Mother's Urhan while Ideen was Mother's Dear Ideen.

She said: "Don't come back to me until you have found him." That bundle of bones issued commands so authoritatively that one would melt with shame.

I said: "I can't be at his beck and call day and night, Mother. What am I to do with the shop? Believe me, I am fed up with him."

"Get out."

But where could I go? I said: "How am I supposed to know where he is?" I continued: "Don't you appreciate the fact that I have taken him to the doctor on numerous occasions, that I look after him all the time, that I give him newspapers, that I pay for his tea, that I take him to the barber, and that I take him to the bathhouse? Well, I'm a human being too. I have to have some respect and dignity." But she would not be calmed by any sort of argument. I sat beside her so that she could tell me whatever she wanted to, shout, pull my hair, slap me and, if I were lucky, eventually leave me in peace.

She said: "Whatever it is, it is your doing. But remember that you have done an injustice to yourself as well."

"That's not true, Mother. What have I done wrong?" I pulled the blanket over her legs and poured her some water from the jug. I put the glass in her hand and she threw it away with such ferocity that the room was filled with pieces of broken glass. She said: "Where is my Ideen?"

He was playing a *zanboorak* with street urchins behind the walls of Anooshirvan School. I held his hand in order to take him with me. He said he would not come. Like a little child, he let himself be dragged along, getting dusty. With his greying hair, he looked like a stubborn old man who knew nothing but stubbornness and who always looked no more than five years old. I said: "Don't behave like this. Think of how big you are, Ideen."

He stretched his neck and brought his head near mine: "What's the matter? What's happened?"

I quickly slapped him: "You, big imbecile! I'll teach you a lesson so that you behave properly."

"Don't say such things, brother. My head is bursting."

"I'm not saying anything. Mother says you should come home."

"Mother?" He hesitated for a moment. Then, as if surrendering to destiny, he forgot about the *zanboorak*-playing children and came with me, taking big steps. He now paid no attention to the children's noise.

I said: "You should come with me to the shop, to the souk. You should stay where I can see you until we go back home together. Understand?"

"There is so much noise in my head that it feels like a coppersmith's workshop." He put his hand on his chest and continued: "Something is stuck right here. It has lodged itself here and is getting worse all the time. "

Mother suddenly slapped me. I jumped up, with my eyes wide open: "Why are you hitting me, Mother?"

"What poison have you made him eat, you disgraceful man?"

"He's crazy. But what makes you say things like that?"

She uttered such a heart-rending shriek that I felt my skin was cracking. She said: "Since that night, yes, that very night… You'll be punished for this. You are doomed."

Symphony of the Dead

I had to resist and not let her find out the slightest thing. She did not believe my word. So, I decided to pretend to be ill for a while in order to earn her sympathy. She did look after me. She did the cooking and reminded me to take my medicine. But, every now and then, Ideen would suddenly burst out: "Ouch, Mother." Mother scratched herself with her fingernails, became highly concerned, wailed in a high-pitched voice and talked with a low-pitched one. She talked to herself. But the person who sat in front of us looked like a statue sculpted out of a huge chunk of stone or lead. He was not like me. He was really ill. The more he tried, the more he sank. He was dishevelled, had a wrinkled, Tatar-like face and a head as heavy as a mountain. He was a man who could not hold his head upright. He became delirious and talked nonsense. My heart was pounding. Mother looked at me in disgust for a moment and, eventually, said: "You have done what you have done. Now at least tell me what you have made him take so that can I try to find a cure for it."

What could I say? I remained silent, as I had always done. Mother would then say: "If God really acts as God, he will give you the punishment you deserve."

"Don't curse me Mother. Think of my youth. I am only 29 years old. I still have many hopes and many wishes." I was not aware that I was crying. And I am not aware now that I am crying because of pain, fatigue, cold and hunger. I always feared Mother's cursing. But her curses never affected me. She herself was always ill. From about the same time she developed breathing difficulties and became bedridden. From day to day, she looked more distressed and more broken. She lay down between her white bed linen with her frail, bony figure and just snored. Summoning what little remained of her strength, she would say: "Ideen... Where is my Ideen?"

Under the now familiar plane tree in the cemetery, he was sitting beside Ida's grave. I always looked for him and found him, aware of the painful fact that I was not Mother's Urhan. What I had believed had turned out to be quite true. Even years earlier, I had known that popularity was more pleasant than any amount of wealth. I could read this even in the porters' looks. And still now they, porters and other people, like Sooji more than they like Urhan. Even Father, with all his hatred for him and despite the fact that he insulted and ridiculed him in his absence, could not behave normally in his presence. He had respect for him while he pointed out his weaknesses. He was forced into saying: "What are you doing, boy?" without having said: "You cowardly lout."

"I have not got anywhere with poetry. So now I make wooden boats."

"Go on. Make boats so that we can see what territories you will conquer."

This man, who used to be preoccupied with poetry and literature and whose rubbish used to be printed in newspapers all the time, had become a fully fledged carpenter following Ida's death. He played about with wood and, when confronted with tree stumps, looked for something that none of us either found or identified.

Mother's behaviour, however, was different from Father's. She could not hide her feelings. She betrayed what was in her heart. In between the weak breathing that was about to come to an end altogether, she tried hard to say: "Ideen…Ideen…"

Near Shoorabi, right here, he crammed his pockets with his old newspapers. He even pushed them into his socks, under the elastic of his underpants and inside his trouser legs. In addition to all those, he held a few newspapers in his hands. I said: "You have come here again, you big imbecile?"

"I am also a human being, at least sometimes, brother."

"May you end up in the mortuary. Come on and get in the car."

He no longer laughed. He just blinked, looked around and then remonstrated: "Let us go on foot, brother."

"I have hired a car. I have already paid for it."

"You know that I get dizzy and nauseous in a car."

I grabbed his shoulders and threw him on to the back seat: "I don't give a damn. You have made your bed; you have to lie in it. I'm a busy man. I can't be held back by you all the time."

When we reached the entrance to the souk, I called the porters and told them to help us. He had screamed and shouted so much along the way that he had become too weak even to moan. There was foam around his mouth. His eyeballs looked so white. We laid him on the floor in the hall. Esmayol wanted to bring him into the shop. I said: "There is no need to do so." He kept insisting, but I wouldn't let him. I said: "I don't give a damn about what people say. But if he pees in the shop, we will be unclean down to our bones." Esmayol drew a line round him with his packing needle. It was a perfect outline of a body whose pain would stay in the ground and not rise. Esmayol then washed Ideen's face with cold water. He took him to the end of the hall and poured him some tea. Subsequently, the porters surrounded Ideen. But he was giddy and not quite conscious until night. When we arrived at home, he started crying as soon as he saw Mother. I knew that he wanted to torment Mother. And Mother, in order to torment me, put her arm round his neck, kissed him, combed his hair, changed his shirt and clipped his fingernails. I, standing at the doorstep and dying from hunger, did not know what to do. What would the better option be: to stay or to go? Mother sensed my presence for a moment. She turned back and just looked anxiously at my hands and feet.

Symphony of the Dead

The wolves' howling was closer now. There were wolves all around the place and they howled in unison. They would not fall silent for a moment. Besides, the cold was killing. The cold had often frozen horses and cows to death. Some years back, they said, they had found a frozen shepherd who was still sitting on top of a rock and gazing into the distance. Urhan got up from the corner of the stable. He was shivering, not out of cold or fear but because of something he could not identify. He shivered quite noticeably, as if he had been connected to a live wire. He pounded the stable floor with his feet a few times. It was no use. The previous year, three people had been found frozen in a car, a young couple and their child. They had wrapped their child with all of their own clothing but had not been able to fight the cold off. The nose and the mouth of the three-year-old girl had frozen and all of them had icicles like stretched crystals hanging from their eyes. Urhan moved his hands and arms, did his buttons up and began to move his limbs again. He moved his feet quickly up and down while he was standing on the same spot. He did this for quite a long time. It was no use. The howling got nearer and nearer. He blew into his cupped hands to warm them up. Where are you Sooji? Oh, Sooji!

He had shouted. He had screamed. Had he roared and wept too? He had no idea. He also had no idea why he had set out at that time of the day either. But he did know that loneliness had given him even worse nights than this. He already had plans about what to do when he saw him. He wanted to tie his hands and feet quietly, tie a tight noose around his neck and just leave him there. But now, he himself was a captive of snow. It was a cruel snow and there was no end to it. The sky had been angered and wanted to bury the whole world under snow, like a child who buries an ant alive and, as soon as the ant comes out, buries it again. There is an endless supply of earth and there is more than enough to bury an ant. Any struggle would be futile.

All these matters apart, where was Ideen? Wherever he looked, he saw Ideen. This time, he was looking for Ideen not for the sake of Mother but for the sake of his own torn and weary heart. Mother was no more. So she could no longer say: "Where is my Ideen?"

In the ramshackle hall near the house, facing Lord's Electric Fan Factory, a rejected, hopeless lover sang a Turkish love song so beautifully and Ideen cried so readily and whole-heartedly that it was easy to realise that he had been reminded of Ida. On that day too, it had been snowing. The streets had been flooded and the workers of the Electric Fan Factory were trying to divert the course of the flood by placing sandbags here and there.

I said: "What are you doing here, you big imbecile?"

He said: "Come and shed a couple of tears for your dead. May God bless them."

I said: "I have searched everywhere: Mashd Abbas's teahouse, the cemetery, the area behind Anooshirvan School, Akhavan Garden, the salt marsh and so on. I have been all over town and its surroundings. And now I see you in here. Don't you think you're supposed to let me know where the hell you go?"

"It's a long time since I started coming here."

We left the abandoned god-forsaken hall into which a punishing wind blew from openings and cracks here and there. I grumbled: "We can't go on like this. I can't have to look after you. I can't scour the world to find out where you are."

"Then chain me again, brother."

While Mother was still around, it was not possible. But following Mother's death, I used to chain him up. I chained him to the railings on the upper floor and scattered old newspapers in front of him like grass in front of a sheep. He played about with them and fell asleep while sitting up. He slept so soundly that I thought he was dead. Now I said: "Would you like that?"

"Oh, brother! The days are the same but times have changed. Would you have believed that Ida, our own Ida, could one day set herself on fire?"

Now, it was he who insisted on being chained. It was a peculiar insistence that tormented him day and night. It was not Mother's insistence. Mother had been resting under tons of stone and ice for many years. So no disgusted gaze could focus on Urhan's hands. Nor could any disgusted mouth issue orders: "Ideen. My Ideen."

He lifted his head from the wall against which he had been leaning. He looked outside in the direction of the wolves' howling. The snowfall was now more intense. There appeared to be no end to it. The sky looked intent on finishing with everything. It was intent on depositing such an unforgettable load of snow on earth that, for many years to come, people would refer to "the year of the great snowfall". It would be like the years when we dug passages through the snow to open up a way to the street. The narrow alleys had already had too much snow. In addition to that, people sweeping their rooftops added to the huge pile of snow, so much so that people could not open their doors. Mother was unable to heat the rooms and a deep depression fell on all of us. Father asked: "What could Ideen be doing in this severe cold?"

I replied: "I don't go into the basement room Father, do I?"

"But a villain like you would surely know what he does at night."

"He reads books."

Oh, let him read. I wish Father would not prevent him from reading. Where

Symphony of the Dead

are you Ideen? Sooji? No. The shouting rose from the depth of the throat of a wandering animal. It was as if it moaned, or perhaps howled. Every second the wolves got closer and closer. He leaned his head against the wall and summoned all his strength in order not to die. The sound came from just behind the walls. Mechanically and without looking, he took a cigarette out of his coat pocket, intending to light up. But he had no matches. He threw the matchbox away and pressed the cigarette between two fingers until it was crushed. He blew into his cupped hands. The moisture froze on the skin of his hands. Sooji! The wolves could now be heard from behind the walls. There were five or maybe six of them. They all stood on their hind legs and let themselves fall noisily. Hunger was translated into a roar and landed with pain. He said: "My head." Then Ideen ran into the shop and called me with delight: "Brother! Brother!"

"What's happened, boy?"

He pointed at a woman who was accompanied by two pretty, fair children. He said: "Brother! This is my sister-in-law."

I looked carefully. It was my own wife. It was Azar. She was buying nuts from the shop facing ours. She had a son and a daughter. Azar had done up her daughter's hair in a pony-tail. Every now and then, she cast a furtive glance at our shop. I had not seen her for years. Until that day, I had thought I was sterile and that I was not attracted to women any longer. But when I saw her, I felt that I dearly wanted her to be my wife. I really wished her to be my wife right on that day, right at that hour. And now, too.

As she was leaving, she paused in the hall for a moment in order to call her son. She then held her children's hands and left, with a sweet smile like that of a lover at dawn.

Ideen said: "My sister-in-law." He smiled in such a way that he seemed as if he was about to cry.

I said: "So what?"

"Nothing. It was my sister-in-law."

"Get lost." And I pushed him away.

"Okay. I'll go away." He picked up a handful of melon seeds and went back to the end of the souk. He sat on his usual tin box and pulled his blanket over his legs. After that day, I saw Azar once more. At the entrance to a cinema, she was straightening the lapel of her husband's jacket. I could not see the man's face. But Azar's jolly face and her honey-coloured eyes were so alluring. She was taller than I was. Whenever I wanted to slap her on the face, I had to stand on tiptoes. I used to slap her two or three times a week. But she appeared to enjoy it. She gazed at me in cold blood, blinked, stared, smiled and stared again. And I was tempted to slap her again.

In the divorce court, I said: "We have come here so that I can divorce you."
"Alright."
"Sign." She signed. On the following day, she came home to collect her belongings and leave. Like Father, I did not want to talk about the matter. I remembered Father who sat on his sheepskin rug, under the weeping willow, with complete peace of mind, cut his watermelon into big slices, gave one slice to me and said: "Don't talk about this corpse."

The stable door was forced open and a howling wind blew in a lot of snow. The white light emanating from the snow lit up the opposite wall. The wolves' howling could now be heard from within the stable. They had broken the door and come inside. They were right behind him, all six of them. They howled and moved back and forth. Oh, how hungry they were! He wished he had a piece of dried bread to throw at them. Where are you Sooji? Oh, Sooji!

He said: "It tastes good. But it feels like eating lead."

I said: "You don't know this Mr Boyook of ours. He's a master chef. Go on. Eat! This is a heavenly dish."

"What do you call it?" He ate two spoonfuls and looked at the remainder on his plate with reluctance.

"I don't know. It is a rare bird. Mr Lord eats this dish every day."

"I suppose it's quite expensive too." He ate another spoonful.

"Eat as much as you want. Don't think of the cost." My heart was beating fast.

"Why aren't you eating yourself?"

"I've eaten already."

"Have a mouthful at least." He ate some more. My heart was beating fast. I clearly noticed that he was afflicted with hiccups and that his eyeballs seemed to be jumping up and down in their sockets. He pointed at his chest and said: "It is stuck here. It's heavy…like lead." He then held his head in both of his hands. He moaned, moaned and moaned. He then said, calmly: "Oh, God!"

The wolves had surrounded him and were ready to attack. It was their habit to form a circle, gaze at each other and then, enraged with hunger, rush at the victim who had been taken off guard for a moment and tear him up. An hour later, just a few bones would be lying in the snow. They panted and he could feel the warmth of their breath on the back of his neck. One small movement, and they would jump on him. It was for this reason that he dared not move his head away from the wall. He closed his eyes and roared in anticipation of being torn apart. Ideen! Ideen!

Suddenly he fell silent. He turned back. He saw no wolves. He heard no howling.

Symphony of the Dead

The sun had risen. Thick, white clouds had fully covered the sky. They appeared to be making sure that there would not be the slightest gap, lest Urhan see just a bit of the sky. The world was all whiteness. He looked around. All he could see was snowfall, faint daylight and pure whiteness. The only other thing was a dried-up tree in front of the ruins of the teahouse. He remembered that he had once stood under that tree and pointed at the town with his outstretched hand. He stood there once again, facing the broken door of what used to be a lone but warm and friendly teahouse. When we descended the hills, we could see the blue-green waters of Shoorabi. But now, everything looked dead. The falling snow had no intention of stopping. It continued loading and overloading the vast expanse of earth.

While standing beside the tree, Urhan surveyed the direction he thought he should follow. He set out. With every step, he went down into the snow up to his knees. The hubbub of the town appeared to come from a particular direction. He listened carefully. No. He could not tell the direction of the sound. He continued straight ahead. He saw Sooji in the distance. He was approaching him. He was wearing the green woollen sweater that Ida had knitted for him, an old overcoat and Father's *papakha* that had lost much of its colour and turned pale.

He said: "Hey, brother, what direction shall we follow?"

Sooji tore up his newspaper and scattered the pieces, throwing them up. They fell like snowflakes. He said: "All in the same direction. Eight abreast. Forward to the cold of Moscow!"

"Hey, brother. Where are you going?"

"Don't follow me, brother."

"Why?"

"Leave me in peace. We are old men now."

Every other one of his teeth was missing. In some places, he even lacked two out of every three teeth. Instead, brown stumps had remained in his gums. I suppose he could utilise them to chew his food. A single hair out of every three had turned white. I said: "Would you like me to make you a little room in this very souk so that you can stay with Esmayol all the time?"

He was leaning his left foot against the wall and watching the street. It feels just like yesterday. But it was 11 days ago. Today is Monday. On that day, it was snowing. Ideen looked sad. I said: "You are now in the 42nd year of your life. It is about time for you to be concerned about yourself and to behave properly."

While he was watching the street, he suddenly began trembling. He held his head in both hands and said: "I am going to vomit." He then pulled his newspapers and scraps of paper out of his coat pockets, from under the elastic of his underpants and out of his socks. He scrunched them into a ball and dropped it into the brazier in which something was burning and giving out smoke. The brazier was in front of Martha the beggar. The newspapers and pieces of scrap paper wriggled, twisted and went up in smoke. They reminded me of his books that we burnt in the courtyard. It also reminded me of the basement out of which a raging fire rose. And I suddenly felt Father's nervous laughter and his words: "Eh! This is the devil's spirit that's burning."

He said: "It was these very things that ruined me." He moved off.

I called him: "Ideen!"

He did not turn back. I followed him. I grabbed his hands and pushed him against a tree. The snow lying on its branches fell on us. I asked: "Where are you going?"

"Somewhere else."

"Where?"

"I don't ask you where you go, do I?"

I slapped him on both cheeks. I noticed that his hands trembled and his eyelids flickered. Imitating Father's authoritative tone, I said: "Get back into the souk."

He was spellbound and just kept looking at me for about two minutes. I felt ashamed and gave up. I looked down. I then saw him moving off once again. I was not wearing my coat. I was feeling cold. Nevertheless, I followed him and got hold of him again. I asked: "What's the problem, Sooji?"

He exclaimed: "Sooji?" He wore an air of childish sadness on his face and looked at the trees. He kept looking up in the manner of a little child. I think he was about to burst into tears. He bit his lip. He then faked a cough and tried to look serious.

I said "Ideen" and I laughed. I thought he had regained his health and could understand things like normal people. Once again, I laughed with kindness.

He asked: "Why are you laughing? Is she dead too?"

"Yes, she died many years ago, about a year after Father."

"In that case, we must go."

"Where?"

"We must find out how the dead sleep. It's a mystery."

"Go back. I want to talk to you today."

Once again, he scanned me from head to toe. He narrowed his eyes and gazed into mine: "What do you have in mind this time?"

I was completely truthful. I told him that I had no plan in mind. I had an uneasy feeling, felt ashamed because of the fact that I had never considered him a respectable human being during those 14 years. I had never realised that I felt I lacked something when he was not around. As soon as he set foot in the shop, I frowned at him and shouted: "You here again?"

He would put a handful of melon seeds in his coat pocket and, with a furtive and playful look like that of a child, run to the end of the souk. Esmayol regularly poured him tea. He also served him broth and kept his makeshift heater, his brazier, hot. So long as Ideen was around, it did not occur to me that I might miss him. Now, I knew that he would be around anyway. Nevertheless, I felt I needed to talk to him. I don't know why. Perhaps I simply longed to communicate with someone familiar who was, at the same time, one of the family. I said: "Let's go." And I pulled his hand.

He withdrew his hand and moved away once more. I was feeling so cold that I could not follow him again. I just shouted: "Was that your final word?"

"Oh, brother! Desolation knows no bounds now. One must pack up and go." He went.

He walked on and on. He thought that by following a particular direction for hours, he would definitely reach the town and save his own life. He walked on. He turned back to assess what distance he had already covered. The teahouse ruins looked even more ramshacklē when it was further away.

He said: "Oh, brother! Desolation knows no bounds now. One must pack up and go."

He was shaking with anger. I said: "I'll make a man of you. I'll teach you such a lesson that even the birds in the sky will weep for you." I returned to the shop. He disappeared ten days ago. And I, being tied to him, was now a wanderer in the wilderness. Today is Monday. But there were other days too. He said: "I must go."

I said: "I hope it is for auspicious reasons. Where are you going, pray tell?"

"Where? I am going to kiss the master's feet."

"You're talking nonsense, aren't you?"

"My master has summoned me again. His samovar is boiling."

I knew that he would be going to the Shoorabi teahouse. But in the past, when Father had just died and Ideen worked in the shop in accordance with Father's will, whenever he said: "One must pack up and go", I replied: "I am fine in here. You go if you want to."

He said: "You are wrong if you think that you'll see me leave." He was so exhausted that he looked like a lifeless bundle deposited behind the counter. My back was not strong enough to carry such weight either. Besides, I had toiled for 12 years in that bloody place. I had swept the place clean and carried full sacks. I had carried sacks of pistachio nuts and melon seeds up and down those stairs so many times that, now, I wanted him, too, to toil for a few years so that he would realise the value of life and livelihood. I had told him all these things so that they would be indelibly inscribed in his mind, so that he would not suddenly think of himself as a man of letters suited to sitting at a desk and doing nothing else.

Twenty-three sacks of sunflower seeds had been stacked in front of the shop. They had formed such a huge pile that we could not see through the window. I said all the sacks had to be carried downstairs. He put all of them on his back, one by one, and carried them to the basement warehouse, down 40 steps. When he had finished, he poured himself a glass of tea, sat on the floor, stretched his legs and drank the hot tea in one gulp. Big drops of sweat had covered his forehead and the area under his eyes. When I looked at his navy blue trousers and his blue shirt that were soaked with sweat and stuck to his body, I was reminded of myself who sweated even more than he did, because I was overweight. I had said: "Father, I have carried these sacks down 40 steps and up 40 steps. This is not fair." There was now no question of fairness. He, having just arrived on the scene, was putting his hand on all I had. Father, unfair as he was, no longer had anything to lose. So, on his deathbed, he said: "Whatever there is, it should be shared between the two of you." That night, I burnt from within with a high fever, became delirious and talked nonsense. I was wet with perspiration, with no-one around even to hand me a glass of tea. That day, he had forgotten to shake the dust off his clothes. He also looked a bit thinner than usual. I knew that, exhausted as he was, he wholeheartedly wanted to say that he could not stay there any longer. As Father had said, he had no business flare. Nevertheless, he had to stay in accordance with Father's wishes. He said: "Brother! Desolation knows no bounds now." He finished his tea and sat on a step at the front of the shop. I had no idea who was in his thoughts. About half an hour later, at the exact moment when the cuckoo of the clock chanted four times, that pretty Armenian girl came to see him, as she had done every day. She said: "How can you look like this?" Ideen brushed the dust and sack threads off his clothes, took his jacket off the hook and put it on. He asked: "Would you like something?" The girl picked up a handful of dried peach slices, a handful of pistachio nuts and a handful of salted melon seeds and put them in her handbag.

The girl's hue was curiously violet. Or, at least, that was how she appeared to me. Her eyes shone so intensely that an onlooker would feel embarrassed. With every turn and twist of her body, a wave of smooth, blonde hair flew through the air and I no longer saw either of them. It was as if her hair formed the wings for their flight. In times to come, that girl turned and twisted all the

Symphony of the Dead

time in my mind, leaving a memory of an opened fan of hair, violet hues and a pretty smile.

How could I dare ask where they were going? Even when I told Mother, she frowned and said, so that I would shut up forever: "Is it any business of yours?"

Late every afternoon, I was alone in the shop at lighting up time. Every day a new idea came into my head. But he paid no attention to my new ideas. He would agree neither to take his share in order to pursue his studies nor to work with me full time in the shop. I even suggested that he could keep completely away from the shop and just take his share of the earnings. But he said; "My conscience would not allow me to do that."

"Don't talk about something you don't have."

"Don't be rude."

"Then don't complain later on."

"Try not to damage our brotherhood."

"I piss on this brotherhood." Although I knew that he was head over heels in love with that Armenian girl, I wanted him to say so himself and to beg me to let him leave the shop in the afternoons. Father had not been able to bring him to his knees. I wanted to complete his unfinished task. I wanted to behave in such a way that would compel him to kiss the hinges of the door when he entered the shop in the morning, to be under my control and to follow me back home at night. But the more I tried, the less successful I was.

I said: "How long do you want to play with wood for?"

"Until I get to grips with it."

"How long do you want to read books for?"

"Until the day of resurrection."

He stood in front of the cracked mirror at the end of the shop, tidied his hair with his hand and combed his moustache. The cuckoo of the clock appeared four times. Mechanically, I looked at the door to watch that Armenian girl come up the staircase. She would always arrive at that moment, pick up a handful or two of something and leave with him. On that day, I called him when he was at the door and about to leave: "Wherever you go, have me in your thoughts."

Enraged, he cast a glance at the girl and, then, at me. He said: "You're really malicious, Urhan."

I said: "Young lady, tell this prince to keep away from my life."

She said: "Where is your life, sir?"

I blushed with embarrassment. But I feigned indifference and told Ideen that I was prepared to buy his share of the business. He answered: "Urhan, whenever you think about money, you lose your humanity."

"I'm not thinking about money now, am I?" After he left, I said: "You're always malicious, even when you're asleep."

He stood facing the wall and closed his eyes. But his mind was filled with a nightmare in which all the dead whom he knew had funny faces or figures. Father walked. Mother was out of breath and made a wheezing sound. The tall, good-for-nothing Jamshid, leaning with his foot against the wall and waiting, said: "Let's go and have a good time." Every time he saw Urhan he would open his eyes. But when he looked at the wall, all he saw again was wilderness and snow. There was just freezing cold and the endless white of the plain and the hills. He saw Mr Lord. He was approaching the teahouse with his leg covered in plaster and his iron crutch under his armpit. The tip of his crutch made a repetitive hollow noise, as if it had been covered with a piece of cloth. With every step forward, he cast a glance at the teahouse and relaxed by breathing out a lot of vapour. He was wearing his formal black suit complete with tails, a white shirt and a maroon bow tie. Whenever he wanted to be serious, he pursed his lips in such a way that one would think he was sucking sweets. Right now, he was sucking his damned sweet. He said: "I have come from the necropolis."

"You have come out of your tomb after so many years. What for? What do you have to say?"

"Are you still alive, Mr Urhan?"

"You can see that I am alive, can't you? Come and have a look… But, believe me Mr Lord, I don't know how to spend the rest of my life if I survive this frozen hell."

Father said: "We know how the market works, Mr Lord. We keep our finger on its pulse."

Mr. Lord replied: "Your own pulse is under our finger, Mr Urkhani."

I laughed. Mr Lord said: "This son of yours is clever. He understands economics. But the other one, who has been entrapped by poetry, is a complete fool."

Father said: "Well said. Well said." Some time later, he told me that there was no doubt that we were both stubborn and intransigent. He then turned to Ideen and told him that, as the British put it, he was a complete fool who had not even as much wisdom as an ass.

When Mr Lord was about to leave, shaking hands with Father, he said: "Don't think about the past hundred years. It would be in your best interests to be under our guidance." He laughed. He laughed again. And again. And now, with his broken leg and his crutch under his armpit, he had come to see Urhan. I said: "Tell me, Father, why do the dead not leave us alone?"

Symphony of the Dead

No. An iron blow had struck the earth and the thump of a heavy, plastered leg was about to shake the heart out of it.

I thought it was the sound of a crutch, with a piece of cloth round its tip, hitting the earth and shaking its heart.

He closed his eyes. He then saw Mr Lord running. He was running fast, with a thump and a bang. Snowflakes spiralled down and landed on the ground. Thump, bang, thump, bang. He said: "Stop it, Mr Lord."

He pressed his hands against his temples. What pleasant heat! No, my God. This is not fair. Ideen! Ideen! Where are you to witness that I am now all on my own and that the world freezes over every night. It looks as if all the people in the world are dead and I am being punished for everyone else's fears. A nauseating headache had lodged itself behind his eyes, right in his forehead. He felt a bitterness in his mouth. He sensed that his mouth smelt foul. He felt that he had half sunk in snow, like the ruined teahouse. He put his hands in his coat pockets and set out anew. He was weak and impatient with hunger. As far as he could remember, he had never missed even a single meal. But now, he had eaten nothing since midday the previous day.

Today, it is Friday. It's a pity that human beings, unlike some animals, cannot store their food inside them to ruminate every now and then. Father said: "Don't forget to earn and save something for when you move to the eternal world." But we did forget. I said: "Didn't you promise never to come to the teahouse again?"

He replied: "Life is an old tradition, brother."

"Get moving. And don't talk nonsense."

"Women make two kinds of sounds: low-pitched and high-pitched. They talk in a low-pitch and scream in a high-pitch."

"What woman?"

"The breeze rising from Lord's electric fans will one day blow all of us away."

He always thought that the one-hundred-gram weight in our shop weighed more than one hundred grams. And he said: "Monsieur Sooren's coffee is stronger."

I told the lanky Jamshid: "Hey, you long stick! Are you following the route taken by those who buy with credit instead of with cash?" He preferred not to have been seen by me. Later on, he said he had intended to pay me a visit at the shop without prior notice. He never did.

The more he walked, the less he seemed to be approaching the town. Where was the town then? The edges of his lips itched. He put his fingertips to his lips and, for a moment, he felt his warm breath again. He also noticed that he had developed cold sores.

Mother said: "Before you fully develop cold sores, hold a copper saucepan on the area. It will subside."

He was no longer strong enough to stand up. There was a sharp pain in his bones and his toes cried with pain. He was too weak to walk. He could hardly take a single step forward. He really wished just to drop down somewhere and fall asleep. Nevertheless, he changed direction and set out again.

Ideen said: "Brother, we will have 7,000 years at our disposal in order to sleep. Sleep if you like. Just don't look at the light. And never insist that I should sleep as much as you do at night."

I asked: "How many hours of sleep are needed by youths of our age?"

He retorted: "How many hours of reading are needed by youths of your age?"

"We can't go on like this. We must divide our room. But the partition can't go this way. It has got to go that way so that it will exactly halve the window, half for you and half for me. I intend to place a vase on my half of the windowsill and pour the remainder of my drinking water into it."

He said: "One cannot understand the meaning of life if one has not read fiction."

"What are you looking for?"

"Myself."

He was looking for the town. Not necessarily his own town. He was looking for any town where he could find a piece of bread and where he could take shelter against the freezing cold. But there was no trace of any human being. Nor was there any trace of any animal so that he could split its belly open, thrust his hands inside and take something to eat out of it. The hubbub of the town appeared to have died down under the snow. He sat on the snow, held his head in his hands and curled up into a big ball. The shepherd who had frozen stiff while sitting on a rock had been found with his mouth open and his open eyes betraying deep anxiety. He had no doubt shivered, then sat on a rock and, eventually, accepted the fact that he had to die. When death arrives, one regains one's original dignity. Father died with a particular dignity, with his usual awe-inspiring air. We had made him lie on the floor of the large upstairs room in such a way that his feet pointed to Mecca. He was in death throes from eleven o'clock at night until midday the next day. Mother was sitting next to his head, reciting from the Koran with a sad, incomprehensible tone. Every now and then, she cast a glance at Father's pale face and pressed her lips together. Then, her entire body shook. She hid her head in her chador for a moment and continued to recite from the Koran. I was sitting on Father's right and Ideen on his left.

Symphony of the Dead

Ideen said: "Is there really nothing that we can do?"

He rubbed Father's hands between his, occasionally wiped the sweat off his forehead with a handkerchief and, every now and then, poured water blessed with the dust of holy shrines into Father's mouth. Father's face was yellowing. It was the sort of yellowness that one would feel uneasy to look at. Whenever he vomited, I left the room to fetch something or to breathe some fresh air. I told Ideen: "I'm a weak, squeamish person. It's all too much for me." By the time I had returned, Mother would have cleaned everything with a damp cloth and Ideen would be still holding Father's hand. Ideen appeared to be asking me something with a particular movement of his head. I said: "It's no use. It's all over."

Father turned his head gently towards me and cast a glance at my collar. As I had undone the buttons of my collar, I thought he meant to tell me to do them up again. But it was hot and I was feeling nauseous. Ideen said: "Sit down." I sat down. When I held Father's hand, he had already passed away. It was midday and the voice of the muezzin reverberated everywhere. Mother, lying on the floor, cried loudly.

He felt he had regained some strength, like the last vestige of strength that sometimes manifests itself. He stood up, shook the snow off his clothes, turned round and looked in various directions. He was hoping to see the silhouette of something manifest itself in the distance. The only thing he could see were the ruined walls of the teahouse lying on his right-hand side. There seemed to be a red signboard there as well. He put his hands in his trouser pockets and began to walk towards the teahouse. He said to himself: "Don't think of your hands, Urhan." He did not.

We left home to attend the funeral. Father placed a bunch of flowers on Mr Lord's coffin. In the afternoon, we were astounded when we saw a van being loaded with electric fans as usual. There was a sticker on every fan: "Mr Lord has passed away. Let us remember him with respect."

I asked: "How?"

One of the workers said: "He was a great man. That's all. Let's just appreciate that." He ran, albeit slowly. He could not walk. Nor could he stand. And then he noticed that he could not run either. His face was touching the snow and his hands had plunged into it. He got up, shook the snow off his clothes and began to walk again.

Ideen said: "I have greater respect for Master Delkhoon."

I wondered why Mr Lord manufactured electric fans and not heaters. And I wondered why he had not set up his electric fan factory in Abadan where the climate was hot. It was probably for these very reasons that Ideen said he could not respect him. For four years, he did not see Ideen. And by the time he returned home, Ida, too, was lying in the cemetery. That was what brought him back to the shop. And that was why Father embraced Ideen, put his head on his shoulder and said, sobbing: "We have lost Ida. You should not leave us alone."

"Very well, Father."

"Where have you been, my dear son? You look so old."

He arrived back in front of the teahouse. He shook the snow off his clothes, pounded his feet a few times and went into the stable. This time, he had to have a better idea and follow a different direction. It would be a good idea to wait for the snow to stop falling and only then to set out. He could then walk on and on until he reached some town or other. But I did not mean anything bad when I said: "Sooji! All the people in the town know that you are mad. Do you know that yourself?" I just wanted to know what sort of situation he was in. He pulls a newspaper out of his trousers and reads: "Everybody is dead silent. The city has been abandoned by its inhabitants. The trees have burnt down. The women have turned to prostitution. They cannot find even a loaf of bread and they wonder how they can warm themselves. Only at one extremity of the city, in a green, lush garden, Hitler and his mistress live a quiet life. This is a photograph of Hitler pointing out the conquest of Belgrade. In front of…"

He suddenly disappears and comes to this teahouse. That is the only thing wrong with him. I said: "Shall I chain you to the railings of the veranda again?" I then fetched a chain and a lock and fastened him to the railings. When I came back home at night, he was asleep. The courtyard was full of ravens and cats. They all flew away or ran away as soon as they saw me. A horrifying silence then fell on the house. I said: "Get up, Ideen. I have brought you some broth."

He opened his eyes. Overjoyed, he suddenly attempted to stand up, forgetting about the chain. But he had to crouch again. He said: "My brother."

He had wet himself. I said: "Let me untie you." I did. I said: "Eat some broth."

He asked: "But where is my sister-in-law?"

He had not asked this before. I said: "I divorced her six months ago."

"Don't try to trick me. It will take you six months to prove it."

"To prove what?" I sprinkled water on the veranda. I was reminded of Yousef and the fact that we could never sprinkle water where he sat. I then began to move away in order to go to bed. Ideen would not touch the broth. The air felt hot. I said: "Eat."

"In this country, the law applies for 24 hours or, at the most, 48 hours."

"In that case, go to bed."

He moved towards the basement. On his way down the stairs, he asked: "What happened afterwards."

"After what?"

"This photograph shows the city of Belgrade almost completely in ruins."

I snatched the newspaper out of his hand and said: "That's enough. Don't read any more."

He also had a fairly good voice. He sang Turkish love songs. Mashd Abbas came out of the teahouse and said: "If I'm not wrong, I think we are one month into spring. He always begins to sing at this time of the year."

But what I thought was that he sang when he saw swallows flying. That thin, feeble muezzin had placed his index finger in his ear and kept shaking his head. I said: "That's enough. Don't chant any more."

We were holding Ida's memorial service on that day. After four years of absence, Ideen had reappeared. He was looking at us in astonishment at the entrance to the mosque. He began to weep as soon as he caught sight of me. I sensed that he had had a hard time and I noticed that he looked so devoid of any vigour. He was thin and pale. His hands trembled and there were wrinkles on his forehead and around his eyes. He looked even older than Father. He said: "Ida?"

I answered: "Yes. Ida. And Father is over there." I took him to Father.

He crouched at the entrance to the stable and stayed there, waiting for the snow to stop falling. He now wished he were a beast of prey. A warm hide would be covering all his body and whenever he wanted food, he could invade the crowd. There was a child over there, next to the water tap and leaning against the railings of a flowerbed next to the road. He kept bending and stretching. People quickly passed by. I said: "Don't you want to go home, Ideen?"

"Let me wait until this crowd disappears."

I was standing on the step at the entrance to the shop and paid no attention to the porters' laughter. Ideen said: "Tell me, brother. Where do all these people get spoons from?"

"Some eat with their hands."

He then fell silent. He looked as if he had been relieved of some concern. The crowd passed by. One could smell freshly baked *barbari* bread from the adjacent alley. One could smell Turkish coffee too. But the coffee shop was far away and Monsieur Sooren had a daughter who surely wanted to get married to Ideen. In times to come, I always thought of trying to find that Armenian girl. The more I enquired, the less I found any clue. She had disappeared into thin air.

But just three or four days ago, a priest entered our shop. He appeared to be a stranger. He said: "Excuse me brother. I am enquiring about a tall man with greying hair and Tatar-looking eyes. Isn't he your brother?"

The priest himself was pale, thin and tall, with greying hair. The skin under his eyes was bluish. I asked; "Why?"

"At Sheikh Safi Crossroads, he has thrown a stone and broken the traffic lights. He has now been arrested."

I felt happy, as I now had some news of him after several days of his absence. But, until that day, he had never even hurt a child. He minded his own business and it was completely out of character to break traffic lights. I asked; "Sooji?"

The priest said: "Maybe. I have not heard this name."

I accompanied the priest to Sheikh Safi Crossroads. It was snowing on that day too and I had forgotten to take my papakha. I put my question to the policeman who was posted at the crossroads. He knew me. He knew Sooji too. But he told me that a dangerous madman had broken the traffic lights. I asked: "Sooji?"

"No sir. It was a dangerous psychopath. He has been arrested."

On our way back to the shop, the priest asked me where Sooji was. I said I did not know. He said that, for a long time, he had been looking for a man who had previously been a carpenter and who had disappeared without trace.

I said: "That's my brother."

"Where do you think we can find him?"

"I, too, have had no news of him for quite a few days. He has disappeared."

"Why?"

"I don't know. He sometimes just disappears."

"I see! What can be done?"

"Who are you and why do you want to find him?"

"I am his daughter's godfather."

That was the first time I was hearing such a thing. I exclaimed: "Daughter?"

"Yes. Don't you know?"

"Don't I know what?" Someone went running past and I fell into the snow. The priest held my hand and helped me to get up. I said: "I don't understand what you mean."

"Can we talk in your shop?"

We went back to the shop. I sat at the desk and he moved his chair closer to the heater. He looked tired and worried. But he was a meticulous, disciplined person and he talked slowly. He said: "Your brother's name is Ideen Urkhani. Is that right?"

"Yes."

"He has a 15-year old daughter whose name is Elmira Urkhani. Her mother's name is Sormelina. Mr Ideen Urkhani's identity certificate is with us."

Father's lineage had extended, reaching a point that I had never expected. I said: "You should give his identity certificate to me."

"Why should it not be held by his daughter?"

"What daughter? He himself is superfluous."

I was angry. But the priest maintained his normal calm, shook hands with me and left the shop. Before he left, I said once more: "You should give the identity certificate to me."

He replied: "We will meet again." And he left.

He took the rope out of his overcoat pocket and cast a glance at the wooden beams of the ceiling. For a moment, he thought it would not take even five minutes and that the torturous shaking and trembling would soon be over. But he knew that the world would never come to a standstill. Ideen would resurface, wear a brown suit, wear a violet tie with his beige shirt, go to the nut sellers' souk in Ardabil every morning and become the sole owner of so much wealth and so much grandeur. Perhaps he would hold memorial services on the seventh day and the 40th day of Urhan's death. But, afterwards, the world would go on and town would be as noisy and as lively as it has always been. In due course, everyone would forget that there used to be a person called Urhan. No. Oh, God. No. This is not fair. Sooji is undboutedly no more than just a mask, feigning madness. Perhaps he deserves it. People live only half of their lives. I belonged to the first half and he to the second. But I will stop him. All the property is officially mine. Neither the house, nor the shop, nor the apricot orchard... no... nothing is in his name. All he owns is a grey-green suit, a second-hand *papakha* and a borrowed little room that looks more like a cellar than a room and that is seven steps down from the courtyard. Its walls were damp. Father brought in builders. They chiselled away the old, swollen plaster and resurfaced the walls with cement. It is not unpleasant. I slept there one night. It is cool in summer and pleasantly warm in winter. But one would sleep there frowning. Everything is dark and gloomy in there. Sleeping in that room is like sleeping in a tomb. Father is lying in his tomb frowning, with the same sort of frown that he always had for Ideen. But now, the roots of the tree at the cemetery have wound themselves round him so tightly that he cannot budge. The roots have invaded the folds and crevices of his body and sucked his sap away. It is for this same reason that some trees are always frowning, so much so that one would think one owes them money. And I have such a dislike of the people to whom I think I am indebted. I said: " Ideen, you have not been made to be a businessman. Father is no longer around to prevent you from doing what you like. Would you like to go to university? Would you like to continue your literary studies? I will pay your expenses."

"No. Not at all."

"Why? Why are you so stubborn?"

"Because now it's too late and, besides, I don't want to disregard Father's wishes."

"When you give up business, the will would automatically be null and void."

"It's alright for me for life to go on as it is. I no longer have the energy or the enthusiasm for studying."

He would not compromise. He worked hard, as hard as a porter. He left the shop every day at four o'clock in the afternoon. He did not complain either. But he would not consent to an amicable settlement or to the sale of his share of the property to me. I had spoken my final word and he had said that we should not make our dead family members turn in their graves. On the other hand, Mother, who was constantly ill, would not allow us to officially register our property. It was then that I made my decision and left for Astara. I had heard that in the forests near Astara there were two octogenarian spinsters who could give sound advice on how to conduct one's life. They were said to have cured sterile people. A woman said that she had been unable to become pregnant for years but that, following her consultation with the grand old ladies, she had given birth to 11 children so far. Ayaz the policeman said: "She recites a particular incantation as a result of which a secretly bigamous man can rest assured that his two wives will not know of each other and that, furthermore, the man can sleep with them simultaneously in the same bed without them seeing each other." Another man said that although he had been born blind, he could now see better than anyone else. So, why shouldn't I attempt to solve my problems in the same way?

When I arrived there, I was told that one of the grand old ladies had left for Russia and that the other was not far from breathing her last. She looked pale, yellow and disgusting. She had numerous long strands of pleated white hair that looked as if they had taken root in the soil. She resembled a skeleton covered with a layer of skin. I placed my banknotes in front of her in a row. I noticed that her eyes sparkled like rubies. I said: "Tell me."

She began telling my fortune with chickpeas and, subsequently, with bones. She then used her astral chart. No conclusion could be made. I placed a few more banknotes in front of her. She tried fortune telling with smoke. She placed a dried leaf, looking like an open hand, on fire. Suddenly, the leaf made a moaning noise and black smoke rose up high. I saw with my own eyes that the smoke fluttered its wings, not knowing on what branch to perch. I laid a longer row of banknotes in front of her and said: "Tell me more."

"There is someone in your life who hinders you."

She then used water to foretell the future. Looking into an earthenware bowl of water, she went through every member of my family. She recalled my whole life. She pulled Father out of the bowl. She then pulled Mother out. She expressed an extremely low opinion of Ideen. And the more she tried, the less she could revive Ida. I asked: "What about outside the town, with a club?"

"No. That would be wrong." She howled like wind blowing through a bed of reeds.

"Shall I throw him down from a cliff top?"

"No." She roared with a dry, vibrating sound. And she moaned again: "No-o-o-o." She stretched the end of her words.

She remained silent for a few seconds while she gazed at me. I said: "Tell me."

She then foretold the future with prayer beads. Again, it was inconclusive. I said: "Shall I poison his food?"

"No, no. That would be wrong." She then guffawed so loudly that I could not believe my ears. She said: "You haven't eaten swallows' brains, have you?"

I ran. Along the stretches I had to go on foot, I ran. And along the stretches I had to be carried by motor transport, I suffered. I went through Heyran mountain pass. It was a winding dirt road. Eventually, I ran as far as home. It was towards the end of summer and I had to wait until springtime for the swallows to appear. I placed a calendar on the desk in the shop and went through a page a day. It snowed. The ground became slippery with frost. The ravens on the pine tree chanted "Snaw! Snaw!" and springtime appeared to have no intention of arriving. As if I had run all through winter, I felt the arrival of springtime earlier than anyone else. Early in the morning, I went to the mountains around Veela Darreh. Before sunrise, I picked up a white sack and climbed a mountain. When the sun rose, I found out where their nests were. The swallows flew above my head in swarms. They fluttered so near that I could raise my hand and catch a few.

He felt he needed neither motherly love nor fatherly kindness. He shouted. He shouted in order not to be afraid. Once again, he heard the wolves' howling from a distance. They were approaching, trotting. Their mouths were open and their eyes betrayed hunger. He cast a glance at his hands and noticed that there was blood around his fingernails. He felt a sharp pain in the bones of his hands. Curiously, the periphery of his eyes burnt with heat.

I pushed my hands into the nest, grabbed five of them in one go and dropped them into the sack. They kept chirping. I pushed my hand into the nest again and, this time, picked two. I then saw a large flock of swallows that rushed out of the cave like black smoke. I carried the sack on my back and walked to Mr Boyook's teahouse. There was not a soul there. There were only a few owls gazing out of the little windows and doorframes of that castle-like building. I knocked at the door and called his name. There was no response. I knocked again. I then heard footsteps from behind me. I turned round. I saw a man with a handlebar moustache and wearing sturdy, black Wellington boots. He was holding two rabbits that had had their throats cut. I said: "I want to see Mr Boyook." I noticed he was lame in one leg.

"What is your business with him?"

"I have to see the man himself."

"I am Boyook. Talk to me."

It was the middle of the springtime. Even the swallows trapped in the sack chirped. I said: "I…" I suddenly forgot everything. When he passed next to me, I felt that he was twice as big as I was. His hair was smooth and comprised two colours: White and silver. I asked: "Have you got tea?"

"You mean you have come all this way just to have tea?" He opened the door to his teahouse.

He removed the wooden bars from the doorframe and we went inside. It was fairly cool inside. The vapour rising from the samovar hit the ceiling. I sat on a bench and looked at the paintings on the wall. They showed Rostam and Akvan the Demon[22].

He asked: "Have you caught starlings?"

"No. Swallows."

He poured me a glass of hot tea and asked: "Swallows? What for?"

"Foreigners catch these swallows, stuff them and put them on their shelves and mantelpieces."

"I see!"

"There used to be a man, called Mr Lord, who had a factory behind our house. I learnt this from him. I want to stuff these birds. But I don't mind killing a couple of them so that we can eat them."

Before he put the tea down in front of me, he poured out the water that had gathered in the saucepan on the floor and held the tea-glass in front of the window to make sure the colour was acceptable. He said: "A few years ago, I

Symphony of the Dead

made a dish of braised swallows for someone. It was so delicious that he was astounded."

"So you know how to cook them."

"I am a master of the art."

He placed the rabbits on the table and slit their bellies open with a big knife. Then, when he was separating the skin from the flesh, he said: "The guy came for the dish again last year."

I said: "I have a guest."

Vapour as white and as soft as the rabbit's hide rose from his blood-stained hands and from inside the rabbit's belly. He asked: "Who is your guest?"

"You don't know him." I poured some tea on to the saucer in order to cool it and then drank it.

"I am a master of this art."

"Have you ever eaten the dish yourself?"

"I have just about tasted it, but as for eating..." He picked up a cigarette with his hands, still blood-stained, and lit it: "No."

"I want a proper meal."

"To tell you the truth, cooking this bird is no joke. It takes a lot of effort. But the dish I cooked for that guy was highly praised by him. He could still taste it for a long time afterwards."

As I was finishing my tea, I noticed that he had skinned both rabbits. They just looked like two pieces of lean, smooth meat on his worktop. I said: "I would like you to cook us the brains as well."

"The brains?" He gazed at me: "But beware of eating it yourself!"

"I know. It also takes a lot of trouble and much expense. But I have a very dear and valued guest." At the same moment, I felt a shiver down my spine. I felt a stabbing pain in my bones and, unusually for me, my hands trembled.

"Give me the bag."

He took the bag from me and said: "Beware of eating it yourself!"

When I was handing the bag to him, I sensed that my tongue had become so heavy that it felt as if it was stuck to the roof of my mouth.

He left the stable and looked around while he felt as if a feverish pain was boiling out of his temples. His heart beat fast. He concentrated all his strength in his eyes so that he might see a black spot in that white wilderness.

Where was the end of this wilderness then? What time of the day was it? No, my God. This is not fair. I was not wearing my overcoat. I wanted to bring him back. I wanted to chain him up again. And, now, I want to wind a rope round him. It's about time. He has lived his life and I do not think he would want anything more. If I tie him up right here, to the stable door, he will be among the dead within a few hours and with no further ado. Right at that moment, I would tell him: "You have a pretty daughter, Ideen. Did you ever know that?"

A blonde girl of mixed blood will emerge one of these days from wherever she is. She will ask: "Is this my father's shop, sir?"

I will ask: "Who is your father?"

"A madman." It is ridiculous. It really is ridiculous. Father, too, was a peculiar type of person. A few months after his death, I felt like paying a visit to his grave. It was a horrible autumn. All over the town, the streets were covered with fallen plane tree leaves. The leafless trees of the graveyard had been invaded by ravens. Big flocks of God's horrible, black creatures had perched on the branches in such a way that one would think that a theatrical performance was going on in the cemetery. I went round its high, gloomy walls and entered it through its green, two-leafed door. Once you are in there, you are always followed by about a dozen beggars. One of them pulled so hard on my jacket that it was about to tear. I said: "Get your hands off, you silly ass." All of them ran away. Father's grave was on the right-hand side of the cemetery under a young plane tree. Its fallen leaves had covered it. I pushed the leaves back with my hand and read the inscription on the tombstone. I then stood up and gazed at the necropolis. Every now and then, someone arrived and someone left. Some, standing up over the graves, moved their bodies to and fro.

I said: "Are you witnessing our plight, Father? Don't think that yours is the only necropolis. The world outside is another one. To hell with everything and everywhere. To hell with us. To hell with this so-called brotherhood." I sat on the tombstone and continued: "Look, Father! I carried sacks of pistachio nuts down 40 steps and up 40 steps. I did this for many years. You yourself were witness to that. Your God, too, is a witness. I can't put up with the situation whereby this lout, having barely arrived on the scene, can own half of your estate. Why didn't you give me what was rightfully mine? Why did you give what was mine by rights to someone else?"

I picked up a stone, knocked on the tombstone a few times, scratched a star on the tombstone and said: "I have no respect for him, Father." Bending over the tombstone so that the beggars and the passers-by would not hear me, I said: "He is worth less to me than a rusted *real*." I never achieved my desire of having a second entrance built for the shop, to create a shop on the corner of two lanes in the souk and to have a big, bright shop to myself with a board bearing my own name.

A feverish shiver was driving him mad. His teeth rattled and his chest shook. He suddenly felt hot. He put his hand to his forehead and noticed that

Symphony of the Dead

it was alarmingly hot. He knelt in front of the teahouse, in the snow. He struggled to get himself into the teahouse, but a funny sort of weariness prevented him. He then saw the sky become smaller and rush towards him all at once. He saw himself wandering in the sky. He pushed his hands into the snow, picked up a handful and placed it on his forehead. Well, well. Today is Friday. There were gentle waves on Shoorabi's surface. Father's skin was tickled in the water. He said: "Well done, Urhan! Rub it on." And I did rub and massage. I picked up a packet of pumpkin seeds and headed for the basement. Ideen was lying on his bed. He was probably asleep. There was a book lying on his chest. I started to crack the seeds and deposited the shells on his chest. That was all I did from midday until evening. I buried him under a pile of pumpkin seed shells. Mother was on the staircase, holding a tray of tea-glasses. She asked: "What are you doing this for?"

I replied: "For fun."

Ideen woke up and rose from beneath the shells. He asked: "Who has eaten the seeds?"

I explained: "I just wanted to see how it would look."

Mother was not amused: "You should be ashamed of yourself."

Ideen frowned. I had not seen him looking at me for many years. Well, I'll now give Father a good rubbing and a proper massage. But he went up and up, like a kite. Why are you pulling on my trousers, you damned fool? Is this the way people die then? If no-one helps them, they die. The earth gets smaller and rises. You then swell and swell until you grow as big as the earth. Then you burst. No, my God. This is not fair.

He said: "Throw a blanket on my back, Azar." His teeth rattled all the time. He then said: "Throw a big quilt on my back, Azar." He felt an opaque liquid had covered his eyeballs. He was feeling hot. He did not see the snowflakes that fell on his face, settled and melted. He said: "Throw it on my face." He then made a superhuman effort, sat up and stared at the ground. He had become an animal that was looking for its nest. There were icicles hanging from him. He lay on the ground and went into the snow, head first. He went further in and covered himself with a layer of snow. He then pulled himself out again and sat up. He looked around and just about managed to stand up. Now he could walk. He was wet all over and felt like a ball of snow. But he could walk.

He could see Shoorabi over there. In his mind, he pushed back the snow on the surface of Shoorabi. He could now see Shoorabi with gentle, blue waves. He limped to the reed bed. Where are you, mad *Mirza* Ideen? No. Where are you, Ideen? Mother said: "Bring him here, you fool." She talked to herself in a low-pitched voice. Ideen was sitting in front of her, like a stone statue. Mother said: "What have you done to him, you shameful man?"

He had now reached the dry, untidy reed beds. A refreshing cold breeze caressed his face. It was the first time that he was enjoying the cold weather. Shoorabi dared not even budge under the snow and the reed bed no longer looked like the United Nations. Dishevelled and disturbed, it looked like it had subsided into a sloping side of Shoorabi. He sat right there and, with a stentorian voice, he said: "And here we are at the United Nations. But there is no trial." He wanted to pick up a flag, but he could not reach one. He felt like eating a flag. I said: "Eat bread instead of drinking tea."

There was no more strength left in him. He could not even move his hands. He fell down like the flags. He looked around. Everything was dead silent. He was being buried under the snow. He saw the flags that had fallen in silence and were being buried under the snow. He then saw Mother who had descended from the sky. She was pulling on Urhan's thumbs with both of her hands.

He said: "No, Mummy. No."

Mother said nothing. She just laughed. She laughed with kindness.

He said: "No, Mummy. Is this what is meant by fairness, Mummy?"

Mother kept pulling on his thumbs, severely. He thought: "I might fall. I am not seeing what is in front of me, am I?"

He said: "Life has become so hard."

Swallows flew and danced in the snowfall, scattered, flocked together again, formed a single black spot and went further and further away until they looked like a beauty spot on the face of the sky. Oh, how yellow the sky was! And how thick was the smoke rising from the chimneys! The ravens' place was on the branches of the pine tree. They woke him up every morning when they chanted "Snaw, snaw". Two of the ravens sat on the wooden mast holding the radio's aerial, exactly facing him, above Foroozan's house and that of the other neighbour. One of the pair arrived earlier and pecked at the foot of the wooden mast of the aerial on which the other one would later perch. When the second one arrived, it was unbalanced and moved to and fro on the tall, cross-like aerial. It eventually fell off and flew into the branches of a pine tree.

Mother would not let up. She kept pulling hard. Urhan thought he was shouting. He pushed his feet into the mud on the shores of Shoorabi. He was looking for a foothold in order not to fall. He was going further into the mud. Mother was hanging down from the sky. The wind waved her purple skirt.

Tell me, Father. Have you ever run from winter until springtime? You people are dead. But I have run from winter until springtime, eyeing the sky and the sun all the time.

Symphony of the Dead

His eyes resembled those of a man who, after enduring a long famine, had now just drunk water to quell his hunger. He felt he was seeing Shoorabi from the depths of the swallows' nest in the tree trunk, without knowing whether he himself was alive. No. He was dead. And he did not know that he was dead. Inadvertently, he put his hand into his coat pocket and pulled out the rope. He shouted: "Ideen! *Mirza* Ideen!" But no voice came out of his throat. He said: "Don't kill me."

He said: "Don't kill me."

I said: "Don't be afraid. I'm not going to kill you."

"In that case, do kill me. But don't do this to me. I still have many unfulfilled wishes."

"You will achieve your wishes."

"You are a malicious man."

He suddenly remembered that the nut shops in the town owed him money: a lot of money. He had cheques that he had not cashed. He had to turn back and collect what was owed him. Otherwise, they would keep the money and disappear.

I said: "You are ruining my life, brother. What am I to do with you?" I went through ten sleepless nights. I kept visiting the basement. But he was never there.

Nothing can be more tragic than this: I am going to meet my end before I have found Ideen. This is my destiny, I suppose. But it is not only I who is drinking this hemlock. Ida, too, killed herself. She probably did it because being away from Ideen made her depressed. She was submerged in her own female thoughts and fantasies. What could be done? Ideen used to say: "When the body temperature reaches 42 degrees, one is dead. You should believe, then, that the body temperature of the dead is 42 degrees."

He said: "No, Ideen. I won't kill you. But I don't want you to kill me either."

He then moved gently into the water. It was warm and a thin vapour rose from its waves. Snow fell silently. And the sky was so beautiful.

"Let me die of my own accord, my dear brother."

He felt like sleeping. And he did sleep. He slept soundly. And the rope was so close to his head, so straight and so taut on the water surface that any passer-by would think: "Oh, my God! A man has hanged himself horizontally in the water."

Glossary

Aftab-e Sharq – The Eastern Sun, a newspaper
Ashhado a'llaa Elaaha ella'llaah – I testify that there is no god but Allah
Ashhado ana Aliyyan vali o'llaah – Specific Shiite affirmation of faith meaning 'I testify that Ali is the guardian (ie. the immediate successor to the Prophet Mohammad) appointed by God'
Ashhado ana Mohammadan Rasoul ol'laah – I testify that Mohammad is the messenger of God
Ayat – a special prayer that is recited when there is a cause for being frightened or sensing danger, such as during an eclipse, an earthquake or a flood
barbari bread - A richer, thicker and bigger version of pita bread
chador – long veil worn by woman which covers the head
Chris-dom-Koloft – Fat-tailed Chris; a play on Christopher Columbus
Dayee – Uncle
dorostkar –'honest' in Persian
fesenjan – an Iranian khoresh or stew, the ingredients of which are usually chicken, ground walnuts and pomegranate puree
hajji – a Muslim who has made the pilgrimage to Mecca
Inch peses – Armenian for 'how are you?'
khakshir – a herbal medicine
Kolbeh Choobi – wooden hut
korsi – a large, low, wooden table over which blankets and quilts are spread and under which a heater is placed. In old times, this heater was a usually a brazier slowly burning lumps of charcoal. Family members sit, lie or sleep under the quilt at the four sides
Laa Elaaha ella'llaah – Islamic affirmation of faith, meaning: There is no god but Allah. A funeral is one of many occasions on which it is chanted. It could, however, sound inappropriate during the funeral of a non-Muslim
Lava – Armenian for 'good'
Mahoor – one of several systems of musical notation in the realm of traditional Iranian music
Mashd – The titles Mashd, Mashdi or Mashti are shortened versions of Mashhadi, referring to someone who has made the pilgrimage to the shrine of Imam Reza (the eighth Imam of Shiite Moslems) in north-eastern Iran
mirza – is the contracted form of Amir zadeh which means a prince. But the word has been overworked and has gradually acquired other meanings.

Here, it is apparently used to mean a scribe, or a man literate enough to write letters and documents for the illiterate for a fee
Norooz – the Iranian New Year, usually coincides with March 21
papakha – Russian-style sheepskin hat
sangak – A long, triangular, flat loaf of bread baked on hot pebbles
seer – measure of weight equivalent to about 75g
tooman – Iranian currency. Ten *reals* make one *tooman*
Uz ishidi – an Azeri Turkish phrase meaning: 'It is his own doing'
zanboorak – A makeshift musical instrument, looking somewhat like a tuning fork or Jew's harp
zanbouri – literally meaning waspish, are oil lamps with incandescent filaments giving out as much light as a medium electric bulb. They make a humming noise, hence the name

Explanatory Notes

Numbers in the text indicates a translator's explanatory note below.

1. Shoorabi is the name of the lake, literally meaning salt-water
2. – Ardabil is one of the main cities in the province of Azerbaijan, north-west Iran. It is now the administrative centre of East Azerbaijan
3. Mount Damavand is a dormant volcano in northern Iran. It is permanently capped with snow
4. "You burnt a feather for me..." This is an allusion to a fairy tale in which the burning of a feather signifies summoning someone or a desire to see them
5. Oroumiyyeh is a city in north-western Iran. It is the administrative centre of the province of West Azerbaijan
6. The kings of Qajar Dynasty ruled Iran from 1787 to 1925
7. Reza Shah was the first king of Pahlavi Dynasty. He reigned from 1925 until his abdication in 1941, following the Allied occupation of the country
8. 16 September 1941
9. Delkhoon can be a real surname as well as a pseudonym. It literally means 'of bleeding heart' or 'having a bleeding heart', implying dissatisfaction with one's lot or with the society as a whole
10. Mansoor Hallaaj was an Iranian mystic (sufi) who lived during the ninth and the tenth centuries AD
11. Sheikh Safi-od-din e Ardabili, a sufi guru, was the most notable ancestor of Safavid kings who ruled over Iran during the 15th and 16th centuries AD
12. Nima Yooshij is generally regarded as the father of modern Persian poetry. He began his, then, revolutionary departure away from classical poetry as early as the 1920s but attained his highest degree of acceptance and acclaim in the 1950s. He died in 1959
13. Sa'adi and Hafez, both natives of Shiraz in southern Iran, are among the most prominent poets in the realm of classical Persian poetry. They lived in the 12th and 13th centuries AD
14. In many regions, banging pots is a superstitious reaction to an eclipse
15. Seyyed is the title of those who can trace their ancestry to the prophet Muhammad

16. Unlike Nima Yooshij (see Endnote 12), Shahriar, a contemporary of his, only occasionally composed modern poetry. He was an Azerbaijani poet who lived in Tehran for most of his life. Almost all his works were in Persian. He had, however, composed one long poem in Azeri Turkish, which was regarded by many as a masterpiece
17. Ali-ibn-Abi Talib was the Prophet Muhammad's cousin and son-in-law. For the Shiites, he is the first of the twelve Imams (rightful successors to the Prophet Muhammad). For the Sunnis, he is the fourth, and the most venerable, caliph. Imam Hassan is Imam Ali's eldest son and his successor as second Imam. Imam Hussein is Imam Ali's second son. He is the third Imam of Shiite Muslims
18. Mount Sabalaan is a dormant volcano in Azerbaijan, north-western Iran
19. The Allies, having occupied Iran and having used the Iranian railways and roads for the transfer of British and American armaments to the Soviet Union between 1941 and 1945, bestowed the title 'The Bridge of Victory' on Iran
20. Barmaki Dynasty (in English: The Barmecides) were an influential family of Khorasan Province, north-western Iran, in the ninth century AD. Their most prominent member, Ja'far Barmaki, was the grand vizier of the Abbasid caliph Harun-ar-Rashid in Baghdad. But he fell foul of the caliph and, subsequently, he and most members of his clan were killed
21. Amir Arsalan is a character (a young warrior and a kind of superman) in a popular Persian story of the same title probably written in mid-nineteenth century
22. Rostam is the name of the legendary invincible warrior in Shahnama (The Book of Kings), the great work of Persian epic poetry composed by Ferdowsi (10th century AD). Akvan the Demon is another legendary figure in the Shahnama